THE SONG AND THE TRUTH

THE SONG AND THE TRUTH

HELGA RUEBSAMEN

Translated from the Dutch by Paul Vincent

ALFRED A. KNOPF   NEW YORK   2000

THIS IS A BORZOI BOOK
PUBLISHED BY ALFRED A. KNOPF

Originally published in The Netherlands as *Het lied en de waarheid*
by Uitgeverij Contact, Amsterdam/Antwerpen, in 1997.
Copyright © 1997 by Helga Ruebsamen

Publication has been made possible with the financial support from the
Foundation for the Production and Translation of Dutch Literature.

Library of Congress Cataloging-in-Publication Data
Ruebsamen, Helga.
[Lied en de waarheid. English]
The song and the truth / by Helga Ruebsamen;
translated from the Dutch by Paul Vincent.—1st American ed.
p.   cm.
ISBN 0-375-40261-6 (hc.)—ISBN 0-375-70277-6 (pbk.)
I. Vincent, Paul.   II. Title.
PT5881.28.U35 L5413 2000
839.3'1364—dc21   00-023274

Manufactured in the United States of America
First American Edition

I

IN THE GARDEN OF DEWI KESUMA

(1938–March 1939)

ONE

Every day, as soon as the sun went down, tiny lizards climbed up the walls of our veranda.

"Look, the *tjitjaks* are here."

The night people lit the lamps, in the rooms and on the veranda. The ladies who'd come to tea took their leave and went home. The day was over, and night was beginning.

My mother accompanied her guests as far as the *waringin* tree and waved to the visitors and their children as they left. I stood on the veranda listening to the sounds coming from the Lembang road. I could hear the cars driving uphill, up the mountain, where the sun was already asleep in the volcano. Or hear them driving downhill, to Bandung, the town where the zoo was and my father's clinic. There were often parties in town, and the cars drove faster then.

My mother came back; I could hear her singing before I saw her. She didn't hurry, she sauntered along, stopping now and then, so that the bright spot she formed in the darkness grew larger only very slowly. When it reached the point where I could make out more than the color of her dress, I could also see her platinum blond curls and even her bright eyes. By then she was so close that she could touch me.

"Well, we've got the veranda to ourselves again," said Mummy. She stretched out on the settee and beckoned to me. "All those visitors," she sighed, "and never anyone you can talk to."

The *tjitjaks* had found their places. On the ceiling they had frozen into wooden ornaments, but they pounced like greased lightning on any insects that strayed close to them.

The lamps burned in the rooms and on the veranda, so that night could not descend on us.

The night abolished the distinction between inside and outside. At night it was cool and dark everywhere. Everything was safe—people, animals, and plants—beneath a dark dome as large as the world.

When the sky, the earth, and the water had attained the same dark hue, the *toké* arrived. I waited for the *toké* every night. He was the big brother of the *tjitjaks*. I did not need to go to bed before the first *toké* had called.

By that time all the other nocturnal creatures were there: flying foxes, crickets, bullfrogs. Their noisy concert was in full swing.

The *toké* rarely showed itself, but every so often it called out its own name loudly, so that we and other *tokés* knew where it was. The more often the *toké* called, the more luck it brought. Everyone could hear it, including us. The moment the *toké* started up, we would stop talking. We counted under our breath. One . . . two . . . three—it went on for ages.

Would there be another call? Yes, one more. Quickly on: four . . . five . . . six . . . seven. Then it became more and more exciting, because once it got to nine, the luck would really start flowing. If the *toké* called twelve times, we would have long life, many brave sons, an enchanting daughter, and a vast fortune.

Later my mother told me that the night before we left for Europe, the *toké* had called thirteen times.

When the *toké* had called a few times, when scarcely anyone else was talking on the veranda, I was taken to my room.

At night a new life began for me. Once the sun had set, I no longer needed to remember what had happened during the day; the night erased the hard white things just as the sponge on my mother's blackboard erased her chalk letters.

At night I could say and do what I liked. I needed only to see it in my head and it happened. If I wanted to get up and go outside to see the moon, I was immediately lifted out of bed and taken out in someone's arms. The night people petted me, laughed the whole time, and asked nothing.

I was given as much pink syrup as I liked by the night people, and soft green sticky cake to go with it. I was allowed to touch everything. I was allowed to watch everything.

Whenever I said anything they cooed cheerfully or clicked their tongues admiringly. They never asked me anything, but they always answered me. We chattered away, the night people and me, whether or not we understood each other's every word.

Night people had the names of the work they did during the day: Babu the nursemaid, Kokki the cook, Djahit the seamstress, Djongos the houseboy, Kebon the gardener's boy. They had other names as well, which had a singsong sound; I knew those too.

I never had to say them out loud. All I had to do was think them, and the night people came. During the day everything was different.

The mornings approached, the dark dome of the sky first became translucent and then cracks appeared in it, to let the light through. Sometimes it was a slow process, sometimes it was so fast your eyes could not keep up.

If I was still outside, as it grew lighter and lighter around me, I would run back to my room and wait in bed for the day to come. As soon as it was fully light the gods, who had gone wandering in the night, returned. People in paintings and photos could roam around freely at night, but at the crack of dawn had to be back in their frames.

I tried hard to learn by heart all those names, of the gods and the people in our household.

There was a god, with no name, who was the god of Granny Helena. He had brought her here, because he watched over marriages and births.

My mother and my aunt had been born here, under the watchful and all-seeing eye of that one god. They were convinced that they belonged in the Dutch East Indies, because this god had so ordained.

But this god, in his lax popish way, had nevertheless allowed Granny Helena, their mother, to run off to England with an itinerant painter and stay there with him for good. Fortunately my mother and my aunt were cherished and brought up by Poppy, Granddad Bali's new wife; they had not been abandoned. Poppy had introduced them to other gods, who also did a good job, perhaps a better one than that one god with all his patron saints. From then on that one god was on an equal footing at home with the other gods, who were older and native to the country.

We regularly lit candles before the statue of the Virgin Mary, while we scattered flower petals around Buddha's feet. Mary was on the same table where he sat smiling, a little way off. The fat amber Buddha sat facing the door to ward off evil.

In the hall was the god Vishnu in all his splendor, seated between the wings of the long-legged bird Garuda, which in turn stood on a tortoise, the symbol of time.

Garuda was a gigantic man-bird. Apart from massive wings and a great plumed tail, he had a pair of human legs with bird's talons on them, and human arms and hands, in which he held

Vishnu's feet. Garuda was Vishnu's steed: he carried the god everywhere.

I asked if we had been brought by Garuda too.

"No, there was no need, we were born here."

Garuda was the great bird of good fortune. He had a proud, cheerful face and pointed, razor-sharp teeth.

I would often climb onto a settee to reach him and, without anyone seeing, stick my little finger into his beak, to feel his massive, jagged teeth. Each time I tried to see how long I could keep it up, how long I dared. I was only satisfied when red teeth marks had appeared in my little finger.

Sometimes, before the sun had even risen and the morning was still white, my mother would get me out of bed.

She dressed me. I had to wear socks and shoes with buttons that I loathed and took off as soon as I had a chance, together with the socks. Things were not arranged fairly in the world: most people who I knew were allowed to walk around barefoot the whole time. Very occasionally they would wear light sandals, which they could kick off whenever they liked. Why did I have to put such tight things on?

"If Daddy sees you walking around barefoot, he'll be sad. Bare feet are very dangerous, it seems. You mustn't do it, it's dirty and dangerous."

The shoes, the socks, putting them on and walking around in them: a daily punishment, though I had done nothing wrong.

"Why is she allowed to and not me?" I asked, pointing, although my mother said I must not point, at Babu Susila who always forgot the shoes when she dressed me.

"Susi isn't allowed to either, but she forgets to put on her shoes, because she's got so much on her mind, much more than me," said Mummy. "I have nothing on my mind, I just have to dress you so beautifully that everyone will say: Look, there goes the prettiest girl in the world."

My mother wanted me to look like a doll. She fiddled around with me, trying to make me look like those dolls that I never played with. But it did not work with the clothes and even less with my hair.

However hard she tried, however many cuddles and pinches she gave me when she dressed me, I was never pretty enough for her. It made her lose heart. Finally she behaved almost roughly, as she tried in vain to get my hair into shape.

"It's like a feather duster, it's a disaster, a breeding ground for vermin, I'll have to buy a steel dog's comb, what's going to become of this? Who in heaven's name do you take after?" I heard her whisper.

"Will we have to cut it off? Will we have to cut it off, Mummy?"

I had heard them talking about this; children who had lice had to have all their hair cut off. I had once seen a child like that in its mother's arms, in the carrying sling or *selendang.* There were blue worms throbbing under the bare stubbly little scalp. I shuddered when I thought about it.

"We can try it. But will it help? It may get even worse."

I became as sad as she was. I would never come to any good.

"I give up. What a funny little creature you are, yes, you, my darling monster," she exclaimed in mock despair. She gave a short snorting laugh, a laugh she used when she teased me. It was better when my mother teased me than when she was angry with me. But I never knew exactly when she was teasing me and when she was serious.

"Do you know what the trouble with you is?" She stretched, but did not say what. (Hoping that it might miraculously come right, I allowed my hair to be washed as often as she wanted without protesting. And for her I would have kept my tight shoes on all day long, I think, as a token of my love. Everything that hurt me gave my mother pleasure, so why shouldn't I have gladly borne the pain in my feet?

Or are these memories false? And is it true what she says, "Child, I had to chase after you all day long with your shoes. I couldn't do a thing with you!"?)

Once I was dressed as well as I could be, we went to see my father off, as he drove away in the car with the chauffeur at the wheel. Because Daddy was away so much, at first I found it difficult to believe that he really lived with us and for a long time I even thought his bed was at the clinic and not at home.

He wasn't a day person, because he was not there during the day. He wasn't a night person, because he was often not there at night either. He came home or he left, and those were important moments. Waving him good-bye was a solemn event, during which my mother did not want me to cling to her or put my thumb in my mouth.

My hair had been brushed with much pain and effort and a large ribbon had even been put in it, but my father ran his hand through it and messed it up again. He ran his hand through my hair, lifted me up, kissed me on both cheeks, looked at me, and said in a serious voice, "Stay healthy, my child."

The clinic was in town at the bottom of the road down from the hills. My father made sick women better, but how he did this and why, I had no idea. Mummy said that we did not need to know. She also said that he often looked gloomy because not all of the women always got better; sometimes they died, and that made him sad.

When the car with my father in it had driven off, my mother and I kept waving until the last bit of it disappeared from view. We turned and walked slowly back home.

The house where my memories begin was in the garden of Dewi Kesuma, who had been a princess until she had been turned into a stream by the gods. The stream wound its way through our garden. Dewi Kesuma was crystal clear and charming, except in the rainy season, when she became swollen, and flooded.

Farther on stood the *waringin* tree, which had once been a prince. It was so large that it could be seen from a long way off. It was at the front of our grounds, near the entrance. It cast its shadow over our garden and part of the road, which led from the town to the hills. In the hills, amid the blue mists, lay the volcano Tankuban Prahu, an upturned rowing boat, under which a fire god slept.

If our house had been an animal, it would have been an elephant. With its head turned toward the road, the elephant lay waiting for I know not what. The two white pillars by our front door were its tusks. Above them were tall oblong windows, its dark, wide-open eyes that looked out at the world with curiosity.

Its bulging cheeks were the outbuildings and its fat rump facing the mountains housed the storerooms and kitchens. Here, in these rooms where it was darker than in the rest of the house during the day, there was activity day and night. We did not see much of it, but smelled and heard all the more. The splashing of water and the spitting of fires, the hissing and steaming of dishes and infusions. Above all, the smells of spices being heated. Here people were chopping, cutting, kneading, and cooking. Here everything was first dragged in, then laid out, inspected, and finally prepared for us. My dog rooted about between the rotting piles of rubbish, which were packed together under banana leaves. He was called Teddy-Bali, because I had been given him by Grandpa Bali.

The dog had another name: we often called the dog "Here boy . . . *kebon!*" Teddy Kebon . . . "Here boy, Teddy . . . *kebon*," because the dog and the kebon, the gardener's boy, were never far away from each other. When we called they both came running up.

In Bandung I had two mothers.

One was called Hélène and the other was Auntie Margot, who lived with us and was a sister of my mother's.

"I'm your mummy, and Auntie Margot is your aunt."

I knew that perfectly well: one of my mothers was called Mummy, the other was called Auntie Margot.

However different the two of them were, they were so attached to each other that at some moments you could not keep them apart; they had intertwined. In appearance, though, they were not at all alike. Mummy was tall and thin, Auntie plump and broad; Mummy had light-blond hair with little curls, and Auntie a bush of dark frizzy hair with gold highlights.

They both took good care of their skin; one's was milky white, the other's golden brown. They rubbed each other with cocoa butter; they squeezed each other's pimples; they examined each other devotedly, putting their faces close together. As a result their eyes, which were the same brown color as our pond, had developed a slight squint. When their faces were so close together, you could see that they were not alike and yet somehow were. I felt excluded when, arms linked, they walked up and down for whole mornings and had long conversations that no one was allowed to hear.

We strolled round the grounds, where there were trees, not all of whose names I remember. There was a hibiscus hedge, there was a flamboyant *kembodjas* and *melatis*. Above them all towered the *waringin*, which in a former life had been called Pangeran Djamodjaja.

"Go and stand under the *waringin* and listen hard to what Pangeran tells you," said my mother, and she sat me down by the tree with my back to its trunk. "Now pay attention and listen," she ordered me.

I could do nothing but watch the two of them, my mother and my aunt, full of longing. Watch as they walked away from me, looked round at me a few times, but then forgot me, exchanging their secrets, heads together. Two whispering goddesses.

My mother and my aunt walked circuits and now and then disappeared behind trees and bushes, but always reappeared just in time, just at the moment I was about to start screaming. They hadn't changed a bit, although I was always afraid that in those few moments they had been enchanted and I would no longer recognize them. Fortunately, though, they were still my mother and aunt. Their dresses fluttered around their legs, they giggled, they laughed behind their hands.

Sometimes they would wave briefly at me as they went past.

"Just look at that dear child, *senang,* as good as gold, by that tree."

"She's such a sweetie."

Finally they would come and get me.

"What did the *waringin* tell you?"

I said nothing.

"That's not much, is it?"

The conversations I had with my mother and Auntie Margot were full of incomprehensible words, which filled my head like stones or snakes. Names were mentioned that I did not know. What was I to make of them? Names of other people, of other mothers and fathers perhaps, I didn't know. They were secrets.

"Lulu's not very talkative today," said my mother.

"Then she's her father's child."

"She's mine!" cried my mother. She threw her arms around us and wedged me snugly between their bodies. The three of us rocked to and fro and my mother said, "How I love you two! Yes, I do!"

"And we love you, yes, *betul,* we certainly do, yes, we love you," said Auntie Margot in her deep voice. It was like dark chocolate.

I felt the bellies of mother and my aunt against my head, much softer than the trunk of the *waringin*. I felt soft too and suddenly I knew what the tree had said.

"Moo . . . ma . . . moo . . . mmmaymamoo."

I roared it with relief. The faces of my mother and aunt bent over and hovered above me, red and with eyes wide open.

"What's wrong, darling?" asked my aunt in a worried voice.

I jumped up and said, "Moo . . . mow . . . may . . . mully. That's what it said."

My mother let go of me and took a step back, no, two, three steps back and covered her eyes with a hand as though she could not look at me anymore.

"Do stop it, Lulu, what kind of spectacle is that?"

"That's what the tree said, it really did." She turned away from me and spoke to Auntie Margot.

"No lack of imagination."

"And we don't know who she gets it from." My aunt said it teasingly and cheerfully and gave me a soothing pat on the back.

Auntie Margot was a nurse, and she worked in my father's clinic, but she didn't work there every day as he did.

Sometimes a horse and trap came to collect her in the late morning. Then my mother and I would drive with her and get out at the zoo. We waved at Auntie Margot and she waved back, until we lost sight of each other.

Some days my aunt had no time for a trap, she had to go in the car, and the chauffeur came to fetch her, because there was an emergency in the clinic. "I've got to get a move on, *ajo*, come on, I've got to hurry."

My mother said, "Why does she wear herself out so, my sister, always working for others, again and again? Let her stay with us. I miss her so when she's not there."

Then I would be there to keep Mummy company. I lived for that, during the day.

I loved looking at her: she was the most beautiful woman in the whole world. Everything about her glittered when she talked. I could never hear the stories she told often enough. For me repetition did not detract from a story; on the contrary, each time it gained in significance and color. All the exciting stories that she knew or had read, all the fairy tales and poems, she read them aloud many times and kept telling them to me afresh. In my mind it was not me experiencing the adventures, it was all happening to my mother.

I believed in it so much that I sometimes screamed, "Look out, look out" when I was afraid that she would be pounced on by the monster she was telling me about. Then she would say with a serious expression, "Shh, Lulu, quiet, darling, you can't change fate. That's just how the story goes, that's how fate is."

I would fan my mother to keep her cool when she sat writing in the morning. In the afternoons we would have a pillow fight. Every day we played school.

My mother first taught me the letters and then she made words for me. She wrote them down, large white letters one after the other, which squeaked on the blackboard that she had put on the veranda. Only when I had recognized all the letters and all the words was my mother satisfied.

Apart from that I did not do much. When Mummy no longer wanted to be cooled down, when she had praised me enough for being so clever and remembering all the words, she would lie down and read on the veranda.

I wandered through the grounds and when I got tired I rested on the warm boulder by the stream.

I closed my eyes, and sometimes I played rain. Rain was good, everyone said. The day people said it and the night people too. Everyone was always longing for rain. We would stand outside in the rain with upturned faces. We took off our clothes. We splashed back and forth along the path that became muddy and softer and softer.

I turned my face upward and listened to Dewi Kesuma. The princess who had been turned into the stream whispered dreamily on, and her sound was like water and wind. Almost always she gurgled in a friendly way, sometimes she babbled cheerfully, and very occasionally she roared.

Only at night did she assume her human voice, and then she laughed and talked in her water language. Mostly I could not understand Dewi Kesuma, but I could at moments when I was half asleep, half awake. Just before I fell asleep, she would start her story, and she would go on with it while I slept. I remembered her story and could repeat it the next day and tell it in turn to my mother and my aunt.

Mummy said that the princess was happy that there was someone living here who wanted to listen to her, even though it was only a little girl with lots of imagination. It made a great impression on me. I hadn't even really tried to listen to the stream, it had just happened; in fact, it happened by itself.

"But she's calling the *waringin*, not me, isn't she?"

"Yes, that's true," replied Mummy. She smiled for a moment and went on, "But that *waringin* the whole time, oh well, it knows her stories by now. It's been hearing them for thousands of years, you see."

Auntie Margot nudged her and said, "Those stories remain as good as ever, Hélène, even if you hear them a thousand times, even if you hear them for a thousand years."

Whenever I sat by the stream, I would start dozing. Dewi Kesuma's whispering made me sleepy, and sometimes I nodded off.

I would wake with a start when the sun got too hot, or there were loud day sounds.

During the day people's voices sounded louder than at night. At night I had to whisper because I mustn't wake anyone up.

During the day the *kalongs* and the *tjitjaks* slept, the *tokés* too, but no one cared if we woke them up. When I spoke softly anyway, Mummy told me to stop showing off.

The *waringin* also told stories that were a thousand years old. I stood with my back to the trunk and tried to listen, but did not manage to understand. The day went on and I returned to the gallery, where my mother was still lying reading. I crawled into my father's chair and stared straight ahead.

Day covered the grounds, the sun was right above it, a white shaft surrounded by the dark green of shady plants. Anyone who ventured into the shaft, I feared, would be struck by the light and the heat and become paralyzed. I was going to risk a game with the sun.

The sun hummed and buzzed and always tried to penetrate everywhere, to force its way in through the shutters. It always succeeded in finding a chink somewhere and hunting out creepy-crawlies and dust in the room. The rays were like long, grasping fingers and I hid behind the table or behind a chair so that it could not grab me. Sometimes I also pushed the shutters open, although that wasn't really allowed. Then I ran out, to see if the sun would slip into the room, whether it would plunge eagerly in. Then I could lock it up. I needed only to run a little way off and look back quickly over my shoulder and there it was, everywhere at once, but I never managed to catch it.

When the day was over, we would look at the sunset. We would wait for the cooling darkness. On the orange horizon strange spectacles were acted out among black masses of clouds. Mummy described what was going on up there in dramatic tones.

Nestling in my father's wicker armchair, I listened to the stories about royal children and dragons. Daddy always came late anyway.

When he finally got home, he would come and sit with us on the veranda, but usually he did not stay long. He had an attaché case with him from which he soon produced white and light-blue letters. He chatted with us a little, asked if everything had gone well, and then read his letters. It was exciting watching him, I thought, because he gave a kind of performance, with gestures and exclamations, which revealed what the letters were about. If his gestures became too brusque and his exclamations too loud, my father could not keep in his chair. He said that he wanted to read a few things again quietly, but there was nothing quiet about it.

He would leave, taking the letters with him, so nervously and hurriedly that he could not hold all of them in one hand. As he walked off, thin colored sheets fluttered around him. Almost before they fell they were caught by the *djongos*, who always squatted on the stairs and instantly leapt up when my father rose. I should also have liked to leap up and run after my father and pick up his letters, and I often tried to, but I never managed to beat the *djongos* to it.

My father strode off swinging his arms. "Look, there goes Groucho Marx," said my mother and grabbed her handkerchief to smother her laughter. I didn't know who Groucho Marx was. I thought my father looked like a *wajang* shadow puppet.

With his black hair and white face, he looked like the puppet I knew from the *wajang* plays, although we of course didn't have puppets like that in the house because they brought bad luck. My mother would not even allow me to say that my father was like one, because even that brought bad luck. I no longer said it aloud, about the *wajang* puppet, but I did go on thinking it. As I watched him go, I almost thought it aloud.

Many people I knew, my mother, the ladies who came to tea, their children, were like my dolls. They had blond curls, blue eyes, and white clothes. Some said "Mummy," just like a puss says "Meow." They closed their eyes the moment they were lying down. They slept the whole time. I was frightened that I would become just like these dolls, who didn't experience anything. In that case I'd rather be a *wajang* puppet who had lots of adventures, even if that was dangerous.

Whenever my father went off, my mother grumbled about his clothes, which hung too loosely on him.

"Isn't he just like a scarecrow?" she would say. "That silly wide suit would look better on a scarecrow! It's a sight."

On the contrary, I liked his clothes; they were white and flapped, and I could recognize him by them from a long way off. When he got closer, his gold-rimmed spectacles also loomed up, glasses like no one else wore. I never tired of seeing how they slipped down when he read his letters. They usually slid to the tip of his nose and as he read he would look over them, with his eyelids lowered, so it looked as if he was searching for them.

"Daddy, they're on your nose!" I would shout.

"Thanks a lot, darling Lulu. Where would I be without you?"

Once I asked if I might put on his glasses. He let me, and I suddenly saw everything in sharp focus, brown edges to the plants and gray dust on the floor. I got a shock and pulled off the glasses. In a flash I had also seen that my father had lines in his face and gray hairs in his black mustache. He had more furrows in his forehead than Kokki One-Tooth, and he was ancient.

"Didn't like it, I expect?" asked my father with a smile. Without glasses, he laughed with his own face again. The gray hairs in his mustache had disappeared.

When my father did not go off to read his letters, or came home early, he would ask us what we had eaten. While we were telling him, he sometimes raised his head suddenly and cried out, "None of it's any good."

"What do you mean, Cees? We're not going to start eating Dutch here, you know. For heaven's sake, don't inflict that on us."

"Better not," said Auntie Margot too, and she usually nipped the quarrel in the bud by explaining to my father at length what was wrong with Dutch food.

"*Makanan belanda* doesn't taste right here and it swells up and makes us feel bloated. Unless it grows here. But even then it takes years for it to adapt so it can't do any more harm."

Whenever Auntie Margot explained anything, she stood on tiptoe, and if she was wearing her nurse's apron she would take that off first.

My father said, "Did I say anything about Dutch food? Vegetables and fruit are what I mean. I couldn't care less where they come from, even if you pick them on the moon."

"On the moon chickens grow on trees and cauliflowers walk around freely," said my mother, but when she saw how upset he looked, she quickly said that they would take on a second *kokki*.

"We'll get one from Daddy's. But be careful, even though he's a vegetarian, our Daddy has a bloodthirsty nature."

It made her laugh in the way that I sometimes tried to copy, sniggering into a handkerchief that she pressed to her nose. At those moments it was as if my mother knew something that no one else must know.

My mother did not want my father to talk about food the whole time. She herself ate almost nothing: a chocolate or two in the mornings and a little *rudjak* fruit salad in the evening. Apart from that she drank black coffee and water from the fridge all day long.

"Pure lunacy!" my father called it. My mother asked if he wanted to stuff her full of rice, so that she would grow like her plump sister Margot.

"You should have married Margot, dear Cees. Mother Mimi advised you to."

My father raised his hands to heaven, uttered a barely audible word that none of us could make out, and lowered his hands so that they landed on his head.

"I've nothing more to say," he said, looking glum.

He made lists of what we should and should not eat. He gave the *kokkis* a list to hang in their kitchen.

"And you think they can read it?" asked my mother. "And even if they could, it wouldn't make any difference."

At the beginning when my father asked me what I had eaten that day, I had always listed everything, whatever it was. Whether it was tasty titbits from Kokki or candy from the Chinese. But when I realized that snacks like that did not put him in a good mood, I preferred to tell him what he wanted to hear. Because the list was never completely true, in fact it wasn't true at all, I turned it into a poem. In poetry it didn't matter if things were true or untrue.

What I sang sounded very good: *Apel dan pisang ikan ketimun ajam ketang.* (Apple, then banana, fish, cucumber, chicken, and sticky rice.)

We both liked the sound and rhythm of the words, and my father would sing along. In order to make it even more authentic, I added a drawing of apples, fruit, a fish, and a cucumber. He would hang the drawing on the wall behind his desk in the work pavilion.

"What's that?" asked my mother when she saw me making a new drawing, with different fruit this time.

I told her. "It's food for Daddy."

She frowned, but a little later started giggling.

"Oh yes . . . Now the penny's dropped. And where are the cakes and the chocolate milk?" She had to get her breath back before she could go on, but couldn't stop laughing. "And those cream horns and that gorgeous ice-cream pudding?"

The huge papaya which I had already drawn in outline, and which I was coloring in with two greasy crayons at once, orange and yellow, loomed up at me. It was as though I were being swallowed up by the huge mass of the orange-colored fruit, which enveloped and smothered me. I stopped coloring and rolled the crayons away. Something was wrong. The tone of my mother's remarks told me that something was wrong, but what was wrong, I couldn't understand. The papaya would put my father in a good mood, I was sure of that. And it was just as certain that the cakes would upset him.

Was I to give my father a drawing that made him sad instead of happy?

"Can't I give him that?" I pointed hesitantly at my papaya, which took up a whole page of my drawing pad.

My mother bent her head, her nose touching the paper.

"There's nothing wrong with this papaya," she said after a while. "I've smelled it and it smells good. You go ahead and give it. And in a little while we'll have a slice too. Yes, that's what we'll do."

"And the cakes?"

She leapt up. "You can draw them too later. On another piece of paper, and you won't give it to Daddy, you'll give it to me."

TWO

There were days when my mother dressed me even more carefully than usual. On such days it was as if I were a royal child who had to be shown to the people in full regalia.

My mother tickled me to make me laugh, but I couldn't laugh. The further the dressing progressed, my mother too felt less and less like laughing.

Once it had got to the point when I strode dutifully up and down in front of her, dressed in my embroidered skirt with lace and ruffles, my hair combed up high, she would suddenly burst out with unexpected passion: "Goodness gracious, how on earth can a normal child play in clothes like that?"

When Auntie Margot was at home, my mother would summon her as well, although my aunt was just on the point of leaving for the clinic in her light-blue uniform.

"Just look at the kind of theatrical clothes Mama has sent again. Where's her common sense? What is she thinking of?"

"*Bagus*, lovely!" said Auntie Margot, and she sounded embarrassed, as though she weren't saying what she really thought.

"What a nice blouse, really, a picture, and is it a good fit?"

"You don't have to ask the child that, you can see it with your own eyes, it's a formal thing, you can see it's not right for a child, let alone for that little fidget. This is for a ship of state."

My mother went on fuming. I tried to calm her down in every possible way, and so did Auntie Margot. We did our very best to calm her down. What was wrong with her?

"You're not going to send this back, Hélène, you're not going to send it back, are you?" pleaded Auntie Margot.

My mother stamped her foot. "Because I never send anything back, more and more comes." She wrung her hands. "She's forgotten what children's clothes are like. She never knew anyway. How could she? She didn't even know her own children. She'd left before we got dresses like this. She lives with her painter's fantasies. Ermine jackets and bombazine smocks." There were tears in her eyes.

Auntie Margot said as cheerfully as she could, "Can't we just try? Perhaps these dresses are tougher than you think, come on."

She squatted down beside me and whispered, "Louise, we're going to play a new game. You pretend that you are a tea lady in your lovely dress. *Mevrouw*, will you come and have tea with us? Or have you just been?"

My mother screamed, "A tea lady who comes to have tea with us? Has she got to play one of those? And imitate those frumps and hussies as well? I see more of them than I want to as it is."

But if Auntie Margot wanted to play in this game, then I was prepared to imitate the visitors, who came to disport themselves in all their splendor, bringing their chubby children along with them. Stately and big-bellied, I pranced back and forth, fanning myself with an imaginary fan and speaking in a high-pitched voice, "Phew, *mevrouw*, the heat today! I just can't get used to it and I can't cope with it . . . if only there were some rain . . . and that poor little thing . . . !"

". . . hasn't cried for days, *njang ketjil*, little darling," Auntie Margot joined in and burst out laughing. "You see? *Terlalu bagus*, very good." She beamed.

I could play for hours with Auntie Margot when she had time. We never got tired and she dreamed up something new every time.

"Tea ladies" was one of those new games that we were to play frequently from then on, because Granny Helena's clothes were at least of some use then. I kept inventing new ladies, sometimes tripping around and sometimes taking long, storklike steps as if I were on high heels. The next time I would push the toy pram with all the dolls in it wearing exactly the same sort of dresses and shoes as the ladies and children who came visiting. On another occasion I brought my toy dog with me, which was on wheels. He was called Teddy-Port Said. He came from there, and my father had bought him for me because I wasn't allowed to look after my real dog, Teddy, myself. Nor was I allowed to keep the monkey with me that I had been given by Granddad Bali at the same time as my real dog. The Balinese gardener's boy, who had looked after the two of them on the way, had stayed with us. We should take good care of that boy, who could make gold grow, wrote Granddad. According to my mother, Granddad's presents were never right, just as Granny Helena's were not.

Whenever there were boxes or baskets from Bali or England, it spelled trouble. Mummy fumed and raged the whole day. She simply smashed the statues and vases, having first lifted them oh so carefully out of their crates full of wood shavings and then carefully unwrapped them from their many layers of tissue paper. Hundreds of wonderful shards in all colors of the rainbow on the floor of the front gallery.

"Better *rusak* than sent back," Auntie Margot would groan, looking at the havoc for a few seconds and then putting her hands over her face. "But it's from Poppy, sis." Or she would say in her deep voice, "Let's allow Mother her happiness, can't we? Are we grown up or not?"

Such remarks made my mother even angrier.

"It's easy for you to talk, she may not even be your mother."

Auntie Margot covered her face with her hands, spreading her fingers to be able to see what was going on anyway.

I saw her lips moving and caught her hoarse whisper, "Throw and sling as much as you like, but don't send them back, you hear, don't send them back."

I can't remember my mother ever sending anything back. She didn't send my real dog back, nor did she return the Balinese gardener's boy with the flashing eyes who could even make gold grow.

Without my mother giving any indication that she was aware of it, my dog Teddy-Bali lived in the servants' quarters and I visited him every night, for as long as I could. During the day I taught my toy Teddy. I taught him all the things a real dog does.

The monkey had disappeared into the trees in the garden, but according to my night people it came back when it heard the music of the *gamelan*. The monkey was inhabited by the soul of a musician.

The night people appeared in the early morning to do all kinds of things: they cleaned the house, they swept the paths in the garden, and they came and asked what shopping needed to be done.

Mummy didn't want to manage the household; she preferred to leave it to the night people who served us. Sometimes she tried to be a better lady of the house, under the direction of Auntie Margot.

"Hélène, you must *manage* the household."

"All right then, you tell me how I'm supposed to *manage* it," replied my mother gamely.

"To start with, you give the orders in High Sundanese."

"Oh yes, orders? Oh dear, I really don't feel like it. . . ."

"Don't bother then," said Auntie Margot in resignation.

She clapped her hands and gathered the night people around her. My mother and I stood at the edge of the circle and heard her speaking forcefully in her chocolatey voice. We listened with the others and involuntarily marched on the spot in time with the sounds. We marched in single file, with rhythmical, clear movements, but above all not too fast. I went off into a trance, saw Auntie Margot a head taller than everyone else as if in a dream, even leaving the ground, in her white dress, the only thing that was white about her, surrounded by the night people who were so much more like her than my mother or I. It made me proud of my aunt and at the same time sad, because I would have liked to be just like the night people.

My mother and I stood there until the circle had disappeared. The night people had gone back to work. And Auntie Margot, once she had finished what she had to say, had come back down to earth. She walked toward us with a happy face, because it had again gone well.

There were also days when things didn't go well. Then there was a vague quality about the circle, which made it seem larger and fiercer and more tightly knit, as though the night people were keeping an animal in their midst that no one must see, that they had to keep quiet. Their faces were not polite and passive, as usual, but rigid with tension. They closed their ears to Auntie Margot.

I could never see the animal, but when it was there I knew immediately. My mother felt it too, because every time I sensed that invisible presence, she would say abruptly, "Come on, let's go."

She chivied me along. I dawdled because I would have liked to stay to find out what kind of an animal it was.

"Who have they caught?" I asked.

"Caught?"

"Yes, he's in the middle of them. Who have they caught?"

"They haven't caught anyone. I think it's the other way round: they're caught themselves."

"Are they caught?"

She answered, "I don't know."

"Will it all come right?"

"I don't know. Fate goes its own way."

They were my best friends, the night people. I knew their turns of phrase and their ways of doing things almost better than those of my mother, my aunt, and my father. The night people weren't always caught.

At night they were free. They took me with them. From the night I knew their soft, shadowed faces that I could stroke with my fingers as much as I wanted, which I did in order to absorb them in the hope of becoming like them, dark, invisible, silent.

During the day they did not lift me up and I was never allowed to go with them. They had a lot to do and mostly they looked right past everyone with a smile. However, at those ominous moments, when the circle was large and angry, in the clear light of morning, the night people had wooden masks on. But it always came right again eventually.

Auntie Margot would trot up to us, clapping her hands, gleaming with pleasure.

"Everything's been properly fixed again, Hélène dear."

"Gosh, sis, what would I do without you?"

"You don't have to do anything without me," buzzed Auntie Margot, "we're always going to be together, aren't we?"

They linked arms and walked on, with me behind them.

Auntie Margot soon turned round to me with a smile.

"And what is Si Lulu going to do?" she asked. "Is she going to the store with me to learn how to manage things?"

"No, not to the *gudang*. She's just got her new blouse on. Lulu and I are going to the *waringin*, to say good morning."

"Oh, but that's very important too," agreed my aunt, beaming. "If not more important!"

In the mornings my mother sat on the veranda reading or writing. She was always dressed in fairy-tale gowns, with jewels that sparkled even in the shade. She wore them round her neck, in her ears, and round her wrists. She fanned herself and without even putting down the pen she was writing with, which is why things often went wrong.

If the fanning went well, her writing hand would slip off the paper and there would be ink stains on the tablecloth. If she was able to make the pen glide swiftly over the paper, she would wave the fan rather aimlessly in the air. Then I was allowed to take over fanning from her. I was allowed to do it for her. As I remember, it would keep me amused for hours. I would sit as quiet as a mouse in a chair on a pile of cushions, at the same height next to her, and when I noticed her skin was starting to glow, a sign of the heat, I would fan faster, but unobtrusively, so as not to disturb her. It was fascinating to watch words rolling out of her pen. Each word crept out like a living being: elephants or dwarfs, bats, giants, cats, or birds.

One would flow out of it elegantly, another would come hopping out, and a third would take ages, moving as slowly as a snail. All these words formed an endless parade, a procession without music.

When my mother finished writing at the end of the morning, she put away her notebook, the inkwell, and her pens, deep in the chest whose two drawers were locked, so that mocking spirits couldn't get their hands on her stationery.

In the afternoons my mother would sometimes take me with her to her room and put me in her bed. She would lie down next to me and leaf through some photo albums. She would tell stories to accompany the photos, or we would play games like pat-a-cake and recite rhymes. We sang songs.

I loved her bed: it was much bigger than mine, and the sheets smelled of flowers. The bars of the headboard over which the mosquito net was draped were decorated with white and green ribbons, white rosettes, and light-green bows. Mummy told me they were the ribbons from her wedding bouquet.

On the bed there were at least six or seven pillows, not even counting the bolsters, of which there were two. I thought one was for me, but one day my mother said, "Give me Daddy's bolster for a moment, and we'll build a fort."

"Daddy's bolster?"

"Yes, that one. Pass it over."

It still didn't dawn on me that my father slept in the same bed. I'd never seen him in it. I could no longer concentrate on the building we were making.

"Are these pillows mine, Mummy?"

"Yes, we want lots and lots of pillows. Here, count along with me, we've already got one, two, three. You take this one and I'll take that one and now we'll have a pillow fight."

She threw the pillows around the room like a madwoman, she jumped out of bed and danced around in her shiny shift until she was all red. "Pillow fight, pillow fight, come on, throw something, keep throwing. If you run out of pillows, then throw something else."

She simply hurled her hairbrushes and combs as hard as she could onto the stone floor. After the fight she lay on the bed quite motionless.

"Now don't pester me for a bit, darling, Mummy's tired."

One day the rosettes and bows had gone. Since I had occasionally asked if I could have them, I was disappointed.

"Who got the green ribbons?"

"*Personne.*" She put her finger to her lips and looked around. "I mean: no one. I got rid of the ribbons because they were bringing bad luck. I didn't even realize. I shouldn't have kept my wedding bouquet, I should have given it away."

"Who to? To me?"

"To Auntie Margot."

"Not to Granny Helena?"

"To Granny Helena? She's my mother, silly. Mothers are always married, you see. Although . . . although . . . well this is getting too complicated, you'll hear about it another time."

This was a magic formula I knew very well. So I would hear the story again one day, and I was glad, because I liked hearing stories more than once. Things I was really familiar with gave me confidence. Everything changed so often anyway.

The wedding bouquet, which in my eyes was a sad monstrosity with its hosts of shriveled flower heads, had first occupied a place of honor on the table of Kwan Yin, so it could bathe in her glory. But suddenly it had simply been banished from the house, and sent off to the rubbish heap to be burned. When it had done nothing wrong.

"Oh yes it had, it was bringing bad luck."

"But why?"

"Once you're married, you don't need a bridal bouquet anymore. It's unnecessary and it gets bored and starts brewing mischief; that's the reason."

"What's married?"

"Daddy and I are married. Mummies and daddies are always married. Uncles and aunts aren't always married, though they sometimes are. Granddads and grannies are married too. Do you understand now? No? Doesn't matter, you'll hear about it another time."

"Is Granny Helena married?"

"Of course she's married, otherwise she couldn't be my mother."

Granny Helena didn't look married, or like a mother. She

hung in an extension of the bedroom, where all my mother's clothes also hung and where there was a very large wardrobe full of shoes and clothes belonging to all of us. Granny Helena was in a painting, she was large and white and bare on top, although she also wore a long skirt that came down to her feet, which were also bare. She was standing on a rock in a foaming sea; you could see only a small bit of that. Granny was staring straight ahead, but she wasn't looking at us, she was looking over our heads. She had long curls of golden hair surmounted by a large hat with a bird on it. It had cobalt blue feathers, and its head and wings were slightly raised, as though it were about to fly off. There was something strange about the bird, but I didn't know what. I never dared to look at it for long.

"Can Granny Helena do magic?" I asked my mother. The question suddenly occurred to me, not because Granny looked like someone who could do magic, quite the contrary. She looked more like a tea lady, a visitor who was a little sad because she had to stand in the water with her lovely frock on. So it wasn't the right question.

"Shh," cried my mother, "if she could do magic, she'd be a sorceress. Never say that, never say anything like that about Granny Helena."

She looked almost angry. "Whatever gave you the idea she's a sorceress?" she said, and immediately declared solemnly, "Granny Helena is my mother. You don't talk about mothers like that. A mother," said Mummy, giving me a piercing look, "is someone you honor!"

"It's because of the hat," I mumbled, frightened of causing another outburst, but instead my mother now gave a hearty laugh.

"You should have said that straightaway. Yes, that makes good sense, on top of her hat there's the blue bird, which everyone looks for on distant journeys, but no one finds. Because it's simply at home with you. That's why! Do you understand?"

Sometimes we walked toward the painting: each time you looked at it, it was different. The closer you came to it, the bluer it got. In the white foam of the sea there were monsters, if you asked me, and one of them was gnawing at Granny's toe. My mother pointed. "Have a good look at that hat; can't you see anything special?" I peered as hard as I could, but I couldn't make out anything except what I'd already seen. The bird was sitting there with outspread wings on Granny Helena's head. Whether it wanted to fly away or not, we couldn't tell.

"I know what, have a closer look." Mummy helped me climb onto the wardrobe, giggling as if we were up to something naughty. As I stood up straight, she put her hands firmly round my calves. "Now look carefully, I'll make sure you don't fall."

I almost fell anyway, not out of clumsiness, because I was good at climbing. I was always climbing into and on top of everything, as my mother knew perfectly well, but I almost fell over in astonishment. If my mother hadn't held me tight, I would have tumbled backward off the wardrobe.

The bird had a human face, and not just any face, but the face of an old woman laughing. And how! As if she would never stop. The bird looked like my father, but I must be imagining that, because though my father was old, he was not nearly as old as that old bird woman, and I'd never seen him laugh like that.

My mother lifted me off the wardrobe and put me on the ground.

"Did you see the doll?"

I was dizzy, but before I could ask anything, my mother was already telling me: "Now you've met Granny Mimi."

"Who's Granny Mimi?"

"Your father's mother."

How could a hat be my father's mother?

Granny Mimi was a mother who could make hats herself. She had made this hat for my other granny. Granny Helena lived in England, and Granny Mimi lived in Holland. I'd get to know my grannies if we ever went there. When were we going then? That was written in the stars. That was all she would say, and I didn't dare ask anymore.

"I got a beautiful hat like that from Mimi too. She made it for me," my mother went on. "It's even more beautiful than Granny Helena's hat. Mm. Don't you think that's wonderful? I expect you'd like to see it, wouldn't you?"

"No, no, no!"

"What? Don't you want to see my most beautiful hat? My hat is even more beautiful. . . ."

On the top of the wardrobe with the mirror was the hatbox, pushed right to the back, so that my mother would have to get a chair to reach it. I quickly sat down on the chair, to stop her looking any further.

"Now what's wrong? Get out of my way for a moment."

Outside brooded the heat that always crept up on us during our siesta. The blinds were down, but the sun tried ceaselessly to find a way through chinks and crannies and always managed to project whole rows of specks of light across the bed and the floor and along the walls, through which I often jumped and hopped because I mustn't be touched by any of the dots, or a terrible fate would befall me. I hoped my mother had lost the hat. Just imagine if there were another face in it?

My mother walked up and down the room, opening the door of a wardrobe, a drawer. She was looking for something.

I finally had to ask.

"Does your hat have a face too?"

"A face? No, of course not."

I might just as well not have asked. I would only know for sure when I saw for myself. My mother was often wrong. She forgot a lot too. That's why she said all kinds of things that afterward turned out to be quite different.

Just imagine if this hat had Granny Helena's face on it. Perhaps it was quite normal for hats to have grannies' faces on them.

This afternoon, when my mother couldn't find her wedding hat and cleared out the whole wardrobe and threw more or less everything that was in it on the floor, Auntie Margot came into the room. She'd tapped on the door and called, "What's the reason for all the commotion in here? Are you having a party?"

"Look out, Auntie Margot!" I took her arm and pulled her to one side, because as soon as she crossed the threshold, the sun splashed all over her white kimono. "Mind the sun, mind the sun!"

The last person to whom anything terrible must happen was Auntie Margot.

"Oh sweetie, what a thoughtful, darling child you are. But shouldn't you two be asleep? What's going on here?"

"I'm looking for my wedding hat." My mother was squatting next to the mountain of clothes and pulling everything out of the bottom drawer. She looked up at Auntie Margot over her shoulder. "Would a wedding hat suit you, Margot? Isn't it time for a wedding hat for you?"

"Wedding hat?" Auntie Margot said the words pensively, as if she'd never heard them before. My gaze was fixed on the ground, where a mountain of material was rising before my eyes. My mother added to the mountain with everything she found in the drawer; I saw it climb higher and higher, more and more bits of cloth, perhaps scarves or blouses or sashes. Once the bottom drawer was empty, it was the turn of the wardrobe shelves. Items of headgear floated down one after the other, feathers trembling.

"Hélène, what do you need your wedding hat for?" asked Auntie Margot, still in a tone of astonishment. She saw me looking at the mountain and looked with me. She clicked her tongue. "*Aduh*, what a mess, just look!"

My mother suddenly leapt up holding something that was translucent white with a touch of light green.

"Got you!" She tried to put the thing on the head of Auntie Margot, who gave a cry.

"Be careful! Don't do that, Hélène. That brings bad luck, you know."

My mother slapped her forehead. She flinched as if she had hurt herself.

"*Aduh!* Didn't think of that . . . " she stammered.

"Oooh, be careful!" they both cried and bent down to get the hat, which had fallen on the floor.

Auntie Margot picked it up and went into a corner of the room, where she raised it high above her head with both hands.

"Hélène," she cried, "there are things that even you can't force."

My mother made a contrite pout. "I'm not forcing anything. Everything comes as it's meant to come."

"True," said Auntie Margot. "Whether it's meant to is another matter, but it's true that everything comes."

"And Felix is coming too!" My mother sounded cheerful again. "He's coming, you know, it's a fact, Mimi wrote and told us. It was in her letter to Cees."

"I'm not sure," mumbled Auntie Margot. "He hasn't written to me himself."

"When he's here, we'll give a party."

"Let's see if he comes first."

"He's definitely coming."

"And if he comes, will I be happy? I don't know anymore. He never sends word."

"Oh sis, that's not true."

"He doesn't write letters," sulked Auntie Margot.

"You know he's not much of a writer. But he sends masses of postcards, he sends piles of presents. Sis, you don't say nasty things like that about the man you're going to get engaged to."

Auntie Margot bowed her head, as though she were ashamed.

"How do you know I'm going to get engaged? Engagements lead to marriages." She spoke softly and added even more softly, "Is getting married all that sensible, I wonder?"

"What are you driving at?" cried my mother, suddenly flaring up.

"Nothing, nothing, what do you think I'm driving at?" Auntie Margot hastened to avert the disaster that was once more impending.

"You said getting married isn't sensible. Why did you say that? You said getting married isn't sensible. What did you mean by that? Did you mean me by any chance?"

"What makes you say that? I meant Felix and me."

Auntie Margot's cheeks were flushed, and she looked unhappy. I rushed over to where she was still standing in the corner. I put my arms around her waist and tried to snuggle up to her, but first I looked helplessly at my mother. How could she make Auntie Margot so sad? We all adored her.

I saw my mother coming slowly toward us, but fortunately she didn't look angry.

"Oh, sis! Do you want to stay alone forever?" she asked in a tiny voice.

"I'm not alone, how can I be alone? Look around you. Hélène, tell me honestly, am I alone?"

"No of course not! Of course not, dear Margie! You're never alone, because we're always with you!"

She put her arms around Auntie Margot too, around both of us. Because she was taller than we were, we felt her breath descending on us, and when she started speaking, every word was like a warm raindrop. My mother sang rather than said the words, "Roses wither and ships sink at sea, but we shall love eternally."

THREE

Felix arrived out of the blue as if by a miracle. He was suddenly standing there in our garden. I had never seen him before.

When they first welcomed him my mother acted bashful, almost timid. She kept quietly in the background, bit her nails, and stuffed half of her handkerchief in her mouth. Auntie Margot rushed into Uncle Felix's arms, and my father too was enthusiastic. He called out happily that we would have good use for the newcomer. The first thing I heard the visitor shout was: "That tennis court drives me bananas!"

He shouted it with his arms still around my father, looking over my father's shoulder, laughing. "Bananas are all that court's good for!"

My father said that that would change from now on.

"I can play with you. Those lazy girls prefer sitting on their fat derrieres, their *pantat berat.*"

He laughed as cheerfully as my new uncle.

My mother stamped her foot at the *"pantat berat,"* dropped her handkerchief, and drew herself up to her full height.

"Cees, how dare you!"

"Fiery Hélène! I almost overlooked you," chuckled Uncle

Felix. Whatever he said made my father laugh. Uncle Felix was his youngest brother.

Daddy continued in heartfelt tones, "So you've come to make sure that tennis court finally gets some use."

"We prefer swimming," my mother hurled at the laughing pair. "We like cooling off a bit. We prefer not to wear ourselves out."

"That's the first I've heard of that," crowed Auntie Margot, rocking back and forth, from one foot onto the other, causing her whole body to bounce with pleasure. "Of course we'll play tennis."

"Right, you go ahead. I'm not."

"Can I play too? Can I play too?" I asked. They didn't listen.

"We can get the court cleaned up," said my father.

There was an argument about it anyway.

"And what about our swimming pool then?" snorted my mother.

The tennis court, next to the work pavilion, was all higgledy-piggledy, overgrown with papaya and bananas. In my mother's eyes it was a shambles and good for nothing. Apart from that, the shambles occupied the ideal spot for a swimming pool. It wasn't the first time that there had been words about this.

"And what about our swimming pool then? It's a disgrace that we have to go across the street every time. Especially when their swimming pool's hopeless! And we've got plenty of space. I want our swimming pool to be in the shape of a lotus. That's right, then we'll bob up and down gazing at the stars."

My father maintained stubbornly that that was out of the question as long as he had any say in the matter. "Not while there are children wandering about who can't swim."

"But Lulu knows the danger, I promise you: she'll be able to swim soon. . . ."

"There are other children wandering about here."

. . .

"What did he mean by that?" my mother asked Auntie Margot the following morning. "Is he implying I don't watch Lulu carefully enough?" Our morning walks had changed since Uncle Felix's arrival. Mummy was up to all kinds of things, laughing mysteriously and sometimes spitefully. Auntie Margot kept dancing and twirling around the whole time, in her kimono. She was always in a good mood anyway, but now she was so cheerful: "I'm overflowing. . . ."

My mother and my aunt didn't even seem to notice I was there anymore. I walked after them and kept stumbling in an effort to keep up with them; they were going too fast; I had to run. They also tried to talk softly, but their voices kept rising to a pitch.

"Who are all these children wandering about here? Do you know?" It got louder each time, like a bird call. "What children?"

"The servants' children. He means them, your dear husband," answered Auntie Margot.

My mother stopped and stamped her foot on the pebbles, which crunched and flew in all directions.

"The servants' children, those water rats? They dive into the river, they don't need our swimming pool."

"*Suda*, let it be," Auntie Margot tried to calm her. "Cees doesn't mean any harm, you know that."

"I don't know anything." My mother stamped her foot again. "We'll have our swimming pool built, just like that! Who says I need his permission anyway?"

"Oh, *suda* . . . let it be . . . let it be, Hélène."

The women let go of each other, and moved apart. As usual I quickly crept in between them.

"Please tell me about the swimming pool, Mummy," I asked.

"Later," said my mother, "later, darling, we're too tired now."

I was satisfied with answers like that. They were magic formulas.

On the afternoon that Felix arrived at our house, my father went to the clinic. The hellos were over. A celebratory meal had been served, and everyone was still sitting eating.

My father leapt up, raised his hands, and cried, "I almost forgot Mrs. Dee."

My mother always protested. Now too. "Yes, but listen a moment, your brother's just got here. After a six-week journey—"

"And he needs to recover properly."

My mother bit her nails. "Recover? Recover properly? He seems to have recovered pretty well to me. Best take him with you and show him the ropes. Take him with you to see Mrs. Dee."

My father chuckled. "Mrs. Dee isn't up to that."

"That clinic is the joy of your life; you'd rather be there than here."

"It wouldn't do for me to dislike it, would it, darling?"

It annoyed my mother that my father simply went off, without a messenger arriving with a report, without receiving a phone call. Why should he go when everything was ticking over silently down there at the clinic?

"Oh, my big brother, always taking other people's troubles on his shoulders," said Uncle Felix cheerfully. "He's incorrigible. So let him go, fair sisters, you'll have to console yourselves with me."

As we sat on the veranda after the meal, waiting for the sunset, Uncle Felix said in a reflective tone, half talking, half singing, "I know what I'd do!"

He leaned back in the rocking chair. He turned his head sideways and studied my mother. She was lying on her settee but she wasn't resting, she was looking at newspapers. She flipped through them, then threw the paper peevishly on the ground.

"Don't stare too hard, or my face will fall off," she snapped at Uncle Felix.

"Impossible. As impossible as ever."

My mother stood up and kicked at him with her pointed shoe. She missed, because he didn't even shout "ouch," but grabbing her ankle, he took the shoe and threw it nonchalantly over the balustrade into the garden. Babu immediately brought it back. She carefully dusted the shoe off with her sleeve, but when she got close to my mother, Uncle Felix rose from his chair, took the shoe from Babu, and knelt down in front of my mother, on the ground. He looked up at her. He slid the shoe onto her foot.

"There, Cinderella . . ." I thought he said that, but I didn't hear properly.

Mummy sat up in a fury and didn't say a word.

"Can't you take a joke anymore?"

Her face hardened even more, she pressed her lips tightly together and picked at her nails, which she often did, but never as doggedly as now. A drop of blood appeared by the quick of her thumb, which she licked up. There was still a little blood on her lower lip when she said, "You concern yourself with Margot; you're here for her."

"That's right, for who else?" Uncle Felix slowly got up, turned around, and knelt down by Auntie Margot's chair.

"Margot dear, shall we knock a ball about?"

Auntie Margot had sat amiably all that time. She nodded to him with a smile. "It's too late now. How about another time?"

She had forgotten to change after the siesta and still had her kimono on.

"Oh it's never too late for a game," said Uncle Felix.

"Oh yes, dear, that's true, but let's get changed first." Auntie Margot got up, hesitated again, and dawdled just long enough for Uncle Felix to say, "Don't worry, darling lazybones, I'll find someone else!"

To my excitement he turned to me. "Lulu, you! You know it's never too late for a game. Fair maiden, come on, would you like to knock a ball about with me?"

This happened on the very first day Uncle Felix was with us. Had I heard right? I immediately ran to my room, looking for my badminton set. I didn't know what to make of it. No one ever wanted to play with me in the evenings. I always had to wait until the night people fetched me.

From then on Uncle Felix and I played shuttlecock almost every evening. The first time I fetched the bats and the ball, which had such a funny tail of feathers attached to it, but after that, when it got a little cooler Uncle Felix brought the set himself.

After the first few times, which still came as a surprise, I waited for it. In Daddy's chair, on the veranda, even before the *tjitjaks* had appeared on the ceiling. I also prepared myself, as well as I could, for a disappointment. Would this be an evening for playing shuttlecock or would it all go wrong this time? Was it still hot or was it cooling off a bit? Would something else ruin everything? A thick cloud across the moon or, worse still, a storm or fire?

If the game was on, Uncle Felix would ask, "Lulu, fair maiden, would you like to knock a ball about?" The way he said it was a new experience for me, even more so than the game itself.

Fair maiden! No one had ever dreamed that up for me, not even the night people, who gave me lots of pet names.

"Isn't this evening the fairest of evenings for shuttlecock!"

"Don't get the child all excited before her bedtime," my mother sometimes said sternly.

"Physical exercise is a healthy kind of excitement."

"Oh, you think so? Well, well. All right then, but not for too long . . . until the shuttlecock hits the ground, no longer."

We went on playing much longer than that.

Very cautiously at first; we crept over the lawn, like cats. The first bats were already fluttering about; in fact, we could no longer even see the ball with the feathers on it. And then, after it had fallen on the ground somewhere among the bushes and we really could not find it anymore, we simply played on, as if the shuttlecock was still in the air. But it wasn't at all, it was lost. The others didn't know, because we kept letting loose cries like "I say, good shot!"

"Oh, just got it, nearly a mis-hit. . . ."

"Did you see that one coming?" And we made particularly strange leaps that served no purpose.

"Our secret," said Uncle Felix afterward, pinching my cheek. "Just keep it well!"

"How do I do that, Uncle?" I whispered nervously.

"How do you do what?"

"Keep a secret."

"Oh! Look, like this . . . !"

Uncle Felix twisted his right ear, then his left one. "You simply tie a knot in your ears and that's it."

My mother came storming up through the dark.

"What's going on, is this game ever going to end?"

"Look, Mummy, I can keep a secret."

I twisted my ears just as Uncle Felix had done.

"You learned that from a smooth talker." She nudged Uncle Felix with her elbow. "Oh yes, my fine fellow, you help me bring her up."

Uncle Felix moved into a house a little way away, a pavilion that was also close to the stream. He had books and large bottles, and jars like my father, but lots more. During the day he went to the pharmacy at the clinic. Not every day and so many nights too, like my father. When he got into the car to drive there, it was always during the day and he had already first been to see us and say good-bye. The car stood purring on the road, with the chauffeur at the wheel, but Uncle Felix didn't hurry.

"Well then, dear ladies, it's time for a little action again. We're off to mix some poison."

He gave us all a kiss, just above the wrist, and later waved to us from the backseat of the car, his hands fluttering in the air until he had vanished from sight around a bend in the road. He always came back earlier than my father.

"Oh well, why should I get in everybody's way there? I can leave everything to nature, and to good old Driessen of course, with a clear conscience. For form's sake I got the Chinese to fold packets today."

My mother looked glum and shook her head.

"You've deserted again, you have. How can my conscientious husband possibly have such a good-for-nothing of a brother?"

"'I'm always where I'm needed,'" cried Uncle Felix cheerfully. He blew over my mother's hair or quickly tickled her behind the ear. Then he made a deep bow in front of Auntie Margot.

"Care for a knockabout, fair lady?"

They hadn't got around to playing tennis yet, but one afternoon my mother jumped up energetically and grabbed Auntie Margot, who was sitting next to her on the settee, firmly by the arm. She shook her backward and forward. "Sis, I want to make something very clear to you."

She didn't say anything more to Auntie, but turned to Uncle Felix. "Yes, you there! A game of tennis will do my easygoing sister good. Felix, she's a lazy devil, you know. She just sits on her *pantat berat*. But not you, no, if it's a question of a game, you don't mind running! Teach her the game for goodness' sake, tire her out! So she finally sheds all that lazy fat of hers!"

Although Auntie Margot kept cooing happily that she was quite prepared to play some tennis, if she only could understand the game, she kept dreaming up excuses not to have to go to the court, which for that matter wasn't even ready yet. But my mother wouldn't hear of any further postponements.

"Come on!" she urged them. "There's no getting out of it any longer."

"But why? Leave me be."

Meanwhile Mummy made two plaits in Auntie's thick hair. "Cut that impossible bushy mop off, sis, you look like a Papuan."

My aunt shook her head awkwardly with her new plaits.

"I'm not sure, Hélène. It's as if there are two drowning people clinging to my head."

"Now come on inside and put on what I've bought for you. Oh, you'd be a match for Suzanne Lenglen."

Auntie Margot covered her eyes with her hands as though a terrible punishment awaited her, but did go inside with her. After a while she emerged looking sheepish, preceded by my triumphant mother. I also thought she looked pretty strange in the short white dress that stretched tightly around her bulging torso and puffed out around her hips like the calyx of a flower.

"*Terlalu*, this is a shroud. . . ." said my aunt in a flat voice. "A shroud that comes halfway down my thighs. Wasn't there enough material to make a proper dress?"

"I don't want to hear another word about it!"

My mother sometimes spoke in the same stern tone to me. It worked. Auntie Margot leapt straight into action and went off at a trot, jabbering that she hadn't a clue about tennis. She called out that she didn't know how to hold a racket. And what side of the net should she stand on?

"If there were any net in sight, you'd be standing there," we heard Uncle Felix say cheerfully.

It wasn't long before the sound of the bouncing balls and gales of laughter came from the distance.

"Are we going to have tennis lessons too?" I asked my mother.

"No, it's too hot for us, we're water people, we'll have a dip shortly. . . ."

"Let's go and take a look, just for a bit."

"No, Auntie Margot is having a tennis lesson and in a tennis lesson the players mustn't be disturbed, or everything will get messed up."

"If I creep up, very quietly—"

"Darling, you can't, because I've got to write so you've got to fan me."

My mother's word was law. Usually.

The tennis lessons went on and on. The fan felt so heavy I could scarcely lift it any longer. Mummy went on writing imperturbably, the letters gliding onto the paper at lightning speed, forming serpentines and snaking across page after page. I looked at them, but it made my head spin, there was too much squirming. I submerged myself in the little star that she wore in her ear. It was blue-green like deep water, and I tried to get to the bottom. But if she shook her head slightly, I flew out again and landed somewhere on her cheek, which was snow white but also full of freckles, innumerable freckles under the layer of powder. My eyes wandered over her face, at first in an exalted mood but with increasing longing. Once I'd discovered her freckles beneath the powder, I wanted to find everything else that was to be seen, and my eyes probed further and further. Now and then she glanced to the side and fluttered her eyelashes. I don't know if this was a sign of approval or something else, but I didn't stop to think about it for long because I didn't want to let anything stop me. Her eyelashes were the same color as her freckles, except at the tips, where they were painted black.

"Don't stare so hard or my face will fall off," she remarked after a while, and it sounded a little like a plea, not spiteful as when she'd said it to Uncle Felix.

"Can you do that, Mummy? Can you really ruin all the beautiful things just by looking?"

I nuzzled her cheek.

"Yes, it's possible." She didn't sound angry, more satisfied. I wanted to run my nose gently along her cheek, as my father sometimes did, but I didn't dare. Instead I stared for a long time at her nose, which was as small, wide, and flat as a cat's. Without thinking, I finally touched it with my forefinger.

"Don't prod, Lulu, look, splashes all over the paper," she said absentmindedly and went on writing faster than ever. She became more and more like the cat suggested by her nose. She even stuck her tongue out surreptitiously and ran it across her lips, as if trying to lap up the words as soon as she had consigned them to the paper.

I had to control myself so as not to touch the whole time, stroke her nose again, or, worse still, seize that darting tip of the tongue between my thumb and forefinger and pull it out a little farther.

In order to banish these impulses, I started listening as hard as I could to the murmuring of the garden, which was faint but penetrating, and for which you had to keep both ears wide open, so difficult was it to distinguish the music of the different insects and other creatures, let alone actually name the music makers. There were some that hummed and others that rustled and some that hissed or sniffed, but all of them together had nowhere near sufficient power to drown out the shouts and screams of Auntie Margot and Uncle Felix that were getting through to us. It distracted my attention from the garden. What did it mean? I'd never heard that kind of cheering, not even at the fair.

The cries and the laughter came closer. Perhaps my uncle and aunt were playing a game and imitating the sounds of all kinds of creatures; there was giggling, crowing, roaring, and growling.

Suddenly they were standing in front of us. "Tea!" they cried. They maintained they were shattered, but that wasn't true. Auntie Margot was beaming. Her brown skin glowed, and she swayed contentedly back and forth with the racket in one hand and the ball in the other.

She looked a little disheveled, the buttons of her dress were no longer done up, they were almost all open.

I wanted to run up to her, as I always did, and put my arms around her and feel her arms around me.

My mother put her hand on my shoulder and stopped me. "Stay where you are. Auntie Margot's so tired, she can't do a thing, poor dear!"

That's what she said, though Auntie Margot didn't look tired, but rather as if they were just about to start a new game. But Mummy's hand stayed where it was and pressed down more heavily and became hot.

Auntie Margot and Uncle Felix finally sat down in the wicker chairs and begged for tea.

"What are the two of you thinking of, soaking wet and in soaking wet gear? Quickly go and have a shower and change first."

My mother spoke in measured tones, slightly irritated, as though talking to naughty children.

My uncle and aunt shuffled into the house with their arms around each other, and then you could hear all kinds of noises coming from the distance but more softly this time. The splashing of water and now and again something reminiscent of singing. My mother sat upright the whole time, although she was no longer writing. She'd already put her stationery away. She was deep in thought.

I listened to the garden again and almost fell asleep in my father's chair. Suddenly I started, because Mummy was suddenly shaking me to and fro, her curls were close to my face, her nose was almost touching mine. She whispered, "That shower's taking a long time, isn't it? Darling, I'm going to see nothing's happened."

"Shall I go and look?"

"No, no, no, no, not for all the tea in China."

She didn't go and look either, though. She had sat down on the bamboo seat. She stayed sitting where she was. She stared over my head, straight ahead.

After a little while it was not only quiet where we were but in the house too.

Auntie Margot and Uncle Felix didn't come back.

I had dozed off rolled up in the chair, and woke up when my mother said to me impatiently, "The sun's already . . . you see, all right then, you go and have a look. . . ." She'd started writing again at the writing table, and now she stopped. "Go on . . ." I saw her blowing her writing dry on a thin blue piece of paper and putting her pad away in the cupboard that had been made for her, intended for her stationery. She clapped her hands.

Night people came from various directions. My mother and they devoted themselves to the preparations for a late tea ceremony.

I dawdled into the house. But before I could go to her room to look for her, I found my aunt in the side gallery in her kimono. She was barefoot and was singing *pompadom* in her deep voice. She looked the same as always, and yet she was unrecognizable. She looked right through me. She looked like someone I'd never seen. She almost floated as she walked, but I stood right in front of her and thrust my head out so that it bounced against her tummy. She recognized me.

"Hello, sweetie. My darling Lulu tootsie."

For a moment I was frightened she didn't know who I was—she'd never called me Lulu tootsie before—but then she bent over me and lifted me up a little. Everything was all right when she hugged me. She smelled wonderful. Sweet and warm. Her frizzy hair, which was so marvelous to run my hands through, was like a huge bush around her head again. She was glowing. She gave me smacking kisses on my cheeks, and I put my arms as tightly as I could around her. As we let go of each other to gasp for air, I saw the bruise. I carefully put my finger out to it.

"Oh Auntie, you got hit with a ball here."

The spot, on her neck below her ear, was a nasty blue color.

"What's that?" Her hand shot up and she was about to go back to her room, but changed her mind and went over to the big mirror in the hall with me. She stroked her neck and breast hesitantly and didn't want to open her kimono any farther, but I pulled it open at the top and pointed to another spot. She saw it and had another shock.

"Oh dear, oh dear. What now?" Again she closed the kimono as high as possible.

"Do they hurt a lot, Auntie? Shall I kiss them better?"

"They do hurt a bit," said my aunt slowly, "but not too badly."

She pinched my arm reassuringly, kissed me on the head, put me back on the ground, and turned me in the direction that I'd come from.

"Off you go, sweetie. We'll be right there."

Meanwhile the tea table had been laid on the veranda and indeed beautifully, as though there were a party, with my favorite tea service, on which there were all kinds of little men and women wandering hand in hand through a park, over little bridges and down little avenues. It was a gold Japanese service, a present from Granddad Bali, but hadn't been smashed on the floor yet.

"Uncle Felix has thrown balls at Auntie Margot very hard," I said to my mother.

"What's that?"

I described the blue bruises that I'd seen on my aunt, and I made it a little less bad than it was in case my mother got alarmed, but I was still telling her when she suddenly screamed with laughter, so that I realized there was nothing seriously wrong with Auntie Margot.

FOUR

Uncle Felix and my father spoke to each other in a language that annoyed my mother, because she couldn't understand it properly. She felt that Uncle Felix should learn our language better.

"Practice your Dutch," she said sternly. "It's the language of your future wife."

From then on she gave us both lessons, Uncle Felix and me.

I drew a new letter for her every day, with colored pencils, on drawing paper. If I'd done a good job, she clapped her hands and hugged me. She had my letter drawings hung up, on the veranda. "Look, everyone, my clever girl did that." Auntie Margot and my father sang my praises, but Uncle Felix wasn't that impressed.

"The child's got a whole lifetime yet to ruin her eyes and curb her mind."

Particularly when he was there, I was very good at learning. He was also given new words to learn by my mother.

At each lesson Uncle Felix did his best for a while, but suddenly began to invent words for himself; at lightning speed he invented scores of words and insults and let them escape from his mouth with the appropriate sounds. Swarms of flapping birds and clumsy enchanted toads, whatever was appropriate.

"The ships of steamship company Ascension Day steamed

toward Goejanverwellesuis on Twelfth Night! The Hottentot
Tent Exhibition, good God! Don't spout wrath, fair lady, don't
spout wrath."

"Spout wrath, Uncle Felix, spout wrath, what's that?"

"Spouting wrath is what gargoyles do and you find them in
Paris, like this . . ." and then as quick as a flash he drew horrific
and wonderful creatures with folding snouts and wings on large
sheets of paper.

"Uncle, they look like Garuda—"

"Who's Garuda when he's at home?"

I took Uncle Felix by the hand and pulled him along
with me.

"Look, Uncle, Garuda's here and here and everywhere."

Garuda, the legendary fighting bird that fought evil with its
beak and claws and carried the supreme god Vishnu on its back
between its gigantic wings, was always present, in all forms and
shapes, but you couldn't always see it. Once you knew it, you saw
him. I had known Garuda for as long as I'd been alive. He lived in
virtually everything in our surroundings, in clothes and furniture, in household objects, jewelry.

"If Garuda insists on it, the evil runs away," said my mother.

"If Garuda insists on it? Mm, that would be nice. A person
would have to watch his step," said my uncle.

"Yes, as usual you know better, of course."

"Oh, Hélène? The less I know, the more *you* can teach me."

When Uncle Felix was nice to her, my mother got even
angrier.

"It's true you've still got everything to learn," she snapped at
him, "except for dancing and flirting! That's all you can do."

"What's flirting?" I asked.

"Later, that will come later. First we're going to dance because that charmer, that future brother-in-law of mine, can do
that."

I didn't know if these were swear words because although my mother was speaking cattily, Uncle Felix laughed at her and said, "Honored, I'm sure, honored, I'm sure."

"Can I take my shoes off if we dance?" I asked while the two of them chose a record and put it on the turntable.

"On the contrary. Shoes on! Especially when dancing! Look how easy it is."

My mother began waltzing and pulled Uncle Felix with her. He took her in his arms and nodded to me with his head to join them. I didn't. I preferred listening and looking at my mother and Uncle Felix, singing together and dancing across the marble floor of the hall.

"Dance, darling, dance, don't stand there staring! You've got to dance, dance!" Mummy called to me, panting and laughing. "Why shouldn't we dance?" she went on excitedly. "It's almost the end of the monsoon. It's time for a wedding. We shall dance."

Auntie Margot had got engaged to Uncle Felix. The two had refused to celebrate it nicely and festively, said my mother, with cards and a cake with rings on. Auntie Margot replied that it was a festival in itself, being engaged to her Felix.

"That dandy, who wastes our time here with you," my mother observed sharply.

Uncle Felix didn't care what my mother said to him. He always listened with a grin. And nor did Auntie Margot care what my mother said anymore.

"You mustn't be jealous, Hélène, you've got Cees and your darling Lulu," she crowed, "and your darling Lulu."

Since Uncle Felix had arrived, something had happened every day. Like the rain, he got everything moving.

He became my best friend. He could tell beautiful stories. You didn't even need to understand him word for word, because he acted out what was happening. When events became too complicated, he would play a piece of music. He was an accordionist, a poison mixer, a juggler, and a minstrel. He was a prodigy.

He could do everything because he took swigs from magic bottles all day long, and from glasses the others didn't know were there, just he and I.

The glasses appeared and disappeared and made journeys through the whole house. Sometimes there would be one, half empty, on a ledge in the library for a while; suddenly it would be gone, but when I went looking for it I found it again, refilled. In the shower room in the flower tub, or in the hall under the telephone table, or carefully protected behind the back of the Elephant God, I found the secret glasses everywhere.

The bottles stayed in their place for longer, hidden behind books and in the cupboard. There was also a bottle, which I'd never seen empty, that lived in a hollow in the *waringin* tree.

I told Uncle Felix that our *waringin* had been a Javanese prince in an earlier life.

"Well I never!"

Dewi Kesuma, our stream, used to be a princess. Something terrible had happened to this prince and princess, but I didn't know what. No one knew, not even the gods.

They had found out too late and by that time not even the gods could rescue the prince and princess.

Uncle Felix said that this didn't surprise him at all, because when it came down to it, the gods could never do anything. They were too lazy or they came too late or they hadn't noticed a thing as usual.

One day he came up to me with a blue book. He'd been given it by my mother to practice the Dutch language.

"It's in here, look," said Uncle Felix. He pointed to the golden letters on the cover: *"Javanese Sagas, Myths and Legends.* Listen to this.

"'How when the gods had turned Prince Pangeran Djamodjaja into a tree . . .' Are you listening? Pay attention, this isn't rubbish. The gods turned the prince into a tree. It was like this: 'The dead, stiffened body of the prince stood up with outstretched arms and his long black hair fell in thin gray tresses over his shoulders to the ground!'"

Uncle Felix stiffened, and the book dropped from his hands onto the ground.

"Watch closely, Lulu," he said, rolling his eyes. "This is how it went."

He lifted his arms up, hands flapping wildly. He opened his mouth as wide as he could and his head with the rolling eyes fell to one side. He stood there like that and his voice went on telling the story, but I couldn't see his mouth moving.

"Dewi Kesuma, the prince's wife, cried buckets of tears. She saw that her beloved husband was turning into a gigantic tree. He had been a giant of a man, but not anymore. On the contrary, he was becoming a giant of a tree, a real tree with branches and leaves. Roots too."

Uncle Felix dropped his arms and planted his feet so firmly that the earth underneath became churned up. He pretended he couldn't take another step. He couldn't walk anymore. The book lay on the ground, closed.

He went on in a high-pitched voice, "'What good is this life-less tree to me?' Dewi Kesuma cried and she wrung her hands in despair. 'What good is this soulless tree to me?'"

When I'd heard the story often enough, I joined in. Then Uncle Felix would fall silent at certain points, and would wait till I solemnly said my lines, in the deepest voice I could manage.

"This tree is not lifeless. It is sacred and everyone will call it the Holy Waringin."

Uncle Felix continued, "The Kama Djaja, the protector of married couples, descended from heaven. He descended at the spot where the prince lay and bent over the dead man."

He went on like that in an exalted tone for a long time, and I didn't even need to understand the words, I bathed in the sounds as if in a shower of rain, I swayed to the rhythm as if I were in a rocking chair.

When Uncle Felix's voice swelled and boomed out, I knew the passage was coming that appealed to me most: "The dead and almost rigid body of her husband stood up with out-stretched arms—"

"How did that happen? How?" I exclaimed, although I knew. Before he could answer I pulled my uncle along with me to the tree.

Fleetingly I touched the cool trunk, which was the color of elephant hide and under which there was a soft pulse, as if under my own skin.

"Is this the body of the prince, Uncle?" I asked. "Is this really the body of the prince? How did it happen? How did it go on?"

Uncle Felix also dared to touch the *waringin*. He stroked the bark tenderly and now and then he grabbed one of the tough gray air roots. "This is his skin, this bark, and these long strands were his hair. If that surprises you, Lou, although you've heard the story so often, you can understand how surprised that poor Kesuma was, the first time. She couldn't believe her eyes, good heavens. She was frightened out of her skin, right out of her skin. Listen. Dewi Kesuma saw with astonishment how a layer of rough bark had covered the whole body of the prince. His arms were covered in bark too, and from these arms sprouted branches full of fresh, bright-green leaves. Just imagine. Dewi Kesuma shed many tears and then as she cried she had to watch the feet of her beloved husband sink into the earth. Just imagine your feet turning into roots. Impossible to a walk another step. You might as well forget jumping and dancing. His feet became the roots of this tree. The princess went to the tree weeping, flung her arms around the rough bark, and pressed herself against it. Sobbing, she cried, 'What use is this lifeless tree to me?'"

Uncle Felix picked the book up. He gave it to me so that

I could hold it, and paced around the tree making expansive gestures.

"This tree is not lifeless. It's sacred and all will call it the Holy Waringin. And the *waringin* will be holy and will remain so. It will spread its seeds over the whole of Java. A proud tree will grow from every seed. Everywhere these trees will come out of the ground, even in the smallest village. And the Holy Waringin will be the sacrificial tree of all those who live in Java. Princes as well as beggars will place their sacrifices to the gods under its branches. Children will play in its shadow, and young people will entrust their secrets to its trunk in a whisper."

Uncle Felix looked like a floating god, because he could do that too, walk a little way off the ground. Anyone who looked closely could see that he was walking on tiptoe, of course, but he did it with such speed and panache that it could pass for flying. Everyone who heard his voice came and looked, even the night people would come out of every nook and cranny, even the *kokkis*, abandoning whatever they'd been doing.

Uncle Felix's ginger hair fanned out round his head, his eyes sparkled behind his glasses; it was absolutely certain that Kama Djaja had such a pair of glasses and just as pale a face and was dressed in an untidy sarong not tied completely in accordance with the rules, and a cream-colored, rather oversize shirt, which was buttoned askew.

We all looked up, and saw Kama Djaja fly back to heaven with great wing beats, and saw how once he'd arrived there, he became invisible to our eyes. Then we looked down again, to where Uncle Felix was suddenly standing there again with his head bowed, knees bent, just returned to earth.

"When the god Kama Djaja had said all this to Dewi Kesuma he went back to heaven. Did you all see him go?" Uncle Felix grinned up. He waved. "Bye, bye, gods, bye! Back to heaven, off you go." He called it out in a tone as if he were talking to the geese, which were always waddling up onto the veranda or to Teddy-Bali. "Off you go, off you go, shoo, shoo. Fall in! Quick march! Quick march!"

We encouraged him with our glances, nodded satisfaction with our heads, yes the enchantment had been broken and that was just as well.

Uncle Felix looked around him, bowed and said, "My thanks to you all." He came slouching up to me and took my head in his hands. When he was close I could catch a whiff of his magic drink.

"Well Louisee Peasee," he said half mockingly, half solemnly, "now we both know the story of the *waringin*. Oh dear, oh dear, if only it were true."

"And now the stream, come on, Uncle?" I handed the book back to him.

"Yes yes, off we go again. So we've still got the story of the stream. Little Dewi Kesuma. The sad princess who never again left her prince."

Uncle Felix read this part very feelingly, wiping a tear from his eye behind his glasses. I myself was usually crying happily even before he began.

"'She stayed in this spot, her arms flung round the trunk, her head resting against it. In that way Dewi Kesuma fell asleep forever. Her beautiful soul was taken up into heaven and her body became a spring, from which crystal-clear water bubbles, and from which crystal-clear fountains spring.'"

Only now was the story completely finished.

Only now could everyone laugh in approval and nod and point, because sure enough, look over there, they were still together, the princess and the prince, here in the garden with us.

There was quite a distance between the tree and the water, but they could still always hear and see each other, they talked to each other every day and every night.

Listen, here you could stand by the *waringin* and hear how sweetly the stream murmured, and here by the stream you could hear the leaves of the tree giving her a rustling answer.

Uncle Felix was a night walker just like me. At night, on my way to the back garden, where the night people lived, hand in hand with Babu, we often saw him standing there, in his sarong and pajama top, his head flung right back in order to study the heavens. From his clothing you would think he was one of the servants, but from his gleaming lenses and his equally gleaming hair falling over his ears, you knew that it was him, Uncle Felix. My escorts beamed. They attributed supernatural powers to him because of his golden hair and light-blue eyes.

Uncle Felix recognized us too, Babu and me.

"It's full moon, and a man can't sleep then. Hello, lovely Sopia, hello, little Harlequin."

He always knew the names of the night people. He knew a lot, and he could do almost everything.

According to my mother, though, he couldn't think up good excuses when he didn't want to dance or fix a date for the wedding.

"Think of a better excuse," she said, full of contempt. "Say you don't want to dance because you've got a headache. Or a tummy ache, or muscle pains for all I care. But you simply make it clear rudely, without a word, that you don't feel like anything. Perhaps not even marrying?"

"I don't feel like anything. Just wring my neck. Just shoot me."

"So what's the good of that trunk full of dance records? What are you always doing by the gramophone then? That thing's been on all day: English waltz, quickstep, fox-trot, tango this, tango that. . . ." She went up to the cabinet and banged on it so hard that the record screeched. "Why don't you go out more with my dear sister and take her dancing at the club?" My mother stalked up to Uncle Felix. "You've got to provide more distractions and then she won't want to work day and night in that horrid clinic anymore."

Uncle Felix went right up to my mother and took her by the arms.

"Margot is a nurse with all her heart of gold, and she wants nothing better than to help those horrid cases back onto their feet again. Just like Cees for that matter."

He shook my mother back and forth a bit as if he were dealing with a difficult portrait. My mother pulled herself free.

"Perhaps Cees should have married Margot," she said teasingly and menacingly.

"And I you, God help us," replied Uncle Felix, in the same tone.

Then they burst out laughing. Small glasses were put on the table, and I was given my syrup.

Uncle Felix wasn't always cheerful during the day, but late in the evening he was.

When we sat on the veranda admiring the sunset, the usual bottle and everyone's glasses were on the table.

The glasses of Mummy and Auntie Margot had silver feet and large goblets, but Uncle Felix's evening glass was small and round, and he held it in his hand like a Ping-Pong ball. He drank from it calmly, sip by sip, not as quickly as from all the others that were in the niches and in other secret places. He downed those in one go, head back, as he passed. Perhaps he did it so quickly because the magic drink tasted so nasty. I had experienced that for myself. I had once taken a swig from the bottle that was in a hollow in the *waringin*, because after all the tree had divine powers and so made everything in its surroundings holy and good. Nevertheless, the sip burned my throat, and I had to make a huge effort to swallow it. I just managed it. Afterward tears came into my eyes and I felt strange and just sat quietly in the tree until it passed. It was the first time I became invisible. All kinds of people went past without anyone seeing me. No one could say anything about my sitting there because they couldn't see me. My mother walked past deep in thought. If she'd seen me, she would have given me a ticking off because I was sitting on my haunches. I wasn't allowed to do that, squat. I had to sit properly on a chair, with legs down and feet together.

In the morning Mummy and I stood in the shower room in translucent green light. My mother poured water over me with the *gajong*, sometimes she sighed long and deeply and didn't want to talk, but sometimes she sang a song and taught me the words.

We heard the voices of my aunt and uncle.

"Well well, little Margot is not at work for a change, that must mean something," chortled my mother, "and Felix has gone very early. How early they are; what are those two up to?"

"They're eating."

"Yes, they make a lot of noise. Everyone has to hear and see their happiness."

"Can I go and hear and see their happiness?"

"Off you go then!"

Uncle Felix was just hurrying toward the corner of the gallery where the tea chest was. He went over to it with the great catlike leaps that he was so good at and showed to their best effect when the two of us played shuttlecock. Now he leapt toward the chest, which contained his holy relics, as he called them. Just like my mother, he had a collection of pens and inkwells and notebooks: though hers lay on the top shelf and his on the middle shelf. Below that, in a drawer that was always locked personally by her, was the secret, blue-marbled notebook of Auntie Margot.

When Auntie Margot wasn't in the clinic, she always sat singing and swaying in the rocking chair on the gallery in the morning, looking at my mother and Uncle Felix delightedly, as they both sat with pen poised over the paper. Uncle Felix wrote perhaps a word every hour. When that happened, Auntie Margot jumped up and cried: "Have you done it again, you clever boy?" Then Uncle Felix would get up suddenly and start walking nervously through the garden and around the house.

"Do stop fussing . . ." hissed my mother.

"Hélène! You usually say just the—"

"Sssh. *Suda*, let it be."

One day Auntie Margot had an exercise book on her lap too.

"What? Have you started writing poetry?" cried Mummy. "My sister's a poet and wouldn't you know it."

Auntie Margot covered the pages with her hands. "You're very spiteful; surely it doesn't matter what I'm writing. Then you two can be quiet and I've got something to keep me busy too. . . ." She sounded as if she were apologizing.

"Busy with what, may I inquire? What have you got to write about? A diary or something?"

"Or something," answered Auntie Margot mysteriously, and laughed softly.

I liked to sit with them when they were all writing in the gallery. I knew very well that I had to keep quiet, but sometimes a word slipped out. Then Auntie Margot would put her finger to her lips and push the dish of sticky delicacies toward me for me to eat from. Although I wasn't supposed to because Mummy said it would give me little brown stubs of teeth like the oldest *kokki*, I nevertheless took something off the dish now and again and popped it in my mouth because that made it easier not to talk. What were they writing? Why didn't they read it aloud? Why did Uncle Felix write so interminably slowly? They must be magic formulas, which he put down on paper one by one so elaborately and with such concentration and breathing so deeply. It wasn't even writing that he was doing, it was more like drawing.

"Yes, dear Lulu, you guessed again, they're magic formulas, for a doctor."

In Auntie Margot's case the words did regularly flow from her pen. I saw Uncle Felix sometimes glancing sideways with a wounded expression when he saw her turning the page again. Sometimes her fast writing certainly must have annoyed him because then he would say gruffly, "Try a new pen, Margot dear, that one's scratching so badly it's hurting my ears."

"Oh, of course, I'm sorry, darling. I was so absorbed in my innocent scribbling, I'll do it right away. Don't let me distract you, whatever happens."

"Too late." He shut his book with a bang, jumped up, and took me by the hand.

"Lulu, would you like to take a turn round the garden with me? Do you want to join the girl guides? Don't, do you hear. In the girl guides there are naughty akelas. Be careful, be careful. Never join the guides, because the akelas are on the rampage. Don't ever play with an akela because she has a big saucepan and she throws little girls into it and makes them into little girl soup."

Auntie Margot came after us. She leapt off the veranda, losing a slipper, her housecoat blew open, and she had nothing on underneath. She was like my round toy dipper from Singapore.

"Don't you believe him, Lulu. What have you got the nerve to say about akelas, you bad man?"

Uncle Felix went on imperturbably; he pulled me with him and we walked faster. Auntie Margot lumbered along behind us.

"Akela bottles fat girls. Fat girls go into the vinegar and the thin ones she puts into batter and the silliest ones she puts into kilner jars!" cried Uncle Felix loudly, and then he was pounced on by my auntie Margot and they rolled and romped over the grass.

"Like dogs, like *kampong* children? Bah, bah, bah," exclaimed my mother indignantly as she watched the wrestling. Uncle Felix, who was lying on the ground, grabbed her by the hem of her dress. My mother was already immaculately dressed even early in the morning; she did her toilet long before six o'clock, even before we went to see Daddy off. She was there without fail, perfectly groomed, decked out in her necklaces and bracelets and earrings, her face even more palely powdered than it was naturally, her hair brushed till it shone, her eyebrows picked out in little arcs.

Uncle Felix grabbed her by the hem of her dress with one hand, put his other round her ankle, and pulled her over.

"There goes Hélène!"

In the evening she told my father. Surprised and concerned, he had commented, "What are those grazes and bumps? What have you all been getting up to, for heaven's sake?"

"That savage grabbed me and made me fall on top of him!" my mother began, and as she told the story, however angry she tried to sound, she couldn't suppress her laughter.

"I swear to you, Cees, your brother ran amok. First he took Margot for a ride. How dare he, how dare he!"

A ride? They hadn't been riding. All I could see was that tangle of people rolling over one another, which my mother had suddenly plunged into the middle of, her hands messing up Uncle Felix's hair.

After a while Auntie Margot, a little farther off on the grass, had called out urgently, *"L'enfant l'enfant,"* which was usually intended for me. Just when I was getting ready to join in the melee myself, because I thought that was the idea, an end was put to it by her shout.

The three of them had got up and one by one walked off to different parts of the house shaking their heads. The rough and tumble had been as jolly as a birthday, with a cake with candles on it and balloons that burst. I went quickly to the *waringin* to tell it.

After our afternoon nap my mother and I often went across the road to the swimming pool of Villa Isola. We didn't say any more about that swimming pool of ours, which had yet to be built.

For a while Uncle Felix sometimes came running after us in his blue bathrobe with his towel under his arm.

"Mummy, can Uncle Felix come swimming with us?" I asked excitedly.

"Him? Swim? He prefers to watch from the poolside and smoke his cigarettes."

"No, he always joins in and then we can play John Jenny in the Tun," I said, supporting Uncle Felix.

"In the tun? That's all right, but swim? He can't. Forget it, a bit of dipping and splashing, that's all it is."

I sung to myself "Dipping and splashing, dipping and splashing."

We walked across the road, Mummy in her embroidered silk bathrobe, a work of art, she once told me, with her head cocked to one side, "Made for me by Granny Mimi; you're a lucky child, to have such artistic grannies!"

Under the bathrobe she wore a light, almost transparent nymph's costume, as pale as her skin, with a hint of green. I loved her bathing cap, which she always forgot to put on when Uncle Felix was there. It fitted smoothly round her head and there was a picture of a paradise on it, full of glowing trees and big-eyed fishes. But when she forgot it, I didn't say anything, and I sometimes put the cap a little farther away behind a plant, because I liked seeing her even more without it, because I thought it was so beautiful, the way her hair floated around her in the water.

She let herself fall backward into the pool as if she were

sleepwalking, floating down the wide steps. The water received her, and started pushing her gently around, and she let herself float with eyes closed and a smile around her mouth, her short, silver hair fanned out under the water surface; her head was a little like the moon. I shivered and became momentarily dizzy with a feeling that something from very far away had suddenly come very close, just for a second.

One afternoon, when I was sitting on the edge of the pool, at the shallow end, I heard my mother call out something; it was more humming than shouting, and might also be singing to herself.

"Come on then, come here, come to me, come to me."

I could not see her very well, but I suspected that she was floating at the other end.

What she asked sounded very enticing, but although I could already move quite well in the water I had never been as far into the deep end as where she was now. I was only allowed to go there when I had my swimming ring on and that wasn't even inflated. I made some clumsy efforts to blow the thing up myself, but in vain.

Uncle Felix stood a little way off smoking a cigarette on the side. He didn't hear me when I asked if he could help me. She never allowed me to go into the deep end without a swimming ring on. And now she was calling me.

With my teeth chattering and tears in my eyes that I didn't want anyone to see at any price, I tottered down the stone steps inch by inch, deep into the water.

I often dreamed about it afterward, and I still dream about it more than half a century later.

"Come on, do it now. You must learn to have confidence; otherwise you'll never be able to do it." She said that to me so often, although it was mostly about something else, shaking hands with strangers or something like that.

Now she was beckoning to me from the other end of the pool, I thought. I assumed that she had raised her head slightly and was looking at me. What she looked like I didn't know. She was too far away for that. I could imagine: cajoling, teasing, challenging.

"Come on, you love me, don't you? Come on then!"

It was as though she were right next to me, I could hear her so well although her voice never rose above a whisper.

All I could see was her floating shape, at the other side of the pool, her silvery green color, like that of a fish.

"I don't dare, Mummy," I blurted out before plunging helplessly into the water, first going under with a mixture of pain and enjoyment and then suddenly encountering an unknown phenomenon, at once all-embracing and featherlike. My leaden fear fell away from me, and after that burden had disappeared, I lost myself and was absorbed into the universe where nothing about what I knew and understood mattered. I don't know whether I finally came to the surface again by myself after a long time or whether my mother or Uncle Felix, who was suddenly also plunging around in the pool in his wet clothes, pulled me out. It seemed to take a long time, but I don't even know how long it lasted. The first thing I heard when I came back to myself was her voice. "What got into you? What were you trying to do to us, you little idiot?"

She'd flung her arms round me and pressed her face against the top of my head, so that I could see only her neck and breast and a piece of swimming costume. But I could hear how frightened her voice sounded, and I could feel how she was trembling and I realized that she didn't understand what I'd just been through. I still felt so exalted that her alarm or confusion or whatever it was that made her shiver didn't worry me, but, on the contrary, made me laugh softly because I still felt so light and pleasantly languid.

"What? What? Are you standing there laughing? Surely you didn't do it on purpose, you crazy child?"

"Oh, if you only knew how I felt . . ." she said to Uncle Felix, clutching me still more tightly to her.

"Oh, my heart's pounding, you should hear it, I can't get it to calm down."

Just going under was child's play compared to what I'd been through, and I tried to explain it to her.

"What you're saying is all nonsense. You mustn't say it at all. Please hold your tongue. You must never ever do anything like that again. You can already swim quite well, you can stay afloat quite well, but you must never, ever, ever stay underwater for so long again."

I couldn't tell her that I'd done it for her and for her alone, and that I'd just as willingly never do it again for her alone.

Felix held his arms around us and she leaned against him.

"Calm down now, Hélène. The dear child's not disobedient. On the contrary, she faithfully does everything you tell her. She simply adores you."

Did I imagine it or did he continue softly: "And who doesn't, for that matter?"

My mother shook him off and slapped the water with her hand, but it was no longer a game; she was angry now.

"I don't want her to adore me." Slap. "I don't want her to adore. Anyone, me included. You always pay for adoring people." Slap. "And I don't want her to stay underwater for so long." Slap.

Before she could get completely wild and crazy, as she often did, although it had never happened in the water, Uncle Felix said loudly and seriously, "Do you know that everyone here simply throws his children into the water? That's how they all learn to swim."

My mother calmed down. A faint smile appeared on her face.

"We'll make peace," she said. "We'll do a water dance." She took both our hands and pulled us with her, in a circle through the water.

"John Jenny in the tun
John Jenny in the tun
See a hoop around it run
John Jenny
John Jenny
and the tun's
not worth a penny."

FIVE

Uncle Felix liked the tea ladies. He told them stories and joked with them. He performed new songs for them, which he sang or played on a mouth organ. The tea visits lasted much longer than they used to, the visitors stayed until long after it was dark, and I didn't know what to do with myself. I couldn't go on looking at their babies, which were in prams or baskets. Sometimes I just wandered aimlessly in the grass a little. Sometimes I was given a glass of pink syrup. "Drink it up quickly before Daddy comes."

My mother and Uncle Felix and Auntie Margot sat laughing and talking with the visitors on the veranda. Occasionally I had to join them and tell them what I'd done that day or what word I'd learned. Suddenly I couldn't remember. I didn't want to say, with all those people there, some of whom I didn't know, as they'd never been before. Sometimes I crept away and left my syrup untouched.

"What are you doing, Lulu? Where are you?"

"I'm looking for Teddy."

"Teddy's sitting here in your own chair, silly."

I knew she meant my toy dog and not my real dog, the one I was actually looking for. But I came back obediently.

I sat there again on my best behavior, until I finally heard the familiar sound of the car, then I charged off the veranda to greet my father. Since Uncle Felix had been there, Daddy usually didn't come and sit in our circle. At most he came and stood by us to say hello to the people there. When there were tea ladies, he talked to them for a moment, but in a fairly absentminded way. These days he confused all their names, according to my mother. After exchanging a few words with the visitors, my father said to Uncle Felix, "Would you do the honors from now on, brother."

Most evenings he went straight to his pavilion after he got home. I tried to grab hold of his hand the moment he got out of the car, but I wasn't able. He carried his briefcase in one hand and in his other hand often a book or papers. Then I simply walked with him, not next to him, but a little ahead of him so that he could see me properly. At first of course I'd stayed politely behind him, because my mother had taught me never to get under people's feet, because they might stumble or fall.

But when I walked behind my father, he didn't even know who was there, the chauffeur or the *djongos* or Teddy or me. That was how absentminded he was. Sometimes he was so lost in thought that he went the wrong way. So for him it was actually better for someone to get under his feet so he didn't get lost.

"I'll show you the way, Daddy."

"You show me the way, that's right, tiny tot."

After that there was silence. When I wanted us to start talking, the best thing for me to do was to ask, "Shall I tell you what I've eaten today?"

"Yes, you do that." He made a noise that was a little like laughter. "Tell me what you've eaten. No, shall I try to guess? Chocolate pancakes with vanilla custard."

"No!"

"Well, you tell me then."

Sometimes we'd reached the group on the veranda by that

time because we had to pass it, and my mother picked up our conversation.

"Did you ask what she ate? Do you want to know? Our brave girl drank three mugs of cold chocolate and a cream slice. Did I say *a* cream slice? Louise ate three, one after the other. Shall I tell you something else?" And then roaring with laughter she told him all kinds of stories about things she and I had done and which I had totally forgotten. "Your buffoon of a brother absolutely had to go to Lembang today, so we went to Lembang and then straight on to the zoo. Phew, it was hot! So then very stupidly we had lemonade with ice."

"Did we go to the zoo? Did we go to the zoo? I don't remember!" I heard myself saying in complete astonishment. "No, we didn't go."

"Lembang takes the whole morning, children. I don't think that's a very good idea at all, so you haven't even had a proper rest."

Auntie Margot emerged yawning from her siesta. But as usual she was immediately ticked off by Mummy. "First of all, take off that silly apron, sis, then you can talk with us. Oh, it's like a hospital here and it smells like one, or is it you, Cees?" She didn't wait for an answer to her questions, but went on talking. "Why don't you get changed, like we do? Well, if you must know, we just dropped into the zoo for a short while, but it was much too warm, and anyway Louise walks round in a dream during the day."

Uncle Felix cleared his throat, as he did when he wanted us to look at him, and when we looked it made him behave even more stupidly and pull funny faces.

"Hmm, hmm! I simply want to say that where she is, her soul is not, Lulu's soul is often elsewhere, where it's probably even nicer than here."

After such statements Auntie Margot looked at us lovingly and then kissed me.

"Are you already as absentminded as your father? Were you even walking around daydreaming at the zoo?"

I wanted to tell him that we hadn't been to the zoo at all that afternoon, but in the swimming pool at Villa Isola.

My mother called out to us to be quiet, because she had heard the *toké*.

"Let's listen carefully. The *toké*'s calling. Shh. Count very quietly."

It was an early *toké*, a baby perhaps, and it called only three times.

"Now off to bed as quick as a flash, Lulu."

"Oh, come on, she's been walking around in a daydream the whole day," my father observed. He put his hand out to me and took me with him to his room. "Would you like to see Servus Poldi for a moment?"

I always wanted to see Servus Poldi. It was floating in alcohol and lived in a glass jar.

In the evening my father sat writing and reading in his study, and the few times that he sat with the others in the group, in his own chair, where no one else except me was allowed to sit, not even by accident, he said very little. He sighed and frowned as he read the letters that came by air from Europe. Most of them were light blue and translucent, like butterflies. I sometimes stroked the envelopes to see if they would later give off the fine powder that lay on butterflies' wings. They weighed scarcely anything, and you could make them sail through the air, but Mummy said you mustn't do that and so did Auntie Margot. The letters were a mystery.

Something strange had already happened to a letter from Granny Mimi. This letter had had babies. I knew, but my mother wouldn't let me tell my father.

A letter was good when it stayed unopened. As long as

Granny Mimi's letters were still in their little house, everything was fine. But when my father went to his pavilion to open them, then they revealed themselves as the long, fluttering white and blue butterflies, which must be poisonous, because they caused so much unpleasantness.

My father crumpled them up in his fist and simply walked up and down his gallery with them, his forehead deeply lined, jaws clenched, and emitting a faint growl.

The letters arrived after my father had already left for the clinic. Mummy slid them quickly backward and forward in her hands: "Oh dear, oh dear, there's another one, another one from Mimi." Then she would put the letters for my father into a pile and this one special letter on her hat shelf for a while, a day or a week, so that my father didn't have to get all sad and upset the same evening.

When my mother had fallen into a deep sleep during the afternoon siesta, I would drag a chair up to the wardrobe and stand on it to look at this letter, which was still lying on the shelf. There was one that had been there for a long time. It was light blue and bulged a little, fairly innocent from the look of it. I tapped it cautiously with my forefinger. You must never do that with poisonous insects, but I'd asked Auntie Margot if a letter was poisonous and she had assured me that it wasn't. My mother shrugged her shoulders at my question: "That all depends."

Such answers were no use to me.

The longer Granny Mimi's letter stayed on the hat shelf, the more I imagined that it had grown. It had grown fatter and occasionally it sighed.

If I tickled its tummy, it released tiny light-green clouds of an unfamiliar aroma, vaguely reminiscent of the perfume my mother dabbed behind her ears when she made herself particularly beautiful. The letter was making itself extra beautiful for me, because no one was looking at it. I made a bed for it out of a satin beret that no one wore anyway. I made sure that this nest was put a little closer to the chinks in the cupboard, so that the letter could get enough air. Perhaps the letter would have babies, perhaps not. But while I was still in doubt, the bomb burst.

That was what my mother called it, whispering to Auntie Margot: "*Aduh,* the bomb's about to burst, Mimi's written another letter. Hasn't she got anything better to do? Cees is wondering what's happened to her previous one."

"Where is her previous one then? Wasn't it delivered?"

My mother folded her arms, bent double, and screamed "Oooo . . . oooo . . . oooo . . . *Aduh.*" But this cheerful outburst ended in lamentation. "Oh dear, delivered, but not given, oh dear, what am I to do now?"

"What! Didn't you give Cees his letter?"

"Oh yes I did, yes I did, but not for a little while. For tactical reasons."

"Pah! You forgot the letter."

"Sunday! I gave it to him on Sunday."

I was sure she hadn't. My mother and father had stayed indoors almost the whole of Sunday; they'd spent hours looking at photos and sticking them in, talking excitedly and laughing, and whenever I'd come in, one of the two had said, "What's wrong? Do you want to ask us something? Mind you don't touch anything. When we're finished you can look at the album." The photos were spread out in rows and in piles. On the black dining table, on the smaller tables, even on the chairs. There were photos wherever you looked. But nowhere a letter, I was certain of that.

"Are you sure? Why didn't he read it then?" asked Auntie Margot.

"Yes, sis, that's a good question. The letter's not there anymore, so I've given it to him!"

"Have a proper look."

"Listen, if the letter isn't where it was, then it's gone; it hasn't grown legs, has it?"

I was dying to tell them that it had. The letter had grown legs and more besides. It was a long time before I could interrupt them with my good news.

"Oh," they said in chorus. "Now we're getting to the bottom of it." They took one arm each, and the three of us flew to the cupboard. My mother, who was tallest, jumped onto the chair and with a violent sweep cleared the whole hat shelf. We waited below with outstretched arms, ready to catch the things, but everything fell on the floor, hats, boas, scarves, and rolled-up belts that suddenly uncoiled to their full length, like snakes. I called to my mother urgently that she must be careful in case the letter had had babies, like Teddy-Bali.

"Babies? What are you going on about now?" She was holding the gold-colored beret in her hand, squeezed into the shape of a banana.

I screamed, "It's in there, it's in there, be careful!"

"Where?"

"In that banana."

My mother raised her hands heavenward and dropped the beret; it thudded onto the ground and I saw immediately that the letter was still inside, it looked as if it been inflated, it bulged so, but Teddy had been like that for a while too.

"Look, it's fat, Mummy."

She stared in amazement at the swollen grubby thing in the beret.

"Is this a letter? Lulu, tell me, what on earth has happened to this?"

It was as though none of us dared touch the letter. When I cautiously extended a finger toward it, my mother pulled my hand back. "Leave it alone!"

"If you ask me, it's mildew," said Auntie Margot.

"Mildew? Then everything in the wardrobe's ruined."

"Couldn't it be moths? Mimi is surrounded by old bits of cloth, perhaps she was sitting writing her letter among her old rags?"

"Mimi, moths? Old rags? Don't let her hear that! She'd murder you."

"Dutch moths. It's possible, isn't it? But they won't survive here, sis, don't worry."

"Oh stop it. Moths in a letter? It's impossible."

"Paper moths perhaps."

"Look how the thing is bulging."

"Look out, look out," I cried, but it was already too late, my mother had grabbed the letter resolutely and opened it with her razor-sharp nail file. I bit my lip so hard that I could feel it for days. I didn't really dare to look anymore, but I couldn't help it. There were babies, but they hadn't come out right. All kinds of creased photos, in a horrible pale color and with serrated edges, emerged. My mother stared at them.

"Oh look, how lovely. Photos of Felix and Cees," she peeped up at last, sounding very anxious. Her head and her shoulders drooped, but not for long: suddenly she straightened up and said radiantly, because she'd just had a brain wave, "That suits me fine. We've just spent all day Sunday sticking photos in, but there's a whole pile we haven't finished, and these will go nicely in with those."

"You're just going to slip them in at the bottom of the big pile?" asked Auntie Margot. "But you can't just do that, he'll notice. Cees always notices everything immediately."

"Oh yes? Do you want to bet? He doesn't notice a thing, as far as I know. He never notices."

If no letters had come, my father buried himself in the newspapers. Some of the papers were delivered; others were sent "from Europe." He never said what was in the papers, but he sometimes shook his head wildly, crumpled up the newspaper, suddenly unpicked the wad again and stroked it smooth, rolled it up firmly, and took it in his hand, as if it were a stick that he wanted to hit someone with, and then he went to his room muttering softly to himself. "Good heavens, God help us, it's already so late," my mother would whisper.

Next to his own chair there was a table with a carafe of water on it and a large glass next to it. Even when he was not sitting there, the carafe was filled with fresh water and put down, the glass turned upside down next to it on a lace doily. My father always drank water. Every so often, when he was sitting reading or working or talking, he would take a glass, pour water into it, and drink it in short gulps. Never anything but water. Not even when there was a party.

"We can celebrate your birthday with a glass of gin, can't we? Just a drop, Cees, a person has to relax occasionally." My father replied that as far as he was concerned, there was nothing more wonderful than water to relax with. Water, the most precious thing on earth. We ourselves were made of it anyway, we were more than half water. My mother contradicted my father and said that we were more spirit than water, and then they squabbled for a bit with Auntie Margot sometimes supporting my mother and sometimes my father.

When Uncle Felix lived with us, he challenged Daddy; he always contradicted everyone anyway, usually teasingly, but sometimes very seriously, coming close to anger.

Whenever this happened, my father looked at him benignly and he smiled, but shaking his head as if he wanted to believe Uncle Felix but really couldn't. He looked at me like that when I told him what I'd eaten.

"Oh, brother, *alle Theorie ist grau*," shouted Uncle Felix repeatedly. He crept up with his dancing gait, the bottle raised above his head in an attacking position. "Because we're half water, we are sad and sluggish. Our water half dozes off and is a stinking, stagnant pool, that longs to boil and seethe on the fire! Put some fire in those lame limbs of yours, brother. Have a swig! This stuff isn't called firewater for nothing. Come on, follow the unerring senses, not the defective intelligence. Cast those stupid papers aside and let Mimi's letters look after themselves."

Uncle Felix could say a hundred times, "Laughing and loving life is healthier than all that reading, if you ask me," but in my father's case it did no good. Daddy would laugh amiably and say, "That's what I like to hear," or "If only that were true." Then he would drink a glass of water.

He went on reading his letters and frowning and made sure that all the papers were saved for him.

After a while, when my father was on the veranda with us in a mood like that, everyone stopped playing the fool, and people spoke more and more softly and slowly. Finally everyone sat and sighed imperceptibly.

Uncle Felix occasionally jumped up and said in a pompous voice, "The doctor prescribes: a piece of music. That'll make this company perk up." He went over to the gramophone. He put a record on. He stood with his arms outstretched and said in a velvety voice, "Aha, Franz Lehár . . ."

As the first notes sounded, Daddy looked up and said gloomily, "Umpahpah!"

Whenever my father came home very late, there were "complications" at the clinic. In that case the chauffeur would bring Auntie Margot home alone, if she'd been to work. Since Uncle Felix had been there, she went with him almost every day. She told my mother about the "complications" but spoke so softly and quickly that I couldn't follow. I did see Mummy putting her hands over her ears and acting, with her eyes glistening, as if she didn't want to hear at any price. When Auntie Margot had finished, she would cry plaintively, "That's quite enough, thanks! I don't want to hear anything more about it! It's bad enough being married to a fanatic like Cees, and then to have another chatter-box of a nurse as well!"

My mother sat down on her high chair on the veranda, played with her long necklace with her slim fingers, raised her cigarette holder to her mouth, took small puffs with pouting lips, and carefully blew out clouds of smoke that were as large and fleeting as my soap bubbles. Then she tapped her foot on the ground to attract more attention.

"I must tell you all something . . . ," she puffed out together with her cigarette smoke.

We always expected the most awful news, such as: there's a catastrophe about to happen, there's a tiger prowling around the house, the volcano will erupt, a curse has been put on us, but she said, "Margot, Felix, I think that engagement of yours simply must be celebrated. We'll throw a party. A fancy dress ball."

"What? What?" cried Uncle Felix. "Dancing all evening and then through the night? In our Sunday best? Or even worse, got up as Napoleon? As if we hadn't got enough to do, we're swamped with work all day. Really, I'm happy when I can sit here occasionally with nothing to do."

My mother turned to Auntie Margot.

"So what does he do then?" she said with a wink. "I'll sum it up. He only plays tennis with Cees these days. He doesn't dare to play with you anymore for fear of his glasses. . . . You did knock the lenses out, it's true. Our noble soul thinks horse riding is cruel to the horses. It's too warm for walking, and the distances are too great for cycling."

"He swims with you two, doesn't he? But believe me, we're usually too tired for anything when we get back from the clinic after such a long day."

"Oh, that clinic. I'll be in it myself soon. I'll be your principal patient, and you'll finally have plenty of time for me."

"No, not a bit of it," said Uncle Felix, "we need all our time for the beautiful Mrs. Dee."

My mother jumped up and whacked the paper that Uncle Felix had just spread out on the stone balustrade.

"Mrs. Dee! Hah, she makes you all jump through her hoops. I don't want to hear another word about that spoiled rich monster. I'd rather you told me, you idiots, when we're going to celebrate your wedding."

"Oho! That's not for me to say," replied Uncle Felix.

My mother looked surprised.

"Margot! Are you dragging your feet again?"

"Hélène, it'll all be all right."

"She's the queen of my heart," said Uncle Felix, "and she's the dearest and best nurse in the world. She's a gem in our clinic. It'll be a crying shame if I alone have to take up all her time."

"The queen, the dearest, the best, a gem," repeated my mother in a strange tone. She stopped talking to take a deep breath, looked at the ground, and burst into tears. "If only someone would say nice things like that about me occasionally."

Auntie Margot had been sitting rocking with me in the rocking chair. She had just raised her legs to pick up momentum, but this crying reduced us to silence, she with her legs still in the air and I with my arms around her. I held her firmly and pressed my head into her bosom so as not to be able to see my sad mother.

Uncle Felix walked off.

We stayed behind. We watched Uncle Felix stroll past the side wing to the work pavilion where my father had gone quite some time before. He didn't hurry; Uncle Felix strolled more than he walked. He also looked around and at the sky, but he didn't look at us anymore, although he stopped occasionally to wave at us with two hands, without turning round to look at us.

"What a good-for-nothing he is!" muttered my mother, between two sobs, but her voice was already almost back to normal. "Any grocer can see that I'm having an attack of nerves, and the one person who should know is too damn lazy to give me some valerian. Calls himself a pharmacist, and he's just a pastry cook, a German pastry cook just like his pa."

She came over to us and leaned against us.

"Margot, don't put it off any longer. Get married, for goodness' sake, sis. Marry that merry pastry cook. How marvelous to be able to have such a carefree and lazy life. Why didn't I choose one like that? One of those happy-go-lucky types, the sort you can have fun with."

Auntie Margot said nothing, I heard her humming, and because I was sitting right up against her, the melody penetrated through to me, and, as if automatically, I hummed along with her.

"She sits there singing as if she hasn't a care in the world. You nitwit, you dope, you headless chicken. You were born for happiness, and you just throw it down the drain."

"Not a bit of it, sis! Felix and I are getting married, that's for sure."

Mummy went on and on. I couldn't stand the trembling of her voice; it was as if she might start crying again at any moment.

"That's exactly what I mean: that it has to be that clown of all people. Shall I list all the proposals you've had? They've beaten a path to your door, with bunches of orchids, and roses. Red roses galore. You've had all the chances in the world, but you've thrown your life away."

My aunt put me carefully down on the ground, led me to my father's chair, and only then did she flare up. Breathing heavily, she turned to my mother.

"You've got it all wrong, you know. Felix is the one for me. I love him; I won't hear a bad word about him."

"Oh listen to that. So when can we finally expect the wedding?"

"You seem to be in more of a hurry than we are," said Auntie Margot.

"Well, people are starting to say some funny things behind your backs."

"They just gossip for all they're worth."

"It affects our good name, the clinic's too."

"Oh Hélène! We're going to get married, you know, but I sometimes have my doubts. I don't mind telling you." Auntie Margot looked at her sister sadly. It now seemed as if it was her turn to start crying. "Am, I really cut out for marriage?" she asked, her eyes already brimming with tears.

"What else would you be cut out for then? Nursing for the rest of your life? Nursing other people's children forever?"

"I don't know. I like my work. I'm scared to give it up."

"Oh, even better! Looking after other people's children and not your own?"

"Being a mother seems almost too hard a job to me."

My mother paced around like a tiger in a cage; she didn't scream, she walked back and forth silently with great padding strides, and that was even worse than screaming and crying. Finally she threw herself down on her settee and made cycling movements in the air.

"Don't start all over again, sis, don't say it again." My mother was gasping. "It's much too hard a job being a mother. So you say. But how come you know that already? Can you tell by looking at me by any chance?"

I sneaked a look at my aunt and saw her standing there half crying and half laughing.

I remember that these outbursts always happened before the rain came. In anticipation of the rain, the arguments became fiercer and the shouting louder. Once the violence of the rain had finally erupted, all the human hullabaloo seemed futile. Everything was washed away by the rain—the arguments, the reproaches, the spiteful words.

"Oh rain, rain, let the rain come soon, please!" I would ask the *waringin* tree when things again got so bad with my mother that she didn't even need anyone else to argue with, and she growled and raged all by herself.

What was the matter?

I had no idea.

I could ask her. She would say that it was about all life's wretchedness rolled into one.

All life's wretchedness was rolled into one, always just before the monsoon.

Auntie Margot and Uncle Felix went on a trip, and it lasted for two days. According to Mummy, the whole town was scandalized. "It's already been transmitted on the grapevine. Time, place, and action, all public knowledge. Bandung, the Paris of Java? It makes Marseilles look like Lourdes."

Apart from its being a scandal, everyone had been "worried out of their minds" all night long.

Even my father had become involved. He'd driven back to town with the chauffeur to look for the pair.

Hours later he'd returned, more cheerful, but had not been willing to say anything except, "Everything's fine, don't worry, they're both quite grown-up enough."

The lilac orchids were delivered for Auntie Margot early in the evening.

"Exactly the color of the polka dots in my dress; oh Felix, how thoughtful of you."

Auntie Margot twirled round awkwardly in her airy gown, which made her look very different from the sturdy cotton she usually wore. Her plumpness was accentuated; she was just like the Grandma in the painting, and she was almost completely bare on top. She quickly threw a thin shawl around herself. She looked so anxious that it made me feel frightened too.

My mother had to pin on the corsage, because Auntie Margot couldn't manage it.

"Aren't we a clever nurse," they both joked at once.

Finally Mummy managed it, and she stretched her fragile frame high above my aunt and strolled gracefully around her, making a few adjustments to her hair with languid gestures. Finally she pursed her lips: "Yes, I'm satisfied; what do you think, Felix? This beautiful orchid is far better than that eternal red flower in her hair."

"Better my hat, it's all wrong," stuttered Uncle Felix, and the next moment he disappeared to make a hurried round of his glasses.

Auntie Margot must have heard, because she tore the corsage off her shoulder with a desperate gesture and went deep red.

"Careful, careful, you'll ruin the chiffon," cried my mother.

Before getting into the car, Auntie Margot suddenly ran to the hedge on her wobbly heels, picked a closed hibiscus flower, and simply stuck it just behind her right ear with a hairpin, as always.

"The child of the *dessa!*" muttered my mother disdainfully. She stood with the spurned orchid in her hand, and I suddenly saw how much this fragile violet flower resembled my mother, with her intensely pale skin, which in the evening light contained a hint of green.

The car drove off, crunching the gravel. My mother forgot to wave.

"He couldn't even arrange a proper corsage for her. The idiot chose one that was really for me." She flung the orchid on the ground.

Felix and Auntie Margot didn't come home till the following afternoon.

It had started pouring with rain on the evening of their trip, and it went on raining. They walked blissfully through it hand in hand.

They looked disheveled, but they glowed and laughed. At first they couldn't get any words out, they were laughing so much.

Felix walked onto the veranda, still laughing, toward my mother and was about to say hello or perhaps give her something, because he put his hand out toward her. My mother brushed it aside angrily, and Uncle Felix, accidentally or deliberately, stroked her cheek. She immediately grabbed his hand and quickly sank her teeth into it. The blood spurted out, I screamed, but it wasn't that bad, it didn't spurt, it dripped. Taken aback, Uncle Felix looked at the drops of blood, with his finger raised.

"A tiger's bite. I hope I'll survive this," he said, half admiringly.

"You should be ashamed!" screeched my mother; yes, she really screeched, and although we were used to a lot from her in the way of fits of temper and outbursts, each time we thought we'd never heard her as bad before.

"*Suda. Suda.* Monsoon! Monsoon! Calm down, it's all right, Hélène. Hélène, it started bucketing down there," Auntie Margot said to her. She tried to sound reassuring, but her gaiety burst through. "It suddenly started pouring down there, my oh my!" she crowed. "We stayed in the Preanger Hotel, you know. We had to. You couldn't even drive a car anymore. In separate rooms, of course." She swung her case exuberantly, and Uncle Felix put his arms around her.

"The die is cast. This spitfire and I are getting married."

"The idiot, yes, the idiot suddenly picked me up and carried me over the threshold as if we'd just come from the wedding, ha, ha, ha, and I said to him, 'We're not married yet.'"

Uncle Felix hugged her even more tightly, took a deep breath, and lifted her up.

"And listen, Hélène, just listen," cried Auntie Margot, thrashing about with her feet. "We're getting married in Bali. First our birthdays, and then we're getting married. In February."

SIX

Auntie Margot worked during the day, but sometimes she had already returned and suddenly had to leave again late in the evening, for an emergency. I couldn't contain myself and pleaded with her, "Auntie Margot, you will come back, won't you? You will come back?"

"Of course I will, toots, of course I'll come back. I always come back to you."

I couldn't imagine life without Auntie Margot. She was always ready to play with me, even when the others were too tired. I could ask her anything I liked, even more than my mother. Auntie Margot never got angry.

I liked sitting on her lap best because she felt so soft, as soft as two cushions. My mother was very narrow and you could feel her frame, and with her I didn't dare move because I thought that I might break her bones with an awkward movement. I never sat on my father's lap.

When Auntie Margot was working during the day, I had a mother less. In order to make it up to me, my aunt devoted her day off, when she had one, entirely to me.

My father had been seen off and driven away; my mother had gone back to bed. Before Uncle Felix went to the pharmacy, he would pop in to visit us. Then Auntie Margot and I would see him off, but Uncle Felix was usually not with us this early.

Auntie Margot and I installed ourselves on the veranda. There was always immediately something of a party atmosphere; even at this early hour we had a glass of *susu* syrup.

Sopia came by with her new baby, which she was carrying in the sling. Auntie Margot said he was becoming a fine boy. I was astonished: I thought the fine boy was rather pathetic, being all scrunched up, with his little fists under his chin as if he were frightened of something. And besides, he was dribbling.

"You were like that too, you know," said Auntie Margot. "You were like that too as a baby."

I couldn't imagine it. The baby was like the creatures in my father's big glass jars.

"We were all like that once, when we started," Auntie Margot told me.

"No we weren't."

"Yes we were."

"It's impossible, Auntie Margot."

"It is possible. It's one of life's secrets."

At the side of the house the *kebon* rolled the garden hoses out toward the young plants around the tennis court. Before Uncle Felix invited me for shuttlecock, my father and his brother usually played a game of tennis. We sometimes watched them, but there was no fun in watching, my mother thought, because "the two of them act as if their lives depend on the game."

Auntie Margot didn't play tennis anymore. I sometimes played shuttlecock with her now, but she never went on once the shuttlecock hit the ground.

"What are we going to do today, Auntie Margot?"

"Oh, today I don't have to worry about anything," she said, moving up and down in the rocking chair. "*Jam karat*, a day off! Can you hear, the wind has woken up too, can you hear it swishing through the trees?"

"Swishing?"

"Sometimes I can't tell if I'm awake," Auntie Margot went on dreamily. "Sometimes I think I'm still dreaming and sometimes I have bad dreams, but then I hear the wind and I feel it and I think: Luckily I'm awake and back with both feet in my earthly paradise."

She smiled at me and reached up to the sky with both arms. Then she stretched out all her fingers one by one, and made movements with them as though she were playing a piano in the air. She yawned at length, suddenly put a hand over her open mouth, and cried, "Dear, dear, what manners" and smiled at me again.

"What are we going to do? You're asking me? You say, Lulu."

Auntie Margot was always willing to listen to all my stories and answer any question. On her day off she was prepared to play any game that I dreamed up.

She was the most cheerful of all of us at home, always, as long as I could remember, but she was doubly cheerful now Uncle Felix was there. In February she was going to get married to Uncle Felix in Bali, where my Granddad and Poppy lived.

Auntie Margot couldn't tell stories as well as my mother, and she didn't know the answer to almost everything like Uncle Felix and my father; but if she didn't know something then she made a joke of it, and her stories were always lots of fun and always ended happily. When I wanted to, I was allowed to dress up in her clothes and wear her high heels. If I asked her if I could try her pearl necklace on, she would immediately put it round my neck. "*Bagus*, on you!"

Auntie Margot was inexhaustible, at home and also, or so my father told us, at the clinic. He praised her so often that Mummy sometimes said, "Ah, it tires me out listening to all this. . . ."

"I've never seen Margot tired," my father would say, as if he hadn't heard Mummy's remark.

"No, she doesn't get tired, because she doesn't have a husband

and a child clinging to her skirts. She's as free as a bird. She doesn't have to worry about anything."

My father said nothing. My mother cried theatrically, "I'm driven to despair the whole time."

"By whom, Hélène? By what?"

"By all of you."

"Don't you worry," Auntie Margot would say reassuringly at such moments.

We never ran out of things to say and sometimes played all through her day off, even in the hottest part of the afternoon when all other people and living creatures took a siesta.

Everything was still, inside and outside. The blinds had been lowered, and my mother was lying in the white and green bedroom, which I was never allowed to enter without knocking. Auntie Margot and I crept past, fingers on our lips.

The silence of the siesta, in which no one appeared, was a bit like the silence of the night except that in the afternoon it was much lighter and hotter.

We played a lot that day, Auntie Margot and I. We played hide-and-seek, changing trees, tag, and dressing up, and after that animals as well. We were chickens, geese and toads, dogs and cats, owls and lizards, cackling, yapping, barking, creeping, winking, and crying softly and hoarsely, "Toké . . . toké . . . toké . . ."

In this heat, in this silence, shouldn't Auntie Margot and I play the game with the black dining table? We were feeling listless, and perhaps that game would put some life back into us.

It was a tense and exciting game, the table game. It seemed much more exciting than shuttlecock, and I would have liked to go on watching it for ages, but as soon as I saw it, I wasn't allowed to stand still for very long. My night people quickly pulled me along with them, and we ran off.

I thought of it and asked if Auntie Margot knew the game.

"Another new game? The table game? Ping-Pong you mean?"

"No, it wasn't Ping-Pong."

"What table game then? I'm not sure I know it. Tell me! Tell me!"

"It's the black table game."

"The black table game?"

I nodded.

"What's that, tootsie? I don't know it."

"They're demons, Auntie Margot, they're enchanted and that's why they act like that." That's what the night people had told me. I giggled with excitement, and Auntie Margot giggled with me.

"Really? What do demons do then? Show me."

"Yes, I'll show you, wait a moment."

I climbed onto the table, lay on top of it, on my back, with my arms spread out and my knees raised, and I squirmed. Now and then I threw my legs high in the air, I clenched and relaxed my fists and banged the table with the back of my head. Then I rolled backward and forward, moaning softly, because I had to accompany everything with those strange noises that I'd caught snatches of in the night, fearsome screams and intense groans, growling and panting and squealing like young puppies.

"And you have to do it without clothes," I said finally.

Auntie Margot looked at me strangely, her eyes glittering.

"Tell me again, will you?" she asked me as if she didn't understand.

"But it's not difficult."

She made me tell her again and show her again.

Then she asked, "How can this be?"

She'd sat down on a chair, a long way from the table.

I jumped off the table, went over to her, and tried to pull her with me.

"It takes two to play. Come with me."

"*Aduh*, what kind of funny game is this?" My aunt blushed.

"Here!" And I ran to the table again and knocked on it.

Auntie Margot got confused. She was about to laugh and yet didn't. There were blue worms pulsing under her skin.

"What people do that?" asked my aunt, half jolly and half indignant. "What people do it then? What people do it here?" She bit her lip and had to fight back her laughter.

I suddenly wasn't so sure anymore, I'd only been able to watch the game for such a short time.

"What people do it then?"

"Mummy does it."

Auntie coughed into her hand.

"Mummy?"

"Mummy and Uncle Felix."

Auntie Margot rested her head against the arm of the high chair and breathed in and out deeply.

"Just as I thought," she muttered, so softly that I couldn't quite understand.

I went over to her and looked at her, and saw her breast was heaving. There was something the matter with her, but I hadn't the slightest idea what it could be.

"What's the matter, Auntie Margot? Is something the matter?"

"But when does it happen?" She looked at me helplessly.

"They do it when the moon makes them into demons."

She spluttered, "*Kalang kibut!* You're completely overwrought, child! Tell me honestly, tell me honestly, Uncle Felix isn't there too, is he?" She threw her head right forward, so that her hair hung down to her lap like a thick curtain, and she stayed like that so that I couldn't see her face. I could hear her talking.

"Surely it wasn't Uncle Felix?" she asked flatly.

Then I had to tell her again and show her again, but she no longer even looked, she sat behind her hair with her head hanging down, and halfway through she interrupted my performance with a loud cackling laugh. She gave another cry and suddenly ran off, out of the dining room, into the dark hall, to the side gallery, to her room.

I watched her go and followed her slowly, too flabbergasted to make a sound.

Auntie Margot had charged into her bedroom and shut the door behind her and as I stood outside, I could hear muffled sounds coming from within. Perhaps this was a new game, I thought for a moment, with a vague hope, but I no longer dared to believe it. Something had happened, but I didn't know what. There were gods prowling around our grounds that I knew nothing about.

After a little while I knocked cautiously on the door and said very softly, "Auntie Margot, Auntie Margot, listen, it's me."

There was no answer. Only after I'd knocked harder, even pounded and started shouting louder, did the door open ajar.

"Darling, I'm too *sakit*, you know." She looked at me, with her still troubled face in which her eyes had now become very red and small. "I'm a little too ill at the moment. Tootsie, be a good girl and go to Sopia." She was crying.

"Can I come in, Auntie?" I insisted. Her appearance frightened me. This was no longer a game. I wanted to get into her room to be with her, stroke her and console her, but she closed the door again and now I heard her turning the key on the inside. That had never happened before. No one ever locked their door. Not even my father, although there were enough things in his pavilion that no one must touch.

"Auntie's very ill," I said to my mother when the water was splashing over me in the shower room.

"Yes, why didn't she give you a quick shower?" she asked in astonishment. "What have you been up to to make you so dirty? You look as if you've been rolling in the mud."

I had been, with Teddy and the young puppies.

When Auntie didn't come back anymore, I'd gone to play with Teddy-Bali and the *kebon*. The *kebon* had shown me the litter of three small puppies, all looking like Teddy. Then I'd been allowed to help to put food into a basket for the *kebon*'s idol. He had shown me how to burn the incense sticks. I could remember it all, but it also seemed like a dream, a dream that had intervened between the incomprehensible events.

"What on earth did the two of you get up to, you bandits?" asked Mummy curiously. I was clean again, with a blue ribbon in my hair and white pajamas on. I told her we'd played lots of games. I hesitated about the table game, but then told her that we hadn't even played the table game and that Auntie was still sick.

"How sick?"

"She locked the door of her room."

"Oh, is she in her room? Then she doesn't want to be disturbed."

My mother shook her head, and smiled.

"She's never really ill. You were probably too hectic for her; you don't know when to stop."

"Shall I call her?"

"Oh no, you won't do anything. Daddy will have to take a look at her in a moment, if it's really necessary. We'll let her have a nice lie down, the darling, she'll be back again soon."

But Auntie Margot didn't come back.

My mother and I ate together at the black dining table. Every evening the table was laid for lots of people. I didn't even know who came later. We often ate before the others arrived.

I never stopped to think where the guests sat, but that evening I did. I looked at the empty chairs and didn't sit down where I normally sat; I didn't want to, because it was too close to the forbidden spot.

"What are you wandering around for like that?"

"Can I sit somewhere else?"

"Yes, why not, as long as you finally sit down."

It took a little while before I found a safe place, in the corner, close to the door.

"Are you finally sitting down? Then I'll come and sit next to you."

Because I ate little and my mother even less, we simply sat there next to each other for a while, drank a few sips of water, said a few words to each other, and moved the cutlery back and forth a bit. We rocked our legs under the table, argued for a joke whether we should have pudding or an ice, and then we'd finished.

All that time the night people walked around the table, filling our glasses and lifting up the lids of the dishes. I always preferred to guess what was under the lids and talk to the night people, but I was never allowed to, because then I was keeping them from their work.

This time I passed the ritual at table in silence.

Just like every other evening my mother and I went and sat on the veranda. My father wasn't home yet, but Uncle Felix had arrived meanwhile.

"Fair maiden, do you feel like a game of shuttlecock?" he asked me.

For the first time since I'd known him, I shook my head. I felt too burdened. The events of that afternoon with Auntie Margot were weighing down on me, and I didn't know how I could get rid of the feeling. I sat in my father's chair, the only one not connected with the table game, but sitting in his chair didn't help because instead of disappearing the wretched table game began to grow and grow in my head. It assumed such monstrous proportions that I couldn't see anything else except the table game and what happened in it, and it got so bad that it was a great effort not simply to look at my mother or Uncle Felix.

"She's worn out," my mother said to him. "She's been playing with Margot all day long."

"Aha, and now she's no use for me."

"Is Auntie going to come and sit with us in a little while?" I ventured.

"Oh, don't worry about her, darling. Of course you've exhausted the poor darling again, but she's strong, you'll see." My mother sounded cheerful. "She's the strongest of all of us!"

"Isn't she very ill?" I whispered.

"No, not at all. All right then, just to put your mind at rest, I'll go and take a look," said my mother; and in her teasing tone she added, "If we have to wait for the doctor, we'll still be here tomorrow morning. Felix, what do you say?"

"I'll go with you, Hélène, and wake up our lazybones."

"Listen to who's talking."

Talking cheerfully, arms swinging, they walked down the side gallery to Auntie Margot's room.

I sat on the veranda in my father's chair with my hands over my ears. I didn't want to hear. It was like the barking of dogs that sometimes rang out for hours and hours on strange stormy nights.

It was coming from Auntie Margot's room. It went right through everything. However tightly I pushed my hands over my ears, their voices sounded louder and higher and louder and came closer and closer, till I saw both of them charging out, toward me, and I dashed out of the chair, into the room, through the hall to the dining room to the dining table, which still looked so innocent under its white cloth. Now I was sure they would no longer believe me.

My mother found me by the place where we had just been playing soldiers with the knife rests.

"What's this I hear?" she cried, as she came toward me. "Do you spy on people at night?" She grabbed my arm and shook me angrily back and forth. "It's not true! Say it at once!"

While I was still hunting for words, she gave me such a box on the ears that my head started buzzing. It was the first slap I'd had in my life.

She looked so angry, so terrifying, that I ran off without a second thought. I got out of there in a hurry and it's quite possible that she called me back or chased me, but I knew the way behind the house, where the servants lived and where none of us often went, much better than she did.

My dog and I waded through the water of the stream, which I'd chosen as a guide. We were on our way up, toward the volcano.

In the afternoons I often went to Dewi Kesuma with Teddy-Bali, but I'd never gone as far as this. There was still a little light left, but it wouldn't be long before it was pitch-black. Yet I had to go on. I no longer knew the way, but that didn't matter, since I had no intention of ever going back home again.

In the direction of Lembang lay the upturned boat, under which the summer always went to sleep. We didn't cross the asphalt road, and didn't drive in a car or a carriage as we usually did, but went through the fields and the vegetation, which became thicker, almost impenetrable. Was this already the jungle perhaps? You had to be very careful of the jungle, I had learned. Here dangers constantly lurked, snakes, vicious monkeys, carnivorous and poison-spurting plants, headhunters, and perhaps a tiger. Evil had crossed my path because I had imitated a demon on the black dining table that evening, and because of that had become one myself, for all I knew forever. But in the jungle it was warm and comfortable, and here and there there were cheerful and friendly people, doing perfectly ordinary things like collecting leaves and cutting branches, and if they were old ladies, chewing *sirih* leaves, and no one looked angry because I was walking through the water barefoot with my dog. On the contrary, they all wished me a good journey in their fairy-tale language.

I thought it was better to live here than in a house, where there was big, dark furniture and where the bed had to stand with its legs in four deep buckets of paraffin, so that no vermin could climb up. Here in my jungle the vermin slid up and down tree trunks and leaves in the last light of the sun, gleaming and flaunting their rainbow colors. They were like moving jewels and they meant us no harm. It was Teddy who wanted to go back after a while. He wanted to turn around; he raised his snub baby nose in the air and cried softly. But when I went on, he went along with me. Imperceptibly the playful stream, which babbled so cheerfully, turned into a menacingly foaming river that wouldn't tolerate us but tried to sink its sharp yellow teeth into us. The water spirits who lived here were not friendly to us; they grabbed intruders by their ankles, dragged them along for a while, and then smashed their skulls on the stones. We were forced to move onto the bank, where the ground was boggy and covered in thick vegetation. I almost didn't dare go any farther, because I sank deep into the ground. Now that the river could no longer get us, the earth was sucking us down.

"You're not frightened, are you?" I said to Teddy. "We've no need to be frightened, not of the water and not of the earth, not of the dragons or of the spirits of the air."

Teddy had gone on ahead. He was bulky and slow-moving, and I stayed as close as I could behind him. We had great difficulty making headway, since we had to keep pulling our feet out of the mud. Sometimes I thought I saw snakes darting away out of the holes I made with my feet. Sometimes I sank in a long way and had the furious rushing of the river in my ears. We seemed to be making scarcely any progress. But we were, and we kept climbing. The river was going down; we were going up. The ground was getting harder; the water flowed over stones here. When I looked round and thought I saw a glimpse of our house through the thick greenery, like a white dot, it surprised me that it was still standing there, as though nothing had happened. I thought I saw our house, but I wasn't happy.

Teddy was finally content to stay quietly at my side. We sat down. The earth bore us again, as always. I didn't want to go home, but I didn't want to go up the mountain either. We might fall into a crater and burn in the fire. Back along the river to where it became a stream wasn't possible either, because that was the direction of home. There was nowhere left to go. We were sitting on a stone that was still warm, looking at the setting sun. When it was fiery red in the sky and black on the ground, I saw lots of great fireflies swarming out over our land. I heard only later that they were people with torches. I looked at the scene below me; I could make out great black silhouettes against the backdrop of heaven, behind which the fire would go on smoldering for a long time, orange and purple plumes against a slowly darkening background. It was a *wajang* shadow play for the giant of our mountain.

Only when my father got close did I recognize him. He was riding a baggage pony, and both his legs were hanging almost down to the ground. He called out something. He called my name, Lulu.

I wanted to answer him, but my voice didn't want to.

The gardener's boy always whistled Teddy in a special way and I heard that whistle many times too, and when I did I always held the dog tightly. Finally I let him go. He didn't shoot off.

He strolled slowly ahead and kept looking back with his childlike face, so I crept behind him, barefoot; I'd dropped the buttoned shoes on the way and hadn't picked them up again.

"Thank God, there she is," shouted my father. Now I couldn't make head or tail of what was happening to me. I was received like a long-lost darling, hoisted onto the horse, kissed, and raised aloft. The night people cheered and clapped their hands. We went back home in festive procession.

"Is Auntie Margot all right again?" was the first thing I asked.

My father said, "We're so glad you're back; it's the first good omen today."

"Is Auntie Margot all right?"

"Yes Lulu, everyone's all right," said my father, but he sounded so gloomy that I felt like crying again. When we reached our house we got off the pony; Daddy took my hand and we walked across the grass in the direction of his room.

My mother was sitting on the veranda with her white kimono silhouetted dimly in the darkness. She made no move. I didn't dare to go to her.

"Lulu's back and everything's all right," said my father as he went past.

"That's good," I heard my mother say tonelessly.

"I'll take her to bed. Get some sleep, Hélène."

Not a word came from the veranda.

My father lifted me up and sat me on his arm. That didn't happen often.

"What do you think? Shall we go to my room?"

Daddy and I had already gone quite a way down the path to his pavilion when a tiny sound almost like a child's voice reached us. It was my mother calling after us, "Good night, both of you, darlings. See you tomorrow, see you tomorrow, see you tomorrow."

After my father had laid me on the bed in his study that night and sat in the wicker chair with my favorite book, *Andersen's Fairy Tales*, none of which I understood but which made me cry anyway, I suddenly asked, as he read "The Nightingale" and the tears rolled down my cheeks, "What did I do?"

He read on for a few sentences, his voice slower and softer. He put the book away and looked at his palms. Then he turned them over and looked at the other side.

"You didn't do anything," he said finally and looked at me, "Nothing wrong, just remember that. It was all a big mistake."

I felt my ear and the side of my head, the places where I could still feel the first slap in my life.

"Is a mistake a slap?"

"A slap?" My father didn't seem to have understood. "What slap? What are you talking about?"

"Mummy gave me a slap."

I pointed to my ear. Perhaps I knew, as I told him, that it would have been better not to; perhaps in the meantime a vague notion had formed in my brain that something happened to things the moment you talked about them, that they became bigger and more dangerous. The things you talked about took on a life of their own, jumped up at you and bit you on the nose.

"What are you saying? A slap? Did you get a slap? How? Where? Tell me exactly."

He picked up a torch and shone it in my ears, eyes, and nose, which was nice and tickled and made me burst out laughing. There was a tap at the door and Mummy slid into the room, lithe and elegant in her kimono, but less self-confident than usual. She seemed confused. She had a red glass in one hand and a cigarette in the other and looked at once frightened and angry.

"I saw light. What's wrong? What's Louise doing here?"

"Hélène, you hit her." My father stood with his back toward her.

"Hit? I gave her a tap, because she . . ." She didn't finish her sentence.

"You know what I think about that."

"What? You believe her story?" She smashed the glass close to his feet on the stone floor. Daddy turned round and hit her on her cheek; it sounded hollow and sharp at the same time.

"Right, now we're quits."

She said nothing. She just stood where she was and closed her eyes. She still had a cigarette in her hand. The blue smoke curled up along her body. She stood there for a while, her white powdered face held high, then turned and ran off.

The night people had swept up the slivers in my father's room. It had taken them a long time; they had a sacred respect for broken glass: it was dangerous, it brought bad luck, it had to be cleared up down to the smallest sliver, and they searched every last nook and cranny of the room.

My father had lifted me onto his desk; he was sitting below me in his chair. I had put my feet on his knees. We sang songs, I can't remember which. When the floor had been cleared of slivers, he picked me up and took me to my own bed. He would sit with me until I'd fallen asleep, he said.

My room was in an extension of the house and there was always someone squatting outside my door and that someone always had taken me by the hand as soon as I woke up and lifted me up or carried me off to the life of the tropical night, where things were more hectic and noisy than during the day when the burning sun slows everything down and finally paralyzes it. At night it was cool, and as soon as the strange singers and the strange musicians, invisible during the day, piped, the party could begin. The daytime commandments no longer applied. Now the spirits and sorcerers were in command. Those who were not frightened of the darkness, and did not allow themselves to be intimidated by singing and strange figures they'd never seen before, had nothing to fear.

Since my trip through the jungle my night companions had to guard me and ensure that I did not leave my room.

That same turbulent night, in which so much had already happened, my mother came into my room.

I woke up and looked for my father's figure in the wicker chair next to my bed, but the chair was empty, and instead of that she was standing so close to me that I could touch her. I sat up with a start, but she wasn't the avenging goddess that I expected. She sat down on the edge of the bed trembling, her head bowed; tears ran down her cheeks, and she hugged me again and again.

She whispered nonstop into my ear and I couldn't make proper sense of her words, but what I understood was that she was asking *me* for forgiveness. She kept asking urgently, "How can I make it up to you, tootsie, darling, Lulu, dolly, tell me?" She had goose pimples and shivered and crept into bed next to me, pulling the sheet over both of us. She raised her hands and banged her head hard several times. I became terrified again.

"Don't do that," I cried, pulling her arms down. Mummy put them around me.

She whispered, "Nothing's happened, you must believe that."

I repeated her words, "Nothing's happened, you must believe that." So softly that I could scarcely hear it myself, I asked her, "What's that? Believe?"

"Believe? That's a secret. You can't see it and you can't hear it." My mother's voice sounded so sad that I wished I hadn't asked anything. "It's often better just to believe. But you don't have to believe everything that you hear or see."

I understood less and less.

"Did something bad happen to Auntie Margot?"

"Nothing bad happened to Auntie Margot. I wish I could explain it to you, but I can't. It's too difficult. Later, later, perhaps."

We lay together, dozing off and sobbing, until we heard voices outside, hostile at first, then helpless.

"Oh my God, will this ordeal never end?" cried my mother. "I brought all this misery on this house through my own stupid fault. What am I to do?"

When the commotion outside didn't stop but instead grew in intensity, we crept out of bed.

On the veranda against a background of leaping shadows, a struggle was in progress into which we dared not venture. It was like a struggle between gods. I couldn't understand what was said, I couldn't follow the gestures, and the intricacies were shrouded in semidarkness. My mother said nothing.

As we walked away, I looked around and saw Uncle Felix kneeling on the ground in front of Auntie Margot, and her grabbing him by his hair and pulling him to her, before immediately giving him a shove that made him fall over.

"I think you're lying, man," she cried.

SEVEN

My mother was ill and stayed in her room all day. She did not emerge until evening, and then lay down silently on the settee on the veranda.

I tried obstinately to get back into her favor. I was allowed into her room sometimes, and then I would play there with my dolls to give her pleasure, although I found them such prissy creatures. But I didn't show my dislike, and I invented whole stories about Liselotte and Desiree. She listened to them with a sad expression. While I was performing my puppet show, she sat up in bed, but I wasn't allowed to touch her. When she stroked me for a moment, she still kept me at a distance. "Not too rough, I've got a headache, so we must talk and act softly."

"When you're better, can we go swimming?" I asked her because I knew she loved swimming. We used to swim every day.

"Oh yes, we'll go swimming again one day, darling." Tears came into her eyes. I wanted to console her.

"And then can we sing 'John Jenny,' can we, Mummy?"

She listened to my pleading for a few seconds, then crept back under her sheet. In a muffled voice she sent me back to my own room.

After that I made sure I didn't ask her anything more and didn't get too close to her.

My father and I weren't angry with Uncle Felix, but the others were.

When my father came home in the evening and sat with us on the veranda for a while, he would say pensively: "Felix sends you all his regards."

His remark hung there, buzzing around for a long while. I should have liked to ask, "When is Uncle Felix coming back?," but I didn't dare. Perhaps my mother and Auntie Margot wanted to ask too, perhaps they wanted to know too: "And how is he?" But as far as I can recall, they didn't ask anything either.

There would be a long silence on our veranda. It was as if my father had thrown his words into a deep well, and whenever you thought they'd gone for good and it was time to talk about something else, they suddenly bobbed up again. Because my mother or my aunt, one of the two, would sigh, "Oh yes, Felix."

Then my father, holding his hand to his forehead, would say anyway, "Of course, he's doing very well. He's doing a lot better."

After another long interval my father said, "He's stopped drinking."

I looked at the ceiling, where the *tjitjaks* were appearing.

It was so quiet on the veranda that I could hear Daddy shift in his chair. And shift again. I could hear him emptying his glass of water and filling it from the jug, in which no ice cubes were tinkling anymore because they'd melted. The *djongos* had hurried up to take the empty jug; my father walked to his work pavilion with his glass, passed the back of my chair, and stroked my head, without saying anything. He sat writing at his desk in his study until deep into the night, with his head very close to the paper, his glasses on the end of his nose. Once when I went past his room in the night with Babu Roslin, I saw that he'd fallen asleep.

I had to laugh; his head was lying on the paper like a great *rambutan* fruit.

My mother was reading. She read and read. Every week a packet of books was delivered to her from the bookstall. She read during the day and in the evenings too on the veranda. She had a lamp hung up especially for the purpose, on which there appeared the stupidest and fattest *tjitjak* that I'd ever seen in my life.

"It's not a *tjitjak*, it's a *toké*," said Mummy with a deadpan expression. As if it were the most normal thing in the world for a *toké* to show itself. I didn't believe her, but said nothing. This *toké* was as big and fat as my lower arm and had bulging eyes as big as Ping-Pong balls that stared straight ahead. Large and small flying insects, everything disappeared inexorably into its jaws.

I'd heard that one must never look a *toké* in the eye.

"Who did you hear that from? Who told you that nonsense?" I'd forgotten. Perhaps I'd made it up for myself, the idea that a *toké* was a secret creature, which shouldn't be seen, but only heard.

I cried, "It's not a *toké*, because it doesn't call out its name."

"It's a *toké*." My mother went on reading, regardless of what I'd said and indifferent to what was happening around her. Even when she answered, she went on reading.

"It's not a *toké*, it's a dragon."

There were pictures of dragons in my book of fairy tales: they were dreadful creatures that breathed fire. They appeared to everyone all the time, but they never ever called out their names. They roared or breathed fire. They never brought luck; they brought lots of bad luck.

"All right, have it your way. It's a baby dragon," said my mother. She didn't look up from her book.

So that meant we were having bad luck. It meant that evil spirits and demons were in control of our household. However often everyone said that we weren't having bad luck, and that it wasn't my fault.

Auntie Margot told us that she'd sent Granddad a letter saying that she wanted to come to Bali anyway although the wedding wasn't going ahead.

"Why are you going there anyway? What's the point of that?" cried my mother.

"I want to go to see Daddy. To talk."

"What is there to talk about?"

"He's our father, and he always knows what to do." She looked at Mummy apologetically.

"Insufferable daddy's girl!" cried my mother spitefully.

"Who's the insufferable one here? If you ask me, it's you," stammered Auntie Margot.

"Don't imagine he's going to read your letter."

My mother said this triumphantly. The bully never read letters, she went on. Certainly not letters from his own daughters. Perhaps they were opened for him by his intimates, perhaps they read him the amusing bits, but he never answered them.

I wanted nothing better than to see him in the flesh for once. I'd never seen a granddad.

"Can I go too?" I asked my aunt.

"Good idea."

"Oh yes, you go then," flustered my mother. "You go, the two of you. Just leave me all alone."

"You're not alone, you've got Cees." Auntie Margot said it almost as a rebuke.

She wouldn't be dissuaded from her plan by anyone. The preparations for her journey caused a lot of work and talk and activity, so that the excitement over things that had happened and that nothing could be done to alter anyway subsided automatically.

·   ·   ·

Auntie Margot had the telegram in her hand and waved it about.

"Granddad Daddy wants us to come, yes, toots, you too."

She grabbed me and did a dance with me. She was cheerful again. Everything seemed as it used to be, but still it was different. She was so strangely cheerful . . . had she been drinking out of Uncle Felix's bottles?

She giggled and waltzed around unsteadily. She soon let me go and danced on with her parasol. Then she cried out with a loud laugh, "Here goes . . . ," drove her parasol into the ground by its point, grabbed hold of it, and swung around it like a top.

"Well, just look at our performing elephant. My, the tricks she can do," cried my mother in a cutting tone.

Auntie Margot rushed at her, with her hand raised. Mummy grabbed the hand quickly and put it against her cheek. In a tragic voice she said, "Go ahead and hit me, sis, hit me, yes, I've deserved it."

Auntie Margot looked even sadder than my mother.

"Would you like me to start hitting you?"

"You're going to Daddy with Lulu. The pair of you are leaving me in the lurch. That's bad enough."

These moods swung quickly, and by the following morning my mother had already come up with something new.

"It's good that you're going, so I can recover."

"And so can we," replied Auntie Margot.

Auntie Margot was changing. She was becoming a different Auntie. She was becoming a little like the ladies who came to visit us, hectic, posh and tinkling, and always well dressed. She no longer smiled vaguely like the Buddha.

In the past when she came home she always slipped straight into her kimono, and then she could glide across the gallery like a lazy cat, listening to the goings-on around her. She always stood still for a long time wherever she went; she ground up fragrant leaves of plants in her fingers, smelled them, smiled, and stroked my hair. If she hadn't already kicked off her sandals under some table or other, she lost them casually on the way.

Now she suddenly no longer wore such lighthearted, comfortable sandals but real ladies' shoes with heels and straps. She kept spraining her ankles, but she kicked pebbles with them for no good reason, as if she thought it was necessary. Uncle Felix would never let me throw pebbles or kick them, because the spirits slept in the stones.

Auntie Margot picked flowers at random to put in her hair, but if she wasn't able to do it immediately she threw them on the ground without a second thought. It happened again and again.

I froze: it was unbearably hot that day, and I was standing in a tub of water in my swimming costume while a *babu* sponged me down. I wasn't supposed to get out, but I got out anyway and ran to the hedge to pick up the flowers that Auntie had thrown on the ground. No one said anything about it, but I simply jumped out of the tub and ran across the grass in my bare feet. I picked up the flowers. Spirits slumbered in flowers. I first put them in the tub in the water and then carefully stepped back in. They floated round my legs and touched me gently. I didn't dare ask my mother if spirits could drown too, just like little kittens and people. Mummy was sitting on the veranda in her kimono and on her desk was a pile of pale velvety paper, which she was frowning at.

"Beautiful laid paper. Perfect. It was meant for the invitations. But now!"

"Now you can simply write and tell everyone that the party's off," said Auntie Margot furiously.

"But no one knew anything about it." My mother gave a deep sigh.

"That's true!" Auntie Margot sighed even more deeply. Tears glistened in her eyes.

My mother went on quickly, "Shall we make it a different

party? When you come back, to celebrate your return. A fancy dress ball? Shall we give a fancy dress ball? Forgive and forget?"

Auntie Margot, who on other occasions was the soul of amenability, pounced on Mummy's address book, grabbed it, raised it aloft, and swung it to and fro high above her head.

"You still feel in a party mood; do you dare say that?"

"Give it back! Put it down!"

"If you feel in a party mood, then I know why."

"You're going to Daddy's. That's a party for you. Can I do what I want?"

"Oh, oh, oh, you certainly want me to go. And I know why."

It went on like that until Auntie Margot leapt onto the front gallery like a puppet from a puppet show, in her shiny black high-heeled shoes, in her red dress that twirled and undulated around her body. All I could think of was the fire dancer I'd seen at the *pasar gambir* fair, who had wobbled through a sea of fire on black wooden stilts and suddenly dropped into the flames with a horrid cry.

"Don't start again, Margot, not again, will you? It's all untrue anyway."

In the tumult my mother had still managed to take her nicest fountain pen out of the tea chest, the emerald green one with the black circles and the gold cap, in which a bird was engraved, not Garuda, but a sacred bird from Holland. She was already setting out her inkwells in front of her and deciding on the colors.

"Margot, calm down," she said solemnly. "I'll write a letter to Daddy and give it to you to take to him. I'll write and tell him that he must give you some good advice. Now the question is, what color shall I write to him in? Red? Unfortunately red's impossible, don't you agree? It's supposed to be the color of love, but in fact it's the color of passion. And has passion got much to do with love?"

"Yellow!" cried Auntie Margot, putting her hands to her mouth like a horn. "Yellow, the color of hatred and betrayal!"

"You can't see yellow on ivory-colored paper," whispered my mother with her head bowed. Her short white hair fell forward, and as I watched red blotches in the form of clouds welled up in the nape of her neck.

Horrified, I put my finger on them. She didn't move; she was like a statue.

"Hélène, Hélène," said Auntie Margot comfortingly, "calm down, why don't we let the matter rest? Good idea. We were going to keep smiling, weren't we?"

I looked on and everything passed before my eyes at high speed. The images were jerky, reappeared and tumbled over, ran upside down, as in a Charlie Chaplin film I'd seen that kept breaking and was projected again with everything topsy-turvy. Unreal images, which have conformed to loom up, each time in a slightly different constellation, for more than half a century now.

My mother, like the actress allowed to play the queen, sits magnificent on her throne in the middle of our stage. Decor, props, which could be cardboard. Our veranda, on which our life took place. The furniture polished till it shone. Snow white rugs and cushions embroidered with colored silk, the lamp made of Murano glass, the parasols that leaned against the wall with their yellow heads, their gold-colored fringes. All the decorative plants, enclosed in brass pots that were too small for them, from which they would fortunately soon burst out. Their mightier green companions encouraged them, waving and giving secret signs of complicity.

Having run away from this scene, I can see myself on the edge of it, at the bottom of the veranda steps, in a bathing costume, in a tub full of water, where I am being lovingly sponged down, or having water carefully poured over me with the *gajong*, or sprayed gently with a garden hose as if with a wagging tail by the *babu*, who had concentrated totally on this task and didn't utter a word, so that I experienced her care like a natural phenomenon.

In my tub I listened to my mother, worried about my

drowned flowers, while above my head the conversation continued about the question of whether or not there was ink of a
color good enough for that bully on Bali, so that he would have
to read this special letter. After a long time, I intervened in the
discussion with the courage of despair. "Gold, gold, gold, gold,"
I screamed. Gold was the most beautiful thing there was in all
fairy tales. The letter we took with us must be gold.

"Gold, gold, gold," I shouted, pulling myself up on the balustrade of the gallery.

"Louise, stop that. Take your wet hands off."

"A drop of water never killed anyone." The voice of Uncle
Felix sounded behind us.

I turned round in surprise. "Gold!" I shouted at him exultantly.

Uncle Felix was back. He was suddenly there again, just like
that. It was as if he'd flown in. I hadn't heard or seen a car.

"How did you get here?"

"I walked, Hélène, down the long, long Lindenlaan," he
replied.

Auntie Margot rushed off, disappearing like a flash across the
lawn in the direction of the stream. As she went she wriggled out
of her shoes; with one foot she peeled one shoe off, the other she
kicked off, as she used to, and then ran on in her bare feet. Uncle
Felix ran after her, and I saw him catch up with her.

I climbed onto the stone balustrade to get a better view. After
they'd stood there shouting and moving about for a while, Uncle
Felix suddenly left our garden with his head in the air.

"Then you must believe what you want to believe," he
shouted. He didn't say good-bye to anyone, he didn't even wave,
he didn't look around once.

Auntie Margot watched him go. She was still looking in the
direction in which he had disappeared long after he had gone.
Finally she came over to us.

Not till she was close to us could I see properly, and I was shocked at how her face had fallen. Her round face seemed to be made of rain-soaked mud, her forehead and eyebrows, the drooping eyelids, her cheeks, her chin, everything seemed to be sliding off her like dark ooze. As she trudged up the steps of the veranda, she said in a mournful tone, "He's gone."

"Straight back to the bottle."

"Hélène!" Auntie Margot folded her hands and looked up as if wanting to appeal to all the good gods. "That's not true! You mustn't say that; that's not true."

Although I occasionally asked very cautiously, I was never again allowed to go with my mother for our afternoon siesta.

From then on, when the afternoon began, I was taken to my own bed and sometimes I sat up in it the whole time. Sometimes I fell asleep.

That afternoon, when the air was so warm that even the butterflies had difficulty getting through, I'd been sitting up for a long time and looked around me and still nothing happened. Then I had got up, crept out of my room, stepped over the sleeping Babu Roslin, who was lying on her *tikar* by the threshold, and had made my way cautiously to Uncle Felix's house.

I walked along our stream, downhill, till I reached the pavilion where Uncle Felix lived and where he had his terraces of medicinal plants.

And there he was; he was lying rather than sitting in his low wicker chair, among his plants. They were larger than ours, and some of them looked very different. Kebon-Bali was squatting a little way off, staring broodingly straight ahead, but he often did that. Something was troubling him, but I didn't know what. Did he come here every day to look at Uncle Felix's medicinal plants? I knew for certain that he wasn't allowed to water them, he wasn't allowed to touch Uncle's plants; no one was.

With each breath through his nose Uncle Felix made a mournful humming sound. I looked out on his crown, from which long streamerlike curly hair twisted, with a golden glow over it as if it were bathed in light. He was sitting among his plants, which shared his life with him and some of which, with their ginger-colored, strangely serrated leaves, even resembled him.

The plants were close together in their stone pots, large and small mixed together. Uncle Felix had written their names on cards, which he had pushed into their earth.

I tiptoed up to the wicker chair, where there was a zinc bucket on the ground, with a bottle in among the ice cubes that had already half melted. I bent down to grab the bottle, but first ran my hands through all the foliage and immediately a mixture of strange smells swirled around me, bitter and sharp, with a touch of sweetness, but so sweet you could almost taste it. Bitter and sharp returned a moment later, and if you breathed in the dark, fiery odors deeply and kept the air down for long enough, it eventually made you dizzy. How long would I be able to hold out in this vortex? It was a long time before I wanted to free myself, but I didn't allow myself to get carried away since I had to watch Uncle Felix, who didn't see me because he didn't give any sign of life and sat motionless in his chair. I couldn't stand here any longer, I had to go to him. I had to tell him I wasn't angry with him. He had a half-filled glass in his hand, which he held at an angle, and which therefore was gradually emptying onto the ground.

I was so nervous that I couldn't whisper very well.

"Uncle Felix!" I stammered.

The *kebon* looked up, saw me there, and nodded at me earnestly. We were friends. I was about to ask him something, but he rose and left, resting one hand on the stone edge and leaping over the balustrade without a sound. He had gone before I

realized, like a great black cat. On the other side of the balustrade there was a hoarse sound, a kind of bark, and I realized
that Teddy-Bali had been waiting there all along.

When I reached my uncle, and got so close that I could touch
him, I tried to attract his attention again.

"Uncle Felix, are you asleep?" I blew the words toward him a
few times through my cupped hand so that they could slip into
his ear, as he always did with my mother and Auntie Margot.
"Uncle Felix! The glass is spilling!"

A sudden jolt went through him. He raised his head with a
jerk, straightened the glass, looked in it, and drank it down in
one. He kept hold of it with white knuckles and looked woozily
ahead of him.

I heard the glass crushing, heard it digging itself into his
hand in thousands of fragments, drawing thousands of droplets
of blood.

"Away," he muttered, "get away from this damn place." I
thought he said that, but the words were not easy to understand;
they were like a soft groan or growl. It was as if Uncle Felix
could no longer speak. Soon he would no longer be able to move.
I closed my eyes tight shut so as not to have to see his body being
covered in long gray tresses.

"Pity of the gods," I heard him say.

He didn't see me, though I was standing next to him and
could touch him with my hand.

"We chose our own Persian life carpets again," he grumbled.
"*Meshugge* as we were!"

His breathing became louder and meanwhile he looked at his
wounded hand, as if he'd been branded by an evil spirit.

I went closer to him.

"Dammit, we chose our own carpets once again."

With his foot he swept together the slivers that were lying on
the ground, without looking at them.

"If only you'd chosen a better carpet, lad."

He crushed the splinters with the sole of his shoe.

"Uncle Felix," I said more loudly.

"Choose a better carpet, that's number one. Where's that damned *kebon* got to?"

Uncle Felix whistled between his teeth. Exactly on the last note, the gardener's boy was back. He'd leapt noiselessly back over the balustrade, but I hadn't seen him. Perhaps he hadn't even gone away; perhaps he'd stayed in this place the whole time. Waiting till he was called, and only then appearing again.

Uncle Felix spoke to him urgently. "Good story, you must hear it too, you good-for-nothing."

"What story then?" I asked his ear. I believed I was invisible too, that I would be able to fly away out of my body if I flapped my arms up and down.

"It's the same old story, the same old story." My uncle looked at his bloody hand, turning it this way and that, then grabbed the bottle out of the bucket and put it to his mouth. He drank in great gulps, pausing only to take a breath. "All that nonsense about those Persian carpets, the story's not worth a straw."

With the tip of my forefinger I stroked his shoulder and then his arm, which hung down limply, and I tickled him a little. The material of his shirt was soft, and in some places it was damp. I wanted to ask what exactly he meant by that nonsense about those Persian carpets. I was going to blow words into his ear, but I didn't have to, he'd seen me.

"She has perched by me like a little elf. Hello, princess, as long as you're there, perhaps there's still hope for me."

I asked about the old story of the Persian carpets.

Uncle Felix shook his head.

"It's a disgusting story, and it's not nice at all, dammit. It's enough to make you cry."

"But it has a happy ending," I said hopefully.

"It doesn't have a happy ending." Uncle Felix made a grimace. "It doesn't have a happy ending." He put the bottle to his lips but thought better of it, didn't take a gulp, and wiped his hand with his sleeve.

"Mummy says all stories have happy endings."

Uncle Felix put the bottle on his knee; his white trousers were covered in the stains of his blood.

"Perhaps Mummy's right. For all she knows."

"Yes, Uncle?" I asked. "Does this story have a happy ending, the one about the Persian carpets?"

"Yes," answered Uncle Felix with an expansive gesture. "If we could swap, it would have had a happy ending. Would I want to swap places with you, *Kebon*? Do you want to change places with me?"

"Tell me, Uncle."

"That's a tall order." He looked at the bottle.

"Will a drop of that loosen your tongue, Uncle?" I asked after a while, and was about to get another glass for him.

The *kebon* had already conjured one up from somewhere and put it down on the table. He must have gone into the room, taken the glass out of the cabinet, and then come out again without my noticing.

"Out of the question!" Uncle Felix suddenly spoke with a contorted face and tried to stand up. It was a big effort for him to produce each word that he spoke. They were like stones falling from his lips.

"No more drinks to loosen the tongue. I know that carpet. I'm going to try a different one. What do you think of that?"

"Tell me, Uncle."

"They finally took pity, those gods! They could no longer bear to see the suffering on earth. What did they dream up? They laid our line of carpets down in a square and said: Anybody who's not satisfied can come and swap. There were carpets of all kinds there, all together. Skimpy ones and small ones and very big ones and sumptuous ones. Seedy ones and beautiful ones. 'If what we've supplied is no good,' said the gods, 'we're very sorry.

Exchange your old rag for a better one! Go ahead and choose a better carpet. People, throw your old carpet away, and take a new one that you do like. Without burn marks, beer, or bloodstains.'"

Uncle Felix's hand wandered over the table and came to rest near the glass, which he tapped with his nails.

"The carpet of a teetotaller, I'm going to try that one. What do you think they did, Lulu? Did the people choose a beautiful new carpet without stains or holes?"

"Yes, Uncle, they were happy."

"Are you sure?"

"Yes, Uncle, absolutely sure."

"Not at all, no, princess, you're wrong! What do you think happened? Get ready for this. We were all desperate to have our own carpet back, what do you think of that! Our own carpet. Our own very own *nebbish* carpet. We thought it was the most beautiful thing on offer, so the story goes. Can you believe that!"

I didn't know what to believe. Uncle Felix went on.

"I'm going to do it differently. Louise, just you watch and you too, *Kebon*! Come here, you two are witnesses, I'm going to surprise the gods."

He handed the boy the bottle that he'd been holding in his hand the whole time: "*Kebon!* Pour this life water as an offering to the gods. Give it back to them. Let them enjoy it. They can keep their consolation prizes."

The gardener's boy dithered, and stood with the bottle in his hand, looking embarrassed. I asked, cheerful because we were going to play a new game, "Are the gods allowed to have the life water, Uncle Felix?"

"Yes, and be quick about it, or I'll change my mind."

"Can Dewi Kesuma have some too, Uncle?"

"Dewi Kesuma? The stream? Yes, of course, I'm sure she'll have good use for it."

We took the bottles out of Uncle Felix's pavilion and walked to the stream with a full bottle in each hand.

After the *kebon* had opened them, we poured them into the clear water. Not all at once, but as slowly as we could as if we were making a sacrifice, in great seriousness. Funny though we found the experience, we tried to hold back our laughter. We walked back and forth several times to fetch more bottles.

Uncle Felix had bound a handkerchief around his hand, and sat on his stool pulling faces. "Shall I come and help you?"

"No, Uncle," I cried in alarm, "we mustn't get any blood on the bottles."

"That's true. Well? Is she pleased with the treat, our Dewi?"

"Yes, she's pleased. She's very pleased with the new life water."

"Bravo. That's what I like to hear!"

There was very little water left in the stream, because it was the end of the dry season. There was a tiny trickle of water at the bottom of this bed, but this small amount leapt over the pebbles with a kind of bravado, as if already rehearsing for the great flood. It surprised me that the stream hadn't colored with pleasure. It just leapt a tiny bit higher, and babbled on as before, but contentedly.

A few days later, in the early afternoon, it started raining, for the first time in ages. I ran to my mother's room and pounded on her door.

"Come out, Mummy, it's raining, it's raining."

I was so excited that I had completely forgotten that she no longer wanted to be disturbed and certainly not when she had a headache. Nevertheless, she appeared.

"That's a surprise," she said. "Everything will be all right now." She even put her arms around me.

We went to look at the rain together on the front gallery. She gave me a nudge, indicating that I could go down the steps, into the garden, and get completely soaked by the rain, splashing through the wet grass in bare feet, even though I had a dress of Granny Helena's on.

"Go out into it, darling; you want to, don't you?"

I ran with my arms outstretched, head thrown back, mouth open, through the rain. I circled across the garden; it felt as if I were flying. Whenever I passed the front gallery, I saw my mother's white ghost standing there, swaying to and fro as if she were a flower on a long thin stalk. When I got to the *waringin*, by the big gate, I saw that it was pelting down where we were but not on the other side of the road. There was a shiny curtain of water jets precisely around our garden. At the front it stopped just beyond our *waringin*. The paving stones on the road were dry. I'd never seen this before and ran to my mother to tell her, but when I got to the gallery, she wasn't there anymore.

"Mummy! Mummy!"

"Yes, here I am." Her voice sounded muffled but close by, and a moment later I saw her there, a little farther along the gravel path. She was unrecognizable, with her hair streaming wet, barefoot, just like me. She held up her arms, in the wide sleeves of the kimono, so that the rain could pour into them. With her head thrown back and her mouth open, she let herself be completely drenched by the rain just like me.

The downpours continued until late at night. I was woken up when the uninterrupted noise of the falling water stopped and suddenly all kinds of animal noises rang out, shriller than usual.

Had the rain stopped because the bottles were empty?

I went on wondering until I couldn't stand it in bed any longer. Roslin was sleeping on her *tikar* mat at the door of my room. She never really slept properly, I knew; she dreamed with her eyes open, but this time she must have been very tired because she had her eyes closed and almost all the wrinkles had gone from her face. I stroked her arm, shook her, but she went on breathing deeply and calmly. There was a drop of spittle on her cheek. I brushed it away with my finger, and she still didn't wake up. I had to go out by myself.

The moon appeared, at the same time as a red glow above the volcano.

White figures danced down from the mountain.

I didn't know whether they were living creatures or ghosts or mists. I only knew that I had to take Dewi the bottle still owing to her. Then it would start raining again.

I crept as quickly as I could to the hollow in the *waringin*, put my arm inside with my head averted, because just imagine if it was inhabited by a greedy spirit that tried to bite my arm off. I was trembling with fear, but I had to do it.

I couldn't feel anything; I felt again, again nothing. Finally I put my head in the hollow and looked around, as well as I dared.

The bottle had gone.

EIGHT

In my aunt's eyes Granddad was comparable with the god Vishnu, who clears up all the old rubbish and ensures that everything can begin again. Like Vishnu, Granddad assumed many forms. In the photos that stood in silver frames on a little table in Auntie Margot's room, he could be seen in constantly changing manifestations. In some photos he was wearing clothes from the dressing-up box. He always towered above everyone, and however he stood or sat, his black, piercing eyes were always looking at you. In many photos he had a rifle with him, including the photo where he was sitting on a settee together with the enormously fat night woman who was called Auntie Poppy. On Granddad's side his rifle leaned against the settee.

"Does Granddad shoot with the rifle?" I asked after I'd heard that you could shoot with a rifle, even better than with a catapult. I knew what a catapult was, and I could fire wads of paper; I'd learned that from Uncle Felix.

"Oh yes, Granddad shoots if he has to," said Auntie Margot. It sounded as if she admired him. Uncle Felix had made a catapult from a forked tree branch and a piece of thick elastic. He had put a row of bottles on the balustrade, and I was allowed to shoot at them with corks. I hadn't hit any, but my uncle had knocked them all off.

"Scandalous! All on target!" he'd cried.

Standing at Auntie Margot's table with the photos on it, I told her about our catapult. Immediately I saw her face fall: she didn't like the story at all. She didn't want to hear any more stories about Uncle Felix. In my confusion I asked the first question that came to mind.

"Does Granddad shoot at empty bottles too?"

"Bottles?"

I was afraid she was going to cry.

"Does Granddad shoot at animals too, Auntie Margot?" I didn't want to hear the answer and anyway I knew it already: I'd seen Vishnu standing with his boot on a dead tiger.

"He shoots tigers if they're dangerous because they've eaten human flesh." Auntie Margot sounded as if she was making excuses for him. Again I let my gaze wander over the photo where my granddad was sitting on that little settee together with the fat night woman, and I realized that Granddad had to take great care that this Auntie Poppy wasn't eaten by tigers. She looked like a laughing elephant.

"Granddad never shoots elephants," I observed.

"Never," cried Auntie Margot. She grabbed me and whispered in my ear, "Heffalump, heffalump, he's so clever, he's no chump, who can say, who can say, that eggs are something he can't lay?"

"What?"

"Again? Heffalump, heffalump . . ."

"Can I say it aloud now?" I asked after practicing the new words for a while.

"Go on then, go and say it to Mummy."

I ran off along the gallery and through the house with my newly acquired song.

My mother was sitting reading. I recited my verse as nicely as I could. She didn't look up from her book, but the corners of her mouth went up—a miracle, she was smiling.

"Yes, yes, I can hear that ridiculous nonsense. We learned that from Daddy."

"When are we going to see him?" She went on reading, without looking at me, and shrugged her shoulders.

"Just you wait until Auntie Margot is ready for you to go."

"Does Granddad shoot people?" I asked my mother. Finally she looked at me, in irritation, with a line between her eyes.

"Is Auntie Margot telling you that? That's all a lot of claptrap of hers."

"Doesn't Granddad shoot?"

"He shoots, but he misses."

Some gods flew off their earthly pedestal in order to soar much higher, to regions where the eye cannot reach. According to my mother Granddad did everything that God had forbidden, just for the hell of it. In my eyes it elevated him to the throne next to God. The fact that he had Poppy with him night and day, who smoked opium and was wrinkly and fat as an elephant, made him even more awesome. They were two gods from Bali, my Granddad and Poppy.

The preparations for the journey took ages.

First Auntie Margot packed everything, in cases and baskets, then she unpacked it again. She wanted to do everything herself, but my mother said that was crazy. So Auntie Margot mobilized all the night people and urged them on as they worked for her: packing, unpacking, packing, unpacking. She stood by laughing and sang strange songs. She no longer cared about anyone. She joked with us all day long, and no longer went to the clinic.

"First I've got to get over all that's happened, haven't I?"

In the evenings Auntie Margot was still in her kimono. If tea ladies came to visit she said, "Much too preoccupied with our journey to change."

My mother wasn't in very good sorts yet. She appeared late in the morning; she had blotches on her face and just sat and read. No longer in a beautiful dress but in her baggy pajamas, which were white in the morning but gray by the afternoon. She no longer wore jewelry.

She sat hunched forward in her chair, with her head resting on her hand and the book on her knee. When she read a newspaper, she let it fall on the ground before she'd finished reading it. The newspaper fluttered down, and my mother, so it seemed, went on reading for a bit, in the air.

She never lay on the settee anymore. The latter stretched its round, flowered arms out to her in vain. I sat on it carefully to console it.

We no longer ate at the black dining table that still shone as it had always done because it caught the light from the two top windows, the elephant's eyes. If the moon shone in, the dining table looked like a dark, deserted pool. I felt sorry for it, because it was no longer allowed to serve anyone, and everyone gave it a wide berth. In order to cheer it up, I sometimes put my dolls on it, but they always returned to my room even before I did.

We now had dining tables all around the house, and anyone who wanted to could follow the sun from meal to meal, in the morning in the east gallery, in the evening in the west.

It was a big improvement, because it was less formal than it used to be and you could make a mess and spill as much as you wanted to. It no longer mattered.

I made more of a mess than before, because I scarcely ate the food, which too often had inert lumps and slippery strands in it. Lukewarm, sweet meat, which groaned under my teeth the only time I bravely tried it. According to my mother, I lived on fruit and vegetables.

"We simply can't get her to eat anything else."

"Fine," said my father.

"She looks like a ghost."

"Ghosts don't thrive on vegetables and fruit," he said, sounding put out.

My mother stood straight in front of him: "Don't you ever want to talk about anything else? Always about food? Wouldn't you like to say that I've got such a nice dress on? That I put on specially for you?"

My mother was angry, but she pressed up against Daddy. He took her by the shoulders and pushed her a little away from him. "I know nothing about dresses."

"Because you're just not interested," said Mummy accusingly. She pulled herself free and left us.

My father rubbed his forehead, as if trying to brush off a mosquito. He took me by the hand and walked with me to his room, where we sat down as was our custom since the time I'd run away. He on the chair and I on his desk, so that I could put my feet on his knees.

All the drawings that I'd made for him were hanging on the wall of his room. Apart from that his walls were covered with photos of people in dark clothes, whom I didn't know, drawings in ink on yellowed paper, incomprehensible prints and newspaper clippings. Then there were the shelves with large jars on them in which strange creatures lived. Their names were written on the labels that were stuck on the bottles, in curly letters that I couldn't yet read. So I didn't know what to call them when they had turned around rocking lazily and suddenly looked at me with one of their many golden eyes. Or touched the glass with their fins, as if they wanted to escape. But they weren't fish. Or some of them actually were, so my father said. He explained that a human being assumes many forms before it comes into the world.

The night people had sometimes told me about all the shapes

in which the soul had to manifest itself before it could disappear into nothingness, happy and relieved.

We were rocking on a wave that covered the whole world. In it our souls bobbed too, changing all the time, as a one-eyed creature, as a fish, a human being, elephant, frog, it didn't matter. Everything that lived was only temporary anyway. A fish that lay gasping on dry land might be a bird the following day.

I got a shock when Daddy told me that the creatures in the jars were no longer alive. Their life spirit had disappeared. They didn't move anymore, did they?

In my opinion, though, they were moving, however slowly. What's more, I could swear and I maintained through thick and thin that Servus Poldi waved to me every time. He had lived in a woman and now he was rocking in his jar. Women had such creatures living in them, and men too, but much smaller. I thought I had a Servus Poldi in me too, to whom I could talk about everything.

My father said that these creatures could no longer wave, no longer look around, no longer move of their own accord. They were sleeping the eternal sleep; that was all they could do and they were only there to be looked at by us.

I knew that there were moments that came in the short, dangerous period of dusk, at the times of sunrise or sunset, when the soul hastened to change from one shape to another. At those moments, I knew, I had seen it, the poor chickens from which the soul had just departed for a little while disappeared and were slaughtered.

"Are they morning chickens?" I said with effort. It seemed to me inconceivable that a creature should be forever without a soul, because then it could be slaughtered at any time.

My father shook his head. "They're not chickens, know-all."

He laughed a little, tried to act as if it were all a joke, but it was clear to me that the night people knew more about it than he did. He knew a lot, but not everything.

When I asked him if there wasn't a soul in those creatures, whatever creatures they were, my father said that unfortunately he didn't know what a soul looked like. "Who does know?" he asked kindly.

"I know. Like a fish or a bird."

"Oh, is that right? Are you sure you aren't telling me a fairy story?" He pinched my cheek, tickled me under the chin. I wasn't telling him fairy stories. Hadn't I learned from my night people and from my mother that a soul can assume all the shapes that the God in his wisdom and all the other gods can think up?

I told my father how sometimes in the morning twilight when I woke up and it was still very early, it wasn't really light yet, how I saw my own soul curling up out of my body like a fleeting, transparent ghost, like a plume of blue smoke. I saw my soul fleeing from me or just making an excursion or looking for another shape, who knows? I had to get out of bed as quick as lightning to get the soul back; I had to run and make sure I didn't stumble. I had to move fast, to grab hold of my soul before it hid in a bird, which would fly so high that I would no longer be able to reach it. My own story made me breathless.

"Calm down, calm down," said my father soothingly, holding my shoulders and rocking me to and fro. "Those are only dreams."

One large wall of his room wasn't a wall but a bookshelf, where thick leather books stood behind glass with gold or silver letters on them that I couldn't read. My father sometimes took a book out of the case to look at it, and when I asked if I could look too, he said, "Yes, go ahead and look; you look, even if it won't mean much to you yet." They contained pictures of things I couldn't even recognize.

"There are enough things that you don't have to know yet." He smiled at me. "Be glad."

My mother on the other hand was always happy when I did

know something. So in Daddy's room too I did my best to get to know as much as possible. Every time that I sat in his room and made a drawing for him, I observed everything around me very carefully and that was why, when he was looking for something, I could almost always tell him where it was.

He would mumble something inaudibly to himself, and I would jump up and ask eagerly what the thing he was looking for looked like.

"Oh, just go on with your drawing—"

"Is it red, white, or blue?" I cried excitedly, and then we made a game of it, I-spy-with-my-little-eye, and of course I saw what he was looking for first, because I had remembered where I'd seen it, slipped under a pile of books or lost among the notebooks and papers on his desk.

We didn't play any other games; my father was too busy for that.

My mother had told me that he was too busy with other women and children, who were sick and weren't getting better. Or who had been born dead or even hadn't been born at all.

Because he had no time, my father almost never read to me.

But once he made up a game, the eye game.

On the eye chart there were drawings and letters, which became smaller and smaller as you went down, so small finally that you sometimes had to put your nose right up to them to be able to make them out. I wasn't supposed to do that, Mummy said, put my nose right over the page.

Daddy put the largest board down outside on a table with a pile of books behind it, and we sat a long way away from it, next to each other, in our chairs in the room.

"Can you see the drawings?"

"Is it a game, Daddy?"

"No, it's an eye test."

I whizzed through the rows.

"That's good," he said. "Very good, that was quick.

"Now I'm going to point to them all mixed up. And you just say what you can see. You can draw it too. Wait a moment, a stick." He went over and stood by the board and he raised one arm in the air, probably to show me a plant stick, that I couldn't see with my own eyes but whose length I knew perfectly well, in addition to the fact that it was made of bamboo. From the movements of my father's arm I deduced approximately where he landed with the stick on the eye chart, but it got too difficult to be able to guess the letters and the pictures without a slip.

I couldn't possibly do what he asked. He might just as well have asked for me to fly for him, first quite low and then a little higher each time.

"I don't know anymore!" My despair was great enough to admit it. With my mother I was allowed to come out with "I don't know" only as a last resort. Then she would call out sternly, "*Tida bisa tida mau tida ada tida tau.*" (Can't, won't, am not, don't know.)

And sometimes she also cried out in a low voice, which sounded much more mysterious: "Can't do is in the cemetery, but won't is still walking around fit and well."

Now I muttered almost inaudibly, "I don't know."

"That doesn't matter," said my father consolingly. "You do know, but I don't think you can see it properly. Come a bit closer."

In an attempt to make up for it, I rattled off all the rows of letters, plus the pictures of toadstools and gnomes, that I could remember from the board.

"Oho, you know them by heart, so that's how it is." With a laugh he put the stick away so he could clap his hands. "Good, really clever of you, darling."

He took me on his lap, which he seldom did, produced a handkerchief from his sleeve, and dried my tears.

·   ·   ·

The preparations for our trip to Bali dragged on and on. Grand-dad obviously thought he had been kept waiting too long, because he sent a car to pick us up. One fine day a large car with a chauffeur stood on the gravel path, and more cars followed it into our garden. There were people in the front, and it was full in the back too.

They were women and boys I didn't know. After climbing out of the cars, they rattled away in strange languages, laughed loudly, and commanded our night people to help them unload. They climbed back into the vehicles to grab packets and cases, parasols, baskets, boxes, fruits, and plants. So much came out of the cars that I stopped counting. All kinds of things happened at once. Another car drove up slowly, one that was towing a large wagon with a cage on it. What was in it? Dogs, monkeys, a pony perhaps?

The cheerful women visitors carried their objects—the baskets, the boxes, and the cases—outside, put them down every-where, on the grass, on the gravel, on the steps of the staircase up to the front gallery. And then the servants started lugging them about, whereupon the visitors chased after them until they grew tired of that and turned around to get even more things out of the cars, so that there were piles of additional luggage. The piles went on and on. The whole world was in them.

Besides cloths and carpets and bags and packets and loose pillows and blankets and robes and rolls of paper, there were bulging baskets full of fruit. Papayas as big as babies, colossal durians and jackfruit, *salaks*, mangosteens, they all lay there and a little later disappeared to the kitchen, leaving us behind sur-rounded by a gamut of sweet smells.

The people teemed over the garden like ants, but suddenly everyone had unpacked and was installed in our house, in the pavilions and the outbuildings. Strange, dark women were already fanning themselves in the galleries in the wicker chairs, titbits were put out on the tables, little children were bawling in hammocks, and the dogs had each been given a bone to gnaw in their own corner of the garden.

I'd never seen anything like this before, with so many things and events going on at once. I didn't know this was possible and looked at it openmouthed. It was like a circus.

"Just look, he's overwhelming us. He behaves like a king! King, emperor, marksman, major, nobleman, beggar man . . ." observed my mother.

"Trencherman, fake, bankrupt. I know all the things that are said about him, but they're all sour grapes," sniggered Auntie Margot.

The circus had descended on our garden, without a tent, but with dancers and snake charmers. It hadn't come to entertain us; it had come to fetch us. It had scarcely arrived; I felt it was not even a day before it left again and took us with it, Auntie Margot and me. I began my first journey.

I stood under the *waringin,* with my mother; I wanted to grab her hand, but she blew her nose loudly in a handkerchief. She needed both hands to dry her nose.

"Off you go, darlings, you go, go on, don't worry about me," she groaned, through the handkerchief. "When you come back I shall have a big surprise for you."

"A surprise?"

"Yes!"

"For me?"

"For all of us."

My mother went on crying, but I wasn't sure if she was crying because I was going. Without her noticing I stroked her body with my fingers and then with the same hand I stroked the bark of the *waringin.* No one must notice.

"Now, now, I don't want to see any tears," said my father, and he lifted me up and put me in the back of the big car, next to Auntie Margot.

The *kebon* sat in the front; he smiled at me, and pointed furtively down below; at his feet sat Teddy-Bali.

"This isn't a punishment, this is a treat," said Daddy. "And it'll be such fun! You're going to stay with your grandfather in Bali for a while, and then you'll come right back to us."

I started crying. Everyone hastened to console me.

"Bali isn't far, you know," said Auntie Margot. We were already off.

"It won't take us more than a couple of days to get there. That's just a little while, if you think about it."

What was just a little while? And I didn't know what, who, or where Bali was.

"It's over there. Where the Blue Mountains are." My aunt pointed. During the trip she kept pointing at the green, blue, or hazy distance that extended in front of us.

"There's Bali! No, a teeny bit farther; yes, we'll be there in no time."

Gradually I got used to the journey, because no one in our party was upset by the chaotic motion of car travel, the getting in and out, the sleeping in strange rooms and beds. All the other members of the motley troupe, the strange creatures, the smiling boys with a flower behind their ear, behaved no differently from the way they'd behaved at our place for that one day. They ate, they played games, they talked in low voices, or they sat with their eyes closed smiling or dreaming a little; they fell asleep and snored softly; they woke up and they smiled again and said a few words from time to time. I saw Kebon smiling virtually the whole journey since the first time that I knew him. He'd never been so happy. He was going home.

·　　·　　·

Granddad and Poppy lived in Bali, the land of the night. The night rose from the black sea, which waited impatiently all day until the sun dived into it. The water lay still but trembled at the edges, where it kept strewing lines of shells over the glowing sand with a modest whisper.

"Yes, this is the Java Sea; this sea here is always calm, not like the ocean on the other side. It's good here, you know, you can go in; you're not frightened, are you?"

Granddad, who was so big that I could only see his face properly when he squatted down by me or when he lifted me up, took me on his arm and simply walked into the great black lake with me and just plopped me down in the water a little farther on.

I was too frightened to scream, but I didn't have to, because the warm water caught me and cushioned me as he let go. I sat there with my knees drawn up and floated. I floated for the first time in my life. In Bandung I'd never floated in the swimming pool, because I quickly put my arms and legs out to keep myself above water. My mother maintained that I was such a fidgety and stubborn child that I refused to float calmly. I preferred to sink like a stone, she said. With Granddad Bali there was no way of refusing. And I couldn't sink either. Floating was automatic here. I couldn't sink like a stone, even if I'd been stubborn enough for it, even if I'd wanted to.

In Bandung I could always do lots of things like sitting, walking, running, rushing, flying, lying, and standing. Not on Bali. Here you could only float. You floated as if you were soaring. Perhaps you floated and you soared because there were no mornings with writing lessons here and no afternoons with afternoon naps. The mornings and the afternoons were no different from each other in Bali, everything merged with everything else.

The sun did go down, although we didn't look at it from a veranda, and the sun rose again, although we were still sleeping in our beds or on the ground. Everything simply went on as though we weren't there.

Auntie Margot said, "I belong here, I want to stay here."

"And what shall we do with the bridegroom?" asked Grand-dad in his easygoing way. "Shall we leave him where he is, pickled in alcohol?"

Auntie Margot lay still in the hammock.

"So you think everything in the garden's lovely?" she asked indignantly.

"There's nothing new under the sun. Always a storm in a teacup," said Granddad. "Storm in a teacup." He shouted again furiously.

"Ah, let it sort itself out." Poppy, who was sitting next to Granddad, tapped him on the nose with her fan. "It'll soon be right again."

Granddad and Poppy lived in so many houses that in my memory all those houses are linked into one long, untidy procession. First we were here, then there, now we were in the mountains, next we had a view of a lake. Mostly we were at the seaside in a house on the black sand.

The sun was there during the day and the sea, that expanse of water that went on for as far as you could see, and was there always, day and night. During the day with the fierce sun in it, and at night with the moon that bobbed up and down. At night there was fire everywhere; there were torches and flares, candles in the galleries, and there were usually power cuts. There was always food being roasted somewhere, there was always rubbish being burned somewhere else. There were lots of noises; in the mornings it was the cockerels and at night it was the familiar tropical concert. If there was somebody shouting somewhere or suddenly a lot of heated argument, I didn't get worked up about it, because it flared up and died down again.

I didn't talk a lot here. I became languid and lazy, which I wasn't allowed to be at home. Here I was. No one taught me any new words.

Granddad went into the sea every day and took me with him. I felt like shouting with joy at this sea, which belonged to Granddad Bali, but no sound came out.

"You're thinking very hard," said Granddad on one occasion, "but I can't hear anything, and I can't read thoughts either. Tell me what you're thinking."

I shook my head.

"Don't you want to say? It doesn't matter, sing a song then."

I looked at him, puzzled.

"Do you want to know what song? You've got to think up a song for yourself. Listen to me!"

Granddad sang a long and incomprehensible verse in a strange language. It boomed out across the waves. It was a shame that it came to an end.

"Yes, it was better than Richard Tauber. Now it's your turn."

I stood thinking about it, until he said, "Just sing normally. Tra-la-la is a song too. . . ."

"Tra-la-la, tra-la-la-la-la."

"That's fine, yes, that's a lot better. You haven't lost your voice at all."

When we'd finished tra-la-la-ing, I asked if Granddad was going to teach me some new words.

"New words? No, you've got to look for those yourself; you're bound to find them."

NINE

Although I didn't ask about them, Poppy reassured me every day that my father and mother were fine and that I could go back to them whenever I wanted.

"But perhaps you'd like to stay with us for a little longer?"

So this was "staying." *Staying* was a new word, but no one showed me how to write it. I tried, but I couldn't. As soon as I got my mother's first letter, I realized that I would only be able to make drawings for her, since I hadn't any new words.

I sometimes imagined what it would be like if everyone I knew in Bandung—my mother, my father, Uncle Felix, the night people and the tea aunts, everyone who sat on our veranda or in their pavilion or wandered through the garden—were suddenly here on Bali. If everyone were sitting here, around the fires, or walked into the sea to float for a bit. If no one talked anymore, but just sang.

Time passed, and it became more and more difficult to sustain my fantasy. At first it became vaguer and paler and the people in Bandung became shadows, phantoms in my head. When I could no longer even recall their faces, I received a letter. Everything that I'd experienced in Bandung was instantly clear in my mind again. I didn't even have to open the letter for that. Perhaps it might be better not to.

It was an unforgettable event, my getting a letter, because I'd never believed that anybody except Daddy could get letters.

This first letter was delivered in the beach house; a man on a bike brought it. The letter was light blue, just like the letters that flew from Europe to my father in Bandung.

I didn't dare open my letter, but left it sealed, and first took it to bed for a while, under my main pillow.

"Sweetie, the letter's from your mother," said Poppy now and then. "Why don't you open it, and I'll read it to you; come on, because we'd like to hear the great news as well."

I shook my head stubbornly. A letter was safe as long as it remained unopened. I'd seen that from my father's letters. As long as they were in their cocoons, there was no problem.

His face would stay calm and sometimes he would smile at us and tease us a little for eating the wrong things again, and more because my mother and aunt were busily engaged in what he called the white and black arts. But then he would go to his pavilion to open the letters, and they caused unpleasantness. My father crumpled them up and held them in his fist like a ball and paced up and down his gallery with them, with deep lines in his forehead and jaws clenched.

This didn't happen with all letters, but it did with lots of them. I decided to take no chances and preferred to leave my letter unopened. I didn't open the letters that followed either.

I received a letter every two weeks in Bali. I stopped putting them under my pillow, because they got creased there, but kept them all in a nest that I'd made out of my underwear, on a shelf in my wardrobe. Whenever we moved to another residence, I took them with us, nest and all. I put them in the bottom of the wicker valise that contained my other clothes and my other secrets. Wherever we went, I always took my letters with me, from one house to another, but I didn't open them. And now I knew why I didn't. The evil eye mustn't read them.

Poppy herself had said so, shaking her head and asking rather teasingly, "Are you frightened the evil eye will fall on them, sweetie?"

I could deal with my other secrets in a more carefree way, because they'd been seen and used by other people and the evil eye had had ample time to fall on them. One of my secrets was a remnant of *obat* medicine in a dark brown bottle that I sniffed to remind me of Uncle Felix, and the other was Tinka's lipstick, which she'd thrown at me almost angrily because she didn't need it anymore, since she would never dance again.

Tinka's lipstick was beautiful, but Tinka herself was even more beautiful. She was the loveliest person there was, even lovelier than my mother. I always thought that Mummy and Auntie Margot were the most beautiful women in the world. With Granddad Smit on Bali, I realized that there were many more such beautiful creatures.

To be honest, they were perhaps even more magnificent than my mother and my aunt, with lots more silver and gold and much longer hair, such long hair that they could sit on it. Granddad had so many of these creatures around him that at first I couldn't believe my eyes. At first I turned my head away in embarrassment if such a fairy came near me. But I couldn't keep it up; there were too many of them, and they were there the whole time.

Anyway, we had to look at them, said Granddad, because that was what they were for, and if no one looked at them, they would disappear forever.

Tinka, who was the most beautiful of them all, had a round, tea-colored face with upward-slanting eyes that hovered between golden brown and green. She was like my favorite cat that crept across our garden, soft and haughty, but she was also just as timid and hot-tempered as other stray cats that would never allow themselves to be stroked.

Tinka gave me a wide berth until one afternoon we both landed on Poppy's lap. Tinka sat on one thigh and I sat on the other; it felt soft and springy as my *guling* bolster. Poppy didn't have a long trunk like an elephant, but she did have a large, wrinkled nose, which made her look like the Elephant God whose statue stood on the hall table in our house, next to the telephone. Poppy sat there as cheerful and sturdy as he was; she had her pipe in one hand and titbits in the other, and wore a sarong and *kebaja*. She sat bolt upright on the ground, in the lotus position, with her knees apart and the soles of her feet close together. Her feet had such thick calluses on them that they were like the soles of a shoe.

In the triangle that she made with her legs, there was room for our feet, which to begin with we kept as far apart as possible. I stared at Tinka's supple, elastic feet. She could do everything with her toes that I could do with my fingers. She could spread them wide apart like a fan, she could move them one by one, backward, forward, and sideways. She could pick up everything with them, even grains of rice. She could write in the sand with any toe she chose, one or more words. She wove the words together, writing with her left foot or her right. She picked up a fountain pen, thin as a straw, and put it behind her ear with her foot. She could also walk past the hibiscus hedge on her hands, pick a flower with her toes, and put it in her hair.

"This is so easy," said Tinka, who simply went on talking to me while she was walking on her hands. "I can teach you this too, even though you're just a stupid child."

(She did teach me and we often practiced together, but that was years later. In Holland we walked on our hands on a patch of grass, where there was also a stop for a yellow tram. The people stood at the stop and looked at us as we showed off our party tricks. They didn't admire us, though; they were scandalized.)

Sitting cross-legged, glued to the ground, I saw the gold and fiery red creatures release themselves hissing from the fire and shoot forward like twisting flames. I held my breath in horror as raging Titans with hair standing on end and feet kicking with impatience came to earth again, and I bent my head shyly when smooth water nymphs rose naked from the pond and splashed us with water drops. Their dripping hands ran playfully over us. Looking down, I saw toads scuttling across the churned-up ground between the stalks of grass with little pans of sticky rice and their banana leaf full of tangy titbits and cardboard boxes full of sweets. They popped all kinds of things into my mouth and into my hands and quickly pinned jewelry on me and, giggling all the while, garlands of glittering stones, I remember, and a white flower, the smell of which overpowered me. But I was safe on the lap of Poppy, the old woman who looked like an elephant, but who also looked like a Buddha. She and I experienced the spectacle and the events as if we were sitting in a rocking rowboat on lapping water and now and then she cooed that I should join in: just jump in, come on, off you go, there's no need to be frightened at all. After all, I was one of her little doves. The elephant woman was so dark and fat that during the day, like a great tree, she cast shadows in which I could play.

I believed that like the *waringin* she was a thousand years old. Above my head was the reassuring sound of the smacking of her lips as she sucked the long pipe that was always in the middle of her heart-shaped mouth and around which she simply went on talking and laughing as if the pipe were a kind of long tusk of hers. She was enveloped in sweet clouds of smoke, and when she took her little turns round the garden, with one person holding her parasol for her and another fanning her with a big fan, you could see a translucent blue trace hanging in the air for ages afterward. Poppy couldn't simply go in through any ordinary door; Poppy needed a double door. "As befits a princess!" said Granddad.

Poppy slept on a mat, not a bed.

When you sat on her lap, or leaned against her from the side, she felt like the softest divan full of cushions. I sat on one of her thighs; on the other thigh sat Tinka in all her glory, who the first time we saw each other gave me an angry look. In night language she asked what I was doing here. I understood only half of what she was saying. Poppy launched into a story of which I understood absolutely nothing, but it made the girl so uncomfortable that she didn't even look at me anymore and ran away fast.

"Tut tut tut," said Poppy to me. "She'd rather burst than bend. She has moods, she has *tinkas*. She won't listen, that little aunt of yours."

Was this dancer, who could do everything, an aunt of mine?

I can still remember the feeling of joy that surged through me. I knew the tea ladies in Bandung, whom I was sometimes allowed to call Auntie, weren't real aunts of mine, like Auntie Margot. But I was losing her a bit, here on Bali. Auntie Margot sat talking to Granddad in the early morning and at night she was still talking. She told me it was about what she was going to do with her life. She was now an aunt who no longer had any time for me. So it was about time I got another.

"Is she a real aunt?" I asked hesitantly. "Not a tea aunt?"

It really seemed too beautiful to be true.

"Yes," said Poppy, "word of honor, she's your *real* Aunt Cristina."

I hoped that she would be aunt for me alone. "An aunt, like Auntie Margot?"

"An aunt, like Auntie Margot, but you don't have to call her Auntie, because she's only seven years older than you."

"Auntie Dancer!" I said, full of admiration. In the evening I'd seen Tinka and another girl wrapped stiffly in golden clothes with sad and angry faces, performing a complicated, rapid dance.

"Oh no," muttered Poppy sadly. "She'll never be a dancer. But she'll learn lots of other good things, that's why she's going to leave us soon."

I felt as sad now as I'd been happy before.

"She's going away?"

"Not from you, but from me. She's sailing with you; that's what's been decided."

I couldn't believe my ears.

"Are we going to sail?"

"On the big boat." Poppy took the pipe out of her mouth. Tears rolled from her eyes, which happened quite often when the smoke had irritated her.

"Cristina is sailing with you on the big boat."

"We're going back to Bandung on the big boat?"

"No, no, later. First back to Bandung and then on the big boat. All the way to Europe."

I'd never heard anything good about Europe. Strange grannies lived there. Poisonous letters came from there, which made my father furious. I'd never been on a big boat before.

I returned to Bandung with two aunts, Auntie Tinka and Auntie Margot. The monsoon was almost over, but it was still damp and hot. We made the return journey in a convertible with an open top that could be put up when it rained. We sat at the back, Tinka and I, and Auntie Margot in the middle. Each of us had a big picture book on our laps, which we didn't look at.

Auntie Margot put her arms around us and said, "Why don't we just look around us, dear children, those are beautiful pictures enough, don't you think?"

We closed our books, but I didn't reply, because if I said anything, I was frightened I was going to cry. Tinka was already crying, without wanting us to notice.

The chauffeur drove slowly, because Auntie Margot had said that that was better. We would have less trouble from potholes and we could see something as well. But when Tinka jumped out en route, because she suddenly decided it was too far away from her home, Auntie Margot told the chauffeur to drive faster so the journey wouldn't seem so long. The top was put up, even though it wasn't raining. After we'd managed to persuade Tinka with the greatest difficulty to travel with us, she lay down on the floor and no longer looked outside. She sat up again only when we cried out that she really must look at the procession.

We stopped for a procession of children who were wearing little hats of silver paper through which their large stuck-on hare's ears protruded. They were carrying silver-colored lanterns in which candles were flickering. Behind them came dancing men.

"The Chinese are celebrating the New Year," said Auntie Margot. "The Year of the Tiger is over and now the peaceful Year of the Hare is beginning, can you see?"

In Bandung there were the night letters and a baby.

My father walked up and down the veranda in the night with the letters. They made him sad and furious. They were even worse than the ones before, and they no longer looked innocent and elegant, like the "light-blue butterflies that came flying over the seven seas," as Uncle Felix had called them, demonstrating to us with his arms outspread and his hands flapping.

These last letters were monstrously thick and sometimes brown. There were some that were so fat that they'd burst out of their skin en route. A pile of newspaper cuttings bulged out of their torn covering, which made my father furious before he'd even read a word of them.

"It's happening again."

He didn't show the cuttings to anyone but withdrew into his pavilion with them. According to my mother, to spare us his gloomy moods.

Whenever new letters and clippings came, my mother went to her bedroom, where she fussed over her new baby. He was called Simon and was my brother, but I didn't believe it, because I thought he was too small to be a brother. In my eyes a brother was as big as Uncle Felix, my father's brother. Uncle Felix didn't come to see us anymore; he'd gone to live somewhere else, much farther away from us. He lived down in the town, next to the clinic. We once drove past and Auntie Margot pointed out the house and said, "So there he is, very convenient, so close to his work." We never visited him at home.

This little brother had replaced Uncle Felix, but it wasn't a good swap. I missed my uncle, but I didn't tell anyone, because I didn't know who wanted to hear. My father missed Uncle Felix too, because he often went to visit him.

"Cees will be late; he's out with Felix," said my mother on those occasions.

"Rather him than me," muttered Auntie Margot.

"You don't mean that, sis."

"That's no business of yours."

The *kebon* from Bali was no longer there. He'd stayed in Bali with Granddad, together with my dog.

Day in, day out, Tinka and I sat together on the new American rocking couch that stood on the veranda. Before I went to stay in Bali, my mother had promised me a surprise.

We thought that the American rocking couch was the surprise, but Mummy said, "No, don't be silly, the surprise is Simon, your new little brother. Say 'hello, darling Simon' to him."

We heard my mother walking around in her side gallery, which these days was partitioned off by a wicker screen and a row of pot plants. We heard her singing behind the wicker and twittering to Simon and saying whole sentences aloud, as if he could already speak, which he couldn't.

The *babu* who had slept in my room now lay on her mat in front of the door of my mother's room, and when I asked when Roslin was coming back to me, my mother said, "She's not coming back to you, because you've got Tinka. She'll keep an eye on you."

Tinka and I went out into the night. We squatted in the bushes and watched my father walking up and down in his pavilion. Occasionally he would throw something across his room, which sometimes broke, we could hear that; we didn't know what, as we couldn't see what it was. We saw how he was wrestling with his thoughts and listened for a bit to his grumbling and cursing, which wafted out in bursts, sometimes too faint to understand, sometimes louder. Daddy was now another animal in the nocturnal concert. After our sorties we went to eat in the servants' quarters, where they always expected us. Only when the morning broke through the dome of night did we return to our beds.

We no longer took siestas. We preferred to sit on the stones by the stream and let our feet be rinsed by the water, which was again in full flood. When I had sat for long enough, I practiced walking on my hands on uneven ground. Then we tried to lure the baggage ponies, which grazed on the green behind our garden, to us with sugar cubes taken from the sugar bowl.

If my mother sometimes heard us making a fuss in the afternoon, she would appear, mostly with Simon on her arm. She stood in the side gallery and called to us, "Remember, you noisy pair, this little chap needs a lot of sleep." But she wasn't angry with us, not even when we imitated her, giggling, "Little, little, little chap."

Once Mummy came out of her room without the baby. She wandered down from the veranda, crossed the lawn, shuffled up to us, put her finger to her lips, and whispered that we must be very quiet. She looked as I most liked seeing her, without my brother. She looked like my mummy again, not like someone else's mother too. Although she wanted to turn round again quickly, I tried to keep her with me for as long as possible. I hung on her, grabbed her hand, and when I couldn't, grabbed her by the sleeve of her kimono and asked her all the questions that I could think of at that moment.

"Do we have to be quiet, Mummy, is Daddy sick?"

"Daddy isn't sick. Simon has to sleep; otherwise Simon will get sick."

"Will Daddy come and sit with us on the veranda soon?"

"Daddy wants to be alone with his thoughts."

"Why?"

"He's got to wrestle with his thoughts."

"Why does he wrestle with his thoughts?"

"Otherwise they'll sour our life."

"What is sour?"

"Make black."

I saw my father's thoughts in front of me; they had the shape of evil spirits. They soured our life.

My mother sighed and freed herself from me; she ran away from me to get back to her room as quickly as possible, with Simon. She didn't want anything more to do with us, not with me and not with Tinka, and not even with my father.

·   ·   ·

Almost every evening that I can remember of our last months in Bandung Daddy walked up and down his gallery talking to himself in strange languages and punching the air with his fists and swearing. He fought his battles, and I got to know the apparitions threatening my father very well. I made drawings of them. As far as you can call them drawings. I made some wild scribbles at random, aimlessly, on the drawing paper with my brown and black color pencils, until apparently almost by themselves, carcasses appeared with goggle eyes and sharp claws. I went to my father with them and asked if these were his thoughts.

He hung my drawing on the wall, laughed for a moment, and looked at it with wrinkles in his forehead.

"Are these my thoughts? They really look like them."

In my fairy-tale books I set to work even more eagerly and conjured up dark figures that attacked everything that crossed their paths. Daddy's thoughts crushed Hansel and Gretel and squeezed little toddlers to death. They pounced on Sleeping Beauty and Little Red Riding Hood and finished off Goldilocks. They even whisked away Old Mother Hubbard, who wasn't scared of anything and was very vicious, under their gray hoods.

"Do you want me to sit here calmly nodding in my easy chair while over there my family are being driven into the sea?" shouted my father one night. He was furious. It wouldn't have surprised me if he'd woken the Fire God in the volcano with his roaring.

It was the first time that he'd battled so fiercely with his thoughts that Tinka and I didn't dare to stay and watch. We crept indoors with our hands over our ears and went to bed.

II

THE VOYAGE

(April–May 1939)

TEN

We were sailing on the *Garuda*. My mother and aunt wouldn't have wanted to travel on any other boat, with any other name. The journey from Batavia to the southern coast of Europe would take six weeks.

Everything would be the same, I expected, as it had been during my stay on Bali. An adventure, which would one day come to an end. When that day arrived, we would reenter our familiar house in Bandung with our old suitcases and new things.

Auntie Margot had taken her exercise book in her toilet case, but she didn't look at it once. I saw it lying there when the case was open, when she powdered her nose. A white bloom appeared over her brown cheeks, and on the blue-and-black-marbled cover too.

My mother did write, every day, just as before. She sat on a chair in our cabin next to the cot of Simon, my baby brother. He was asleep. My mother put the writing pad on her lap and opened it. She had a case containing various fountain pens, and sometimes she took this one out and sometimes the other. She thought for a long time before she started writing. Sometimes she doodled or scribbled a bit. On the cover of her writing pad was a picture of Pierrot. She'd made a bunch of curls of his smooth hair in red ink. They sprang out on all sides from under his pointed hat.

When I asked her, she said that she was writing about the days on board. The days on board formed a long succession, and joined together into one long day. All the days at sea were like each other, so that you knew in advance what was going to come. You could set your watch by them, even the surprises. Dolphins and flying fishes performed their tricks at moments when nothing else was happening. It was as though they'd arranged it with the captain. The elegant creatures disappeared promptly as soon as the ship's bell rang for another event.

The festivities on board were always the same; the passengers concentrated on eating and drinking and dancing and playing games in decorated rooms. There was music; there were streamers, balloons, artificial flowers, flags, and light.

Water and air, wind and waves, sun and moon, days and nights, everything slid past in a reassuring succession that kept us awake or rocked us to sleep when it was time. Occasionally there was an alarming interruption of the gentle breathing of the ocean, just so that we shouldn't think that we were already in the paradisial hereafter. Gray caverns opened up into which the ship disappeared with a moan, until it was forced up again by poisonous green swells, transparent and malevolent, like the wide-open eyes of a sea monster. Our ship floated on them like a speck of dirt. With its long gray nails it plucked us out of its eye and hurled us furiously into the air. We rose and fell and rose again and then, as suddenly as the adventure had begun, it was over. Those who had not been seasick laughed, and putting a brave face on it said, "Oh, we weathered the storm pretty well."

After that life went on as before. The sun rose out of the sea and set in it.

Everyone on board—passengers, crew and performers, and all the children on board too, even the animals who were sailing with us, and there were quite a few of those, tortoises who were pretty sleepy to start with, but even lots of lively parrots and dogs, and there was also a wonderfully spoiled ship's cat on board—all these creatures floated around in peaceful slumber, full of a resigned languor. Nothing mattered. If everything stayed as it was, we would be too drowsy to notice that we'd reached our destination. Perhaps the place didn't even exist.

Like all the passengers, I might have felt protected between the wings of our grumpily humming Bird God, who calmly cleaved the water and was in no hurry to get to land. But I didn't feel protected.

I was frightened that one day the old bird would throw us all out, however much we struggled. He would cast us out onto the land, or simply drop us somewhere.

I'd found a flying fish on the deck, no longer moving, that a minute before had still been sailing through the sky as if nothing could happen to it. It hadn't been rescued by Garuda. It had smashed into the deck. I took it with me and put it in a glass near my bed in our cabin, with its head in the water. It didn't float to the surface. When my mother discovered it, it had to be thrown away immediately because it stank.

I determined to watch my step, which, as I had learned at home, amounted to sleeping or pretending to, not asking lots of questions, and most of all not calling attention to myself. My mother impressed on me every day that I had to be very careful and that I mustn't fall overboard.

The voyage to Europe was called the greatest adventure that I had been able to take part in up to then, and I had already experienced so much, so other people thought. But when I asked about all the things I was supposed to have experienced, they described events that I had forgotten, such as an eruption of the

Tankuban Prahu. The volcano that was a capsized boat of the prince who wanted to marry his mother, my mother explained. The volcano we looked out onto, from our house in Bandung. You remember, don't you?

That eruption, as it was described in the old story, had taken place because under the capsized prow the fire had flared up too high for the wedding banquet. And apart from that? That was what the story said. *Suda,* enough. My mother shrugged her shoulders impatiently: it was nice enough like that, wasn't it? I missed Uncle Felix, who would have been able to tell me what happened next. Would Sang Kurian, who had built the prow for his mother, marry her anyway? Surely it was no accident that the gods had let the fire smoulder in the mountain, on which the rice for the wedding still had to be steamed? In the blue book that my mother had brought with her, there was a picture of Sang Kurian, busy sealing the last seams of the prow. In the distance, in the shadow of a gigantic *waringin,* stood Putri Dajang Sumbi, his mother, stretching out her hands desperately toward the rising sun.

She begged the gods fervently for a reprieve. A reprieve from what? No one on board answered my question.

Some people asked me if we had been bothered by the eruption, or whether we'd gone calmly to sleep in our world full of darkness?

Darkness, closeness, ash rain, and streams of lava slowly seeking out their murderous paths? I couldn't remember a thing about it. Perhaps I'd been dreaming under my mosquito net when it had happened. Or perhaps I had been in a safe place behind our house, in the light of the fireflies, protected by all the creatures that remained invisible during the day but at night assumed shapes and voices. Friends, benign spirits, night people with their own faces and names, which they had to forget again in the morning.

I couldn't remember an eruption of the Tankuban Prahu, but other things were clear in my memory. I couldn't speak about them. I wasn't allowed to say anything about what I really experienced. Tinka and I had to keep our secrets.

Auntie Margot thought we were very quiet and asked teasingly if we'd lost our tongues. I whispered to her that we said so little because we didn't want to waken the evil spirits. She clicked her tongue: there was no need to worry on board, because the demons couldn't rise up here. They were frightened of water, and apart from that they were terrified of Garuda. I didn't believe her.

We sailed on day and night on Garuda's back.

Was it possible that we'd stay at sea forever?

My father had told me that the world was round, like a ball. With his forefinger on the colored globe, he pointed out how we would remain in the blue for a while. Then we would cross a yellow area and then blue again, and finally moor in the green, where we would travel farther by train. The train went over land and stopped at the red and black dots. Such dots, with mysterious names, we would visit on the globe. Colombo. Marseilles. Paris. London. The Hague.

The Hague, which was in Holland.

My mother said, "Perhaps we'll stay there for about a year, but not a day longer, mind. Not over my dead body."

Holland was the old country for her and hence for me too, but my mother didn't like it.

"'Oh land of mist and muck,'" she declaimed, "'not wrested from the sea at my request . . .'" She quoted the words with a shudder and wrung her hands as she did so. She was acting, but she also meant it.

Were mist and muck the names of evil spirits?

No, in Europe and Holland there were no spirits, no good ones and no evil ones. My mother turned up her nose in contempt, as if it were indecent for a country to have no spirits. She knew for sure that there weren't any spirits in Holland, not in that flat, cold country, inhabited by people with hard, sober heads. Spirits received no sustenance or shelter from such people. Never. My father observed testily that she shouldn't be too sure of that. The most malevolent spirit imaginable was being feted in Europe, cheered and welcomed by many people.

In the afternoon I slept, and Tinka was given her Dutch lessons by Mr. de Vries, who was a language doctor.

My baby brother was the only one who stayed the same through all the changes, a grunting piglet. He lay in his bunk laughing the whole time, whether you prodded his tummy with your finger or not.

I didn't pay much attention to him. He belonged with us, but I didn't know him. He couldn't do anything yet except sleep and spit. He couldn't talk, couldn't walk, couldn't play.

"Louise! Simon's only a baby yet, and you couldn't do much either at that age!" Mummy adored my baby brother.

Although he didn't reply, she kept talking to him, while he just lay there gurgling.

"Look at him laughing!" said my mother delightedly. "He seems to know something that we don't. What could it be? What's so funny, you dear darling? Won't you tell us, then we will have some joy in our lives too."

My mother had plenty of joy in her life when she could pamper my brother.

Auntie Margot was busy too with the things that she liked doing nowadays. Like combing her hair, applying lipstick, trying on shoes and clothes, chattering, dancing and flirting, etc.

Sometimes she stayed out all night and didn't come to say good night. According to Tinka, she went to every party that was going. When the opportunity arose because no one was watching us, we followed her. And behind her back we whispered excitedly that she was so cheerful and so beautiful. If Uncle Felix could see her now, he would definitely lift her off her feet again, *betul*, yes indeed. She kept appearing in different dresses. Even during the daytime she changed clothes at least four times.

Tinka and I became friends. Was it Tinka who was looking after me, or was I perhaps looking after her? At the beginning of our voyage I had to hunt for her the whole time because she kept hiding. Meanwhile I met at least ten, or a hundred, other people who interested themselves in me.

"Has that weeping *babu* of yours run off again? Give me your hand, let's go and look for her, the rascal. A fine thing. Shouldn't your mother know that that little devil is hanging around everywhere except with you?"

"She's not my *babu*; she's my aunt. She's called Cristina without an 'h.'"

"Your aunt? Don't talk nonsense, child. I've seen your aunt with my own eyes. That lovely woman, who's so plump. But not as nice and blond as your mother, that's true."

Auntie Tinka was my aunt, although I didn't have to call her Auntie.

She was a daughter of my granddad's. Later she said that she wasn't his daughter. She also said that she no longer had a mother. How much of this was true or not didn't interest me at the time. Now that I'd like to know, it's no longer possible to get to the bottom of it. I can't ask anyone because those who knew all the details are dead. Or old. Or have forgotten. Or don't want to talk about it anymore. She was thirteen, and on the boat she looked like a young woman. In my eyes she was more beautiful than all the princesses in our blue book. She wore her gold-brown hair in a bun, she used lipstick, she dressed in a sarong and *kebaja* of gold-colored brocade.

Granddad Smit had called her Cristina, but without an "h," because he didn't think any Christianity was needed. My mother called her Tinka, because of her funny moods. And it stuck, because it was true about those funny moods.

When I couldn't find Tinka, because she'd hidden away somewhere to cry, I had to go out to explore by myself.

There weren't any night people or night animals on the boat, but there were day people in white clothes. There were plenty of tea aunts and white children and dogs too.

I wondered the whole time where we would end up and where we were heading. Was the voyage taking so long because we had to sail around the whole world? Or couldn't we find Europe?

I'd often traced our journey across the sea on the globe with my forefinger, and sometimes the thought occurred to me that we weren't going anywhere anymore.

The sea was everywhere. There wasn't a scrap of land to be seen. Not in front of us, not behind us, and not to the side either. It didn't matter what direction we went in. We'd definitely lost our way. We'd go on sailing forever.

There were people on board who told me that they'd seen the whole world several times over. Was it the intention we should do the same, and was that why we had to keep on sailing around the globe? That only then would we find the harbor we'd set out from, Tandjung Priok on Java? That only then would we be able to return to our house in Bandung to say, "We've seen the whole world several times over."

I hoped that it wouldn't take too long before our journey back began. I pleaded fervently with the gods.

But before we could return we first had to get to green Holland.

It was a very long way. Java was here, under my finger, and however hard you looked, you couldn't see Holland. You had to cross half of the globe to get to Holland. It was there, on the other side.

· · ·

When *Garuda* put into the port of Colombo, I thought we'd arrived. Everything was as it should be.

The offices on the shore were low buildings; they had flat roofs and were a familiar, grubby white color. Everywhere the dark wooden shutters were closed.

The sultry yellow afternoon light, which I knew from home, shimmered around us. The people visible on the quay lay in the shadow of palm trees and didn't move a muscle.

When the gangway was put down, my father went on shore.

"We're there, hurrah! Can I come too, Daddy?" I asked, skipping with joy.

When he turned around I could see from his face that he wasn't happy; he looked sad. There was no need to ask him if we were there yet—we weren't there, not by a long way.

Our ship was the only one in the harbor. A bird with multicolored plumage flew around above our heads, circling the funnel for a while and squawking in excitement, as if celebrating something. A voice cried out, "Damn it, you nitwit, come here, you bloody animal, quick as a flash or you'll be in the soup." The parrot flew away inland and disappeared from view.

Nothing else happened and still no one moved on the quay. The water in the harbor was dark green and clear, as far down as I could see.

A car drove up at a crawl. There was a bustle of white people in white suits by a white building. I could no longer see where my father was.

My mother was standing at the railing with Simon on her arm and wasn't watching me, somewhere down below by her legs. When my mother and the baby were together, no one else got a look-in. Although my mother held my hand, when Simon was sitting on her arm she wouldn't even notice if I turned into a different child meanwhile. Or a dog or a bag.

Before we had gone to the railing, we had been to the beauty salon, where she had bought tortoiseshell combs and a jar of ointment.

Then we visited the ship's library, where she exchanged books. My mother exchanged a lot, and I asked her if she wanted to exchange me too.

"No, not yet, you're staying with me."

Auntie Margot joined us, with a high-spirited group. The conversation got very giggly and was about things I didn't understand.

I looked up at the white pith helmets of the gentlemen and down at the white silk stockings of the ladies. I was glad that I didn't have to wear those kinds of clothes.

My mother and aunt wore their beautiful dresses and smooth white stockings from early morning till late at night. On their feet they wore white shoes with thin high heels. On the long toes were little pearls, or embroidered flowers. In our house we had a mountain of these shoes, but still my mother intended to buy even more, in Paris. "In Paris you can find the most beautiful shoes in the world!"

"Is Benjamin Silbermann coming on board? Is he really going to honor us with his presence?"

One of the gentlemen asked this; of course I don't remember exactly how he formulated it, but I remember my mother's answer word for word: "Yes, just imagine, we're shortly going to be burdened with his Lordship. God help me."

"But madam! Aren't you over the moon that we're soon going to be able to enjoy his wonderful piano playing?"

"Yes of course. I was only joking." My mother laughed apologetically and dandled the baby on her arm. "But I am afraid he won't play anymore, the great Benjamin."

"There's a whisper that he'll never return to his country."

"He wanted to go to Palestine, but the English wouldn't be moved."

"Uncivilized islanders. Not a grain of feeling for music."

"What a crude world we live in. A brilliant artist like that wants to spend his final years in his promised land, and they won't let him in! On the say-so of a bunch of civil servants."

"Look, they're coming this way. Oh dear, he's too ill to walk."

"Fortunately he doesn't have to walk; your dear husband has arranged for a stretcher."

"Yes, we'll take good care of him. And his loved ones in The Hague are dying to see him," said Auntie Margot in her chocolatey voice.

"Oh, but of course! Mimi will give her old flame a warm welcome."

My mother also sounded emotional.

Last night in bed she had talked differently to Auntie Margot. She'd wondered what poor Granny Mimi was supposed to do with that arrogant wastrel Benjamin Silbermann. He would wreck Mimi's life again, as he'd done in the past.

When they thought I was asleep, my mother and Auntie Margot conducted endless conversations in bed, but I usually only half listened to them.

Mr. Benjamin was carried up the gangway on the stretcher. I saw the procession coming closer and gradually I recognized my father, who was at the front.

I could not make out much of Mr. Benjamin yet, as he was lying with his head under a sheet, with only a tuft of gray curly hair and a large pointed ear protruding.

I hung on to my mother's arm and asked when Mr. Benjamin was going to wreck Granny Mimi's life again.

My mother burst out laughing. "What are you talking about, child?"

I saw the sheet pulled off with a jerk; a large, wrinkled hand pulled it away and a Harlequin's head with gray hair appeared. Nodding enthusiastically at my mother he directed himself in a loud voice to the small throng that had gathered by the railing.

"Hélène! She cackles. She cackles through everything. Through Chopin and Schumann, no matter what. The beautiful Hélène has cackled again. Cluck, cluck, an egg!" He sat up further and started shouting even louder, but Daddy pushed him gently back again.

"Now, now, you're well on the road to recovery, from the sound of you."

"I've eaten and drunk enough for the whole journey," groaned the old gentleman on the stretcher. "This beautiful Hélène is like a glass of absinthe with cat piss."

"You've said enough for the whole voyage," said my father sternly. Surely he wasn't actually laughing forgivingly and in assent? I didn't see this, but my mother did.

She went on maintaining it obdurately, to the end of her days. At first my father contradicted her, but after a while he stopped.

Mr. Benjamin would never return to the land of the barbarians, he told us a little while later. And he didn't want to return to the land of white chocolate either. Anyway, it wasn't his land, it was the land of William Tell, a hero with a bow and arrow. We were going to Holland, but it would be better if Mr. Benjamin didn't show himself there.

Once he started talking to us, he talked nineteen to the dozen. He always said that we shouldn't believe a word we heard. "Listening with your heart and soul! That's better than common sense."

He talked for whole mornings and afternoons, just to us. He said he was sick of mankind. He played the piano and acted for us. He performed Struwelpeter and Punch, he marched up and down, bent left and right, and recited a rhyme: "Left, right, the wretched audience are there all right."

He sat on the sloop deck, on the last section of the rear deck, because he wanted to be as far away from the public as possible.

If he heard voices, however far away, even if they were only soft, Mr. Benjamin would say, "Alarm!" He wrapped his black coat around him and left. At the last moment he grabbed our hands. "You two come with me, for heaven's sake."

He lifted Tinka and me onto the grand piano, which was on a platform in the large dining room. He played the piano when no one else was there, early in the morning, when all the parties were over.

I've never again heard anyone play so beautifully, not even Auntie Flora. Later, at any concert, whoever was playing, I would see the tall, gaunt silhouette of Mr. Benjamin, whose ghost wandered restlessly across the stage, whose wrinkled clown's face laughed or cried, depending on the performance.

In my memory there are two or three days on which he was cheerful. "Today I feel like flying," he said once.

With expansive gestures of his arms he pretended to fly and just at the moment that I thought, He won't be able to do it, he jumped into the swimming pool with his coattails flapping, and didn't even go under, but stayed there floating like a black water lily with a gray heart.

"Again, again!" we shouted from the side as he climbed up the steps dripping wet.

"I owe you one," promised Mr. Benjamin.

My mother didn't want us to spend too much time with him. He gave everyone the creeps with his strange antics. He could simply stew in his own juice.

In the evenings there were parties, and during the day too. Young ladies in bathing costumes came round juggling and next to the swimming pool there was an orchestra. There were always new balloons and streamers everywhere; the silk flowers had been freshened up, perhaps even washed and ironed.

Games were played on almost all the decks. We didn't join in, Tinka and I. If we weren't asleep, we went exploring. We were looking for something, though we didn't know what. We combed the whole ship, and found all kind of things, but it was never precisely what we were looking for. Mr. Benjamin said, "I know what you two are looking for; you're looking for treasure! Who isn't?"

"Where's the treasure?" I asked him.

"I've got one," he replied with a grin. "But you're not getting that."

He said he couldn't give us the treasure because he'd already promised it to someone else. We thought that he'd promised it to the gods. But we didn't ask him.

Mr. Benjamin kept hiding his treasure in different places, because he was frightened that everyone was after it. On our journeys through the ship, Tinka and I looked for places where he might hide his treasure.

He talked to us, but with others Mr. Benjamin usually expressed himself in sign language. He didn't need many gestures to convey the fact that he wasn't in the mood for a chat.

If he saw anyone coming, he would put one arm over his eyes and keep the other extended in front of him to deter people. If people nevertheless dared to address a word to him, he would grumble, "Two-faced."

"What an ill-mannered oaf that Benjamin is," snorted my mother. "Great men have great faults, which is entirely true in his case."

Benjamin had covered his eyes for her too and warded her off with his arm and had totally ignored her.

"What wrong has he ever done you?" asked my father. "He's frightened."

"Of course he's frightened," my mother said excitedly. "Everyone could cheerfully strangle him."

"Yes, people are getting organized. People are cooking something up."

My father wouldn't hear a bad word about Mr. Benjamin and took him under his wing. He even let him sleep in his cabin. Tinka and I once found him on the settee. He grunted and pulled the bedspread over his head, as he didn't recognize us immediately.

Tinka started dancing in my father's cabin, which she did quite often. She knelt on the ground and practiced the movements of her head and hands.

Mr. Benjamin peered at her through the holes in the bedspread. When she stopped, he sat up with a deep sigh and got to his feet. He bowed his head so deeply that his wreath of silver hair almost touched the floor.

The following day Tinka gathered together her golden clothes, which were in her suitcase. She wanted to dance properly for Mr. Benjamin. She wanted to show him all her dances, in her full dancing costume.

"Out of the question," said my mother. "What has the old goat got into his head? Let him go to the Folies Bergères if he wants an eyeful."

Tinka said nothing. She hid her dancing clothes in the lifeboat, in the secret place that we had made, she and I and Mr. Benjamin. He'd also taken his treasure there, which was in a small brown suitcase.

He sometimes sat there crying, and said he had a cold. He smoked his cigars there.

Tinka put her clothes on, as well as she could in the lifeboat, and danced for us on the sloop deck. Mr. Benjamin stood up, threw his cigar overboard, and applauded.

"Come on," he said, taking us by the hand and going below deck with us, "into the ballroom, we're going to do a performance, little bird, you and I. Let the *dummes Publikum* have a good snigger and enjoy themselves while they still can."

My mother said it was impossible.

"Our Cristina isn't cut out to show her party turns on a stage, what are you thinking?" she cried angrily.

"*Quatsch*, all nonsense!" observed Mr. Benjamin, and meanwhile improvised great chords on the piano. "Great injustice is being done to your Cristina with your complete approval."

"How dare you!"

"Has this delicate plant not been deliberately torn up, root and branch? Hasn't she? Is this naïve child of nature being expertly drilled into becoming a little marionette? Or isn't she?"

Auntie Margot interceded: "Let her dance, just let her." Tinka didn't feel like it anymore, and slunk away.

When Tinka wasn't doing dance practice in my father's cabin, she went her own way in the evenings. She didn't say where she went or what she did.

During the day she and I sat with Mr. Benjamin and we talked and quibbled with him and looked at his treasure in the little case and stroked the ship's cat, with which we had made friends.

ELEVEN

As we steamed up the Suez Canal the world was still unchanged. When I woke up, I imagined for a few seconds that I was at home. It was hot, and the air was scented. Outside people were walking about noiselessly on bare feet.

Important people, like my father and the captain and Mr. Benjamin and Mr. De Vries, always wore shoes, even when they were indoors, in their cabin. I preferred to go barefoot, but suddenly I was allowed to do so even less frequently than at home. Every day Tinka put my white socks and buttoned-up shoes on, and every day I managed to free myself of this nonsense and go on my way barefoot.

Everything I had known gradually became almost imperceptibly flimsier and less substantial. Finally it had gone, without leaving a trace. But I only noticed when it had vanished once and for all.

I'd carried heat and tropical scents with me automatically, as though they were extra senses, as though I were equipped with a soft, warm layer on my skin and an invisible extra nose.

It wasn't that I suddenly woke up one day and noticed instantly that I'd lost my special senses. The loss made itself felt gradually.

I could see, hear, talk, and feel, just as before. I could write a few words, and read a few words, and I could even swim underwater for a few yards. Only when I wanted to retreat at a certain moment into my warm cocoon, always as familiarly present as my eyes and hand, did I notice that I had nothing more to retreat into, that I'd been stripped of my skin. I felt as naked as a peeled apple, and looked around me to see where all that skin had got to. Had they left it in one piece, had someone thrown it over his shoulder somewhere on board?

Hunting for it, I ran around our cabin, where there was a big mirror fixed to the inside of the door, in which I met myself. Only it wasn't me, that girl there, who was white from head to toe, with a white face and white lips rushing toward me, that creature without a skin, who had been skinned by heaven knows whom.

It turned out that something perfectly natural, something you thought belonged to you and was inalienable, could just disappear. The warmth had gone. Its place had been taken by that cold, but not really, because cold didn't exist, rather it was just something that was painfully absent, a spiteful emptiness that had to be filled up by us. With blood, flesh, and breath, with our life. This new, absent god, who ruled us from a distance, demanded the utmost of us. He demanded everything of us, not suddenly, but drop by drop, sigh by sigh. We couldn't defend ourselves. The cocoon, the warmth, the protection, the smells, it all vanished into his jaws, bit by bit.

I'd already caught glimpses of Europe, first in pictures and now for real. Blue skies, mountains in the distance, palm trees along the yellow beaches, flowers bulging out of the windows of little houses.

The first gust of cold hit us off the Italian coast. An icy wind had come from the mountains, cutting a path between the sunny days.

"It's a shock to the system, that parting present from King Winter."

It was the first time I heard the enemy's name.

"King Winter?"

"King Winter, and not forgetting his seedy crew." My mother said it with an ominous expression.

"His seedy crew?"

"Fog, mist, hail, icicles, sleet." She made shrill noises and rubbed her hands together nervously.

"Fog, there's fog outside," she warned us.

She hissed between her teeth. "Don't go outside, children, we're not up to it yet."

She wanted us to stay within the protection of our cabin, preferably in bed, with the covers over us. She groaned that the door had already opened and closed a couple of times, so we might have already been imperceptibly overcome.

The moment we had the chance, Tinka and I dashed outside to see Mr. Benjamin and tell him that the seedy crew were there.

We arrived on the sloop deck; I was about to run on ahead, but suddenly Tinka stopped me. She put both arms round me and muttered something, but I couldn't understand her.

I looked in the direction she was looking in, at the railings. A big black bird flew off the ship, and alighted on the gray waves. Now I understood her.

"Mr. Benjamin," stammered Tinka.

"No, no! It was a bird."

We stood by the railings and peered down. There was nothing to be seen. The sea around the ship boiled and bubbled and washed over everything immediately as it always did. It was as though *Garuda* was being urged on. He clawed his way through the sea much faster than usual. We heard his growling becoming louder. Louder and louder, as though he had to strain to the utmost to get out of the white mist. We wanted to shout, but we were literally struck dumb. We were sailing away from the world, or was the world leaving us? In any case the world had gone; it had almost completely disappeared, except for a piece of gray sea.

We stood hand in hand on the sloop deck. I wondered what I'd actually seen. Did Mr. Benjamin fly away with his coattails flapping and alight in the sea, or had it been a bird?

His deck chair was there. The chair was empty, we thought at first. But we'd no sooner thought that than he was sitting there again, Mr. Benjamin. First it was his ghost, but it gradually took on solid shape. Finally he was sitting there, then, his black skull cap on his head, his black coat draped like a cape around his shoulders, his legs stretched out in the thin gray baggy trousers. We saw him sitting there, although we knew that he couldn't be here anymore.

We perched cautiously on the end of the chair, where his thin legs were still lying. Our teeth were chattering with the cold. We breathed carefully so as not to alarm his soul, we sniffed in little portions of air carefully through our noses. Salt from the sea, bitter with tar, the smells of wood and rope. But we could not smell the peppery tang of Mr. Benjamin's cigar, that familiar odor. We could hear his voice, strangely cheerful: "Young ladies, don't forget the treasure in the lifeboat."

He'd said it often enough. "Remember the treasure! It must never fall into the wrong hands. You two make sure of that when I'm not there anymore."

"Who's got the wrong hands, Mr. Benjamin?"

"Everyone! Except for Mimi and you two, that is."

We sat on his chair, and I stroked the rug that always lay over his legs. The rug lay limply on the chair; the chair was empty. I tried to imagine that someone was sitting there, but I couldn't feel anything. No legs, no thin body.

"He *has* gone, he's gone."

"Sh," said Tinka, "don't cry. He's gone, but he'll never be completely gone."

She nodded confidently in the direction from where Mr. Benjamin was perhaps still sitting watching us.

"The treasure in the lifeboat."

I was sure that he'd taken it with him, because he didn't like going anywhere without his treasure.

Tinka let go of me and crawled into the lifeboat, where her dance clothes were too. Almost immediately her head again popped up above the canvas.

"Look! It's still there! Come here."

We had tidied our secret hiding place not so long ago, with Mr. Benjamin's help. He had untied the ropes of the canvas and in so doing he'd torn two of his nails and his thumb was actually bleeding. Then the three of us sat in the lifeboat, I remember. It was raining. Or was it drops of seawater blowing down on us? We pulled the canvas over us. It lay like a light gray tent roof over the lifeboat and the drops, from the rain or the sea, pattered onto it. We could hear them, but they couldn't touch us. Mr. Benjamin drummed the rhythm of the falling drops very fast on his knee.

We were confused for a moment and saw that the case was still there, which meant that he had forgotten it. I don't remember all the emotions that went through us. Disappointment? Excitement? It was as if we were in a trance.

We said nothing as we thought of the treasure in the small brown suitcase, where bottles and jars with silver tops were also stored, hairbrushes, mirrors, and combs. We had been allowed to see the treasure, and even touch it. It consisted of glittering stones, handfuls of them.

It made a crackling sound when you ran your hands through it. It was a mysterious sound, much more mysterious than the crunching of gravel. "You bet it is," said Mr. Benjamin.

We knew what we had to do. Gods are impatient, so we had to hurry.

We hurried. We wrapped the suitcase in Tinka's sarong, a green one, with gold motifs. We climbed out of the lifeboat and made sure no one was coming.

The sloop deck was deserted. Tinka threw the suitcase into the sea.

We watched it go, and it was immediately swallowed up by the water.

"Will it be all right now?"

Tinka nodded.

The ship was motionless. We weren't far from Genoa.

"What's wrong? What's wrong?"

Auntie Margot stuttered. "You must have heard what's wrong. He's done it."

"It's appalling and ridiculous. But what can we do about it?" screeched my mother.

"They say this death is a gentle one," said my aunt.

"The gods will take him to his new country. Really they will."

No one was listening to me.

"But it's still shameful we didn't understand him. It happened under our noses; it's disgraceful that we didn't recognize the signs."

"Oh Margot, you're not going to start blaming yourself like Cees, are you? Shameful? Shame's a question of convention." My mother leaned against Auntie Margot's hip with her own hip. "What was shameful ten years ago is now the height of distinction. Perhaps one day it will be chic to take your own life."

"Stop it, Hélène! Don't go too far, will you."

"Think about smoking cigarettes. It used to be forbidden for ladies; now it's the last word. Let's have one."

Auntie Margot cried out, "Don't you dare. There's a dead person to mourn! And there's a baby here!"

She put her arms round Mummy, and they stood there, rocking to and fro, with the baby between them. They hummed and cooed; they were absorbed in each other as they always used to be.

I wondered if they would notice if I did a somersault on the railing. I was dying to do that. Tinka did it every two seconds and I'd always put my hands in front of my eyes, but still looked between my fingers.

Tinka had always called out, "You can't do that. You've still got a mother."

I decided to test whether it made any difference if someone had a mother or not. With my teeth clenched together and eyes closed, I did a head over heels on the railing. Even before my feet touched the ground, I'd been grabbed, lifted up, and wedged in between the two women. "Must you do that, sweetie?" cried Auntie Margot.

"Do you want to drown too then? Do you want to die too?" screamed my mother.

I gave it a try. She might even tell me.

"What's drown?" I screamed back, "What's die?"

I can't remember what they answered. Though lots of insignificant details stand out in my mind as if it were yesterday.

My mother's and aunt's dresses, their shoes, their hairdos, their scarves, their fans, I can describe them down to the most trivial details. My brother had a silly white hat on, against the sun, which wasn't shining. My mother dropped her box of Egyptian cigarettes when she leapt toward me to pluck me from the railing. The box, with a sphinx on it, is lodged more solidly in my mind than when it lay on deck. I can draw it, even today. What good is it to me? Not much. I'd happily exchange it for what's slipped by me in the way of words and important events.

Memory is an eccentric collector, and manages its collection carelessly. What's stored isn't arranged in order of importance, with an eye to elegant connections. Empty clichés are more accurately recorded than solemn oaths. Insignificant meetings are more carefully preserved than events that proved to be turning points.

We lay for an hour, perhaps an hour and a half, motionless. Off the port of Genoa.

It smelled of tar and fish; the mist lifted, and the coast was bathed in great patches of pale red and dripping brownish purple, the colors of the roofs and the faded bougainvillea of Genoa.

I can't remember how long it lasted, or what we did. We waited. We waited for my father, who was with the captain. We waited until the ship sailed on.

The waiting went on for ages. And it had only just begun.

Perhaps that was when it dawned on me for the first time that it made no difference whatever we said or did. It changed nothing.

It didn't matter whether or not we appeased the spirits with a treasure in a suitcase, with prayers or sacrifices or magic formulas. Everything that happened seemed to have been preordained.

Mr. Benjamin had jumped. The first time, in the swimming pool, he'd waved to us with both hands.

The second time he hadn't even seen us.

My father came back. Drops of sweat were trickling from his thick black eyebrows. He brushed them aside in irritation with a handkerchief that he pulled out of his sleeve. Without drops of sweat his face became even gloomier.

As my father's walk became slower and slower, I heard my mother mutter to my aunt, "It's frightening. Cees is changing before my eyes."

I thought about it. Everything was changing, so why shouldn't my father be as well?

The closer he got to us, the more I could see that he was old, older than anyone. He wasn't as old as Mr. Benjamin, but perhaps as old as Granddad Smit. Not as cheerful: Granddad Smit was a rascal with whom you could go swimming, play ball, and kick up a rumpus.

He was never gloomy.

Daddy came up to us, sad and self-absorbed, as though he found it an effort. I saw that his suit wasn't white, more gray, perhaps grubby even, and apart from that it was crumpled.

"All you need are bloodstains on your cuffs." How often I had heard my mother fuming that something was wrong with his clothes, that he never cared what he wore. He would simply retrieve his old shirt from the washing basket and put it on again. Several times he'd gone to an operation in his pajamas, or so the story went.

As he came toward us, his arms moved listlessly along his body, as if he'd stopped trying to drive away the spirits that were attacking him, but was simply letting them do their worst.

My father lifted me up. I was now too big and too heavy to sit on his shoulders. I hung more or less in the crook of his arm. He smelled of peppery tobacco and toffees. I looked at his big pointed ears and at the broad gray band running across his head, which I had never noticed before, and which may have appeared suddenly, in the middle of the night, in the middle of his head, in his black hair.

My mother complained, "Cees, please don't act as if it's your fault."

I tried to push myself up because I could feel myself sliding slowly out of his arms. My father lifted me up a little higher, and on my head put his straw hat, which fell down over my eyes.

Little green squares of light streamed in through the woven straw; it was as if I were under a tree. I listened to the rising and falling voices around me.

My father made a movement, and we drifted slowly in the

direction of my mother's voice. Then we floated back again, as though my father had changed his mind. He suddenly sounded stern and determined, a tone in which I didn't often hear him speak to us, but did hear him use with other people.

"You must decide for yourself what you want to do, Hélène. I have to go to see Philipp. Do you want to go straight to your mother's in London? Then you must go to London."

"Listen to him. As if I were going to London for my pleasure."

"London Bridge is falling down, falling down, falling down, London Bridge is falling down, my fair lady."

She had taught me the song herself; it was from the story of Dick Whittington and his cat. I remembered that it was white, just like our ship's cat, but perhaps it wasn't. In order to ward off the evil spirits, I sang as loudly as I could, "London Bridge is falling down . . ." until I heard my mother screaming much louder than me.

"Mother was going to meet us in The Hague. Do you remember? But no, now we have to go to London! When I hate the whole clique of them in London."

I took off the straw hat, put it straight back on my head again, and pulled it as far down as possible over my ears, but it was no good. So I took it off again and replaced it on my father's head. Perhaps it might help him. It was sad how difficult things were for him now. He couldn't do anything to defend himself, because he'd lifted me up and I was sitting on his arm. He didn't give me to Auntie Margot, as my mother always did with my little brother when they were going to have a fight.

Mummy fired all kinds of questions at Daddy; she started clinging to his body and his arms like a monkey, so that he had to put me down on the ground. But he kept hold of my hand.

I was turned in another direction with a firm swing.

"We're going to my cabin," said my father.

Auntie Margot was now screaming at least as loud as my mother, and the baby, whom she was holding in her arms, had started roaring so loudly it might have been heard in Genoa.

Simon clawed wildly at Auntie Margot's hair with his little hands. I watched in astonishment as her hairpins fell to the left and right of me, making little ticks on the wood. One after another, like fat raindrops at the beginning of a shower. This rain of hairpins fascinated me, and I looked up and down. Down to where it was gaily tapping and pattering, up to where the dark cloud of my aunt's hair kept widening and kept swirling and trembling.

"Oh look, look!" I cried loudly and squeezed Daddy's hand.

"Come to my cabin, Hélène, Margot, and calm down! Calm down!" said my father in a bogeyman's voice.

He drove us ahead of him to his cabin, where only Tinka and I were allowed to play. We went there when we wanted to be free of all the fuss around Simon, who ruled the roost in our own cabin. Tinka sometimes had to look after him, but she preferred going off with me, and we ensconced ourselves in my father's cabin. It smelled of books and papers and pepper and licorice; it was serious and solemn, dark and quiet. It was so different from in our cabin that we would know exactly where we were, his or ours, even if we went in blindfold.

In our cabin we tumbled into a warm den. Full of smells, which we knew all too well. Where we pushed our way between mountains of clothes and shoes. We smelled immediately that there were cough sweets and bits of *dodol* rice cake on the dressing tables. We smelled vanilla and eau de cologne, tiger balm, rose oil and cinnamon, jasmine and camphor. The pungent perfume of my mother, the sweet smell of my aunt. Fresh smells of washed and ironed blouses. The smell of my brother's nappies, when the washing basket hadn't yet been emptied. Even if the cabin was empty, we knew who had just been there. We could easily guess what had gone on and been done there. A powder paper still on the floor, the smell of my mother's furtive *kretek* cigarettes still trembling in the air, such things told us what we needed to know.

Our cabin gave everything away, while my father's was tight-lipped.

We didn't sit with our feet on the table in his cabin; we were on our best behavior and never shouted.

When we finally gathered in Daddy's cabin on that foggy day, with my mother still far from calm, we saw Tinka lying on the settee, sound asleep, wrapped in the crocheted bedcover in which we'd found Mr. Benjamin that time. But Tinka hadn't put the bedspread over her head. Over her eyes lay a piece of batik cloth belonging to Poppy, so that she could dream about her.

Auntie Margot said in a soft voice, "Look at that darling, she's fast asleep. She must rest. Because she saw it! She saw it with her own eyes!" She dropped her voice more and more, until she was whispering and we could no longer understand her.

She stood in front of the bed with her arms outstretched, as if anxious to protect Tinka.

"Darlings," she said to us almost without a sound, "let's be very, very quiet."

"Good advice. Let's try and be calm for a change," said my father in a kindly tone.

My mother sank onto the settee.

"I don't want to go to London, but I shall have to." She pointed to Tinka, who was still sleeping calmly. "Anyway, she'll have to go; we've undertaken to do that."

"It can wait," said my father, "she can stay with us."

"What, for how long?" cried my mother, as if stung by a wasp. "It's no fun looking after her, *betul.* You need eyes in the back of your head! She's a wild and headstrong girl, and that could set the whole house on fire."

Daddy sat in the chair behind the desk; he leaned back, half closed his eyelids, put his fingertips together, looked over them vaguely, but without focusing on anyone in particular. He said, "I won't listen to this nonsense. Let's stick to the facts."

"Right." My mother said it very carefully. "Tell me, what are the facts?"

She waited for a moment and got up again.

"The facts are, Cees, that my very own mother has once again not kept to what's been agreed and that your alleged father has killed himself."

She twirled back and forth in front of his desk, hands on her back, stuck out her chin, and asked, "What other facts would you like to know?"

While no one paid any attention to me, I crawled into the tunnel of Daddy's desk and saw his brown brogue shoes. They moved like imprisoned, restless animals.

I heard how gloomy his voice sounded, saw his shoes moving and wanted to grab them and stroke them, so that I could get them to be still, but I didn't dare.

"I propose that we simply follow our schedule. There's nothing else to do. After Marseilles we'll go on to Paris by train."

"Paris. What a mixed blessing, seeing Paris again, where we were so happy once. It'll break my heart!"

My father said in a flat tone, "A broken heart, Hélène, we can add that to the list."

The shoes went wild under the desk. My mother sighed, and it was as if she were about to cry; but no sound came out, and it went quiet in the cabin. With my ear to the ground I could feel the floor swaying in response to the muffled pounding of the ship. *Garuda* was under way again.

"After Paris we'll go on to The Hague, because they're expecting us there. Mimi's waiting for us."

I thought of Mr. Benjamin, on his journey to the promised land through the great salty deep. I called up, "Is she waiting for Mr. Benjamin too?"

My father cleared his throat. His feet banged up and down

like crazy. It was no longer safe in my hiding place, and I crept out.

"Let's be glad that we can still move around freely." Daddy sounded serious and hectic. "There may be a war coming. War! Must we start on this too?"

"Who started it? Your Daddy. And our Mummy. They're as bad as each other, those tyrants." Mummy's voice cut right through you. She was like a whole swarm of seagulls. I saw her looking around for things to smash.

"And you! Whatever have you schemed and cooked up with this disastrous journey? While I just tag along after you and now on top of that after Mummy too with a foster child. Oh, oh, oh, why didn't I stay in Bandung?"

"Nonsense, sis," Auntie Margot interrupted her sweetly. "Our daddy also said that you mustn't stay in Bandung alone, and you know perfectly well why not."

My mother blushed; she looked like a scarecrow, although a beautiful one. An elegant scarecrow in her cape edged with white feathers and with white fringes at the bottom instead of sleeves, which made her look as if she could fly. Perhaps she could; she kept flapping her wings anyway, instead of just moving her arms normally.

Her eyes had a wild look.

Little bubbles of saliva appeared on her lips. When my brother was asleep, bubbles like that came out of his mouth too. Great, trembling bubbles slid from my mother's lips down onto her neck. I saw my brother sleeping and blowing bubbles in Auntie Margot's arms. Frogs blow bubbles too, but much bigger ones. Simon didn't look like a frog, which was a shame, otherwise he might have been an enchanted prince. He looked like a red piglet. He was as clumsy and helpless as my celluloid dolls. I could quite believe he was a strange amphibious creature. My mother had told me he had come crawling out of the stream to live with us.

I had decided that he would feel more at home in the stream than in his deep wooden cot.

One night when my mother was asleep, Tinka and I had lifted him out of his bed and tried to take him back to the water where he belonged. The night people had seen us and relieved us of him. They didn't take him to the stream, but quickly back to his bed.

"Right, then. Marseilles, and then on to Paris."

My mother sat with her head in her arms, sobbing.

"London's just a stone's throw away once you're in Holland." Auntie Margot put Simon down and, standing behind Mummy, helped her unwind by squeezing and pummeling her. No one but Auntie Margot could do that.

"Chin up, sis, we'll buy some clothes. Lovely clothes in Paris. Won't we?"

"Oh yes, on to Paris."

"Then The Hague, then London," babbled Auntie Margot. "It's so easy in Europe, everything close to hand."

"That's what a certain Hitler thinks too." My father had raised his head and spat these words out bitterly. "Everything close to hand."

"Cees, don't start off again, no, you mustn't start again." My aunt let go of my mother and made imploring gestures in the direction of my father. "Oh, don't waste any words on that lunatic, *busuk*. What does he matter to us? Please stop going on about him, man. Poor Benjamin's dead just because of that horrid man and he's just a second-rate painter, isn't he?"

My mother, my father, and my aunt were suddenly all talking at once and over the top of each other. Daddy was shouting loudest of all.

It woke Tinka up. She sat up and let the bedspread fall off her, then she stepped out of bed onto the floor and stretched. She didn't bother at all about all the fuss and shouting around her. She stretched all four limbs, all her fingers, all her toes, she made them all longer and allowed them to shake loosely for a few seconds one by one; then she stretched her neck and moved her head without turning it from left to right, all this with great concentration and without paying attention to anyone. It was as if we weren't there. Tinka was my friend, but sometimes she was a stranger.

She picked up her scattered clothes and jewels with graceful gestures and dressed with dancelike movements. Her eyes didn't see us; her face had an animated expression, as if she were concerned with things from a higher existence. My mother fell silent, in the middle of one of her exclamations she was silent, and my father and aunt were silent too.

Tinka slid like a shadow toward the desk where my father was sitting. She kissed him on both cheeks, then floated over to my mother and aunt and kissed them too. Then she came over to me and took me by the hand. She pulled me with her and opened the door of the cabin, which she closed gently behind us.

III

IN THE ROOM OF THE PERSIAN CARPETS

(Summer 1939–March 1942)

TWELVE

The *Garuda* had entered the port of Marseilles. Relatives and friends of my father's were waiting on the quay. Big hats, long coats, black umbrellas. In the harbormaster's office there was a thick letter from Uncle Felix for Auntie Margot. There was a big package for us, from Granny Helena, from which emerged two young ladies' coats in silver-gray summer-weight wool.

My father was nervous. His longing for Europe and his family drove him on, overpowered him, so that he walked too quickly, almost stumbling. But he kept himself under control. He straightened his back. For the first time I saw him as someone separate from us, someone I didn't even know very well, who could leave us just like that. Perhaps leave us forever. He'd lived with us, but his home was here.

He emerged from the shadows, walking ahead of me, with his back toward me. He embraced his family, serious gentlemen, even older than he was, who bowed their heads and talked in singsong tones in a language I couldn't understand.

My father and the men were sad and mournful, probably about Mr. Benjamin.

Tinka and I were dying to go on shore. We walked close

behind Daddy. We stepped ashore curiously and waved to the ship *Garuda.*

We wouldn't be seeing any more *Garuda*s for a while.

So evil could nestle wherever it wanted and was everywhere. In the remains of these dead trees that lay everywhere.

"Dead leaves are quite normal here, they're never swept away immediately. They are always here and these are from last year. But look, there are already new ones on the trees," they said.

We didn't think that the leaves were really new; they were yellow and small and dropped off at the slightest breath of wind.

In the train from Marseilles to Paris it was as if we were traveling by moonlight, but it wasn't the light of the moon. It came from the sun, which hid behind a veil of clouds. It wasn't our burning sun: this one was small and pale. We couldn't believe our eyes when we saw it gave no more light than an ordinary lamp. We raced through the gray light, beneath a sky shrouded in long curtains. No one expressed surprise. These veils of cloud simply hung there, without giving any rain.

"Is it going to rain in a minute?"

"Oh, a little perhaps." My mother shrugged her shoulders. "You never know here."

We saw pale faces and staring eyes as we slid through empty landscapes. The train occasionally stopped at a station with a strange name, where nothing happened. Not until the last moment did a few passengers hurriedly alight. They went off without looking around. Around, ahead, or to the side. They looked at the ground.

"They do that because there may be a cent on the ground somewhere."

We were passing through a long gray tunnel in which we could hear the wind whistling.

"When will we get out of here?"

"That will take a little while yet."

"Where are we going?"

"We're coming from our motherland, and we're going to our fatherland," answered my mother.

"Where is our fatherland?"

"The world is our fatherland," said Daddy. "We don't need a country to die for so we don't need a country to dream of; the world's our home. Citizens of the world, that's what we are."

The long tunnel, with the whistling wind and the cold we found ourselves in, couldn't be meant to stay in.

"Where are we going? When will we get out of here?"

"We're going to our fatherland," said my mother again. My father said more and more impatiently that we no longer had a country. All countries were for passing through. Once you'd gone around the world, then you could start all over again. The globe was our father and mother at the same time.

My globe was in a cabin trunk. The cabin trunk was still on the boat and would arrive in Rotterdam. Where was Rotterdam?

We heard about Berlin, where we would never go, because Berlin had fallen into the wrong hands. I'd never been there. I hoped that my globe would fall into good hands.

Who would we visit on our journey? With a sigh my mother set about answering all my questions. First to Paris, where Philipp, an uncle of my father's, lived. Then to The Hague, to Granny Mimi, my father's mother. She had written him all those letters because she was worried that otherwise she would never see us again.

Then we would journey on to London, where we would take Tinka to Granny Helena, my mother's mother.

"Why is Tinka going to Granny Helena's?"

"Tinka will learn English, a world language. And if she wants to, she can get good ballet training there. She's going to be a credit to all of us." My mother nodded excitedly as she sketched Tinka's future.

Auntie Margot agreed with her. "How proud we shall be of her, *loh*."

We were no longer listening.

Paris, not Berlin, The Hague and then London.

There were many places in the world where we might or might not end up. For us all foreign places were the same.

Meanwhile all the people we knew had changed. So had we. Things happened quickly here; it was because of the cold air and the large number of clothes. We didn't recognize ourselves in our hairy outfits.

The train stopped in Paris, and we looked through the window of the compartment.

On the journey we had misted up the glass with our breath and drawn dolls in the condensation, peering outside through their eyes and mouths. It didn't matter whether we looked at the condensation on the inside or at what was outside. The window glass was as gray and foggy as the rest of the world. Beyond our misted-up window was another misted-up window, it seemed, bigger than ours, and beyond that another, bigger still and so on and so on. As if the whole world were an endless series of ever grubbier windows.

Tinka and I shuffled toward the exit as slowly as possible. We let everyone pass until we were at the back of the queue. No one must notice that we didn't have our itchy coats on. We'd left the furry monsters on the seat of the train. We hoped never to see them again.

Was this our destination? A stone cave full of gray fumes?

"This is the station," said my father. "You'll soon get to know gay Paree!"

The stench of the station was overpowering. It was as if a huge fire had just been put out nearby, one that was still smoldering and might flare up again any minute. There was a black pall of hot charcoal and burned food.

It hit us as if our heads had been covered by a sooty cowl that was even less to our liking than the despised coats—but we couldn't shake it off and leave it behind. We realized we deserved this punishment. We couldn't do anything to make amends. We stared at the ground, hoping to escape even worse vengeance by the gods by not looking at anything. We wanted to hold our noses but didn't.

I can sometimes still smell it: those fiery odors, which escaped from back doors and gray buildings and intertwined to become the invisible battalions of an all-penetrating army. Coal smoke and burned meat.

The houses of the city approached with their faded tints. When they saw us, they retreated. They drew themselves up in a row, shoulder to shoulder, on either side of broad avenues along which cars raced toward us, two, three, four, or five at once. The cars swerved around us at the last moment and moved to the right into another row. Everything happened so quickly that we couldn't count or grasp anything, and it all escaped or eluded us. The images were impossible to capture. Even the paving stones were too smooth for us; they slithered slyly out from under us.

Taxis slammed their doors in our faces and drove off. Then we found a cab and went the wrong way.

We wandered around for ages.

"Do you remember that shady porter, who claimed he'd left a suitcase behind on the platform?" said my mother years later. "But what do you expect, the poverty was terrible in those days, the poor devils had nothing to eat, and besides that they were all Communists. Then we suddenly appeared on the scene, we spoiled people from the tropics, ordering them about in rusty French."

"And wearing fur coats even in the summer."

"What makes you say that? They were stolen, don't you remember?"

We stood there hand in hand, Tinka and I, turning our faces, which were getting warmer, as far downward as possible, because after discovering the theft of the suitcase my mother was broadcasting all our secrets at the top of her voice. We were in the street. She gesticulated as if to get everyone to gather around. She listed the contents of the suitcase in dramatic tones, as if her children had been in it. She described Simon's flannel pajamas, and enumerating her own precious toiletries brought tears to her eyes. She suddenly added our woolen dresses, which we were glad to be rid of, and next thing she'd start talking about our nightdresses, and who knows, even about our starched underwear. We couldn't think of any other way of drowning out what she was saying than yelling for all we were worth. A crowd of people had already formed, pointing at us and grinning.

My mother outshouted us: "The children's coats! The children's beautiful, brand-new coats, the scoundrel has stolen them too!"

We didn't say, "No, on our word of honor, he hasn't got those fur coats." We omitted to say that. Paris was not well disposed toward us.

Whenever I go to Paris, I have the painful sensation of knowing the city from a brief, previous life.

The bells of Paris pealed and said that we didn't belong here. The path rustled past. The railings slipped through our hands. Outside everything was out to get us, and inside things weren't much better.

Fire growled in iron boilers, it crackled and throbbed, don't look into it, don't touch it whatever you do; this fire didn't come from the gods.

"Don't touch, don't touch anything."

We kept our hands clasped anxiously, except when we had to shake hands with someone, which we did at lightning speed.

"Oh, the girls can't make head or tail of it, they're just like frightened birds."

The birds didn't fly through the air here; they sat in cages at the windows. They sat on perches. They looked outside and twittered like mad and jumped up and down.

At the hotel we went up in a lift for the first time in our lives; we were raised from the marble floor, but we didn't fly. We rose laboriously, even slower than if we had climbed up the stairs by ourselves. We were too tightly packed together, in a stuffy, creaking chamber with mirrored walls and a cast-iron door. In the mirrors we saw bits of strange creatures everywhere, here their backs, there their arms and noses, and on the other side their staring eyes and lips, seemingly glued together.

My father didn't sit down in the hotel room where we were going to stay, in one of the fat chairs by the window. He had scarcely looked around the room before he said, "Well, we could have done better, but it'll pass." He went back to the door through which we had just entered. "I have to go and see Philipp, why don't you come too?"

"Go and then tell me what it's like first," my mother shouted after him.

Tinka and I played on the ground, and became absorbed in the landscapes and especially in the oceans in the carpet. Above us we could hear Mummy sighing deeply. Auntie Margot tried to cheer her up.

"Cold herb tea in a silver pot. Typical, isn't it? Those French. Shall we order wine instead?"

"Too early for wine. There's a fantastic new fashion house just around the corner, and we're going."

"The children, Hélène, we can't leave the children by themselves."

"The children are going with us. They need new coats as well, don't they?"

We were now staying with Great-Uncle Philipp, since my father was there the whole time anyway and the hotel was no good. The floor of Great-Uncle Philipp's house was full of the suitcases of Auntie Flora, who had come from Germany, where she didn't want to play the piano anymore because art was being trampled underfoot. She told anyone willing to listen that art was supreme and that the barbarians would not succeed in blackening the name of art. They could burn books—the paper, that is, not the spirit. The howling of the hordes would soon be silenced. Good taste and feeling would triumph. Heart and common sense!

"Open your eyes and unblock your ears, they're full of shit," roared our great-uncle Philipp every time, however often my mother said, *"Les enfants, les enfants."*

"What about it? Shouldn't they get to know life as it is?"

"You're a contrary old cuss and a pessimist."

"A realist," said my father. "And he's right."

At night we heard them arguing. My parents' voices, going from high to low and even lower. About art and a scapegoat and a bloodthirsty herd. It trailed off into tired muttering, sometimes passionate sobbing. In the next room we sobbed along with them.

One night Auntie Margot came bouncing into our room, muttering, "This is too much for me." She blew our noses and took us with her to another room. We climbed three flights of stairs and entered a yellow room, where the wardrobes were the beds. There were no curtains, and the windows looked out onto the street. We saw sick trees, old houses, and dim lanterns in rows, alongside and behind one another.

"Nice view," said Auntie Margot with satisfaction. "Just like Paris used to be."

"Is it nice?"

"Oh yes!" Auntie Margot assured us.

"And the trees?"

"What's wrong with the trees?"

"They haven't got any leaves."

"Oh! Yes, too few, that's true. But the leaves will come back again, I promise you."

"Really true?"

"Really true."

She was her old self again, the most cheerful one. She had had a fat letter from Uncle Felix, which she kept with her all the time. Whenever she had the opportunity she started reading it, clucking and cooing as she did so.

"He's proposed to me, yes he has. We're getting married."

"So we're leaving on the boat again, aren't we, Auntie Margot?"

"Leaving? But, tootsies, we've only just got here."

We had quite a job getting her attention, because she wanted nothing better than to read her letter undisturbed.

"Auntie, is the wedding going to be here or at home?"

"The wedding will be at home, of course. That's obvious."

"So are we going back home very soon?"

"Oh yes, soon."

"When?"

"At the very latest next year."

"When's next year?"

"Oh, when the leaves grow back on the trees, that will be next year."

Every day and every night we looked out of the window of the yellow room. We opened the windows so we could study the branches even more closely. Could we already see them, the green tips, the new leaves? Then it would be next year and then we would be off. We said excitedly to each other, "Yes I can see something, I can see something. I can see it, can you?"

In Great-Uncle Philipp's house there were women and children who played the piano. Everywhere there were large black-and-white photos of women and children at pianos. Fat black-and-white cats walked around. The house was in a street full of shadows, along which people with white faces and black clothes moved. You couldn't see immediately which ones were still alive and which were shadows. People had turned their faces to the ground, as we had. They had cases and umbrellas, folded umbrellas, which they never used, because when it rained, they fled indoors. The inside of the house was black and white, except for our yellow room. All the rooms were tall and dark and smelled of tobacco and the cats. Now I think back, I can smell it again and can see Auntie Flora's grand piano standing there in the lightest and largest room. She reduced everyone to silence when she played, swaying and rolling her gigantic body. She had a large, sweet face, covered with warts and spots. Her eyes bulged a little, and she looked at us in a benign and curious way. She was like the hippopotamus that we knew from a picture, with its head just emerging from the water. It was a hippopotamus in captivity, and lived in a circus and did tricks.

We listened to Flora's playing and sat and waited until she cheered up again, then she imitated the cats chasing each other, across the keys.

"Mr. Benjamin could go even faster," I said to her.

"Of course he could. He was a great artist."

Auntie Flora closed her eyes. "When he played, nectar dripped into your soul."

.   .   .

We could not understand the majority of the people who lived in the house, as they spoke French. Great-Uncle Philipp, who spoke many languages, gave us one French lesson.

"One lesson is enough. Pay attention. I learned this as a little boy in school, before they started pulling the wool over children's eyes: *'Ils naquirent ils souffrirent ils moururent.'* That's all you need to know, that's life."

"What an incorrigible pessimist that man is, don't listen to him."

We looked at my mother inquiringly. We could say the words, but we didn't know what they meant.

"They were born, they suffered, they died." My mother rattled this off sarcastically, and we still couldn't make head or tail of it.

"So what does it mean?"

"There's no need for you to know, there's more to life than that," she concluded in a promising tone.

"What then?"

She wouldn't say any more.

Girls in aprons appeared from every corner of the dark house to make us feel at home; they sang songs and showed us games that we didn't understand. They bought a dolls' house inhabited by tiny monsters that scratched and bit us. The girls cuddled us as hard as they could and messed up our hair. They pinched us, and we went from lap to lap until we could bear it no longer.

Flora asked Tinka, "Dear girl, would you like to dance for me? Would you like to show me an Oriental dance?"

The floors creaked and kept their splinters at the ready, and cold crept out of the windows and walls. We were frightened of the big piano, which was called a grand but had nothing grand about it, and which would come waddling up to us on its bent legs the moment we weren't looking, in order to grind us up with its yellow teeth and tuck us away in its belly full of sharp strings.

The girls in the kitchens fanned the fire so hard that we heard the flames crackling and throbbing in the stoves and ovens. They stayed at a respectful distance. We dared to go closer, as we could stand the heat. We weren't frightened of fire; we were much more frightened of the silent alcove beds, the doors of which were closed at night. And we hated the white bath.

With much clattering and banging they filled a cold, hard white coffin with lukewarm water for us; they called it a bath, and we had to get in. We struggled until we were too exhausted to move a muscle.

Singing all the while, they carried us to the great dark alcoves, which were piled up to the ceiling with woolen blankets, duvets, and cushions. We couldn't get to sleep under the blankets, and on top of that they brought hot stone jugs with sheep's-wool covers. The jugs had to sleep in bed with us, but we mustn't touch them.

We mustn't touch anything; that was better for us. This was impressed on us many times, and we understood.

Outside in the street there was a sour, musty smell when people came past; they smelled of horses and sheep, because they were muffled up in their sheep's-wool and horsehair clothes.

We fled quickly inside again when we saw them, because they sometimes grabbed hold of us. They put their hands on our heads and clicked their tongues pityingly when we said to them very politely: *"Ils naquirent ils souffrirent ils moururent."*

We thought Europe was strange. The chill and the wind, the sun that shone like a moon, the fat white people and the thin gray trees—we couldn't believe our eyes. Black and gray and brown houses and towers and streets and squares and statues, all stone, no trees with leaves on anywhere—it was impossible.

The family had gathered from all over Europe to pay its last respects to Mr. Benjamin.

Gradually they became familiar to us: the uncles and aunts, the cousins, the members of our family, friends of the family. We got to know their faces but couldn't remember their names. Tinka and I were lifted up and inspected at great length, and then put down again.

We could scarcely understand the conversations that were carried on about us. Occasionally a little perhaps.

Where had he left it all, people kept asking, in a whisper and out loud. There was practically nothing left of his wealth. Very little could be found. He must have gone through it all.

We kept our heads down, we made ourselves inconspicuous, and Tinka hid. No one must know what we were thinking. We didn't even know ourselves.

"What's wrong with the children? It's as though they're on fire, they're red-hot," someone observed.

"The dear children can probably tell that we're talking about Benjamin," my mother explained earnestly. "That affects them. They're the last ones he spoke to on board. He refused to speak to anyone else."

"He was a big child and children could sense that," said Auntie Flora, visibly moved.

My great-uncle was always restless and sometimes angry.

"Bad premonitions, Philipp?" my father would ask him regularly.

"Bad experiences, you mean."

He was seldom at home. If he was at home, then the others walked about on tiptoe and everyone was quiet. He sometimes banged his fist on the table and even on Flora's piano. He wandered the streets with all his cameras draped around him and when he returned, he withdrew into a darkroom, where he mustn't be disturbed. If he was in his room working or ranting, the piano was silent. Auntie Flora would sit down at the table and massage her hands; the cats would creep into the garden through the window that had been left ajar.

"I must get out of this madhouse," squeaked my mother. "I've had enough."

One day Great-Uncle Philipp heard her, because my mother was screaming louder and louder through the corridors. He came out of his room and said, "Out of this madhouse? This is a safe haven! But tell me, Hélène, where were you thinking of going? I'll go with you, my little goose, because outside things are *really* bad."

He put a large black hat over his long hair, which was much longer than my father's, and donned a long black coat. My mother didn't want to go, but we did.

We could follow him with our eyes closed. If we opened them again and dared to raise our eyes above pavement level, we could see his figure ahead of us. His hat bobbed along the misty streets. His sleeves dragged more or less along the ground. In his coat were the two fattest black-and-white cats—they were his models and were ensconced in his pockets, which bulged and purred.

We crept behind him at a distance, but close enough to peer at the cats.

Here we are in this photo, hand in hand at the foot of the Eiffel Tower.

Tinka and I are standing next to Auntie Margot, and my mother is behind us, with my little brother on her arm. It was

Simon's birthday, so it was May 27. Here in the photo we have already let go of our birthday balloons.

We watched as their tails became entangled in the ironwork. The balloons couldn't free themselves without our help, but we couldn't reach them. We looked at their helpless red and yellow shapes. It made me feel giddy and I screamed.

"Watch the birdie, watch!" cried Great-Uncle Philipp, to distract us from the balloons and focus us on him.

The shot was fired, the bird stuffed.

For a long time it stood in a silver frame on Auntie Margot's table in The Hague. Later it moved without a frame to my shoe box. It still lies here half a century later, but Tinka has been cut off and lost.

No trace of fear, chilliness, or homesickness is visible in the photo.

"Do you remember that time in Paris?" my mother sometimes asks. She doesn't need the photos. She still remembers everything with crystal clarity. Except what I want to know. "And us at the foot of the Eiffel Tower?" she continues imperturbably. "What fun we had, didn't we?"

I remember that we screamed; I screamed, didn't I? But here it shows me laughing.

On May 27, 1939, the temperature in Paris was only nineteen degrees Celsius. My mother scribbled that on the back of the photo, with three exclamation marks.

Simon was crying because he'd lost his balloons.

We looked up, again and again. In the photo we are standing there openmouthed.

We couldn't move in our new checked taffeta dresses, with smocking and long sleeves. Coffinlike, their lids were screwed down tight up to chin height, and we peeped out of the windows at the top. We had ribbons on our backs, to restrain us. If we tried to run or fly away, we were grabbed by our ribbon.

In Paris kings and nobles had no heads and the trees had no leaves; children had ribbons and collars. Dogs walked around in jewel-studded coats.

We were standing at the window of the little room, Tinka and I. No one could find us and we were talking quietly and haltingly about Bandung and Bali where we had been walking about a short while ago. Sometimes we were suddenly not sure if we'd ever been there—in those places that we called by their names less and less often and that were gradually ceasing to exist—or if we'd just imagined them.

The wind whistled and caught hold of us, here behind our glass. We breathed on it and misted it up so that the world outside became invisible. In the condensation we drew a huge sun and dolls and great trees and gave them our names and the names of gods.

The nights here were shorter than the days; the gray light was reluctant to go away.

In the middle of the day people gathered at tables, big tables on which there were cloths that were whiter and smoother than our bedclothes.

The meal was served on enormous dishes and under silver domes, so large that we were inclined to believe that there were slaughtered infants underneath, as Great-Uncle Philipp maintained.

"What nonsense are you putting into those children's heads now?" asked my mother sharply.

"Go and ask them, Hélène." Grinning Great-Uncle Philipp tapped out a march on the silver dome with his spoon. "Ask all those good citizens outside. They certainly know! They know exactly what's under here and what we're going to tuck into shortly! Those dear people will soon be spreading the news that the fat of their Christian children is dripping from our jaws."

He broke into his hoarse laugh.

To be on the safe side, we decided not to eat another mouthful of this food.

We were in the alcove bed; despite the wool, it was always clammy. We lay close together. We whispered that we could never stay in Europe. Every day that we remained there was a day too many. We no longer even knew how long a day was; the gray light went on and on.

"Where's *Garuda* gone?" I asked my father.

"To Rotterdam."

"Are we going back on *Garuda* yet?"

"No, not yet."

We had crossed the sea by boat, but for all we knew there might be other ways of crossing the sea. Fishes swam from one side to the other, and birds flew. Birds that were free to fly wherever they wanted flew overseas. My father had told us that birds left Europe to cross the sea and to land in the tropics. The tropics, I learned, were where we came from.

Once we found the sea, we would be halfway there.

THIRTEEN

Drawings she did, photos I have of her, her batik cloth that belonged to Poppy, her silver bracelet, everything is stored in my shoe box. Mildewed with damp, with the tears and kisses that did no good.

If they'd asked me why Tinka went back, I could have told them, but no one asked me why she went. Everyone asked me a hundred times *what* had happened and *how.* I refused to say what or how.

Tinka thought she was a *kris* dagger; I didn't make this up.

We talked about it, she and I when we were staying at Granny Mimi's.

Everyone asked how things could have come to that.

There were days that are chiseled in my mind with name and date. I can list them without anything to jog my memory, without consulting old photos or letters.

When I experienced those days, they didn't approach solemnly as the bearers of momentous events. They came, they went. They were part of the whole. Drops of water in a sea that grew imperceptibly colder and changed color.

Or did our water become not colder, but hotter. Frogs thrown into a bucket of boiling water immediately jump out and save their skins. In water where the temperature slowly rises to boiling point, the frogs stay put and boil. Which of us jumped out in time?

On May 9, 1939, the S.S. *Garuda* sailed into the Port of Marseilles.

Great-Uncle Philipp, my Granny Mimi's brother, was on the quayside and captured the moment we came ashore with his camera.

In those photos we're laughing and following each other off the gangway like white geese, happy that we've had a safe voyage and arrived in one piece. We're behaving as if we've already forgotten all that has taken place on the journey.

We'll be visiting family, in Europe, and we'll be staying at least seven months, perhaps a year. We'll be celebrating all over Europe, since we shall be paying birthday visits to every member of our family.

On Wednesday, May 10, we took the train to Paris. It was a Wednesday, I remember it well, because my mother preferred not to travel on that day of the week.

"Wednesday is already quite a long way into the week, but isn't going anywhere. The staff are already getting lazy and lounging about. But their day off is still too far away."

We had to go, because on May 11 it would be Mr. Benjamin's birthday in Paris. He would have been seventy. He wasn't there, but people remembered him.

Seventy, reflected Auntie Flora. "Three score years and ten, but not nearly as old as Methuselah."

"How old are you, Auntie Flora?"

"Artists have no age, darling. The job of art is to triumph over time."

Great-Uncle Philipp turned seventy-two on May 14.

We celebrated it in a Russian café, with Great-Uncle Philipp there in person and with red drinks and red soup.

On May 27 we celebrated my little brother's first birthday. We released his balloons near the Eiffel Tower, and Great-Uncle Philipp took photos.

The following day my father and Great-Uncle Philipp left for Verdun. They called it a journey into the recent past.

"What's the point?" grumbled my mother and Auntie Flora.

"To get it into our heads that we were *meshugge*," replied Daddy.

At Verdun they had both fought in the Great War, on the German side, and they were going to the old battlefield to rake up and lament it all.

We stayed in Paris until the morning of Tuesday, May 30.

We could have gone to The Hague before, but my mother preferred to wait until Tuesday, the ideal day to travel. The other days were no good. At weekends, which began as early as Friday, there were swarms of shady types abroad: adventurers, philanderers, gamblers and day-trippers. On Monday staff still hadn't got used to work and they were tired from their time off. On Tuesday they felt guilty about it, had acquired new energy, and tried especially hard. And on Tuesdays too one couldn't complain about the passengers, particularly if one didn't leave too early in the morning and so avoided the commercial travelers. Wednesday was their day, which was under the protection of Mercury, the god of trade and messenger of the gods. What was wrong with Thursday? The fact that the week was too far advanced, and that one might just as well not go anymore, that there was a general atmosphere of boredom and disappointment to which there was no end in sight.

My mother and Auntie Margot and Auntie Flora, my brother and Tinka and I traveled on the train to Holland.

We arrived in The Hague, at Hollands Spoor Station.

Granny Mimi loomed up on the platform in front of us like a fiery red flare in the darkness. We saw her from a distance; her arms were opened wide. The train crawled past her and she kept flapping her arms and taking great strides.

"Oh, oh, she's bursting with longing for that oaf. But he's not coming yet. The day after tomorrow perhaps. There's only one man for her, and that's her darling Cees." Auntie Flora muttered this as if it were a scandal she was trying to excuse. She stood there as large as life at the window of our compartment taking great puffs on her cigar. She nodded cordially at the people who looked at her, although she assured us she didn't want to be gaped at by Johnny Public for all the tea in China. She would also refuse to give autographs.

"I won't do it! God knows what you're putting your signature to these days."

"Look, there's Celia Zwaan," said my mother and Auntie Margot together. "What a strapping young lady she's suddenly become."

Behind Granny Mimi's skirts galloped a creature that in my eyes looked half horse and half tea lady. Her long blond braid floated after her like a tail.

"Who's Celia Zwaan?"

"An aunt that you two don't know yet."

"Auntie Celia Zwaan!"

"She's our youngest sister, half sister, that is," said my mother. "She lives in Granddad Smit's Dutch house."

"Are we going to stay with her?"

"I don't think so. We're not even sure if the house is still there," said my mother disdainfully.

"How's that?" asked Auntie Margot.

"It was full of those spirit drinkers, wasn't it?"

"Oh Hélène, that was the Anti-Vivisection League; they were teetotalers, if you ask me."

"What difference does it make? Celia's a fanatic. She maintains that she isn't concerned with material things. Perhaps she's given the house to spiritists."

"Oh dear, it doesn't bear thinking about," giggled Auntie Margot.

"Good riddance," my mother laughed. She would go on saying that: "Good riddance."

Ten, twenty, thirty years later she was still saying it.

Granddad's house in Holland stayed intact. It remained open to us under all circumstances. It gave us shelter, again and again, over the years, if we were in trouble elsewhere.

The house was there for us, even long after Granddad had passed on. In the basement, without any interference from us, almost of its own accord, almost without our noticing, our Indonesian room was created, in which I can sit and dream to this day.

Where we reminisce, fantasize, and weave our illusions, and try in vain to thwart reality and transience.

We have always returned there, to our house; we will go on returning there, to Granddad's house in The Hague. Even, perhaps, after we've passed on.

"Celia Zwaan!" said my mother before her feet had even touched the platform. "Don't put yourselves out on our account; we've already booked rooms at the Hotel des Indes."

"*Quatsch*, Hélène!" cried Granny Mimi as loud as she could in her hoarse voice. "For weeks, what am I saying, for months, from the moment we knew you'd be coming, we've been working our fingers to the bone, we've been hounding our staff and our tradesmen. Everything's been arranged, except for lasting peace."

Celia pressed a bunch of white roses into Auntie Margot's hands and gave my mother a bunch of red roses, after quickly removing from it a piece of rolled-up paper that she unfolded with jaunty gestures. There was a whole screed written on it in large letters in different colored inks.

"Dearest daughters, my dear sisters, Hélène and Margot, dearest grandchildren, dearest niece Louise and dear nephew Simon, dear foster daughter Cristina!" She read this out in a solemn, clear voice.

"What next!" exclaimed my mother. "A speech? You're off your head." She grabbed at the paper, but Celia Zwaan leapt out of the way.

"I'll forget half of it otherwise," she exclaimed. "Our mummy advised me to do it this way, as there's quite a lot to say."

"Mummy's forgetting again that we can read for ourselves."

My mother had managed to get hold of the sheet of paper. We saw her eyes racing along the lines, quickly at first, but then slower and slower.

Her lips started trembling. "I didn't know Mummy was ill." Granny Mimi approached and said reassuringly, "Dear child, it's a healthy illness. Although that kind of thing isn't so easy after you're fifty; let's hope for the best." She said it with a broad smile, but my mother went as red as Granny Mimi's boa and threw the paper on the ground.

"Does she really have to do this? Hasn't she got enough already? She does nothing but bear children. It's incredible. And as for Peronel, the old tomcat, they should castrate him. I expect he's strutting around proud as a peacock."

We saw Granny Mimi draw my mother to her and tuck her under her cape, almost smothering her in a loving onslaught.

"Child, watch what you're saying." Granny Mimi hugged my mother firmly to her and moved her long neck back and forth like a watchful bird. "Margot!" she cried and, freeing an arm from my mother, beckoned her.

"Margot, dear child, come here, I want to say hello to you."

The three women rocked back and forth in one another's embrace.

"Did you two dare leave our Felix all alone back in the Indies?" I heard Granny Mimi ask with a laugh. "I don't know how you could do that, Margot, leave your fiancé behind. My spoiled son, he's such a rascal."

"He's written me such a beautiful letter, Mimi. I'll read it out later," said Auntie Margot exultantly.

"Oh, yes please, child. I can hardly wait." Again Granny Mimi looked around her expectantly, her eyes squeezed into splits.

"Where's the rest of the party? Where has my eldest son got to?"

My mother said nothing. She had laid her head against Granny Mimi and closed her eyes. She looked like a little girl, even smaller than my smallest doll, which had been left behind.

"Chin up, Hélène," Granny Mimi consoled her and stroked her cheek. "I'm sure Cees hasn't run off. I'd never believe that of him. The world will have to come to an end before he leaves you in the lurch."

"They're coming on shortly, Mother dear, everything's fine, everything's going according to plan. We thought you might know: they were going to tell you on the telephone."

Auntie Flora's honeyed voice seeped melodiously through all the hubbub; she peered out above the heads of the people who had buttonholed her and with whom she'd got into conversation. She looked so interesting and famous, in her large blue velvet sailor suit, that everyone looked at her with a mixture of admiration and astonishment.

"On the telephone?" grunted Granny Mimi. "Tell us on the telephone? Everyone at our house is stone deaf, or pretends to be.

And anyway, the telephone, that devilish contraption, we don't want to have one put in. Nothing good ever came out of it."

"Philipp and Cees will be coming the day after tomorrow at the earliest."

"The two of them have gone off to Verdun again; that's all we needed," groaned my mother.

"Verdun?" Granny Mimi put her hand to her mouth. "The two of them to Verdun? Haven't they had enough of that wretched misery?"

"Philipp wanted to take photos, I could kill him," my mother exclaimed.

We had got as close as we could to Granny Mimi.

"Hélène, there are suddenly such beautiful children standing right in front of me, I'm going to say hello to them properly." Granny Mimi began a stately descent, like a flamingo landing. She enveloped us in her poppy red silk cape, which she'd first let fan out around her.

She looked deep into our eyes. On her head there wobbled an enormous hat with white and poppy red feathers on it. She brought her mouth closer to whisper something in our ears, but she couldn't whisper; she rasped so loudly that everyone could hear.

"Are you Lulu or are you Tinka, or is it the other way round? Oh, what does it matter! My children, my dear children, come to my heart, both of you!"

There were cracks and grooves in the intense red of her lips; we'd never seen such lips before. Everything was intense about Granny Mimi, and there was a lot of everything. It trembled or was cracked. Corn-blue powder trembled on her eyelashes and there were clouds of chalk-white powder on her cheeks, so thick that we saw figures emerging in them. If we wanted to we could draw dolls in it. We admired her speechlessly: her waving feathers, her lorgnette that hung at chest height, her sparkling earrings, which shook at every cry, the shiny trembling black dot on her chin.

My mother wanted to go to the hotel, but Granny Mimi wouldn't hear of it. Hotels could no longer be trusted. Auntie Flora had had stones thrown at her in a hotel in Berlin.

Lots of relations were staying with Granny Mimi, but there was plenty of room for us. There were enough rooms.

"Receiving guests properly is the most difficult thing there is. How can one constantly make one's dear relations feel at home? I can always tell from their faces that they'd rather be back in their own familiar surroundings. Was man created for adventure?"

"Listen to who's talking," muttered Auntie Flora good-naturedly.

In the heart of the house, in the great kitchen, the aunts manned the ovens. The aunts who didn't want to be in the kitchen prowled around Granny Mimi's workshop. Granny Mimi sent them into the garden to pick flowers. She gave them knitting wool and crochet needles and took them to the conservatory.

The uncles with hats had nestled at the great table that stood in the middle of the kitchen, where they smoked and argued. They drank water from the kitchen tap, slurping it out of the hollow of their hand or using an old soup ladle. They were too lazy to get a glass, fumed Granny Mimi.

They were always talking about justice. I heard my father say, "A just man doesn't have to be an innocent man, and someone who is innocent isn't automatically just."

Great-Uncle Philipp banged his fist on the table and cried, "Caesar is spoiling for a fight again. Why?"

Granny Mimi stood outside in the garden listening; she leaned forward, put her head through the window, and shouted, "Because he got his brains from you lot, that's why."

Then as usual the parties divided into hawks and doves, into yellow-bellies who wanted to flee to North America, crazy idiots who wanted to stand their ground, Zionists, drawing-room Communists, traitors, and fellow travelers. I listened, from behind Granny's skirts in the garden, or upstairs in bed.

The uncles and aunts had traveled to Granny Mimi's because they were on the run. We didn't know why they'd run away or from whom.

Their voices droned on, day and night. At night, they actually became louder; waves of sound rose up in the darkness—like ponderous music—to the blue room where Tinka and I lay in her bed. Always the same sad melody.

Tinka told me that the gods also spoke and sang in her head.

"What do they say?"

"They say I must go back."

Tinka started talking about it, occasionally at first, then every evening.

There were no gods in the thick book of fairy tales from Europe that we'd been given by Auntie Celia. There were lots of wonderful pictures in it, though. Of witches and fairies. Sorcerers and goblins. Talking animals. Great terrors were overcome by human cunning and strength, and occasionally by shrewd heroes who pretended to be swineherds or played the innocent.

Tinka wasn't the least bit interested in these fairy tales. She said people's cunning and strength were not enough. People's love wasn't enough either. People's love had many faces.

I wondered what she meant.

"What do the gods say?" I asked.

She sounded gloomy and serious when she said that the gods knew everything and we knew nothing.

"Your family brought a Javanese wedding chest with them," said Tinka. "Filled with treasure. Jewels, jewelry, wooden statues from Djokja. Gifts for your grandmothers. Your mother and your aunt collected them. They were careful to check that those gifts had no evil in them. Your mother and your aunt know nothing. They took the dagger and the shadow puppets out of the box because they think that they bring bad luck. Those puppets and the dagger are as innocent as white doves.

"But I'm not. I've been sent by a vengeful man.

"Your mother and your aunt think their father is doing a good deed. That he sent me away to become a better person, perhaps a better dancer. As if that were the point! He doesn't give a damn about that!

"We call your grandfather the fire-eater because of his red beard and his conjuring tricks. The gods like jokers and hooligans and so your grandfather has been given a free hand by the gods. No one dares flout his wishes and orders, not even your mother. The only one who dared is the woman who now lives in England. The only one who will understand at once what my coming means. I'm not a gift, but a gesture full of doom and revenge. The fire-eater chose me as he would choose a dagger that brings misfortune. He means your Granny Helena harm; otherwise he wouldn't have taken my name away and pretended that I'm his daughter."

I thought Tinka's story was beautiful, and it was also like a fairy tale, but still I listened to it with fear in my heart. And I believed it too, the way that I believed fairy tales, a little, but never completely. Anyway, you could change a fairy tale however you wanted, as my mother always did when she read aloud and didn't like the story.

So I asked Tinka, clinging to her, please to stay for a little while. We could change the story that the gods told. In a little while we would be going back on the boat. My father would agree to let Tinka remain with us.

"If the gods want to," said Tinka, "they'll let me stay."

·   ·   ·

Real life was different from fairy tales: I had only to listen to the obsessive voices that came through our windows now and then like gusts of wind. Continuously, rising to a pitch, hissing upward over the windowsill. With our eyes wide open we waited in bed for the gods to intervene with their thunder and lightning.

I asked Granny Mimi if the gods spoke to her too.

"Do they just! They're speechless, whatever question you ask."

My father took photos of Granny Mimi with him to the tropics in an old diary. He brought the diary back with him to Holland, but I didn't see the photos until much later.

All the photos that were in it are still there. They are faded, the corners are dog-eared, they're now all in my silver-colored biscuit barrel with flaking pink flamingos on the outside.

Mimi was born in 1872, probably. No one ever saw her birth certificate. She herself constantly gave different birth dates. Up to 1915.

Her eldest son, my father, was born in 1890, in a university hospital in Berlin, by cesarean section, in front of an audience of medical students. In those days it was not unusual for an impoverished, unmarried woman to serve for demonstration purposes for a medical practical. So my father immediately had a large audience, certainly as large as Mimi's companion Benjamin could have wished for at the time. But this artist was conspicuous by his absence. He couldn't afford a wife and child; he had to serve the Muse.

According to ancient custom the child was called Caesar and Mimi believed her child had come into this world to avenge her. He would become an understanding children's doctor, a second Semmelweis. He would never perform an unnecessary cesarean section.

Mimi moved into the basement and photographic workshop

of her brother Philipp, with her child and the old Pfaff, the pedal sewing machine that she was to treasure to the end of her days. Because the Pfaff had brought her luck. Together Mimi and her machine had lived to see her become a famous couturier.

After several years the artist turned up again. His career had gone well; now the Muse served him instead of the other way round. He had fame and money and almost everything he wanted, except for a wife and child. He led, as he wrote to Mimi in a moving letter, a lonely life. He had decided at this late date to make an "honest woman" of her. But Mimi considered his proposal indecent and said no.

She always remained convinced that that was how it was meant to be, because less than a month later she met the merchant Felix Benda, whom we all called the Good German, including me, who didn't even know him.

It was 1893.

Mimi and her brother were busy hanging up photos in a café for his exhibition The German Malaise. It was early in the morning, and an irritable gentleman rushed in and asked the first person he came across, who was my Granny Mimi, for a glass of cognac with a beaten egg in it. Mimi stopped work, sat down at the man's table, and gave him a ticking off. She took him thoroughly to task about his life of dissipation. She couldn't understand what came over her. She'd never done anything like it before.

Opposite her sat Felix Benda, the youngest son of a respectable Roman Catholic chocolate maker and pâtissier. Benda was immediately bowled over by her earthy, rough charm and became so obsessed by her that he kept stammering, "Go on . . . go on . . ." even when Mimi had long since finished pouring out her criticisms, down to the last exhortation, over his head. He would no longer leave her side. He forced her to remain seated and put the child on her lap while he hung up the photos with Philipp.

He also had the impudence to write a clumsy poem on the spot, on a napkin, about her long, black armpit hairs, which gave off the smell of thistle and chamomile, a poem that still hung in Mimi's house on the inside of her bedroom cupboard. Mimi too must have fallen head over heels in love with the man who had wrongly made such a disreputable impression. Though he began this particular day before seven in the morning with cognac and a beaten egg, Granny Mimi could list everything that she'd liked about Benda: his blue eyes; his round cheeks; his calm, yes, call it languor; his dark blond hair, which illustrated this languor by not curling but waving, as if it lacked the energy for such an effort. His friendliness and his unmistakable admiration for her, his loyalty and his cheerfulness, and also his penchant for the good life. Mimi liked all this so much that she didn't hesitate for a second when he proposed. Within a year these two totally different people were a close couple, the child was legitimized and given his stepfather's name. All his life my father regarded Felix Benda as his own father, and idolized him.

Very soon my Auntie Flora was born, but because she, like Granny Mimi, plays around with her age, we go on guessing at the year of her birth out of politeness. A few years after Flora came Felix, everyone's favorite. Flora and Felix were born the normal way, easily in fact. An ironic freak of fate is that the two legitimate Benda children were crazy about Uncle Benjamin, who often stayed for weeks, which they adored. He taught little Flora to play the piano. "She could have been mine," he would say when Granny Mimi was out of earshot.

However, Mimi would never confirm that Benjamin the pianist was my father's father. My father said he felt sorry for Mr. Benjamin, whom he finally accepted as a kind of uncle.

Uncle Benjamin taught the children to dance, to make music, bought musical instruments and gramophone records for them, and once even a barrel organ.

FOURTEEN

We arrived at Granny Mimi's on May 30. Four days after my father arrived with Uncle Philipp.

I stood alone as Granny Mimi and my father embraced fondly. My father lifted Granny up and waltzed around the front garden with her. From the kitchen, from the conservatory, from the studio, women charged toward him, quickly took my father in their arms in turn and were reluctant to let him go. Then it was the turn of the men with the hats on, who hugged him solemnly and laid their heads on his shoulder. My father disappeared in a carousel of heads, hands, shawls, cloths, hats, and clothes. He swirled in and out of my field of vision, without noticing me.

For as long as I can remember, my father was surrounded by women. If it wasn't my mother and aunts, it was the many visitors who came to show themselves off to him in all their glory.

One of my father's great talents was undoubtedly his charm. I have no idea if he was a good doctor. He was certainly no Semmelweis, even though the latter's portrait always hung in his study.

"That man, a gynecologist? Hopeless, he didn't understand a

thing about women. He should never have become a gynecologist, but he became one because of Mimi." My mother talking. According to her he just bluffed his way through.

It seems he could bend over attentively to the patient, who had just told her tale of woe, and then, smiling and with his hands on one of hers, ask her sympathetically, "And what do you yourself think is wrong?"

How did my mother, who was so demanding and so fickle into the bargain, come to marry such a gloomy, ham-fisted man?

"Ah, that matchmaker Mimi did it, but she got it wrong. She actually meant Margot."

My mother did not need to tell me later that besides his good nature it was his very elusiveness that had attracted her, his friendly but troubled persona. His contempt for the good things in life. Everything that other people thought was desirable and important meant nothing to him. He wasn't impressed by her father, the firebrand Lukes Smit, who always invoked the principle of might is right: "The survival of the fittest, my dear Benda; you're not going to try to convert nature, are you?"

My father didn't bow to the might-is-right principle; he believed in the advent of a better world, in which the spirit would dominate nature; he believed in freedom, equality, and brotherhood.

What were we to do with him? Compared with him we were just wastrels, my mother and Auntie Margot birdbrains, Granddad Smit a bloodthirsty libertine, Uncle Felix a womanizer. Even Granny Mimi was in fact a shameless tyrant, who always got her way and made the people around her dance to her tune.

My father was a romantic dreamer, full of good cheer, who lost hope only late in his life. The First World War had not been able to shatter his belief in the goodness of man. It took the Second to do that.

·   ·   ·

We had to be careful with Granny Mimi, my father impressed on us, and not to make too much fuss and noise. She was old and sick, he told us hesitantly. He said it so softly we could scarcely hear it. And we didn't see any sign of Granny being old and sick. She walked faster then we did; she made far more noise and fuss and much more mess too.

She was made of the same stuff as her tough, black-and-white cat with yellow eyes and nine lives, which forced its way in everywhere through kitchen windows to get the best titbits. It stalked the neighbor and stole her beefsteak out of her shopping bag. The cat would then meow triumphantly, and Granny would burst out laughing with the same satisfaction.

My mother had observed in surprise that we had been staying here for quite a while, but that none of the neighbors said hello to us. On the contrary, when we passed, they turned their heads ostentatiously in the opposite direction.

"Mimi has once again managed to make all the neighbors here anti-Semites," said my father sadly.

"Oh goodness, that's not true, is it?" cried my mother. "Has anti-Semitism wafted over from Germany to Holland then?"

"It doesn't waft; it's under every pillow."

Over the years Granny Mimi had got her house into the shape she wanted. She shaped everything that came within her grasp. Honing, crocheting, knitting and sewing, kneading and snipping, planing and polishing until it was how she wanted it, no matter what it was, hats or pieces of cloth, people, children, animals, or houses. The house charmed her so, she said, because it reminded her of herself; it was large, eccentric, and full of fuss. Its joints creaked, it needed lots of paint and attention, but from a distance it looked elegant enough.

It wasn't far from the sea and was being attacked by the salt wind. It had to be repainted every year although that was money down the drain. But it kept a person active, Mimi maintained. No one had wanted to buy the house, and when Mimi moved in it had been standing empty for years. People in the district claimed that there was a ghost.

"Passersby quicken their steps at this place, but whether they like it or not, they freeze and have to stop. It isn't the look of the house or the adjacent cemetery; what roots the spectator to the spot is the flagrant monstrosity of the vegetation in the garden, which looks so exuberant and lush, as only plants can that grow on a bed of corpses' secretions and rotting bones," wrote Celia Zwaan, in her diary. The house provoked such outbursts.

Through Mimi's efforts the shunned house had become a strange showpiece, which besides horror also caused glee. On sunny days walkers sometimes crept closer to point out the details—which in their eyes were undoubtedly crazy—to each other and laugh. Tinka and I thought we were in a castle, which was something like the castles in our new book of fairy tales, on a miniature scale.

It was bursting out on all sides with extensions. Bay windows, balconies, and conservatories popped up in places where you least expected them. From a modest side door, at which tradesmen had originally had to ring, sprang a covered gallery of princely proportions, with an abundance of plants and a fountain of which the Marquis of Carabas wouldn't have been ashamed. This gallery, dubbed the Winter Garden by Mimi, served only those who wanted to go right across the garden under cover to the workshop. There weren't many of those, because the workshop was out of bounds for all grown-ups except my father. Children were still creative and innocent and could inspire the milliner, and we were received there as though every day were our birthday. Our sweets stood in glass jars under the sewing tables. We could sing or read, play with bits of cloth and beads. Or laze about and fall asleep in cascades and clouds of soft and feathery light material. The workshop had a dome-shaped glass roof; there were mirrors, there were settees, there were enormous cushions on the ground. Everywhere there were hairy rugs, skins, and bits of material. Blooming, sweet-scented plants were given shade by large houseplants. Here the moist, warm atmosphere of a tropical greenhouse prevailed. I would later bring the little *waringin* here from Granddad Smit's house to nurse it back to health.

Tinka and I could stand for hours among Granny Mimi's plants. We didn't say anything. We thought the plants spoke to us.

"Don't stand there like pillars of salt, children, go and play."

To please Granny Mimi we rolled back and forth on the ground over the sheets and wrapped ourselves in the poor panther's skin. We played tag and cops and robbers and drew hopscotch squares on the stone floor with big thick pieces of chalk.

She was always sitting there, day and night, always bent over the Pfaff. She could talk with her mouth full of pins, which stuck out from between her lips like glittering bones.

My father would visit the workshop.

"Is this a good time?" he would ask, after knocking.

"Yes, any time, Cees, of course, just come in, come in, don't stand there like an idiot banging on the door, child," said Granny Mimi and the pins fell out of her mouth, so broad was her smile. I always heard and saw the meetings between those two with mixed feelings. My father a child?

"Come in, Cees, but we're working." Granny Mimi got up to vacate a chair for him.

"Don't work so hard, Mimi; why don't you relax a bit," said my father.

"I didn't ask for your advice, lad."

"Mimi was born with pins in her mouth," my father told us. I didn't understand why he sounded so sad. "That's why we don't always need to understand her."

Great-Uncle Philipp took this photo of Mimi when she was about to get married. Look, here she is, squatting on the ground with pins in her mouth, putting the finishing touches to her wedding dress. She is looking over her shoulder at her brother, the photographer, with a crooked smile into which those pins are sticking.

On the back of the photo Mimi has written: "Berlin, 1894, wedding dress, scarlet silk, not white."

Sometimes Tinka went to sleep before I did. I heard her groaning and grinding her teeth in her sleep and wasn't allowed to wake her up because it was precisely in her sleep that the gods spoke to her. So as not to have to listen, I went to Granny Mimi's. I sat down under the Pfaff, where long ago my father had sat. She was working on what were to be her last hats and dresses, at night. Alone in the workshop.

"Why is there a glass roof in here, Granny? There's no light at night."

"At night there's a light that's better than daylight. And besides that, inspiration from the moon and the stars."

"Do the stars tell you what to do?"

"No, darling, only my common sense tells me that."

For one last time she launched a new collection. A veritable whirlwind hit the house. We were bowled off our feet by it, picked up and thrown down again. She no longer noticed us. There were no chalks or sweets for us anymore; she literally walked right over us, stomping through the gallery with piles of swatches and rolls of cloth in her arms on her way to her Pfaff.

"Go to Aleida, children, I've no time for you; go and do some sport and develop your muscles. People have to stand up for themselves in this life. You can get up to plenty of tricks later."

Granny Mimi had promised my mother to find someone who

could make plucky girls of us, real Dutch girls. Sporting and live wires, but calm when necessary. Not easily frightened or easily duped. We who were as sluggish as dormice, and then suddenly exploded like rockets; we excited little madams who made a drama of everything, we must become solid Dutch girls. Fireproof, shockproof, resistant to the North Sea climate and to anything that fate might have in store for us.

When Aleida Bakker first came to us, we were sitting shivering in an overheated conservatory with our teeth chattering. In a heavy downpour we'd got our umpteenth runny nose and were sitting huddled together, wrapped in itchy cardigans. We had dirty handkerchiefs into which we didn't want to blow our noses anymore, and were wondering whether we could blow our noses on the hems of our dresses.

"Hello, my lovelies! My, you're sitting there all sweet and beautiful, like elves in a fairy tale."

"She looks as strong as a carthorse, doesn't she?" said Granny Mimi appreciatively. She pinched Aleida Bakker, praising her all the while, as if Aleida were a dog or a horse.

My mother was already grumbling quietly.

"Just listen to me first, dear Hélène," said Granny Mimi, interrupting her, "I guarantee that with a maid like that everything will be running smoothly here again. So go with complete confidence. You can visit your mother in England with your mind at rest."

"But I had a nanny in mind, someone quite different from this, who can't speak properly."

"Dreamer," said Granny Mimi a little sadly. "What governess with good references will risk working for us these days? A real governess among scoundrels and money-grubbers? A fine lady in our den of cannibals and nun-shavers?"

My mother laid her head on the cushion, closed her eyes, and snorted through her nostrils, but she kept her lips tightly together; she did her very best to keep her words to herself. She wasn't going to contradict Granny Mimi.

"We're not going to start doing that," my father had told all of us. "We're not going to contradict Mimi. In the first place, we don't know anything for certain; and in the second place, she's always right."

Mimi continued her speech, without malice, more resigned. "Yes, you're going to say, I can hear you thinking it: 'Go on, try selling that nonsense to someone else, you pessimistic old bag.' I'd be happy if I could sell anything to anyone else, even if it were only nonsense. But the climate's not like that anymore, dear Hélène. If it doesn't get any worse, we mustn't complain."

My mother sighed, stretched out her arm, and stroked Granny Mimi's shoulder.

"Everything will be all right, Mother, everything passes."

"*Kommt wieder ein Frühling, kommt wieder ein Mai.*"

When Aleida first arrived, we regarded her as an outsider. We had no idea that in her eyes, and in those of many others, *we* were the outsiders. But Aleida Bakker liked outsiders. She didn't judge. She didn't let herself be thrown off course by anything or anyone.

The regal entry of Mimi Rosenblueth at teatime, halfway through the afternoon in the tearoom, had struck everyone dumb, but not Aleida, who jumped up cheerfully from her stool and made a kind of curtsy.

There was no question of anyone giggling at this stiff German bow with wings spread backward. The feat was executed elegantly and with flair. Everyone could see that Granny Mimi was pleasantly surprised. But she couldn't help rasping in her crow's voice, "Well, my little maid, you really haven't a clue: curtsying to an old Jewess!"

Aleida did not sit down again until she was given permission.

"Sit down, little maid, no, not on that stool there, come close to me on the settee. Well now, tell me right away: How did you get these wonderful muscles?" Granny kneaded the brown arms so hard that red marks appeared on them, but Aleida sat and laughed as if she were just being tickled.

She had rust-colored hair with golden highlights, cut short to just below her ears and so thick that it looked like a fur hat. "A natural cloche," said Granny approvingly. "What a lovely head of hair you've got and what wonderful teeth; no wonder you're such a laugher. You've nothing to complain about, believe you me. Just you go on laughing!"

Granny looked at us triumphantly as if she'd made Aleida herself. My mother and Auntie Margot studied the carpet on the floor and said nothing. Mimi turned to Aleida again. "Do you know something, child? Even though you've got such wonderful thick hair, I'm going to make a jolly hat for you, something you can wear on the tennis court."

"Thank you very much," replied Aleida, beaming. She didn't even say "Oh no, you mustn't do that," as we had learned to say to such offers. Aleida said, "Yes, please do, ma'am, I'd really like that."

Mimi got up, strode to the window, and pointed: "Tennis rackets, bikes, and a smart young man, from the look of it. Isn't that Floris Crone, the tennis champion? Isn't he allowed in? Is he your beau?"

Aleida craned her neck to look outside, which made her look even taller and suppler.

"Oh, ma'am, please stop it. Teunis van Vloten is my fiancé."

"Teunis van Vloten? Who on earth is he? Can he beat Floris Crone?"

Hiccuping with laughter, Aleida blurted out, "On his bike he can, 'cause he's champion."

"Champion on his bike?"

"Now this is turning into a sporting conversation, I suppose we can go?" snorted my mother, and yanking Auntie Margot off the settee by the hand, she stormed out of the room with her, almost knocking over Granny, who didn't even get angry but simply said affectionately, "Hothead!"

In the late afternoon Aleida was given lessons on the courts of the Oranje Boven Tennis Club, close to Granny Mimi's house. Granny told us that Aleida was being taught by Floris Crone. The papers wrote about him, and he'd also been on the radio. We'd heard of him too, because the radio was on day and night at Granny's. Aleida would say nothing about him, whatever we asked.

She had asked if she could have every other Sunday off. "Why? It's a day like any other for us," Granny had said.

"But Sunday is a day of rest for everyone, even if it isn't the Lord's day for everyone," said Aleida. "That's why I thought—"

"The Lord really shouldn't allow himself a day of rest at times like these. And you should?"

"Oh, no. We don't have days of rest since our Corie got the Bible water," replied the girl in embarrassment. "And Sunday was never a day of rest for us anyway, because it's extra busy with the boats then. Teunis helps Father and Hendrik sometimes, but because he has lots of races on Sundays, I usually do the work."

"What kind of work do you mean?" inquired Granny.

"The boats, of course, ma'am!" We pricked up our ears. Wherever there were boats was a good place.

·   ·   ·

We sat sucking our Sunday lollies. My father didn't like to see us, so we sat with them under the big table, which had a Persian carpet over it that we had to occasionally lift up at the corner to see what was happening in the room. We kept nudging each other when we discovered something about Aleida that we wanted to discuss with each other urgently. Tinka did that in a singsong voice in our language, but I was starting to forget it, so I whispered in the white language.

In my eyes Aleida was a strange creature, very different from the people I knew. She looked stronger than all of us, with long muscles in her arms and legs. An even more striking thing about her was that she glowed. She glowed and glistened; she sparkled so that everyone seemed to pale beside her. Looking at her was a painful pleasure.

She looked at us good-naturedly with her golden brown eyes, in which joie de vivre twinkled at us. We could see that she wasn't frightened of anything and loved everything. Dared everything.

Suddenly she reminded me of Uncle Felix. I couldn't keep it to myself.

"Do you remember Uncle Felix?" I asked behind my hand.

"Shh, *tida bolé kosong,* don't talk about it, not here."

Tinka only wanted to talk about the past when there were no other people around. "She hasn't even got a cardigan on, do you see?" I said quickly.

"And she hasn't got goose pimples, and she's browner than we are."

She put her arms round me and carefully slid up our thick flannel sleeves a little and first looked at our skin and then peered at hers, which was smooth and colored by the sun, while we had the complexion and the skin of a peeled cucumber.

It was at teatime that we saw Aleida for the first time. Every afternoon there was teatime, when Tinka was there, when my mother and Auntie Margot and my brother were there, and afterward too.

It began after Granny had arisen from her afternoon nap, at about four in the afternoon. Three or four teapots were put out in the large front room with the conservatory that bordered the front garden. The cups and saucers came from many different sets, and because everyone had a preference for one cup or another, it would be given the name of its admirer. So there was Lilienthal's cup and Jongsma's and Dr. de Vries's and the one Gregor didn't like, without us knowing who Lilienthal, Jongsma, or Gregor were. We, of course, couldn't think up new designations because it was Granny who gave the names. Not even Auntie Flora must take it into her head to give a cup a name. My mother's was called Hélène's Chinese Porcelain; Cees's German was my father's. Granny herself had Louise, translucent white with pink roses. I made sure that I didn't get a favorite cup and didn't let anyone see that I preferred one to another. I wanted to try all the cups to find out what they could tell me.

Peronel's cup had a woman's face on the bottom, which loomed up as you drank the last mouthful. I knew who Peronel was. A lot was said about Peronel in the house. Almost all the paintings that hung there were his work. Endless conversations were conducted about whether or not we should take them to England.

Tinka and I were talked about in the same way as the paintings. She was definitely going to England, but it wasn't certain whether I was to go too. Perhaps it would be better if I stayed with Mimi and my father, and with Aleida.

Such discussions dominated teatime, which in fact sometimes lasted for the rest of the day. Tea parties frequently didn't adjourn until it was already dark. Only then did people discover that we had been sitting calmly under the big table throughout, when "children's bedtime" had long since passed.

Late in the evening Tinka and I crept out of bed again and went on playing under a table that was in another room. We had discovered the quiet back room one day when it was raining cats and dogs and the wind was too cold to go outside.

We roamed through the house, and some rooms were full of shouting people, but others were deserted, and all the bedrooms were empty except Granny Mimi's, where there were dogs. We descended toward the kitchen, where we were always welcome, even though the kitchen mustn't be entered without someone present, because there were fires on and quantities of water were boiling there.

In the kitchen there were always the uncles, who, despite the heat, had their long overcoats on, and they called us in or put their heads around the kitchen door, made a joke in some language or other, and gave us apples and a piece of cake.

On this occasion it was cold in the kitchen, and the uncles didn't say anything. There was a strange atmosphere, as though they weren't really concentrating.

The large back room seemed to be an extension of this. There were plants, which dropped many yellow leaves and became bare, scarcely like plants at all. They weren't nearly as well looked after as those in Granny Mimi's workshop. There were no net curtains in front of the windows, or the French doors. At the bottom of the garden there was a view of the tombstones through the sparse leaves of the bushes. Granny Mimi's back garden itself belonged to the dead who lay just beyond it. They could look into the room, and if they wished could walk in and out.

The back room, where we also sometimes played at night, was for them too—that was clear to us at once, partly because the room had been furnished in accordance with their taste, with walls papered in a velvety moss green, covered with silvery mildew. Above the black marble mantelpiece hung a mirror, also mildewed. All the people in the two large paintings by William Peronel were naked and dead.

The settees and chairs in our night room always crept close together. Every night they formed different groups, in circles with their backs to us, their seats and arms pushed together. This furniture never looked completely empty. There were often crumpled newspapers, but we also suspected that pieces of someone had been left behind, an arm over a chair arm, a forgotten leg. Perhaps that was why the chairs groaned and wailed whenever you ventured to sit in one. "We've already so much to bear, our fate is hard enough."

There was a fire in the hearth day and night. Who lit it?

The smooth chairs round the big table felt warm and sticky, as if somebody had just got up from them. There was always a half-smoked cigar already in the ashtray. A fug of smoke hung in the room, and there were the smells of the cemetery. Fire and dust had mixed with earth and leaves and everything that was old and discarded.

The floor was made of dark wood, but you could see only the narrow surrounds. Every inch was covered with rugs. They were laid down here after being banished from other parts of the house. The surplus rugs lay piled on top of each other, always spread out because Granny Mimi said that carpets should never be kept rolled up for a long time. There were so many of them that hillocks had formed in the room. Tinka and I hoped that all our Persian life carpets had been gathered together here so that we could read them.

Granny, I knew, sometimes read the cards here, not for herself but for others. She would almost always complain that it was bad for her heart and her eyes.

If Tinka and I discovered what the life carpets in the night room told us, we would know what was happening to everyone, and Granny Mimi would no longer have to strain her eyes here.

But perhaps I first had to learn how to read the cards before I understood the carpets.

Your house is there
your cross to bear
this you don't prize
here's a surprise
and this will come about, I swear!

On the table in the night room lay a faded cloth that hid us from view. It was just as well that we always sat underneath it, because the night room was not ours alone. The door would often open.

Each time we were so frightened that we didn't say a word. The people who came in yelled and banged their fists on the table.

We found it odd that these people who howled and hissed and foamed at the mouth so darkly could understand each other. It was as if they were playing musical instruments as part of an orchestra. Sounds we could recognize.

Eventually we got used to the strange concert above our heads. As soon as it began, we plunged into the blue, red, and dark areas of the carpet and imagined ourselves in the mountains, in the sky, on the roof of our house, under the ground. We pretended that we had a ship that we could sail ourselves. It looked like our table with its reddish brown sail. The blue areas were the sea across which we sailed back home.

FIFTEEN

Celia Zwaan Peronel was a drawing teacher, and she had asked us to come and stay with her, now she was on holiday, as she would like to draw us, particularly Tinka in her Balinese dancer's costume.

"Is Celia interested in Tinka? Oh, that's a pleasant surprise," said my mother. "Do you know what? It's a good idea; the children will go to the Dutch house for a while. It will make a nice change for them."

Granddad Smit's Dutch house was a big place with an overhanging thatched roof. It was in a long green avenue, tucked away among trees, and was astonishing because it was so round and looked like a beached whale. The garden was enormous, full of profuse shrubbery, overgrown lawns, and knee-high grass. At the bottom there was a summerhouse, buried by ivy. The windowsills of the house were festooned with flowerpots, and orange sunshades arched above the windows.

Eyes closed, the whale looked out over Granddad's pond, which wasn't big enough for it. Ducks quacked in its ears the whole day long. Granddad's wild garden was surrounded by a low stone wall and bordered a very neat, carefully trimmed park.

Here roses bloomed behind fences, and all the trees were in cages. People wandered round along the carefully raked gravel paths looking at their feet, so as not to stumble.

Celia Zwaan lived in Granddad Smit's house. She often sat in the summerhouse drawing the roses in the park.

"Why are the flowers in cages, Auntie Celia?"

"Man is lord and master over nature."

Woods and meadows were fenced off with barbed wire. On it were boards carrying the words "No Trespassers. Keep off the Grass."

Do Not Touch. Danger.

Keep Off! A flash of lightning, the sign of furious gods.

The gods were angry with us, and though we didn't yet know what we'd done, we had to hide from their rage. Stay indoors, like everyone else. No one here simply ventured out, into the rain. Only if there was no alternative did they pop their heads around the corner of the door for a moment or was a window cautiously opened. At many houses I'd seen boards saying "Please Do Not Ring the Bell," "Not at Home," "No Bicycles to Be Placed Here," and "Tradesmen Use the Rear Entrance."

People lived their lives behind windows covered with thin white cloths that kept out prying eyes. In the evenings the heavy top curtains were closed and the houses were strengthened like bulwarks with iron shutters.

When people ventured to the street, they wore mourning clothes.

Celia Zwaan wanted no part of any of this. She wore airy dresses, opened windows and doors wide, and danced in the garden.

Together we roamed for hours through the domain of the fox, walking at a brisk pace through the inaccessible coastal area with its impenetrable thorny vegetation. It was always gray and misty, with smudges of blood red and mustard yellow. A grubby sea gnawed listlessly at the dunes, which were not white, as in the sun, but made of sand the color of ash. From the ash sprouted the marram grass, sharp and blue as a knife.

This landscape did not invite one to laze about; here one marched and hunted and poached. And was silent.

The first thing we saw on entering Granddad Smit's Dutch mansion was the lonely houseplant. It stood in the hall, on a brass table, in a brass pot. It was smaller than we were, and it seemed to be ashamed.

We were alarmed. We had once known this scraggy thing as a giant! The giant had been sleeping in our heads all that time, and suddenly here it was in front of us as a dwarf.

It gave us a sign of recognition. This was the first good omen on our long journey.

We wanted to do something in return, tap its bark and feel its life flowing beneath it, but it was too fragile. It would succumb under our caresses. Its trunk was even more fragile than a bird's leg. We stroked the limp leaves.

"Oh, don't touch it, darlings, it's on its last legs," said Celia Zwaan.

It was some while before it occurred to us what the ailing monster was called. And then we didn't dare to say its name aloud, because was it true, was it the *waringin*?

I couldn't believe it.

Tinka let her hair fall forward, so that no one could see her face and she didn't have to look at anything.

"Auntie Celia, what's the plant called?"

"That one? That's a ficus, child."

Ficus, that's what it looked like.

"Isn't it the *waringin*?"

"Its name is *Ficus benjamina*."

She didn't know. But it was our *waringin*. What had they done to it?

We could only guess. In a flash of clairvoyance or madness we saw our own fate. We would be pollarded, and everyone would forget our names. We'd be left alone in a hall.

In a field thinly strewn with yellow blades stood a notice: "Please Do Not Walk on the Grass."

"What's wrong with the grass?" we asked Celia Zwaan. "Doesn't the grass want to be bothered? Is it sick?"

"The grass can't want anything, the grass has no will. We have a will, a free will, but we don't use it. We prefer to let ourselves go." She put her finger to her lips. "Ssh. Don't tell Miss Elisabeth that we just let ourselves go."

"Who's Miss Elisabeth?"

"My old governess. She's in a little room upstairs. I've shut her up there."

"Isn't she allowed out for a little while?"

Celia laughed softly. Between her pink lips we saw her teeth, which were small and delicate and shone like pearls. "It's nothing to do with me," she whispered, "her will is free; she can go wherever she likes."

Their natural inclination and free will were the most important thing in people's lives, proclaimed Celia Zwaan. But human beings couldn't do anything about their natural inclination, because that was in their blood. We had only to look at ourselves; our blood was mixed and exotic, so it flowed fast in all directions. We rolled all over the globe like pebbles and gathered no moss.

Celia's blood came from the north and was pure, cool, and sluggish. It was attached to its own habitat. It had to warm itself with play and dancing. There was nothing for her to do but keep moving, all day and all night. People could do everything with their will, as long as they didn't allow themselves to be inhibited by religion, class, or clothing.

Celia didn't make us put our shoes on, and she didn't worry about our clothes.

In Granddad's house women in slippers shuffled up and down the stairs and along the corridors. Mumbling old women, with their hair in buns, into which they stuck small knitting needles. They looked at us in a kindly way and nodded faintly with their trembling cheeks, but didn't say anything to us. We asked Celia if the women also lived in the house.

Celia said that she lived here on her own. Miss Elisabeth de Groot didn't count, because she was in Granddad's room under lock and key.

"Celia, we've seen them. They were dusting the stairs."

"Oh, the servants perhaps."

When we sat at table, the old women put dishes down. They also ladled soup into the plates in front of us, whether we wanted any or not.

"Celia, they're here again," we whispered.

Celia looked up absentmindedly from her drawing. Next to her plate there was always a sheet of paper on which she drew while she ate.

"What on earth do you mean, dear children?"

"The women with the buns and the knitting needles. Are they alive or dead?"

"To tell the truth I don't know."

"Shall I ask them?"

"No, I wouldn't if I were you. They might be frightened."

We stayed with Celia in the Dutch house for the last week of July and the first week of August.

Every day we said a few words in the old language to the *waringin* to let it know that not everyone had forgotten it. We wanted to look after it and tried to keep its spirits up. We sang it songs from the past.

In the past it had consoled us; now we were consoling it. Our world had been simply turned on its head, upside down, since we'd set off on our travels.

It rained every day, but no one was happy about this rain. When we woke up, we saw the gray clouds almost touching the windows of our room. We crept up to the top balconies to see if we could grab them. Thin wisps of fog hung in the air.

Celia Zwaan stood down below in her smooth white swimming costume, swinging her legs above her head. Every morning she did her gymnastic exercises outside, whatever the weather.

We tiptoed away from the balcony and went off to investigate. In the house we scoured the corridors, looking for Miss Elisabeth, and tried all the doorknobs carefully. Were we allowed to let her out? We didn't know what room she was in. She might be anywhere, since all the rooms were locked.

In the extensive loft, where Granddad Smit's toy train was set up, you could hear the rustle of the rain in the thatched roof. Celia showed us that the trains really worked. Bells rang at stations and red signal lamps went on and off.

"Don't tell anyone, we're going to stage some accidents."

Giggling, she made the locomotives crash into each other, laid tunnels on their side, and put toy sheep and carts in the middle of the track, so that the trains derailed. We begged her not to do this, because she was tempting fate.

In an attempt to appease it, we let our carriages chuff to the land of the white-capped black mountains with exemplary efficiency.

"Switzerland! You'll be going there too very shortly."

"No we won't, we're going to England."

"You have go to England on the boat," said Celia Zwaan.

Tinka and I looked at her in disbelief.

"Impossible, our boat's gone."

"Where there's a will, there's a way," answered Celia.

.   .   .

Celia liked walking, and every day she took us out with her on her walks in the dunes or through The Hague.

The Hague was different from Paris and London because it wasn't a city, but a village, a creature of fable, an unhappy unicorn. The last of its kind in the world. It had been sitting sadly by the seaside staring after the ark that had disappeared. It was on the point of drowning itself in grief when it had been struck down on the beach by a hunter's arrow. It had stretched out and had fallen into a dream-filled sleep, which might last for centuries. Celia made a sketch and showed us on the street map where the unicorn lay on the coast. The head rested in the dunes, on pillows of sand. Farther on, the horn stuck out into the sea. Closer to us were the legs, and behind us lay the long tail on land. The ivory carcass was the houses where people lived. This had all been lovingly covered with a lace bedspread by the wind. If we looked carefully, we could see the white layer on all the buildings. We could taste it if we wanted. We took a lick and had to admit that the bedspread had been spun from sea salt.

In the late evening we walked with Celia Zwaan toward the sea along one of the unicorn's legs. She'd brought an umbrella, but it wasn't raining. We didn't meet anyone.

"Aren't there any people left, Celia?"

"They're dead or asleep, that's what The Hague is like."

In The Hague I saw for the first time indoor people in the windows of the houses, living an indoor life among their indoor plants. We weren't supposed to look, but we did. We saw the people sitting in dusky light, and weren't sure whether they were alive or dead, as they didn't move.

Between the old tall trees along the avenue there were lanterns, the light from which shined through the foliage. Our faces glowed green in the darkness; we weren't asleep and we weren't dead, but something in between.

·   ·   ·

It was a pitch-black hole that we were peering into, at the end of our evening walk. We could go no farther; we were standing on the sand and the sea came up to here. We could hear it hissing, growling, and saw it for a few seconds. The beam of the light-house swept across it. First we heard its menacing sound, then it was revealed in a flash of light. The sea was dangerously black and gleamed like a *kris*. It was tossing foam at us as a warning.

Behind lay the carcass, in which lamps were lit.

To the side we could see the unicorn's horn in the sea. There seemed to be a fair on. The horn was decorated with strings of light that swayed to and fro in a gentle breeze. People were walking up and down arm in arm, laughing and having fun, leaning over the railings and whistling. They paid no attention to the sea at all. Were we going onto it too? Celia said, "The Wilhelmina Pier is out of bounds for tropical children."

Children who came from distant countries like us, and were still up and about so late, had better not show themselves in public.

Suddenly all the furniture in the Dutch house was covered with white sheets.

"Have they got sheets on because the tables and chairs have to sleep?"

"Tables and chairs don't need to sleep."

"So why are they under sheets?"

"Because otherwise they'll get dusty."

"Does dust make them ill?"

"Well no, oh all right, have it your way, Nosey Parker, the tables and chairs have to go to sleep because we'll be leaving shortly."

"Are we going to England soon, Celia?"

"You'll see for yourself."

We played acrobats on the wooden floor. We were given ballet lessons by Celia Zwaan. Tinka didn't really do her best: the new steps she learned made her laugh.

"My little brownies, I bet you can dance like Mata Hari. The secret of your blood is the natural feeling for rhythm. Let me urge you to defy gravity; it's only a question of will."

It was Celia's wish that we should dance on her birthday. She had cajoled Tinka into giving one last performance of the dance that the gods had forbidden her to do. Celia kept insisting, saying that we were in Holland after all, and the gods of Bali couldn't see this far, so it couldn't do any harm.

Celia accepted my performance as part of the deal. "You do whatever takes your fancy, Louise, it'll be fine. You can do anything because you're still young! You haven't been spoiled by rules and systems yet."

Tinka let her hair fall in front of her face.

"What does that mean?"

"That she doesn't want to," I replied for her. Tinka sometimes didn't talk for hours.

"Why doesn't she speak, does she really not want to?" Celia sounded so disappointed that I had to think of something. I said, "It's impossible because Garuda's not there anymore."

"Who's that then?" Celia asked at first, but then she gave a squeak of surprise: "Garuda? Oh, of course, you mean the bird-god-man."

"The bird-god-man," I repeated with admiration. "The bird-god-man."

"Yes, the bird-god-man, and you know what: he's here in all his glory. Just come with me for a moment, girls. Girls with your funny whims."

She beckoned to us, and we followed her, Tinka still reluctantly. Celia shook her great bunch of keys as if it were a tambourine. She let all the keys jingle and went ahead of us up the stairs, almost to the attic where the trains were. We passed through rooms full of books, through a door, another door, and then up some stairs and some more stairs and through another door and we were in a circular room that was dusty but at the same time glittered and smelled vaguely of *kretek*. Garuda sat resplendent on a windowsill, with his back to the window.

"Ooh, ah!" we shouted loudly. "Ah!" He looked at us with bulging eyes.

"Yes, there he is," said Celia. I shook her arm.

"He has to look outside," I said angrily.

Celia pointed around her. "There are windows all around; he can look out everywhere in all directions."

We scarcely dared look around us. We were suddenly in a piece of the world that we knew very well, but it was no longer as we remembered it. Everything was deathly quiet. Small. Desiccated.

"This is Granddad's shrine," chuckled Celia.

"I'm not allowed in here at all. No one is allowed in here. It mustn't even be dusted or cleared up, as you can see! What a mess."

She strode up to Garuda and took him unceremoniously in her arms. She motioned to us with her chin.

"Ups-a-daisy, girls, off we go. Let's get this show on the road."

The following day was Celia's birthday, August 4. She was twenty-three.

She had put Garuda on a chair in the front row. It was only a wooden kitchen chair—there was nothing else for it—because in an armchair he toppled over. There were at least twenty chairs of all shapes and sizes arranged in rows. The bird-god-man was looking at the piano and the floor, on which we were to dance.

Behind the piano there were glass doors that were open. It

wasn't cold, but it was raining. Inside the light needed to be warm and filtered, so Celia had lowered the orange shades.

Large bunches of flowers had been picked and placed every-where in vases, for what Celia called "our matinee."

The servants would bring in dishes of refreshments and trays of lemonade in the interval.

"Are we having a real interval, Auntie Celia?"

"Yes, you bet we are, what do you think, everything here is tip-top."

When the guests arrived, Celia was still upstairs getting dressed. She was to dance first, as Isadora Duncan.

I came next, with "Improvisation" and finally Tinka, as the "pièce de résistance," not, I knew, with the forbidden dance, but with an unaccompanied "Balinese" dance.

I took the guests to the music room. There were ladies with their hair up and lace blouses, and gentlemen in straw hats and with colored umbrellas. All the umbrellas lay drying on the mar-ble floor of the large vestibule. A fairy-tale fleet with billowing sails.

My father and mother and Granny Mimi and Auntie Margot came, Great-Uncle Philipp and Auntie Flora, who immediately went over to Granddad's old piano to inspect the inside.

"Good God," she boomed, "there are newspapers in it, and I can smell stale beer."

My father said that it wasn't that bad, since they weren't expecting Rachmaninoff, and told her to sit down.

She did so, but grumbled, "Honky tonky, that's all it's good for."

Everything was as I knew it from Granny Mimi's house and it was as it once used to be at our house. Messy and cheerful. Until Casparine appeared.

All the doors front and back were open, and everyone had simply walked in, but not she. Casparine rang the bell.

I ran to the front door. She had no umbrella, wore white

gloves, and rose tall and thin from her narrow shoes with their pointed heels. She was dressed in an immaculate white outfit, which clung soaking wet to her body.

In astonishment my eyes raced upward; she had a round dark face, like Tinka's, but she had boyish, very short black hair, cut much shorter than that of my uncles and my father, even shorter than Aleida's hair. She looked as if she mustn't be touched. But she still proffered me a gloved hand and said in a flat tone, looking over the top of my head with half-closed eyes, "I'm Casparine Smit. Good afternoon, child. Are you Louise Benda?"

I had to think about that. Was I Louise Benda? Had anyone ever called me that before? I suddenly wasn't sure if I was Louise Benda.

"Right, then show me to my seat."

Inside she greeted everyone in general, with a nod, and kept her hands intertwined so that no one could shake hands with her. Auntie Margot had jumped up and gone over to her, as if she wanted to embrace her. Casparine now separated her hands and put them out in front of her, to ward off Auntie Margot.

Casparine didn't look at anyone, but cast a glance at the statue of Garuda and sat down one chair further. She placed her legs very precisely next to each other, rested each of her elbows on an arm of the chair, stuck her chin in the air, and closed her eyes.

"How are your studies going, Cassie?" cried my mother.

Casparine didn't react. After a while she said, "I've finished, Hélène."

"That's good. They must have gone pretty well. What were you reading again?"

"Law," said Casparine straight ahead.

"Lovely! Then we've got a lawyer in the family. We can use one of those."

Casparine raised her chin a little higher and said nothing more.

How were the dances? Celia could do Isadora Duncan very well, and she admired her and had seen her perform. She was such an impressive spectacle with her long, loose blond hair and her bare white top that even Auntie Flora was reduced to silence during the performance. Afterward she thundered, "Encore! Encore!"

"Do be quiet!" snapped my mother.

Next I leapt around a bit in my pink tutu, waving my arms about. Then it was the interval.

Everyone got up and walked around the room and on the terrace, except Casparine, who sat still and stared straight ahead of her. There was lemonade and tart. Flora said that she would like to see the dance again; she couldn't stop talking about Celia's daring costume.

"Good grief, that Celia's a Valkyrie; there aren't many like her."

Without anyone noticing, Tinka had appeared on the stage. She stood close to the piano, in her red, green, and gold dance costume, her head adorned with flowers. I noticed her only because she was transmitting signals or something; it was as though she were standing there glowing. Suddenly a tension emanating from her commanded everyone's attention. She was already dancing, and at the same moment I froze in the position I was standing in. I could no longer move.

Motionless and almost breathless, we watched Tinka dance.

She moved her head, her body, and her arms, but she didn't budge one millimeter from where she was standing. Her feet seemed to be sunk in the ground and yet in bursts it was as if she were raising herself above it. We could hear the music, which wasn't there, ethereal sounds around her, in keeping with the rustling of the garden and the whisper of the rain. She'd never performed this dance before.

Tinka turned away from us and for a long time didn't move. The dance was over, but no one could start applauding.

Casparine Smit stood up, raised her gloved hands, and brought them slowly together a few times. They produced a dull sound, which immediately gave way to loud applause from all sides.

Tinka rounded on us, her face taut with hatred. She tried to say something, move her lips, but nothing came out. Before anyone could utter a word, she left the room, and I immediately followed her.

Casparine's heels were tapping the wood, close behind me.

She touched me briefly on the shoulder and said urgently, "Tell her I understand, tell her."

I turned around and looked at her face close up—it was sweet and vulnerable, a night person's face.

One Sunday afternoon in August, when it suddenly became warm and sunny, the three of us danced once more under the red beech in the garden.

We had wrapped the sheets from the chairs around us and were playing nymphs in the clutches of a faun.

From the garden room came the music of the record that Celia had put on the gramophone: *L'après-midi d'un faune.* With her sturdy arms Celia, the faun, had caught Tinka, who tried to escape from her grasp. The dancers struggled silently, and after a moment it began to look like a real fight, in which both of them panted with effort.

Celia had thrown Tinka to the ground, apparently playfully. Then she took Tinka's sheet off. Celia cooed that it was wonderful when people could let themselves go, but Tinka became implacably angry.

She pulled out Celia's hair, tore her pearl necklace to pieces, and rolled on top of her. With one leg on either side of Celia she held her down. After a while she seemed to have come to a decision; with a dark expression she slowly sat up and I saw that she was wiping tears away. She sauntered off and spitefully threw the piece of the necklace she was holding in her hand into a flower bed.

Celia lay very still, and I saw her smile as if she'd experienced something wonderful.

Some passersby stopped by the low wall to watch, and at the beginning of the dance some of them had encouraged us and clapped their hands, but the mood had gradually changed. They called us names, softly at first, then more loudly, and finally they pelted us with pebbles.

Tinka walked on and without a second look jumped into the pond. At first I threw pebbles back and then I also jumped into the pond, where the water came only up to our waists. Craning their necks, the visitors stood by the wall that divided our garden from the road. A few vaulted it and ran toward Celia, jeering and threatening. Celia awoke from her dream and fled toward the house.

It looked as if the troublemakers would follow her, but as if dispatched by the gods, Auntie Flora appeared. She came strolling along the avenue with a firm tread, carrying a straw hat and a walking stick in her hand.

"*Potztausendhimmeldonnerwetter*, what's going on here?" The voice sounded like an angry gong.

"Go away! Go away, all of you, you barflies and drunks, what are you doing in someone else's garden?" She raised her stick as though about to lash out.

The people scattered and within a few seconds had gone.

Flora strode toward the pond.

With her gloves on and with a grip firmer than I had ever felt before, even from Granddad Smit, she hauled me onto dry land.

Then she took Tinka under the armpits, and Tinka allowed herself to be brought to the bank equally meekly. We daren't resist Auntie Flora.

Everyone spoke about Auntie Flora in capital letters, because she was an artist and also a good person.

She put us on our feet and dried us off with a sheet. Her privileged hands rubbed us warm, removing handfuls of water weed and other unseemly things. When Auntie Flora had cleaned us sufficiently and found us in order, she said softly, "And now I need to give you two a talking to. In the summerhouse."

We crept after her hand in hand, both fitting into the shadow cast by her imposing figure.

"Louise, dear, why did you hit Celia?" she asked me over her shoulder.

"Tinka did it," I said hurriedly, not to tell tales but on the contrary to give honor where honor was due.

"Tinka!" It came from deep down in that huge body; it boomed and resounded. "Oh Tinka, you know how to look after yourself; but do you know that it's better to stay friends with everyone? That we have to compromise and be nice and butter everyone up! Everyone, the whole world and his wife. Isn't it awful and intolerable?"

Tinka let her hair fall in front of her face.

"I know," Auntie Flora went on in a somber bronze voice, "we can't always do that. We're not the sort who can be friends with everyone. But oh, how hard it is for us, we're not bound by anything or anyone."

She sat down on the wooden bench in the summerhouse and we sat on either side of her. She put her arms around us.

"Children, children, what's going to become of us?" she exclaimed.

Our mood was full of uncertainty, which could no longer be banished by dancing or fighting or talking. Every day we were tossed back and forth between despair and hope. How often we'd had to suppress the impulse to run away, now or never, back to our own life, or in any case away from where we were now. If necessary we'd have been prepared to dig our way through the earth if only we'd emerged at the right spot.

And yet today was so warm at last that we had momentarily been thrown off course that morning: Would it stay like this from now on? Would everything become just like it used to be, here too? We soon realized that this would not happen. It was inevitable, it was the same old story: this heat, however moist and promising it might appear, would herald still more new changes.

Our attempts to run away always failed, even before we could undertake them. The gods had something else in store for us than what we hoped for.

Auntie Flora reflected, "Yes, I can feel autumn coming already. But I shan't be here when it comes. By autumn I shall be in the great free land of America. Come with me, Tinka, we two will let our Muses take care of us."

"And what about me, can I go too?" I heard myself asking.

I hoped Tinka would say, "I'll go if Louise goes too."

She said that the gods didn't approve, scarcely audibly, but I heard. Auntie Flora had too, and said, "On the contrary, the gods do want you to." She tried to stroke Tinka's hair, but Tinka pulled her head carefully away, because no one must touch it, not even Auntie Flora. Tinka's head was the place where the gods spoke to her.

"Thistledown, it's the gods themselves who have asked me to take you with me. To North America. Just as Benjamin took me, long ago."

Tinka said nothing.

"Right, then that's settled," said Auntie Flora.

The garden was full of plants that had finished flowering. Butterflies and bumblebees hung motionless in the air as if they'd given up hope.

"Shall I tell you about Benjamin?" asked Auntie Flora when we were silent.

"Yes, we'd like that, Auntie," I stammered.

Auntie Flora hugged us tightly and as a result we could hear her next exclamation from head to toe, we could feel it going through us: "Listen to me."

The tears rolled down her kind, large face, and she told us that she too was a rootless person. Just like us.

"But oh, it was a privilege to hear him play. I heard him in London, where you two are going, unless I can prevent it in time. That ossified place where the people are such mean-spirited Victorians that not even an adder up the arse can put any life in them. You know, that town with its snootiness and endless talk suddenly sparkled and purred like a nest of young kittens. Believe me, the grubby Thames started bubbling over and tinkling, and it wouldn't have surprised me if Big Ben had made a bow. It was as if Mozart were back among us. But Benno wasn't born for happiness; what difference did it make to him if he played for the great of the earth?"

He had been exploited even as a child prodigy, Auntie Flora continued sadly. Dragged from platform to platform and cosseted as a talent, but mutilated as a human being and hence unfit for love. "Which of us aren't, whom the gods have insisted on choosing?"

Auntie Flora sobbed, and we sobbed too.

"Will you promise me, children, that you'll never forget Benjamin? Will you think of him for a moment every day?"

We promised, but I didn't keep my promise.

SIXTEEN

There's no pleasure in fishing the same scraps out of the pool of memory for the umpteenth time. All this raking up hasn't made the fragments of past reality any purer or clearer. Reluctantly, grudgingly, memory yields up the filthy chunks. It prefers to behave like the proud custodian of a beautiful park in which everything is perfectly ordered, where trimming and pruning are regularly carried out, weeds removed, intruders chased off, and humiliating statues removed. Minor triumphs are placed on pedestals. Good deeds are bathed in light.

There is still the occasional land mine, so stay on the paths. It's not safe near that murky pond. Don't start dredging there. It's not like here, where well-spent days sway among blossoming flowers.

There, head-high burgeoning bushes intertwine to form inextricable knots, a whimsical gate above the lukewarm slime, where listless toads mate. But this is no garden of delight. This pathetic mess cannot be shown proudly to anyone. One must keep away or get the hell out. Nothing moves in this ooze except doubt and pain.

But I can't bypass it. We are here to learn, said my granny and my father, from both the good and the bad.

So what comes to the surface?

Pictures I can't take my eyes off of, as I tremble with rage and shame. Objects that I hate and am compelled to keep fingering, still.

Tinka's bracelet, my father's and my uncles' hats, a ginger stick-on mustache, which must be Mannie's.

Mannie liked dressing up, but for fun, not when you had to to save your life. A cap of Noski the lodger's and clothes belonging to my mother and aunt, almost too thin and frivolous even to look at, let alone wear.

Creations of Granny Mimi's, just a couple of old ones. The good ones have all been lost. If we'd lost nothing else, we'd have nothing to complain about.

Letters and diaries, notes on scraps of paper, kept anyway, a handful of ash put into an envelope, together with the green ribbons, all that's left of these fervent love letters. Pages torn from a diary. An incomplete baby book, a pile of meticulously kept account ledgers, the beginnings of a stamp collection. Cuttings from papers, identity papers with false names.

There are mementos that belong on the rubbish heap. I shan't take them there, because they'll come back anyway.

They return with taunting regularity, like warts that have been removed, with redoubled, satanic power.

Scores, hundreds, perhaps a thousand photos. Dug up after the war from Granddad Smit's garden.

For years we literally couldn't be bothered, or let's say we were too preoccupied with our new life, to have them developed.

Granddad Smit had the best of intentions when he sent Tinka to Europe with us. He swore that he had the best of intentions, and no one doubted him.

Only Tinka doubted him. I didn't.

We were back at Granny Mimi's, where Aleida took good care of us. If we were such strapping girls that we weren't sleepy at night, we'd have to devote our energy to sport.

We could feel ourselves becoming stranger and stranger. We had lost enthusiasm for almost everything.

We had already changed. Tinka's chin had become small and pointed and jutted out in a lonely way: it was as if she had to follow this small sharp bone, as if possessed by a spirit whispering things to her that only she understood.

We listened to the voices that wafted through the garden and were borne up through our window by the wind. We listened to the words as they glided down the tablecloth and plopped onto the floor, slid away, and disappeared under the carpets in the night room before we could grab them.

We no longer played at being back home.

Back home and back then were no longer ours. One night, not long after the fight with Celia in the Dutch garden, Tinka said, almost casually, "I've got to go."

"You've got to go?"

"Through the water."

"Through the water, what do you mean?"

"Through the sea." She said it with a shiver. It gave me hope. She was frightened of the sea; she'd never dare go through it.

"In the sea you've got to swim. Can you swim?"

"I'll walk."

"Is it far?"

"Doesn't matter."

"I think it's too far, too far to walk."

"You can see on your globe how far it is. It's not far."

Perhaps it was a couple of days away on the globe, even if it didn't look that far.

Granny Mimi's father had walked from Russia to Poland to Germany and then to Holland.

We asked Granny Mimi how long it had taken him.

"What a question! Why do you want to know that?"

"We want to know how far it is, because we're going to start walking too."

I had told Granny Mimi. She was allowed to know. She wouldn't tell our secret to anyone else. She'd not put the slightest obstacle in our path up to now. Whatever we did, whatever kinds of "strange pranks" we got up to, she approved.

I told her everything, but when I announced that we were going to walk back to Poppy's house and that Tinka had heard voices say that this was the gods' will, she pulled the two of us abruptly toward her. She sat us down on her lap almost roughly, on her crackling taffeta thighs, rocked us to and fro, and started to weep black tears that disappeared into her wrinkles.

"Children, stop it, stop it. Are you completely mad, completely *meshugge*? Just stay where you are. Stay where you are until the boat comes. Till the boat arrives, stay here." Granny Mimi hugged us. "Oh it'll probably all get much better soon. You silly children, giving me such a fright. You must at least have a chance to see snow. You've never once seen snow in your lives. Wait for the winter! I bet you it snows. Snow is so beautiful, you must see it for yourselves. The world becomes white and soft; it's wrapped in cotton wool. You must see that. Then you can go, on the boat."

Her voice curled around us, cocooning us.

The world and the cotton wool preoccupied us for a while. We talked it over, whispering under the table, lying on the Persian carpets, in which we couldn't find any snow.

One morning Tinka said the gods had ordained that it was to be today.

"*You* wait, *you* wait for the snow, I'm going to get started."

"Why so soon?" I asked.

Tinka replied that she had to. Our departure for England was fast approaching. Tinka had begged the gods to postpone it, and three times in succession they had put it off. Now they were no longer listening.

That night I had gone to the blue room where Tinka slept and now where my little brother also had his bed, although he didn't often sleep there. Usually he was in the big bed next to my mother, surrounded by a rampart of pillows.

The uncles were talking in the room of the Persian carpets. We could hear their voices through the floorboards. My father's voice was there too, louder than usual.

Before I went to Tinka that night, I was in my own bedroom, one of the row of white rooms upstairs where Noski also slept, where the barrel organ was and the puppet show. From up there in my room I'd seen Aleida come home very late.

Aleida clumped upstairs, sniffing, soaked through from the rain. She put on the light in the corridor and I saw her blow her nose on her scarf. She had just cycled twenty kilometers on the bike.

Aleida had gone to help her father with the boats through lashing rain and roaring wind. Then she'd put her dark blue coat back on, wrapped her red scarf around her, and come back the same distance on the bike. Another twenty kilometers, through the same rain and storm. To help us and look after us, which she liked doing, out of the "goodness of her heart" as Granny Mimi called it. I was never allowed to blow my nose on my scarf, but Aleida was. I wanted to tell her that she was allowed to do this because she cycled so far to do good, but was too cold or drowsy to get out from under the covers. Aleida came in to me, not knowing that I was awake. She ran her fingertips over my hair. "Just you sleep, lovey, you sleep," she murmured.

When she had gone, I felt my hair; it didn't curl, it frizzed, as my mother always cried helplessly. Now it was full of static electricity, I knew. It used not to be, but here it was.

I'd heard Aleida collapse into her bed with a thud; she hadn't even brushed her teeth, as she did for a long time every night.

The coast was clear. I crept out of bed, put my feet onto the cold floor, and made my hair crackle and looked at it in the washbasin mirror in the corridor. I combed my hair with a comb that was lying there, the thick, rough comb for Aleida's hair, which was smooth and had the same color and smell as the coats of Granny's Irish setters. Aleida's hair didn't crackle; it didn't jump around.

My hair crackled in a wide arc around my head, and sparks flew off it. You could see the sparks in the mirror; you could see the tiny flames leaping up. I made my hair fly around like a firework with Aleida's comb. Tinka must see this. I tiptoed to the blue room where Tinka slept, with Aleida's comb still in my hand.

Tinka was wide awake and said that she had to go. She didn't look at my hair.

I don't know when Tinka was born. I don't need to know that in order to fathom reality.

She was undoubtedly a Scorpio. The scorpion stings itself to death when it believes itself in dire straits.

I knew those cruel games where a ring of fire is put around the creature. It's not a fable, it's a reality.

Oh, astrology. An elegant pastime and parlor game. It's just as easy to blame the gods as to believe the explanations of astrologers and fortune-tellers.

Granddad Smit didn't believe in chance or in gods. A man had everything in his own hands. After the war here was over and the war there was over, he and I talked. In the room with the trains, but more often in the pub. We were on our way to the sea. We were often on our way to the sea, because he wanted to see the place where that rebellious little tyrant had thwarted him. Halfway there, on the Scheveningenseweg, we rested. We took a break in the café, where we often sat till closing time. I was never to show Granddad Smit the spot where long ago Tinka had walked into the sea.

I asked him why he'd sent Tinka away, why he'd packed her off with us.

We could have talked to each other about so many other things, but that seemed to be all I wanted to know from him, and he seemed to be waiting for that question every time. He answered in a voice hoarse with cold or emotion, I can't decide which, but he answered with great conviction that a man of honor didn't leave his bastards to starve.

"But she wasn't your bastard. She was the apple of your eye. You'd singled her out."

My granddad downed his glass. He knew very well. He had played god, and he was one still, a god. One of the white gods, dethroned now, but a god nonetheless. He straightened his shoulders.

"It could have worked. She could have made something of her life."

"Become a lawyer, I suppose, like Casparine!"

Granddad Smit opened his fist, which lay on the table.

His dark eyes turned to me in astonishment. His granddaughter, interrogating him? One doesn't call a god to account.

"She was a born dancer; she could have danced in Europe, but not over there anymore. What do you think would have become of her under that regime?"

Did I say, "Surely anything would have been better than this?"

I kept it to myself. I calculated aloud that if Tinka was thirteen years old when we sailed on the *Garuda*, she would now be twenty-six, now at the moment that my grandfather, who was drunk, and I who was also drunk and, what's more, pregnant, were sitting at a table in Bar 1, a café halfway between The Hague and Scheveningen.

He closed his fist, and banged the table with such force that the glasses jumped.

"Twenty-six, what of it? She's gone, the awkward brat, she didn't make it, for Christ's sake."

In order to console the badly shaken fire-eater—my grandfather whose bloodshot eyes were dripping with water that he brushed away with the words "Damn flu-ridden country"—in order to console him, I said to him, and I meant it, "I know full well you did it out of love, not malice."

He answered at once, "Love? No chance. It was compulsion. Love has to come from two sides."

Alcohol sometimes gives access to the evil fragments of which memory is ashamed, fragments so heavy that they have sunk to where no light penetrates, down to the rocky bed, where they've been hidden away in the basalt caverns that are the source of blackouts, blackouts that healthy, well-behaved mortals know only by hearsay.

No power on earth can gain a purchase on them, these facts that lie there fossilizing. Except alcohol, occasionally. Drunk in large quantities, strong drink is able to bore its way down through all the barriers.

The moon neither dazzled nor warmed us. We staggered on into the wind, or rather we didn't stagger, we battled against the wind, left the wind behind us, left my baby brother on the promenade in his pram.

On that occasion he was sleeping in Tinka's blue room. So we had to take him with us, to ensure no one noticed our disappearance if he woke in the night and screamed. We had dressed him, put him in his pram, and taken him down the long avenue in the darkness.

Later I pushed him back home—no, that's not quite true. He screamed so much that I pushed his pram into a side street. I left him there and went on, as if I no longer had a brother or a sister.

I'd helped her to get dressed in her dancing clothes, her loveliest clothes. Shall I tell you what she looked like before we went? I remember, but I won't.

My brother had woken up. He saw us fussing with the gold clothes and the silk flowers. He could already sit, and sat up in his cot, beaming. He was looking forward to a game or an excursion.

In her shiny gold dance costume she became a different person, and it frightened me. We looked at each other as we crept past the mirror in the hall. We were strangers to each other.

I often walk across the sand and look at the sea. I will see Tinka. I know exactly how many steps we took, how many steps we needed to reach the surf, the point where I had to go back. My brother was in his pram on the promenade screaming, but there was no one to hear him.

Although it's always different by the sea, low tide or high tide, spring tide or neap tide, although the number of steps in the sand is never the same as then, those tracks of ours have not been washed away. I walk in her tracks, I'm always following her, I can't leave her in peace. I want to make her turn around, just as I did then, when I didn't understand fate. It couldn't be woven into our carpet, and if it was, then I wanted to swap. It couldn't be true, I must take my fate in my own hands.

There we go, hand in hand. Not reluctant and unsure, but cheerful, because we know the gods will do the right thing.

If Tinka has to go to England, they'll take her there. If she's allowed to stay with us, they'll lift her back onto the beach.

Tinka couldn't swim. She was frightened of the sea.

So she mustn't go in very far, I whispered to her, the gods would understand her good intentions.

They put her back on the beach. But I didn't wait for her. I should have waited.

She was washed up, but I didn't see her. Was it her, as the others claimed? Did she drown? Did she go that far into the sea, did she dare to go that far?

I didn't see her walk into the sea, at least no more than a meter: the foam of the sea came no farther than her ankles. I walked that short stretch with her, a little way behind her. Then she looked around, over her shoulder, so angry, angrier than I'd ever seen her. She was even more alien than a stranger. Her face was hard and determined. I grabbed her arm to pull her out of the water. I wanted to pull her out of the water; fate wasn't decided yet, we could still change it, she mustn't go. The sea whispered viciously, perhaps invitingly, who can tell: the sea looked ominous in the flashes of light from the lighthouse. I shouted at her that she couldn't go without a boat.

"Go away." She pushed me away, far from gently. She pinched me; she took my skin between her thumb and forefinger, twisted it, and suddenly bit into it.

Look, you can still see the mark, although not very clearly anymore, it's so long ago, but here are the four points, a little way apart, and beneath them another, a small one. The scar is now almost the color of my skin, but for anyone who wants to know, it's a human bite, the most dangerous bite of all.

She forced me to let her go, and she went.

The gods put her back as quickly as they could, so quickly that there was still color in her cheeks, and an old man was still able to give her the kiss of life, an old beachcomber who was wandering around in the night hunting for things that shined in the moonlight. He saw Tinka lying there, shiniest of all. In her gold dress. He tried to bring her back to life—he managed to, I mean. There's nothing I'd rather say than that.

A day that keeps returning, first hourly and then daily, weekly, monthly, and so on. And later on once a year, in all its intensity, and slowly such a day becomes an integral part of life, and it's as though it's always been like that and must have been like that, as though no other pattern was possible, no other way.

NONSENSE!

They left for England on August 22, 1939, not even hurriedly, not as if fleeing, but stylishly, in the proper way, with sad and guilty faces. My mother with Simon and Auntie Celia. Auntie Margot had decided not to go to Granny Helena's with them but to stay with me. I looked so pale. I had to be pampered with eggs and the milk that I hated.

Of course Tinka wasn't with them. The fact that I remember saying good-bye to her so vividly, image by image in every detail, I ascribe to my imagination or to her spirit, which hadn't left me.

"Well, we might as well go now, Lulu. The ship's just a dot in the distance. We're well out of sight by now."

"Where are they now?"

"On their way to England."

> "White swans and
> black swans and
> who'll sail with me till we get to England?
> England's all locked up now
> the doorkey's gone and snapped now

and no carpenter, what's more
can mend it and unlock the door,"

I sang, but it didn't cheer my father up. We walked slowly toward Noski, who was waiting by the car with Dido and Ana, Granny Mimi's Irish setters. The dogs had pointed their long noses in our direction but were not wagging their tails yet. Once we got close to them they would; they would almost knock us over as they bounded with joy.

I would have preferred to run over to the group to play with the dogs for a bit, but realized that I mustn't let go of my father.

His thin, dry hand clasped mine firmly; we were walking along almost touching, my head just reached his coat pocket, which contained his leather gloves, and the fingers occasionally brushed my nose. I realized that my father, who had long legs and always took such strides that no one could keep up with him, had adjusted his steps to mine, which was why we were going so slowly. Should I call out, "Come on, Daddy, let's run"?

I didn't dare. If he were to run, he would go much faster than I could and perhaps he'd disappear from view.

I started walking even slower.

He'd tended my wound, he'd driven me to hospital like a madman in the night, he had been irritated by the bungling, he'd reassured me, and he'd also said, "A human bite is the most dangerous bite of all." Only now, when I was walking slowly beside him, did I try to make him go even slower by almost letting myself be dragged along, did I dare to ask him if her bite meant we were blood sisters.

I was convinced that when she bit me Tinka had swallowed a tiny drop of blood.

"Oh Lulu, what do you expect me to say?"

He shrugged his shoulders, let go of me for a moment, immediately grabbed my hand again, and said, "You don't have to drink each other's blood to be brothers or sisters."

I'd heard the word for the first time the day before yesterday or maybe longer ago. It was an article with photos in a newspaper that was lying around in the kitchen.

"Who brings this disgusting trash in here?" Granny would ask every time, although she knew very well that it had contained leeks and endives. My father and the uncles and Noski, and she herself, spread the papers over the table, smoothed them out, and stood reading them, frowning. When Granny came in, she would say icily, "Why don't you sit down for it?" Daddy would answer, "We're not going to do this rabble the honor of sitting down for it; we're just going to take note of it in passing. I stress: in passing."

"I wouldn't ruin my eyesight on it."

"It can do no harm to know what they're cooking up."

"A lot of good it will do us."

The words "blood brotherhood" had been in one of those papers.

Tinka and I had talked about it, the night before her departure.

We repeated what had been said in the kitchen. Granny and Noski thought it was horrible. "What a barbaric custom, disguised cannibalism, they're fine ones to call other people names."

"Why do they do it, Granny?"

"Those people drink each other's blood in order to be joined to each other forever."

"What's joined forever?"

"Never losing each other again, as long as you live, as if you're sisters—or brothers—of course," Granny had said with an expression of distaste.

Tinka and I weren't sisters; we'd never become sisters. In a few days' time we would be separated, probably for good. Tinka would stay in England and I would go back to Bandung. There was nothing for it but to drink blood sisterhood. Cautiously I'd asked Granny if you had to drink a lot of blood to be someone's brother.

"You don't have to drink any of someone's blood to be his brother!" cried Granny. "Brotherhood is a feeling; those people have too little of that."

"Do you have to drink a glassful?"

"A drop would be more than enough, child, but let them drink each other's blood until they're drunk. That's what I hope, let them slaughter each other, you're going to have a glass of orangeade, you pests, a glass of orange blood! God save our Queen and her country."

Noski brought lemonade glasses, and put his own bottle of light pink drink on the table—the homemade pepper vodka that, according to him, could fell a horse—and in his frog's voice he quacked, "One shouldn't rant and rave about this, children; a queen has blue blood, not orange."

We'd taken our bedside lamp with us under the sheet. We threw off the blankets, as they were too heavy, and sat with our legs around each other and the sheet over our heads. We'd switched on the lamp and it was as if we were floating in a white cloud. We picked the blankets up off the ground again and laid them around us rolled up into backrests, in case we fainted or perhaps died; my teeth were chattering with fear and excitement.

"Shhh," said Tinka, "there's really nothing to it. Otherwise the barbarians wouldn't dare do it."

Tinka said that as the eldest she had to be pricked first; she held the long pin of her brooch close to the tip of her finger and then very gently made a tiny hole in it. "*Aduh*, didn't feel a thing," she said triumphantly, raising the little drop of blood on her finger.

I licked it up. I wanted to know what blood tasted like; it tasted like the ship's railing—I'd almost forgotten what the railing tasted like! I saw our ship in front of me again, *Garuda*.

Tinka put her arms round me and pulled me close. She spoke softly, the words came out hollow, but I understood what she said. She quickly put the tip of her tongue into my mouth.

"Give it back, my blood. A drop is enough, we'll pass it back and forth."

Tinka opened her mouth and I put the drop of blood back in it with my tongue. She put it back in mine. Her tongue crept slowly inside, lazy as a snail. I tried to find my blood and see what she tasted like. Strange and familiar, and then it disappeared again; there was nothing but to look for it again. We fell asleep tasting each other. My mind was at rest: you couldn't become more sisters than that.

I'd always thought that Tinka and I resembled each other, even though her hair and skin were darker.

Only when she was in the sea, and looked around so angrily because I was the only person who could still hold her back, did I see that she was a completely different person. She was a stranger with a cold, hard face. I couldn't imagine that we'd lain in bed together and tasted each other.

She hadn't said good-bye to anyone, not even to me.

I pretended that she would go to England after all and not say good-bye to anyone. Only me. I saw her figure silhouetted before my eyes, saw how she avoided and eluded everyone. I saw how she intertwined her hands just like Casparine and whenever it was her turn to be kissed and embraced, stuck them out as if to ward us off. Anyone who wanted to embrace her or kiss her, or even stroke her, she pushed away. Not roughly or impolitely, but firmly.

It was very difficult to attract her attention. Finally all I could think of was to squeeze her arm to make her turn around so that she wouldn't have to go away.

I bellowed over the quayside at the top of my voice, "Don't go, Tinka, please don't go."

The others looked at me sadly.

Only when she was on the beach ready to embark on the journey, the route that we had found for her on the globe, back where we'd come from, it wasn't that far—only then did I see that she was a completely different person from me. She was a stranger with a stiff, cold face that looked frightened or angry. Was she angry or frightened?

"Don't go, Tinka, please don't go. Why not some other time? So cold now."

She didn't listen.

Tinka would hold her intertwined hands in front of her and not say good-bye to anyone. This time I did go after her; I mustn't be rooted to the spot, this time I must have the courage to do what had to be done: she wouldn't get away this time. On, on, I must go on, if necessary I would swim after her to the ends of the earth, because I could swim. I would dive underwater, look for her underwater, as far as Bali, till I found her in the warm black sea.

I was kneeling on the quayside, the water between the quay and the ship was black; I looked down, to where it was cold and dark.

She was there and she heard me at once and looked at me when I shouted as loud as I dared, "Tinka!"

Her reflection swayed like mine in the water, she came closer and closer to me; she would lay her face on mine and put her tongue in my mouth, her tongue would traverse the inside of me as lazily as a snail.

"Are you out of your mind? What are you hanging over the water for, stop those dangerous tricks. Haven't we had enough disasters?" Half crying, but biting back her tears, my mother pulled me up and separated Tinka and me. My mother dragged me with her over to the rest of the family. Everyone looked at me sadly.

Again I'd failed.

Without much hope I looked around again to see if Tinka would perhaps follow me.

She was standing on the quayside, on the beach, where she always stands, she stands everywhere. In her gold clothes, in her light-gray winter coat that is too long for her. She has a yellow scarf around her waist, flowers around her head, she's dancing. She makes strange movements that lead nowhere and yet do lead somewhere.

I was grabbed firmly by the shoulder by my mother, and was no longer allowed to move.

"Louise, don't stand there dreaming, please, just say good-bye nicely to your brother."

She let Simon, who was sitting on her arm, lean over toward me. For the umpteenth time I was astonished that there was someone who was my brother, when I had not asked for a brother at all. Never. It was virtually certain that there had been some mistake. Now that I knew about sisters and how you became one, I was really indignant that everyone called this my brother, this fat white little fellow with his bunch of strange curls. He could never be my brother. He stank of milk. I didn't want to touch him. I had never given it much thought before, I expected that he'd go away of his own accord, but now he was being insistently presented to me.

My mother kept pushing his wet, purple lips, which trembled and dribbled and pouted, against my cheek. As she did so she looked at me hopefully, and yet with unexpected menace. Angrily I wiped the wet patch from my cheek with my hand. I couldn't obey her anymore, I couldn't start kissing a completely strange baby after I'd been kissed by my true sister not so long ago.

"He's not my brother," I screamed.

"Come on, just say good-bye to him nicely," pleaded my mother. He sat on her arm pouting and dribbling, and she held me with her other hand.

"He's not my brother," I roared, tore myself free, and ran off fast across the quay, zigzagging between the people. I was certain that Tinka would follow me now. We'd hide somewhere. We'd wait until the others had disappeared on the boat. Then we'd go to Granny Mimi's house, where the bed in the blue room was and might not even have been remade yet.

Or—I didn't dare think this, but I did so anyway—we'd quickly find a boat that would take us back to our real house, and then Granny could come and Daddy too. My father had followed me and lifted me up.

"Don't run away, Lulu, we're going to stay together, aren't we?"

"Daddy, is the boat that we're going to go home on here too?"

I could tell from his voice. "Just hang on for a little bit, Lulu, and we'll go back."

I tried again. "Does our boat come here too?"

"No, that boat doesn't come here. Just hang on for a bit longer, Lulu; I don't know how long, but we'll definitely be going back one day."

He said it in a solemn tone and I whispered, "Cross your heart?"

"Yes, cross my heart."

When we got back to the foot of the gangway, my mother and my brother and Auntie Celia had already gone on board. Auntie Margot was waiting for us. She drew me into her arms. She smelled of something wonderful that I couldn't bear.

It was sweet and fierce, but I'd forgotten the name of the flower from the tropics that smells so unforgettably.

She grabbed my hand and dripped something out of a bottle. "Look, sweetie, your little bottle from Bali! Here, wave it about a bit, wave it hard, with your hand. Go on, wave it up and down in the air. See how wonderful it smells."

I moved my hand up and down and suddenly it smelled just like it used to around us. Sweet and fierce, yet soft as in a dream. Yes, it was the *kembodja*, I remembered.

SEVENTEEN

One night Mimi came to the white room where I was lying in bed. I'd been crying, but I'd made sure that no one could hear. I'd bitten my pillow to pieces because I wasn't allowed to make any sound. There mustn't be any more questions. I couldn't answer any questions. Mimi shook me until I lifted the blankets up far enough for her to see me. I said nothing.

She sat down on the edge of the bed and said, "Come on, child, come with me."

She peeled the blankets off me, pulled my pillow off the bed, took it under her arm, and led me out of the room.

In order not to wake those who were asleep, she did her best to keep her voice down, but as a result she actually sounded even louder than usual. It was when she "whispered" that her sound drowned out everything, like the hooter of a steamer. On the way downstairs she switched the hall lights on. We walked past the blue room, the door of which was shut. I didn't want to look. We passed my mother's room, where Auntie Margot was now sleeping. Where was my father's bed? I didn't know. He didn't sleep. He was always sitting talking with the uncles and other guests, in the room of the Persian carpets.

"I'm not allowed downstairs, Mimi," I whispered.

"You've *got* to go downstairs, dammit," she said to me, "how else can you get to my room?"

We went down the hall to her room, the door of which was half open.

"Can I sleep, if you keep me awake with that moaning?"

How was it possible that Mimi, of all people, should have heard me, Mimi who said to everyone that she was getting as deaf as the old servants and who spoke imperturbably through everything and everyone, as if she were the only person in the world who was talking?

While I was reflecting on this, we'd arrived in her bedroom, where there were lampshades and lamps, yellow, pink, and white, which welcomed us like a festively illuminated fleet in the dark sea.

Mimi said contentedly, "Yes, isn't it wonderful? You can look at it for hours."

She pointed to her bed, a great plateau with hills of pillows on top of which she threw my pillow with a casual flip. "Right, wherever it lands is your side, and the other side is mine."

I was about to go straight to my side, when she stopped me.

"Let's enjoy our lights for a bit," she said. We had sat in a knitting chair at a round table, at which there were dishes of fruit and titbits.

I played dumb and looked at the floor, where there was a fluffy carpet, white with no colors or shapes in it. I was glad I wasn't sitting on a Persian carpet that I would have to read. It was warm in Mimi's room, and it smelled sweet.

Her closeness calmed me down, but I didn't really know what to do with this feeling of calm. I preferred to be alone. That was still easiest.

Mimi didn't ask me anything. When I stared at her, I saw that she was enjoying her lamps with a broad smile. She rattled a bit and coughed. In between coughs she giggled and tried to say something. Was I hearing her correctly?

"Time . . . for . . . a licorice."

I wasn't allowed to eat licorice in bed under any circumstances.

"Licorice isn't sweets, licorice is medicine!"

She put a handful in her mouth at once and held the dish under my nose, with more different kinds of licorice than I'd ever seen in my whole life.

"My toothbrush is still upstairs," I said, deciding to sit on my hands, as I used to do long ago when my mother said I mustn't touch something.

"Do you think that I don't know . . . look what's here!"

Oh, on the table was my Mickey Mouse mug, with the Mickey Mouse toothbrush we'd got on the boat, with my half-empty tube of toothpaste next to it. They were all there, partly hidden behind a basket of apples. So she'd first gone to my washbasin and taken my mug and toothbrush as well!

"Come on, take some, my arms will go stiff."

All the lights stayed on when we went to sleep.

"Mimi's bed is like a mausoleum with all those little knick-knacks and rose-leaf petals," my mother had once scoffed. But I imagined it might be quite good fun to be in the grave.

Everyone went there eventually, said Mimi. Some sooner, some later.

"Do we stay there forever, in the grave?" I asked her.

"That's the question."

"What's the question?"

"Where we go to, that's the question," she replied.

Everyone was allowed to come to Mimi's mausoleum—all the people and the dogs and cats too, which were always there before we were. The world was outside and we were here.

Noski regularly lay at the foot smoking his Russian cigarettes. Sometimes he burst into song.

My father sat at the foot of the bed on the other side and occasionally joined in haltingly.

In the evenings Mimi's bedroom was like a stage, on which all kinds of people made entrances and exits. People who had been sitting and talking and picking arguments in the kitchen all day came upstairs. The prosperous gentlemen sat down in the knitting chairs. They had their aunts bring up ashtrays and newspapers after them, they stuffed licorice into their mouths or took an apple and continued the conversations with their mouths full. You were allowed to do that here, talk with your mouth full. Though Mimi had banned a number of topics of conversation, such as war and someone called Hitla.

During the rainy August it didn't get dark, but never got fully light either. It was as dusky in the early morning as it was in the late evening. The fleet of lamps large and small burned the whole day long and halfway through the night. When I was sitting on the bed in my pajamas, on the side where my pillow lay, the uncles and aunts wished me good night. And then they showed me a funny turn, as Granny called it, or a conjuring trick, which usually went wrong.

Auntie Flora had left for North America, but there was no need to worry, because one person after another played the piano, which was downstairs. Not as beautifully as Auntie Flora did, but much louder, so that we could all hear it, even upstairs.

Everyone sat dozing and listening to music, until Great-Uncle Philipp came in late one evening. He'd been traveling and no one had expected him back. He put down a bunch of faded flowers for Mimi and said grimly, "Things look bleak."

"Oh you, you let them fob you off with anything," said Mimi. "What are you doing here, brother? Don't say you've come back on my account."

"There's nothing more to do in Geneva; they adjourned the meeting."

"They adjourned the meeting? Why? Why?"

Great-Uncle Philipp climbed onto a chair and spoke seriously. "Because of the threatening situation. Our Zionists adjourned the congress in Geneva because of the threatening situation." He shook his head and growled, "So what do you need Zionists for if the situation is no longer threatening?"

There was an exchange of words, with all the uncles wanting to stand on the chair in turn, in order to have their say. Finally Granny Mimi drove everyone into the kitchen. We heard those deep voices coming upstairs far into the night.

On August 31 my father and Auntie Margot and I were walking through the woods near the center of The Hague. In celebration of the queen's birthday, I drank orange lemonade with a cube of ice floating in it on a terrace under ancient trees. Auntie Margot had a glass of orange bitter with an ice cube, which she simply stirred with her finger, absentminded as she was. She sighed deeply. "Mmmm, I expect they're having such fun in Batavia now."

We went back on the tram, and I looked out at old yellow houses with great windows that reflected the sun. Everywhere the wind ruffled the red, white, and blue flags and their cheerful orange streamers. The tram went along a quiet avenue, where the crowns of the trees touched each other so that it looked like a green tunnel along which we were riding. We passed Granddad Smit's house, where the flag was also waving, on a tall pole in the garden. I couldn't see the top from the tram, but I still squeezed my eyes tight shut.

Daddy said that he would have a pair of glasses made for me, but there was no hurry. It could wait until my mother was back. I opened my eyes wide and I didn't even dare to think about my mother being back.

"Will it be long before she's back?"

"No, she'll certainly be back in the autumn."

We drank some more orangeade at home.

It was already dark when Noski hit his forehead with his hand and said that in the festive atmosphere he'd forgotten to strike the red, white, and blue flag with the streamer. He should have done so before sunset.

"Will it bring bad luck?" I cried out, and I knew at once that I'd said something wrong, because Mimi and my father looked at me with a worried expression. Was all the bad luck in the world used up?

"Not at all, not at all!" said Noski cheerfully. He took me by the hand and took me outside, to the flagpole in the garden.

"Flags do sometimes bring bad luck, but not if they're still hanging outside in the evening. This isn't bad luck; it's simply bad form!"

The following day there was general uproar because war had broken out. I asked my father if this was bad luck or bad form.

"Both!" he answered furiously. "It's terrible, terrible bad luck and damned bad form." He cursed at the top of his voice.

My father, Great-Uncle Philipp, and the uncles all walked up and down in the room of the Persian carpets. Everyone strode through the French doors that opened onto the garden and then back again. The radio, which was in a corner and had had a large cloth over it, was suddenly blaring out at full volume. I had no idea such a loud noise could come from a radio. It thundered through everything. Hollow, booming voices and waves of sound emerged from it. In the garden the uncles listened to it, with tense faces. Aleida too. The aunts with the aprons, the aunts with the knitting needles, the aunts with cups of tea, they all came and joined us and looked frightened and angry. I didn't dare ask what was going on, and the uncles had kept saying "Shhh" anyway. I didn't ask anything, but looked at Aleida.

"Later, lovey, later," she whispered.

After I had played with the dogs for a while, I strolled back by myself to the workshop. The sun shined warmest here because of the many windows. I waited for Granny Mimi.

She didn't appear. I looked outside and saw her still standing in the garden, in her checked taffeta dress. She stood silently with the company, who were talking their heads off at each other. It was not like her to stay and listen to the uncles' arguments for so long. She never even listened to my father for very long.

The ladies who worked for her, who were usually very willing to talk to me, weren't in the mood today. The three of them sat on the bench in the garden and had gone on mumbling incessantly, "We must get away while we still can."

When no one came into the workshop for the whole morning, I went to Mimi's room and looked round the corner of the door.

There lay my granny, on her majestic bed, with her checked dress still on and her buttoned-up shoes too. There was a cloth over her eyes.

"Shall I fan you, Mimi?"

"No, darling, I'm quite cool enough."

"But that cloth over your eyes . . ."

"A wet cloth is good for nerves."

"What nerves, Mimi?"

"Oh, the war has knocked the stuffing out of me."

I saw the war knocking the stuffing out of us, a huge pig, as round as a globe, coarse and fat. It was pulling an anxious face, because the springs of the upholstery were sticking in its bottom.

My father came in. He'd already sat down on the edge of Mimi's bed when he saw me, on her other side.

"Lulu, why don't you take the dogs outside; Granny must rest."

"I've only just arrived, and so have the dogs, Daddy; we've been outside for ages."

"Yes? Well, go to Aleida, and she can play with you. She's back, you know. She's upstairs in her room."

The white attic had been the living quarters of the two fat servants who had moved away. Aleida had replaced them.

She now had to look after our whole household, said my father. It was brave of her to stay.

She slept in a room the door of which always stood open, and washed in the hall. She didn't mind; she never minded if I came up alone or with the dogs. Aleida smelled of dogs too, and of horses and hay.

I often looked at her while she washed.

I had the best view of the washbasin in the hall from a small white room. There were several rooms in the loft, but when I crept upstairs in the mornings, I preferred this one. There was a window in the roof that afforded a view of the sky. There was a narrow, iron bedstead with a lumpy mattress. Above the bed hung a crucifix with a half-naked Christ on it, which was no longer dusted by anyone. The old servant had forgotten to take him with her. Before I got into this bed, I bowed my head deeply before the man on the cross, who was the son of a god. The servants had done that too. I wasn't very good at making the sign of the cross like they did, because I didn't know exactly where to start. No one in the house was prepared to teach me.

At Mimi's the son of the god was in the souvenir drawer. That was where Mimi kept everything that was precious to her. Such as the portrait of the Good German, who had been her husband, and his gold ring and a watch and a pipe with a long, bent stem. There were also little photographs of Mr. Benjamin at the piano, when he was young and had no beard. There were yellowed letters, some of them with musical notes on them, written in ink that had faded so badly it was almost invisible. Nevertheless, she often looked at these letters, purring with pleasure.

With her eyes squeezed tight shut she'd stand there, not reading but singing. She sang the letters and beat time with her fluttering fingers.

I woke up early in the morning. Granny Mimi was still asleep then. She never noticed me leaving our bed, tiptoeing out of the room, and groping my way upstairs. The sky that I saw through the skylights was still dark blue with night.

Aleida appeared at the crack of dawn.

It was outrageous, the way she leapt out of bed and immediately bounced up and down on the wooden floor, trotted to the hall and back again in her bare feet. She clicked her tongue, yawned with her mouth wide open, and stretched in all directions. She clapped her hands and smacked her own cheeks. She rubbed her arms and her thighs; she kept making the same movements, and she made more and more noise. Aleida began the day with wild leaps and cries.

I would have liked to be the same; I'd have liked to learn how to get out of bed that way too. I would have liked to roar with excitement. Instead, I crept out of bed, was silent and ashamed, and announced my presence by getting in her way. I was immediately given a cuddle, though she didn't even have her clothes on yet.

Aleida cuddled me roughly; her hugs were more painful than pleasant. Yet I was prepared to undergo these torments for as long as I could bear them.

She sat me down on the cork stool that was at once hard and soft.

"Is washing in the washbasin better than having a bath, Aleida?"

"Lovey, I've got no time for bathing, it's already getting on for six."

"If I run the bath for you, it might be quicker than washing."

She leapt up at me, wet as she was, with the flannel still in her hand, and she hugged me again.

"Lovey, aren't you my lovely monkey? Would you really do that for me?"

"Yes, Aleida, I'll do that for you."

She burst out laughing and sniffed and shook her hair, like a dog. She was even more cheerful than all the dogs I knew.

"Then we must try it!" she exclaimed.

"Tonight?"

"Yes, tonight."

I never ran the bath for her. On the day that war broke out in Europe, I was terrified that Aleida would ask me to run the bath for her. As if that wasn't bad enough, she might want me to come and sit in it with her, as she had already announced. "You can come and join me, lovey!" That was never to happen.

War may have knocked the stuffing out of us, but it hadn't put an end to teatime; everything went on as before, for the autumn that followed and another winter.

I made sure to keep out of Aleida's way so that she couldn't ask me anything. Because of that I had to keep away from my father too, because Aleida was always hovering around him at teatime. She kept giving him inquiring looks.

I never noticed her actually asking anything, though. It was because she was ready to wait on him that she looked at him and stayed around for so long. She wasn't normally one to hang around, quite the contrary. She wasn't like the fat German servants who were always in the background arguing about everything and dropping everything and finally, moaning at the top of their voices, knocking over a table. We all loved the fat German servants, but unfortunately they'd left us.

Aleida did all her chores equally quickly and efficiently, as if she were playing tennis. She did tea in a trice. Everything was there before you realized it. Teapots, tea sets, covered tureens of steaming soup, dishes of food, baskets full of biscuits and fruit, *bonbonnières*, vases of flowers—everything was brought in, and Aleida had left again on her nimble feet before you had seen her properly. But she had been there, you could smell it: her sharp scent still hung in the air.

Aleida wasn't easily upset. Floris Crone always said that she was a winner, "Coolheaded and resilient."

I thought they were lovely words, but I confused them. By practicing with Granny I finally mastered the words, "cool-headed and resilient." It meant that Aleida wouldn't admit defeat.

Except perhaps at the hands of Daddy, who didn't pay much attention to her, who was aloof.

Aleida asked if my father disliked her. I replied that I didn't know. "Shall I ask him?" I offered, but she begged me not to do that under any circumstances, so I didn't. It did cross my mind, though, that it might have been better if I had said that my father thought she was very nice and sang her praises. Because he did: he was always encouraging me to go and see her. According to him, I could learn lots from Aleida: tennis and riding a bike and skating, for example.

My father had said for all to hear—and in the kitchen at that, when the stern uncles were still there—"Aleida is a woman with a heart of gold."

In the bed in the white attic room, I first asked forgiveness from the son of the god, and then asked him what crime was more serious: saying things that weren't true, or not saying things that *were* true.

My father said it could do no harm to say everything that you knew, although you couldn't always be sure what was true and what wasn't. Granny Mimi said, "What rubbish, you say what's in your heart and that's always true."

What was in my heart was that it was none of Aleida's business what my father thought of her, because he was my father and not hers.

But when she brushed my hair in the evenings, I wasn't sure if I should say this to her, even if it was the truth. So I thought of something else.

"Daddy likes you, he says you've got a heart of gold and he says—" I was adding more to the list when suddenly the brush scraped spitefully down my bare back. I realized I'd said too much.

Fortunately she didn't ask anything, but said happily, "Look at the sparks flying off it, lovey; just look at all the flames coming out of it. Look, little lovey—fireworks in your hair."

Since war had knocked the stuffing out of us, Auntie Margot was more often sick than well. She kept trying to telephone the whole time but she never said to whom and it was always in vain.

She lay on the settee by the open balcony doors in my father's room, because that was where there was most light and she could at least read. She read almost nothing but letters anymore. She no longer liked books, because all the books that she read made her cry. But sometimes she had to, because "*ajo*, well, it makes time pass a bit quicker."

Auntie Margot said that this room wasn't too bad, but that all rooms in Holland were too dark. She wouldn't have said something like that before. On the contrary, whenever my mother complained about dark and stuffy rooms, Auntie Margot would cheer her up. "It's not too bad, Hélène!"

Now, though, Auntie Margot no longer thought anything was any good.

She was a bit overwrought because of what was going on, said my father.

After my first day at school in Holland I tried to leave my memory behind. I didn't entirely succeed.

Of course everyone asked me after the first day what it had been like. I would have liked to say I didn't remember or tell them I had spent the day in an icy cage, silent and motionless, watched over by a witch, flanked by goblins and dragons.

But that wasn't true. It wasn't that bad, and yet it was worse. There was a fat schoolmistress, with a pout and a singsong voice, who had been nice to me the whole day. She tried everything to get me to talk. She put her silver hair band in my hair, but I pulled it off and threw it on the ground. I'd almost spat at the teacher.

At home Aleida took me by the hand and led me into the garden room, where it was teatime. I pulled my hand away and ran to consult my father about Auntie Margot.

She must have been really overwrought to take me to that wretched school that day. I didn't want to go to school, but she told me I had to. I regarded her behavior as a definite sign of a serious illness. She'd sat next to me on a little chair for a long time, but when the other children went on sniggering and whispering, she had gone. She had heard me screaming when she got to the door. She hadn't come back. My aunt was ill.

I knew that my father made sick women better, and that he later came to us to show us their babies. I asked whether he could give Auntie Margot a baby too so that she'd get better.

"No, it's not as quick as that or as easy as you think," said my father. "Auntie Margot must go back to Bandung as soon as possible, that seems to be the best thing."

"Can we go too?"

"No, we're waiting until Mummy and Simon are back."

"Are they coming soon?"

"When the war's over."

"Will the war go away soon?"

"We hope so."

·   ·   ·

Auntie Margot rose slowly from the settee; her face was wet, with tears or sweat. Her dress was sticking to her.

"Are you hot, Auntie Margot?"

"Oh, nice and hot." She sat back slowly.

"Did it go all right, darling, tell me, come on!"

"Mm," I said, crawling over her and on across the settee to the balcony where Mimi's houseplants spent their time outdoors. There were little palms and flowering plants, with bees swarming around them. The red roses, which began down below against the house, had climbed up along the walls and were wrapping themselves around the balustrade, which they were not really supposed to do because this was the domain of the wisteria. I'd never seen it flower. That would happen next spring, and it would be one big Festival of Blue, Mimi had predicted. I really must experience exactly what a spring was for myself.

"Spring, when the new year really starts and everything comes into bloom. A new beginning!"

Mimi's red roses were called Paul, and she dubbed them her "cheeky boys," which had to be kept in check now and then.

No one had time to keep the roses in check, so they went on up and up undisturbed.

On the balcony, with my back to Auntie Margot, but with eyes in the back of my head, I put my hand on a proudly upward-straining branch with two roses on it. The roses were on their way up, to the room where Aleida slept and I sometimes also slept.

I grasped the branch firmly and felt the thorns pressing into my flesh. I gripped the stem even more firmly and tried not to make any sound. The harder I squeezed, the less pain I felt. I let go of the rose and licked the blood off my hand.

I squatted down on the balcony and let Whitie, Mimi's old black-and-white tomcat, smell my bloody hand. He sniffed and sniffed again, and turned away as if insulted.

Auntie Margot had put the book, which she wasn't reading anyway, on the ground and looked at the display I was giving with sad approval, as if she understood everything. She stretched out her hand to me.

"Was it that bad, Lulu, darling?" she asked a few times with her lips trembling. "Just you come here."

That morning I'd been given a send-off to school that was supposed to be festive. Auntie Margot and I sat on the backseat of Mimi's car in our best clothes; Noski was at the wheel, and for that occasion he had put on a cap and curled his mustache upward.

At the garden gate we were seen off by Mimi and my father. Auntie Margot was allowed to go with me into a downstairs room, called a classroom. The word "classroom" described it perfectly, and I could bounce the word from one side of my head to the other without a sound: a cold, clammy room, with bare walls and hard wooden benches that all faced a gaping black-board. "Classroom, classroom"—nothing could be more heart-less and inhospitable.

"Mm, let's find a nice cozy place for you," said Auntie Margot. A fat woman came up to us and said with a smile that went from ear to ear, "Where is this little miracle going to? Where shall we put her with her long pigtails? Yes, she's a miracle, Hélène's child!" She rattled on. "Imagine our little bluestocking Hélène having such a lovely child. A little pear drop she is, we'll put her right at the front, then we can all see her properly."

"Pear bug." The words crept down the row of children, and in my mind's eye I saw a squashed caterpillar in its last throes.

A little while ago I'd found a caterpillar at the bottom of my milk mug. It was dead. I didn't know it had been there, when I had to drink up the milk. From that day on I no longer drank milk. My father didn't mind, but Auntie Margot and Aleida thought otherwise. They thought it was because of the mug, and had found a new mug for me, a light-blue one on which there was a picture of a child in a hooped skirt. The child in the hooped skirt was drinking from a light-blue mug with a picture on it of a child in a blue hooped skirt, drinking from a light-blue mug, which was too small to see if it in turn had a child with a hooped skirt on it. The mug, which had been found somewhere at the back of a cupboard, was now my own mug, and I drank water from it, and sometimes tea, but never the cold milk that was poured out for me at the breakfast table. As soon as I had a chance I gave that milk to the cat or the dogs or to the little *waringin.*

That morning I hadn't done that, I had left the milk in the mug, but today was so unusual that no one had noticed. There might have been another caterpillar in its death agony, or drowned, in my mug today.

"What are you dreaming about there?" asked Miss Guillaumine.

She pushed me by my arm into the front desk in the middle row, from where I immediately escaped on the other side. I don't remember anything else. After some skirmishes, with Auntie Margot finally letting me have her silk scarf into which I could cry to my heart's content all day long, I arrived back where I'd started, the front desk in the middle row. All morning I kept peeping with one eye at the door through which Auntie Margot had disappeared.

Miss Guillaumine, clapping her hands, said that I was like my mother.

"But my how she could chatter, our Hélène. Not you, though, eh? Chatter, chatter, chatter, our Hélène, and you're sitting there like a block of ice without a tongue in your head."

Miss Guillaumine tugged my hair.

"What pigtails, what pigtails."

All the children had looked at them and laughed loudly.

"We have to get used to the things that are new in our lives," said Auntie Margot slowly, "and then get used to it again when things don't go the way we want them to. Yes, you have to get used to life in general." She sat up again to look at me. "Get used to it, get used to it, get used to it, and especially: have patience!"

I'd opened my hand and wiped it clean on my dress. I knew I mustn't, but I didn't care anymore.

Auntie Margot saw what I did and stopped speaking. After looking at me for a while, she lay down again and pulled the cover over her head. I heard her sobbing.

Instead of saying that I wanted to go back with her, back to Bandung, I lifted the cover up a little and said in her ear, "I don't want pigtails anymore, Auntie Margot. I don't want pigtails."

In December King Winter came. We were given the day off because there was a severe frost and there were winter sports. There was a winter sun that grated on your eyes, and a winter wind that cut your forehead in two. I didn't know what winter was and how long winter could last.

"Shall I tie your skates on? Then we can go for a whirl on the ice," suggested Aleida, in an exultant tone, as if she were giving me the prospect of the greatest pleasure in the world.

"Oh come on, please explain to the girl what that means," Granny Mimi asked her. "The child thinks ice is for eating."

On Frisian skates I learned from Aleida how to slide across the hard black water. At first I struggled behind the cork stool. After that I scrambled along without a stool, with legs that slipped out from underneath me and arms flailing like windmills.

One day my father came too. He skated in curves and made figures of eight as if there were nothing to it. He gave Aleida an arm. They both used the outside edge. I watched them.

There wasn't much to see except the dead trees without leaves and people in woolly hats. You could skate on the outside edge, and in figures of eight, and in curves, and go back and forth across the pond in the woods near the center of town.

I wondered if the fishes would be looking at us, in their glassy element; they must hate me because I kept falling on their roof.

EIGHTEEN

It was Friday, May 10, and war had now descended on Holland too, with a rain of bombs and grenades. It was now close enough to harm us. When bombs came and antiaircraft fire or a hail of bullets, we had to lie facedown on the ground. The war had come through the roof and was raging violently through the country. It was looking for victims. If it saw us, that would be the end of us.

Two days later Auntie Margot left for Amsterdam in a tearing hurry. It was a chance in a million, an unbelievable stroke of luck, a miracle, said my father, that she managed to get a passage on the *Johan de Wit*, the last boat sailing to the Indies.

I didn't have to go to school anymore, as we couldn't venture through the hail of bombs without putting our lives at risk.

When Granny got up, in the middle of the night, to prepare for her last show in her workshop, whether or not it went ahead, or when she spent so long poring over her Tarot cards that even candlelight started hurting my eyes, then I crept upstairs, to the white bedroom, where no one was staying. Noski still had his room up there, but he himself had gone. He had taken people, animals, and cases to safety in the car. He had taken the aunts and uncles with him to the land of white chocolate.

Great-Uncle Philipp and Daddy and I saw them off. Later we put Philipp on the train, as he was going back to Paris. His cats would stay with us, until peace returned.

It was a warm spring day. The sun was shining, and Mimi and I were in the garden feeding the little dog. It was given meatballs from the soup, because it was a war casualty. It hadn't been hit by bullets, but by flying glass.

The dog had slunk into the house one afternoon after the air-raid warning, via the back garden. It stood squeaking diffidently by the kitchen door.

"A war casualty, I'll do something about it, I can't help it," said my father. "Glass in his paw, we can put that right."

Granny sat on the garden bench, and I fed the dog. She told stories about her father, who had sometimes called himself Arthur Regenfuss, the name that he found on a discarded, green-encrusted nameplate in Frankfurt, on the banks of the River Main. "He thought: you never know. A wonderful name like that might be useful sometime. And do you know what that means, Regenfuss?"

I knew and I was just going to say when Aleida came up the garden path with bicycle and all. She immediately turned to Mimi and said excitedly that a board had appeared by the tea-room of the tennis courts saying, "No Jews."

In protest she had immediately turned back in her tracks. She told us about it indignantly, threw her hair back and cried in an angry tone that she would never go back as long as that board was there. That would teach them! They would no longer have a tournament player.

Out of pure habit Mimi had begun her regular speech about the bikes.

"Now we've had a shed built for those machines, with a wide entrance, right by the street, couldn't be easier, so that every Tom, Dick, and Harry doesn't come charging in here onto my lawns with his machine. . . ." Her words came slower and slower, and suddenly in midsentence she said with a note of surprise in her voice, "Well, that's a fine thing, why are they getting involved in that nonsense?"

There was a silence, in which I shook Mimi's knee and said softly, "Rainfoot."

"Just a minute, dear; no, it's not Rainfoot."

She patted my hand, which lay on her knee.

Meanwhile Aleida was talking about a gentleman who had observed that he supposed they wouldn't mind Jews continuing to pay their bills here. He had breathed on his glasses and wiped them with his tie, and then he'd sat and smoked a cigarette under the board.

"But I don't know if he was Jewish."

"Wasn't he Jewish?" asked Granny.

"How am I to know, madam?"

"Yes, you're right there. But he means well by sitting there, whether he's Jewish or not."

"Those signs mustn't be put up," said Aleida fiercely. "Never. They look so mean and miserable, just as if it said 'No Dogs.'" Aleida put her hand to her mouth. "Oh, I'm sorry, madam, I didn't realize, oh, that poor child."

I looked behind me to see what child she meant. Was my stupid little brother crawling around her again, now it was dangerous, forbidden? But that was impossible; he was in England with my mother.

"Sit down quietly, my girl," said Mimi to Aleida, gesturing to the bench, "sit down over there and get over the shock."

"Rainfoot, Rainfoot," I hummed. The new dog lay stretched

out on his back in the grass. I'd fed him and now I was brushing him. He kicked his front paws cautiously as a sign that I should go on. Mimi's cat Whitie had also come up stiffly. The fact that he ventured onto the grass with his old paws meant that it was going to be very warm and that it would stay warm for a long time. Whitie was a better predictor of the weather than the reports on the radio and the barometer in the hall.

"Tell me, Whitie," muttered Granny. "We know it's going to be nice weather, now. But when will this madness be over? Tell me, old salt."

Aleida announced that she had sat down for long enough, she was going to do something, and she lowered the orange-and-white-striped blinds.

"Or are they not allowed anymore either? I've heard they've banned African violets and marigolds from gardens."

Everything seemed summery and calm, unless there was an air-raid alarm. Then we had to go inside as fast as we could. It got brighter and warmer every day. There were no more lodgers in the house. Auntie Margot had caught the boat by the skin of her teeth, and all the aunts and uncles had gone.

Aleida's presence filled my life, so much so that I began to forget everyone, even my mother and my brother.

There was no time anymore to think of anything or anyone else. When Aleida had her household chores to do during the day, I dogged her footsteps. We didn't play tennis anymore, though, because it wasn't a good game for me. I couldn't see the ball coming, and she didn't want to play on, as Uncle Felix used to, without a ball.

On this day, which was already like a summer's day, my father was sitting upstairs writing a letter. Now and then we saw him walking back and forth across the balcony. We heard him more than we saw him, because the wooden boards creaked. Whenever he leaned over the edge of the balcony to look at us, Mimi called all kinds of things up to him. That he mustn't forget to send our love and lots of kisses. She also called up, "And you can say that our fuchsias are coming out. You must write that, because fuchsias are very important in England, son."

"Anything else, Mimi?"

"Do you know there's a 'No Jews' sign at the tennis courts now too?"

My father leaned far over the edge of the balcony, whistled, and pointed with a shake of his head to the "bad" neighbors on the other side of the hedge. What was bad about the neighbors, I didn't know.

"To hell with those neighbors," hissed Mimi. "They can get lost for all I care," she added loudly.

Immediately she said to me, "*I* can say that because I'm an old woman, but *you can't*, do you hear me?"

Mimi took my hand. "Help me with my shoes, darling."

She had shoes on that were bound round her ankles with dark red ribbons. When you loosened the ribbons, you also had to undo three or four buttons. In the past Noski had often put Granny's shoes on in the mornings, complaining that such a vain woman deserved to break her neck on such heels. She tried to kick him when he said that, but Noski held on to her feet firmly. I had seen that, before sliding her shoe on, he brought her foot to his mouth and bit it, softly probably, because Mimi hadn't said anything, she just leaned back a bit and had called in a growling voice, as she could sometimes do, "Talking of vain fellows, I know one."

Mimi stroked the grass with her bare feet, which were so smooth and white that they seemed to belong to someone else.

My mother, for example, who was also smooth and white, all over. Mimi's face was dark, with freckled skin that was cracked everywhere. She said that it was because her face was already almost a hundred years old. Weren't her feet a hundred years old then?

"Oh, they were always indoors, with their eyes shut. They

haven't seen much of the world. If you haven't seen anything of the world, you stay young and beautiful."

And she told me a story about a convent where nuns lived. They were white as salsify under their black habits; they all had the white bodies and the same faces with eyes and little mouths they couldn't even open or shut anymore. My father called out over the balcony, "What kind of nonsense are you filling that child's head with, Mimi? None of it's true!"

Granny answered that it was man's fate to seek in vain for the one truth.

"What is man's fate, Mimi?"

"Man has his fate in his own hands," she said solemnly. "His fate is written in his hand. I'll show you."

I leaned against her and let her read my palms. She carefully followed the lines with her pointed nail, she pointed out lines around the wrist, the children that I would have, successes, she sketched my future as if it were a fairy tale. It was music to my ears; I let myself be lulled by the sounds that flowed through me. She spoke about my life and hers, which had lasted for so long. She was old, look what a long lifeline she had. She showed me the line in her own hand, which was always trembling and which, when she pointed to something, was rather like a fluttering bird. Imperceptibly we'd come back to the miraculous life of her father Rosenblueth alias Regenfuss, whom she liked talking about so much that I knew him almost as well as Noski, who still actually existed, even though he had gone away.

Mimi often said that she would be going away too. She sometimes said with a smile that she still had a bone to pick with Benno Silbermann.

"What kind of bone, Mimi?"

"Oh, that's between him and me."

I asked if she was angry with him.

"Oh no, I forgave him long ago."

"Are the gods angry with him?"

"Oh, I'm sure they're not, they're happy with good musicians."

I thought with relief that we had appeased the gods with his treasure.

Finally Mimi really did go away. Not completely for me: I'd just had time to save bits and pieces of her, but for the time being I had put them in my emergency suitcase, which the bits and pieces didn't mind because they'd never been used to daylight or fresh air. They were the letters and photos and the drawings and ribbons and old flowers that had been on the inside of the cupboard door. I had realized that she wanted me to keep these relics; otherwise she would have destroyed them herself. After all, in her passion for clearing up she'd burned a large part of her own hats and dresses. We'd run up and down from the glass workshop to the bonfire in the back garden, with all the dresses from the new collection, and back hand in hand, hunting for still more booty. Until Daddy had put a stop to it and had taken the struggling Mimi to her bed. She had never got up from it again. But I, who knew the secret way to get into her room, even though it was supposed to be locked, had sat by her bed. Before my father came in, I had time to hide. I heard his footsteps in the hall, his shy footsteps, which stopped now and again, as if he really didn't want to go any farther. But his footsteps were still quick and lively enough then, not weightless and silent, like later.

At each visit Daddy stayed longer with Mimi. I got cramps in my calves from squatting in my alcove by the window, so that finally I simply sat on the floor and let my feet stick out under the curtains. He didn't see them anyway.

First he sat on the pouf near her bed, where I'd also sat. He'd stood up and bent over her; he had examined her, although she struggled. He'd come back without instruments, and she'd first made him show her his empty hands.

"You're not coming to examine me, son. Show me you've got nothing with you; otherwise you can go away again."

He'd sat on the edge of her bed and then he'd lain next to her. They murmured to each other in a language that was like German but wasn't, which sounded soft and floppy, toothless, so mysterious that I understood little of it, although I'd heard it spoken so often above my head, at the big table, by the men with the hats, who could also sing and shout in it. Mimi occasionally shouted too for a moment, but she did so in Dutch because that was clearer and she laughed as she did so, and this laughter sounded hard. I sat wondering if people who spoke different languages would laugh differently in all those languages. That was true: Mimi's Dutch laughter was angular, and the muttering laughter sounded muffled and when you listened more closely was more like crying. They were both crying into the cushion. It got louder and louder, and I put my hands to my mouth so as not to start screaming. I'd never heard my father crying. I didn't know that this was possible, and I was suddenly certain that we were all doomed. I couldn't scream, because I couldn't let Daddy know that I was here. A cold gust of wind pushed me to the ground and I needed to go for a wee-wee so badly that I wet my knickers.

"Oh, can't I stop all that now, my boy? I've seen it all," cried Mimi to my father when he started on about cures in Switzerland, getting better, and new pills.

"How will I get to Switzerland, you stupid idiot? In a plane, I expect?"

"I've heard of routes."

"Oh, nonsense, nowhere's safe anymore. Even if we had

wings, and we haven't, it wouldn't have done any good. The heavens are polluted."

"That'll pass."

"Everything passes. And I've had enough. I've seen it all. Oh yes, do you remember *Bird Flight as the Foundation of Aviation. A Contribution to the Systematic Study of Flight Technology, Based on Numerous Experiments Conducted by O. and G. Lilienthal*?"

"What are you talking about?"

"It had just appeared, Philipp had got hold of it right away, and I read it when you were just about to be born. I hoped that we would be able to learn to fly, oh yes, Philipp, you, and I. O. and G. Lilienthal knew quite a lot about it, but . . ."

"But then?"

In my hiding place I listened intently. I had two wishes in my life, one was a secret and the other was that I would be able to fly.

"And then? Then that gangster with his imperial delusions came along."

"It was our bad luck that he was an expert on the Talmud."

"Excuses. I don't want to talk about it anymore."

"Well, don't then."

"When you were born, the papers were full of song and dance about the visit of the czar. I read that word for word, in order to feel once and for all how people can waste their time."

"You never wasted your time, Mimi," said my father.

"I don't want to read any more papers, full of lies and song and dance, and I don't want to see this life anymore or experience anything else. I've seen my beautiful grandchildren, and I can go with a good grace."

After my father had kissed Mimi's hand and kissed her forehead and left her, sighing and shaking his head, I appeared, lay down on the other side of the bed in my own place, and kept quiet so that she could sleep for a bit without having to turn and cough.

"Open the cupboard, will you, darling."

She was awake. I opened the washbasin cupboard wide, so that we had a good view of the inside of the door.

Together we looked at her treasures, as Granny called them, from the bed. She blew kisses in their direction.

"Go ahead and take them, Lulu. The ones you want, that is. And don't forget my wedding dress. That's for you."

"Are you really going away, Mimi?"

"I'll never go away from you, darling, but this old skin and bone, it's more or less had its day now."

She showed me how slackly the skin hung from her arms and waved it to and fro. "It's finished. Too old. Worn out."

"Get some new skin then, Mimi."

"I'll get everything new, darling *khshives*, in a new life. A new name for a start."

"How's that, Mimi? Can you tell me the new name?" I lay on the blankets kicking my feet in the air in my dress that was still damp. I kicked in order to get warmer but also with excitement. Secrets, revelations, conspiracies—they were becoming my element.

"Germaine Friedensreich," she said with a huge grin. "What do you think of that? What's wrong with Germaine Friedensreich? Nothing, ladies and gentlemen. She is unsullied and pure in heart, soul, and blood."

Granny had closed her eyes and made elegant gestures in the air with her hands. "For a hat for that Friedensreich woman, I shall use orangey blue. So innocent at first sight. A white hood, girlish blue ribbons on her bare plump shoulders, bare with red and black dots. The blue will cover her hard head. You can smash your truncheon on it. Then she has thick, hard straw hair, and on that hard straw-colored hair the eagle and the dove have landed! Can you see them sitting there? They're speaking: 'Where thinking stops, faith begins,' said the dove to the eagle. Said the eagle: 'But the difference is, where you have faith, I still think.'"

She spoke as if she were dreaming aloud, not unpleasantly, but happily, because she laughed a lot.

While she went on with her delirious fairy tales, I carefully took her treasures off the door. The very same day I managed to decorate the cupboard door again with three crucifixes that I'd taken from the rooms upstairs. Around them I stuck all the pussycat pictures that I had.

I flew back and forth and hunted through all the rooms in the house for pictures and decorations for the inside of Mimi's cupboard door.

I gained access to Mimi's bedroom in the secret way, with the iron wire that was under the hall carpet.

I don't know if on that occasion I found time to put on a new pair of knickers. What I can't remember either—though the question now poses itself in retrospect with accusatory force—is whether I asked why that piece of iron wire was there and whether I got an answer.

Three Jesuses on their crosses were now hanging on the inside of the cupboard door. They were no longer alone. I had brightened up their surroundings with pictures of angels, roses, and holiday snaps of strange people.

You had to be nice to Jesus, because he could perform miracles, Aleida had told me. He could do everything; he could even make people rise up from the dead. *Talitha kumi*, was all he had to say, and the dead girl stood up.

When Mimi was dead, my father had opened the cupboard door, lost in thought, as if he were looking for something, and, braying with laughter, had cried, "Jesus! Where have all those come from suddenly?"

He'd sat down, not on the bed where Granny was lying, but on the pouf next to it, with his head in his hands.

"*Talitha kumi, Talitha kumi*," I kept saying. I walked up and down by her bed, on her side. Perhaps it would work with Mimi too.

My father pulled me to him and sat me down on his lap. I was eight and I didn't cry, but he did. I looked to Mimi for advice, and she looked back from the chink that had remained open in one eye. I had the feeling that she was having a bit of a laugh at us.

"Our Lulu's a big girl already and she has to give you a good example, son, blow your nose," I heard her say.

"Let's do 'Talitha kumi,'" I said to my father.

"No," he replied, "we can't do that, because Mimi doesn't want to get up anymore. We just have to accept that she doesn't want to get up." He stopped crying and blew his nose.

It actually felt uncomfortable that my father was sitting by my bed and not at his desk until late at night as usual.

He always sat there reading, in the circle of light from the lamp with the green glass shade. He would support his frowning forehead in his hand and his gold-rimmed spectacles would slide down his nose.

Now his glasses occasionally almost landed in the story of the nightingale, which he was reading to me at my bedside. I was frightened that something would go wrong if his glasses fell onto the page. Many more things had already gone wrong than we thought.

The story had changed because my father read it in Dutch, but with his German accent, which made the emperor and his steward and the nightingale into Harlequins that tried in vain to avert fate with their funny language and funny grimaces. The fact that I couldn't help crying a little again this time wasn't because of the story but because of the sight of my father, who sat there and read although he didn't feel like it, but did so valiantly because both of us were in need of distraction. He brushed away my tears with his handkerchief, even when they hadn't yet fallen from my eyes.

"Don't cry, everything's all right," he said.

"Is it all right to be dead, Daddy?"

"It seems to be peaceful. That's all I know about it."

I'd never heard my father say that he didn't know something.

When Mimi had finally gone completely, all the clothes had been cleared away, the bouquets, the photos, and even the inside door of the cupboard had been stripped of the Jesuses and the new pictures, it seemed as if the house had been abandoned by everyone.

My father sat in the balcony room, which looked out over the back garden and the cemetery, but didn't see this view, because he was sitting with his head in his hands. That was how he had sat long ago in Bandung too. In those days he hadn't even seen me when I walked past him. He sat with his elbows on his knees and his cigarette went out by itself, in his hand.

I was given a tiny spark of new hope.

My hope became even greater when smoke came out from under the door of the balcony room.

"I think we're going away, Aleida."

"Yes, we're going away. But how do you know that, lovey?"

"Daddy's sitting smoking."

IV

THE WETLANDS

(1942–May 1945)

NINETEEN

One night, after Granny Mimi's house had been locked up, we set out on foot for the wetlands. My father and Aleida and Teddy and I.

We moved in with Aleida. Our stay lasted less than three years. Three years is not long in the span of a human life, but at the time it seemed so long I thought it would never end.

The people we lived with often talked about the blessed day that would dawn, "when the war is over." It was said several times each day: "When the war is over . . ."

It seemed as if that would never happen.

When it turned out that the war *was* over, it was like a miracle. No one asked us afterward what we had been through, so we didn't talk about it anymore. It was a miracle that the war was over and we were still alive.

You don't talk about miracles too loudly or too often, or you banish them from the world.

We mustn't look back anymore, only forward.

When she returned to Holland, my mother wanted to know lots of things, particularly what had happened between Aleida and my father. I knew nothing about that.

My mother could scarcely believe that I remembered so little

about our stay in the wetlands. In fact, I didn't remember anything about it. Yes, we'd lived there, for almost three years. Or
thereabouts. That was that.

My memories are like crows, they land in swarms, wherever
and whenever they choose. They either all come at once and
make a shambles of everything, with a great hullabaloo, or else
there's nothing, just deathly silence.

The low-lying house, the garden full of flowers, beyond it the
floating lakes and the river. On the left Oude Verlaat. A little farther on Nieuwe Verlaat. A sluice gate from 1740, its foundation
stone laid by Jonas van Vloten. To the right the outbuildings of
the mill. Our storage spaces.

I have no need to dig up any of this laboriously from the fos-
silized layers of my memory. It's all there, virtually unchanged. I
can go there whenever I like, at will.

The maze with its shady plants.

The canoes, the rowing boats and dinghies, the jetties, the
winter quarters.

New chickens and goats. No more pigs.

In the village, tight-lipped old people.

Aleida's daughter, Dora, whom I don't talk to, which is child-
ish of me. And unforgivable.

At the foot of the dike stands the house with the garden with
the birch tree in it. On the dike the house with the inn. Wicker
chairs and wooden tables on a terrace at the water's edge.

I could see them from my skylight: the chairs, the tables, the
checkered gingham tablecloths, always weighed down with
stones so that they wouldn't be caught by the wind that always
blows here.

The tiled roof is visible from a great distance, gleaming red
in the sun, but not the window of my former room at the front.

I watched the days go by through a small rectangular window, which opened on an arm with four holes in it. In order to look downstairs through it, I had to stand on a stool. People who were tall enough, like my father and Aleida, could look straight through the window. And Mannie. And Mother van Vloten. Corie couldn't. Sister Corie slid through the house on a chair. She couldn't climb stairs.

I would put my head outside and look down, first over the high and then over the low roof. My eye would wander farther downward, past moss green roof tiles, till it reached the brick road by the wide canal. Two jetties and a corner of the boathouse could be seen. By the other house, the inn with the long roof, I could see the chairs and tables where the customers tucked into pancakes with bacon. I never ate bacon.

That was because of Edda, the mother of Barend, and later Barend himself. He was a friendly pig, who had his sty near the winter boats. One day he'd gone, but not completely.

Ernst Haindl rode a German DKW motorbike.

"Damn, a Kraut on a motorized baby carriage, what next?" muttered Mannie.

Heads close together, we peered out of the skylight. I repeated the sentence to myself and counted the incorrect and forbidden words. Three altogether. The next step was to fathom which of them were wrong, and which forbidden.

That was more difficult, but Mannie's lessons were like that.

Mannie was staying in the mill. He had had a breakdown because he had nothing to do anymore and had no view. He used to live in a house near the harbor, where he always had something to do and plenty to see. My father said he was a hopeless case, which is why Mannie always came to spend his time usefully by giving me lessons in life and doing brainteasers with me.

My father lived in the outbuilding. He and I sometimes sat together there with our globe between us on a table. I learned about countries and people, who were all our brothers.

During the day Mannie and I solved riddles. We drew mustaches, spectacles, and beards on the pictures on the photos that we found in old magazines belonging to the Bakker family. We investigated whether something was good, bad, wrong, incorrect, or a miracle. Knowing that was important in life.

The first time we saw him, Ernst Haindl was riding his DKW. I thought it was a big three-wheeler, but Mannie explained to me that it was a motorbike with a sidecar. There was room in it for another German, a beautiful German shepherd.

Perhaps a playmate for Teddy White, my war-wounded dog, who was still being bullied by all the cats. I jumped up to run downstairs, and Mannie caught me by the scruff of my neck at the door. Had I gone mad? Did I want to risk all our lives? I couldn't believe my ears. Yes, I'd heard him right, whispered Mannie, our lives were in danger. An enemy had descended on Holland.

I felt giddy and lay down on the bed in dismay. I hoped against my better judgment that we were playing an exciting game, and it wasn't real. But it *was* real, said Mannie. Just get it into your head: we must be on our guard. It's a matter of life and death. No one must see us and we're no one, and that's that.

We lay on the bed with our shoes on; Mannie had put his arm around me. I stared up at the ceiling, forbade myself to blink, and finally squeezed my eyes tight shut.

Downstairs we could hear Teddy yapping anxiously. I hoped he wasn't putting his life at risk. I wasn't allowed to call him. I wasn't allowed to go downstairs to get him out of trouble. I wasn't allowed to look through the window.

Mannie pulled the sheet over us, up above our heads. We lay absolutely still and took short breaths. We sank down as far as we could into the mattress. After a while, I imagined there would be no more of us to see. Anyone who opened the door of the room and glanced in would see nothing except a neatly made bed that someone had finished off by smoothing down the sheet especially carefully with his hand.

The water lies there as always. As a lived reflection of everything above. Sky, trees, bushes, reeds. The blue hull of my first canoe. Human faces and ducks' heads. The water returns everything, regardless.

The house had, and still has, shiny red-and-white-painted shutters. A new roof has been put on: the new tiles are still free of moss.

At all the windows there were white lace curtains with shapes woven into them, windmills and ships. Those curtains have gone and have been replaced with golden yellow roller blinds.

At the apex of the roof was a weathercock pointing at us.

The surroundings were charming but also menacing because of the abundant dark water that met the eye wherever you looked.

I should have preferred to turn round there and then and leave, long ago, the first time we came here.

You couldn't get beyond this point on foot. The water lay in front and on both sides of us.

We were safe, Aleida had said.

In the garden of the house I saw sister Corie for the first time. She was sitting in the middle of the garden under the tree, a silver birch. She had been deposited beneath it, an agitated, mobile figure tied to a wooden easy chair without cushions but with wheels. It wasn't immediately clear whether Corie was a person or an animal, she was so thickly swaddled in sheets and blankets.

Only her head protruded. From it sprouted a wild mop of hair, which reminded me of a hat of Mimi's, a hat still in the making, but full of promise.

The sight of this gyrating head topped by a hat trembling in time with it caused me momentarily to forget the journey we had made on foot, a step at a time through the dark.

The creature in the chair bellowed. I saw it shaking back and forth, as if trying to stifle an irrepressible fit of laughter. Instead of laughing she started singing. She sang a psalm melodiously and intelligibly.

The singing woman was Aleida's eldest sister, about whom she had said very little. Her stories were mostly about her father, how big and strong and wise he was. Why did Aleida want to steal my father if she had such a good father of her own?

The property was considerably lower than the road we had come along. It was even lower than the black lakes, which seemed to float above it. These mirroring expanses stretched to the horizon.

Behind and to the side of the house the other buildings were almost invisible. They were in dark-green wood and well hidden, merging into tall undergrowth and small but dense spinneys. Nearby I saw the well, the chicken run, the stone shed with its door open. Bicycles, ladders, shovels, and brooms.

Our journey here had begun in the middle of the night. We didn't want anyone to see us. My father and she walked side by side, taking turns to pull the covered cart in which I sat on top of our books, with almost all my clothes on. Next to me, in its brass pot, was Granddad's *waringin*, which I had wrapped in my prettiest scarf. Teddy brought up the rear. By the end of the journey his left hind paw was bleeding again.

Aleida's shoulder brushed my father's sleeve at every step. His leather gloves were in the pocket of his coat, with the fingers sticking out. They couldn't stroke Aleida's cheeks, because her cheeks were higher than mine. When she looked at him, whether speaking or not, she needed only to turn her head to the side, not upward.

She walked even faster than he did and had to shorten her stride a little. Her gait was slouching, but elegant.

It was the walk of the vixen I had come upon in the dunes with her prey. Aleida Bakker wasn't a vixen, but she looked like one.

My father pulled me along in my cart. I saw Aleida reach back with her arm now and then as if to help pull. She did not, because that would have meant putting her hand on his.

When she looked at my father, I imagined the greenish glow of her eyes in the dark, like those of a cat or a fox.

Instead of looking down, at the road, to avoid disappearing into a pothole, she looked at my father the whole time. There was no moon. Perhaps she could see in the dark like a cat or a fox, like me. She did not answer when I asked her how far it was.

In the twilight I saw her sharp fox's face turned constantly in one direction: to where my father was walking. I imagined her flicking her tail contentedly from side to side the whole time, slouching along but with a spring in her step.

She was our salvation, said my father, she was taking us to safety. We were going to hide at her place, because it was no longer safe in The Hague. Not for us, or for Tycho and his granny and father, who had come here earlier and were staying in the windmill next to the boathouse.

I did not understand the point of all this, but I was past caring. I asked no more questions. Of anyone. The answers always boiled down to the same thing anyway. Everything that happened was to do with Europe. Or the war. But often also with the rotten weather, which everyone had to shelter from the whole time here.

·   ·   ·

I had seen the vixen that looked like Aleida in the dunes.

It was quite a while ago. They were all still around then, my mother and my aunts. It happened on a walk. We finally realized we were lost. My mother, Celia Zwaan, and Auntie Margot had been sitting joking with some gentlemen they didn't know in the café where we had eaten syrup pancakes. Afterward none of us could remember the way back to where the yellow tram stopped. We wandered through the dunes in an adventurous mood. It got later and later. In the dusk, on a narrow path overgrown with brambles and impassable for grown-ups, I saw the vixen. She was sauntering off with her prey.

The sun had just set. Celia was rhapsodizing about the lilac and violet hues in the sky, pointing to the purple and mauve glow. The others were looking up and so did not see the impudent way the vixen appeared to me, flaunting her catch. She seemed to be forcing me to applaud her, as I would have done if I had not also seen her prey's still-heaving breast, the jerking foot, one of its eyes turned toward me. Before I could let loose a cry of disgust, she had gone, not skulking off, but with head held high. I despised myself for being unable to do anything to save the bird, which had looked at me with one eye, life and hope still flickering in it. I threw myself down full-length in the brambles. The bird had pinned its last hope on me, but in vain. Later they did not believe I had seen the vixen with her prey.

"Nonsense, child, you're making it up, and anyway the bird would have been dead long ago." Celia Zwaan's tone brooked no contradiction.

"Well, but . . . getting lost can make you go funny in the head," said Auntie Margot, who later teased me by asking how I could be so sure the fox was a vixen.

"I could tell she was."

The fox had had a cheerful, impudent female face, like Aleida. It was light ginger, as a fox should be. So was Aleida.

On our hike to the wetlands I saw that Aleida had only to open her mouth to catch my father. He wouldn't put up a fight, struggle, or squawk. I was afraid I wouldn't be able to save him.

To avert the catastrophe, I shouted to my father and asked him to tell me a story. As long as he was talking to me, everything was all right.

"What story would you like?"

I couldn't think of one. Then I asked if he could think up a new name for the dog. Not a place name, I added in my thoughts. I didn't want us to go to the place where Aleida lived and I certainly didn't want new Teddy to be called after it.

"Why not?" asked my father. It made me start. Had he heard what I was thinking? Or had I said it aloud?

"What about Teddy–The Hague?" I asked feebly.

"No one need know where we're from."

I didn't feel like asking why not. I didn't have the nerve to ask if we would ever go back to The Hague, where Granny Mimi had lived.

We'd never gone back anywhere before, so we'd never see The Hague again. If we thought of a name, it would have to be one with lots of mileage in it. I thought of Teddy White. The little dog had a black ear and a red patch on its back, but apart from that he was all white. Surely it didn't matter if everyone knew that, and anyway they could all see he was white.

When we finally stopped, I asked, "Are we somewhere yet?"

"Yes, you've arrived. You're at my house," said Aleida.

I tried to take my eyes off the rotund woman in the garden, tied to the wooden chair on wheels, the woman who reminded me of our Buddha in the Indies, but in a moving version. It was better not to think of the Indies, because these days it made me feel cold rather than warm. My teeth chattered.

A white cat hid under the blankets that hung down over the woman's chair. Chickens pecked away furiously.

The silver birch extended its branches so as to tower above

everything and see more of the world. We stood still on the road, arms drooping at our sides, at the top of a flight of steps leading down to the house and garden.

"Please make yourselves at home."

I heard Aleida's voice, clear and warm. In order not to disappoint her, I would have to pretend I liked it here, as if I were looking forward to my stay. If I could just become a different child from head to toe, a nice polite girl, I'd be able to manage it.

I would have to invent a child like that for myself.

I came up with Listless Louise.

Apathy took hold of me, and I would soon be asleep. It was as if someone were dressing me in lots and lots of clothes. As someone must have done with the living statue down there. Clothes round me, sheets on top of that, and blankets too. Like her, I would resemble a large, living doll.

Inside the doll the real me was still kicking and spluttering a little, but my teeth had stopped chattering and in my mind I was already feeling nice and warm.

The sluggish creature that had enveloped me took over completely. I closed my eyes and imagined I'd grown so small that I could no longer look at anything and no longer had to make anything up. She was going to do what I could no longer be bothered to do, she was obedient. It was best if from now on she said and did what was expected of me.

She was Listless Louise, whom I had invented. Everything I said myself and had always wanted to say, that we had to go back, back, back, was pointless anyway, and no one listened.

The woman who was also a doll did not laugh so that you could hear her; her mouth was opened in a silent guffaw. A bird could fly into it, one of the many twittering about and landing all over the place. They dive-bombed her head, stopping just short of landing on it, although they could not tell the difference between her and a tree.

The woman in the chair began cackling softly. Or was it crowing? When it became even softer, it was like weeping. It turned into a sad sound between giggling and weeping. The sound wanted to hop away from this garden.

Listless Louise trudged over to Aleida and rubbed up against her. Despite her age, she stuck her thumb in her mouth and closed her eyes.

Breathing calmly, she listened to the twittering of the birds.

I looked through a chink between her eyelashes and saw my father approaching and bending forward to stroke Louise's cheek or chuck her under the chin. But he thought better of it, sighed, and frowned.

"Do you feel all right, Lulu?" he asked in a worried tone. Listless Louise opened one eye slowly, and my father seemed to start. "What's wrong? Is there something wrong?"

Aleida started talking before I could get a word out.

"Would you have a look at our Corie too sometime, Doctor?" she asked.

My father immediately said with relief that he would be glad to.

Two people emerged from the main house, resembling the pollarded willows that grew all around. Though they were old, their age was not apparent from their gray hair or wrinkles, but from the many scars and blemishes caused by wounds and injuries. They moved nimbly, with bowed arms and legs as if still astride their motorbikes. They had introverted faces. They risked their lives in the cause of justice and lost them. Now they are two names on a botched monument.

Sebastiaan Bernard Bakker and Hendrik Bernard Bakker, father and son.

"We might as well show you the er . . . rooms first," said the old man. "*We* might as well do it, 'cause Mother van Vloten'd do it, but she's milking the goats," added the young man.

"We're extremely grateful for your hospitality," said my father.

Everyone acted as if we were coming to stay. For all I knew, we were.

"The, er . . . rooms aren't visible from the road."

"And we don't have much trouble with the occupying forces here generally."

"They do come here sometimes, but only to relax."

"Lucky people," said my father. "No shortage of relaxation here."

"Oh, they prefer their forests."

"We'll use the front door, then we won't have to go round the back through the mud," said Aleida, urging us along, as we were just standing there.

Listless Louise didn't ask any questions, but she didn't turn her head away either. She looked straight ahead impassively. She stuck her thumb back in her mouth and tried to purr.

Aleida put her arm around Louise. "Sweetie, we'll go through the shop first, you'll like that, won't you? A real shop."

I was a little ashamed, because when we lived at Granny Mimi's I had never played with the old wooden toy shop that I had been given by Aleida. But I made myself invisible in the tiniest extremity of myself.

Louise took her thumb out of her mouth and started jabbering.

While the real me did not know how to hide myself away even deeper, while I felt as if it might be better to die, like Granny Mimi, while I wondered what would be the quickest way to die—Listless Louise started jabbering. Louise sat up and begged, presented her paws, let her head be stroked, all at once.

"Oh how lovely," said Louise with a shriek, squeezing Aleida's arm. "Oh how wonderful! Oh Aleida! Oh how exciting, can I really just come and play here sometimes?"

As soon as Louise stopped making noises, she stuck her thumb back in her mouth, like a lolly.

"I'll show you where everything is and then you can have fun helping out in the shop!"

Aleida beamed, tugged Louise's ringlets lovingly, pushed the tip of her little finger into Louise's mouth alongside the thumb. She forced her little finger between my lips. She stretched out next to me, but I hated it. It made me retch. I started to scream, but the scream stuck in my throat and the retching surged in the other direction, downward, back inside me, making me writhe with nausea. My last reserves of strength were exhausted.

Louise took over calmly, as she would always do from now on. Listless Louise put up with the petting and petted back.

She tapped Aleida's little finger with the tip of her tongue, as if about to pronounce a letter. She sucked imperturbably on the finger, as if it were made of licorice, or her own thumb.

"Lovey," said Aleida.

The shop was full of coils of rope. Granny's Whitie was here, her vicious black cat was here, and Great-Uncle Philipp's cats. They were lying asleep on the coils of rope. I knew Aleida had brought them here on her bike in a butcher's delivery basket.

"Look who we've got here," said Aleida, pointing.

You must never lie, even if no one knew exactly what was true and what not, you still mustn't lie, as everyone I knew assured me. My father included. And you must definitely not lie to your own people. Your own people were people who loved you and whom you loved and with whom you belonged and who belonged with you.

Louise didn't care two hoots about anything. She didn't belong with anyone and so she could lie as much as she liked.

She pretended not to know the cats and turned her back on them.

"Rope! Rope!" she screamed in that funny voice of hers, as if rope were the most wonderful thing on earth. "Every color of rope, rope, rope! Reddy-ropey, greeny-ropey, bluey-ropey, yellowy-ropey, orangey-ropey!"

"We've got all the colors of the rainbow in here," cried Aleida excitedly.

While I let Louise dance and crow, I crept around the shop with my eyes on stalks. I came across still more cats, fat cats that rubbed themselves against the counter and cats washing themselves. There were some cats like ours lying asleep on the coils of rope and there were some that themselves looked like coils of black, white, or gray rope. Invisibly, I continued reconnoitering. I quite liked it here. It smelled good.

When I finally started to feel thoroughly comfortable, the child who was making such a fuss calmed down. When Louise held her tongue for a moment, I asked as politely as I could whether Teddy White could come in, with all those cats.

"Course he can, child, them's good cats, they'll give him a good hiding."

A woman with flushed cheeks and piercing blue eyes had entered the shop. She had unkempt, gray hair and wiped her hands on an apron. She had heard my question. She shuffled up to me and looked at me curiously.

"My, aren't you blond, my little pippin. Just as well," she said.

The gnarled man, the eldest one with the steel-gray tufts of hair, had come and stood beside Aleida. He had a weather-beaten, kindly face and greenish eyes; he did not look like Aleida, but then again he did.

"This is my dad," she said, putting her hand on his shoulder. "That there is Mother van Vloten. She's looked after the house since our mother died." Aleida nodded in the direction of the woman with the piercing blue eyes. "That there is my brother Henk. And we've already met our Corie in the garden."

Obedient Louise took her thumb out of her mouth and went along the line of new people shaking hands. She curtsied to all three.

TWENTY

Everything stood still in the wetlands. The sluggish countryside didn't yield up its secrets. It hid itself in rain and mist. Only the invisible cold was always there and permeated everything.

Our hiding places were not heated. In the kitchen there was a coal stove, which was fed by Mother van Vloten. I mustn't go too close; that was too dangerous. When she wasn't looking for a moment, I put my hand on it. If I were quick enough, nothing happened. My hand got warm, glowed, but didn't burn. Fire was friendlier here than water; that bit into me the moment I put my hand in it.

Fire was the only thing that she had a sacred respect for, said Mother van Vloten. It was vitally important, because it brought warmth and light.

Aleida told me that a son of the gods had stolen it from heaven for mankind and had to pay a terrible penance for doing so. He was chained to a rock and the birds of prey pecked out his liver.

And the fire was already there anyway, I said in amazement, it was lying asleep in our volcanoes. What a shame that poor son of the gods didn't know that. He didn't need to fly all the way up to heaven, he could have simply gone to the volcano on a boat.

Had my mother told me that, Aleida wanted to know. Yes, I said, long ago. "Tell me some more," Aleida insisted.

I replied that it was forbidden to talk about the past.

"That's true, lovey," she said hurriedly, "I'm so sorry, please forgive me for asking and just forget it."

She looked sad, as if she were about to cry, which is why I did tell her about the past after all. What I wanted to remember.

The *tjitjaks* and the *tokés*. My dog Teddy-Bali. The tennis court and the swimming pool of Villa Isola. The black dining table, which transformed people into demons.

The black sea, in which I learned to swim.

The light-blue letters from Granny Mimi. The boat *Garuda*, on which we had sailed to Europe.

Aleida listened with her whole heart and soul. She hugged me now and then and cried softly "poor thing" and "gosh."

"I'd like to take you right back there, to the land of the volcanoes," said Aleida. "If only we could fly! If we could fly then we'd fly first to your mummy and your brother. And then? And then to Bandung, to your house where Auntie Margot and Uncle Felix live now."

I shrugged my shoulders.

I replied that we wouldn't go. Mimi had said that my father couldn't fly. She wouldn't want me to fly back to Bandung; she would want me to stay with my father.

"And so do I, lovey," said Aleida, "I want that too."

She said, "Believe me, lovey, it'll all come right."

But it didn't, or did it perhaps?

The water was a friend and foe, said Father Bakker. Holland had tamed the water. The water was like a big, good-natured dog. You gave him his place, and he had to know it. Then he became your best protector and defender. The water would become our friend and protector.

Aleida's father sat me on a chair in the garden and pointed to the water.

Ahead of us was the straight canal, which led via a sluice into the winding waterway. Behind us lay the big lake, the far side of which, with its toy churches and miniature trees, you could see only in clear weather. The big lake had a little one near it, a pond, which you could walk around in three-quarters of an hour. Here I learned to canoe and row. Here we swam, in that summer of the hot days.

Every morning we lay motionless in the green water, Aleida, my father, and I. We didn't say much. The sun rose at the side of the toy church, climbed above the trees, and was reflected in the water all day long. I tried to hold on to the reflection of my face, at the same time as I looked at those of Aleida and Daddy, so that I saw five white faces, two above and three in the surface of the water. I was only rarely able to achieve that feat; probably I never managed it even once.

I had only to whisper that no one must move, and it was ruined. The slightest breath made the water ripple. Yet the image of the five blurred white faces, the white ovals floating in the dark water, was stored reassuringly in my mind.

We were water lilies. Nothing could harm us; we would always come back to the surface.

For as long as the heat wave lasted, we floated in the water.

There were mornings that seemed too beautiful to be true. I couldn't bear it. I would spoil it quickly, before something or someone else did. Slapping the water with my hands, I shattered our faces. I tormented Aleida.

I said that the water lilies weren't flowers, but drowned girls. Girls who couldn't swim, mermaids without tails.

"They're called *wendoleens*. Cross my heart, Aleida, that's what they're called. Look, they're all *wendoleens*."

"Oh, lovey, they're water lilies, they're not called *wendoleens*."

"And I'm not called lovey."

My father took a breath and dived under the water. Before he took a breath, I saw him laughing.

She had combed her hair back and put a wide white band round it. Her vixen's face jutted out eagerly. She swam toward me, the water lapped wildly around her. She made sloppy strokes with her arms and legs; she swam like a vixen.

The vixen that appeared long ago on the dune path where we had got lost, looked at me proudly. She had made it clear to me that she had a prey, which was hers and not mine. I flung myself into the brambles to save the pheasant. I wasn't frightened of the vixen, but nor was she of me. As I lay in the brambles full of painful scratches, she had turned around briefly to me, with the prey in her jaws. She'd laughed at me. Compared with her, I was a slow and clumsy creature. There was nothing I could do.

In the water of the pool I showed the vixen how the otter swims. And I was the otter. The otter cleaves the water without making a sound. It glides and undulates, and is invisible like water.

I dived below Aleida, without touching her. I surfaced close to her. She started and opened her mouth wide, and off I went.

She pursued me but soon had to give up. I dived underwater, grabbed her feet, and pulled her down. She struggled to keep her head above water. I pulled as hard as I could. My father came to her rescue, and they both acted as if it were only a game.

Later, when calm was restored, Aleida started floating. She turned onto her back, and laid her head back in the water. She stuck her pointed nose in the air, and let her tennis balls bobble under her bathing costume. She floated and talked to me, so that I had to look at her.

"Lovey, you know I mean you when I say 'lovey,' don't you?" I dived without answering her. When I surfaced, she went on. "If you say 'wendoleens' no one will know you mean water lilies."

"You know. And so does Daddy."

"That's true, yes," said my father. He swam close to us. I shuddered at the thought that he would suggest we make peace and the three of us sing "John Jenny." John Jenny in his tun with a hoop around it.

"*Wendoleens, wendoleens, wendoleens,*" I cried spitefully.

"Not *wendoleens*. Water lilies."

"Yes, that's right, Aleida, you're right too." My father said it in a friendly way. He didn't propose peace.

Aleida laughed and then she suddenly splashed the water at him with her hand, and he splashed back, at her. I wouldn't dare to do that, splash my father. I'd never seen my mother doing it.

It was high summer, early morning, and the water lilies weren't open yet. I deliberately didn't look at my father and Aleida splashing each other. I dived and didn't surface for as long as possible. I swam between the stalks of the water lilies, with my eyes open; the sun shone underwater. I found myself in a miraculously beautiful world, where I'd have liked to stay, but Aleida was screaming. I could hear her everywhere, even underwater. "Come up, lovey, come now, that's long enough. Lovey, come up."

I swam underwater to the other bank, climbed out unnoticed, and crouched among the bushes. Not until much later did I throw pebbles at her.

After our swim we ate fried eggs in the kitchen with Mother van Vloten. Then we went to our storage spaces, as my new uncle, Uncle Mannie from the mill, called the rooms.

Granddad's ficus stood in its brass pot in my attic room. It got little light, but it didn't become sickly. After the journey in the handcart it had lost lots of leaves, but new ones grew back. I knew because I'd rubbed all the leaves with a cloth almost every day, and I counted them too. Selma taught me to count and add up. She was Uncle Mannie's wife. They both lived in the mill, as did Tycho and his family, in a storage space that was even smaller than mine.

My storage space was under the eaves. I sat there for the rest of the day on a bed and practiced three things.

One was becoming invisible.

Two was not being frightened.

Three was not thinking about the past.

When the day was over, first evening came and then night, which I had longed for all that time. Then I set out for adventure, when no one else was awake.

There were no more people on the water and if there were, they preferred not to be seen.

That night, when I—or was it Listless Louise?—asked her about the past, was the last night that Aleida stayed in the attic room with me. The last time that she came and lay next to me in her nightdress, that she brushed my hair away from my ear and told me in whispered tones to move up a bit.

First three nights went by without her coming, but I still waited. I began counting the subsequent lonely nights, but then I stopped.

She still appeared occasionally, but so seldom that I no longer counted on it. When she came, it actually made me jump. Her coming no longer gave me any pleasure. I pretended to be asleep. I pushed my pillow under the blankets and stuffed my clothes in too, so that it looked exactly as if Louise were lying there.

"You wait for Aleida," I said. "Don't let her notice anything, do you hear." I left sleeping Louise behind and went off.

In the wetlands I got moving and came to life only at night.

I could sit for hours crouching among the bushes in the late evening peering at the lake, watching it go dark along with the sky. I never managed to capture the moment when the contours of sky and water merged. That always happened unseen: water and sky became one. Birds made their last calls and hurried to their sleeping quarters, on the water, in the sky; it was as if they, like people, wanted to get home before dark.

I was never frightened of the dark; darkness proved to be my element.

There were nights when you could drift to the big lake in the canoe, without having to paddle or steer—a light stroke with your hand was enough. Aleida had said it was the wind that did it. Even when there was no perceptible wind, there were currents of air that propelled you forward. I had felt those currents, but my experiences with currents in the water differed from what she had told me about them. She said that all the currents in the water, in the canal, the ponds, and the lakes, even imperceptibly in the unsightly ditches, were determined by the ebb and flow of the sea. You could have the current with you, but also against you.

Schools of fishes took my boat on their backs and carried me to the place I was heading for. They must do, because I always got to where I wanted to go. I could feel the fishes under my boat, could touch them. I could feel their bodies with my hand when I paddled along with them to lighten their burden. In the water I stroked their smooth skin, and they wiggled with pleasure; but when I tried to grab them, they quickly disappeared.

The lake was big, and at night it became even bigger. I set off into it and soon I could no longer see the banks.

On Aleida's chart, the six islands in the big lake looked like a giant's hand that had been cut off and had fallen in the water. The smallest islands were Little Finger and Thumb. They had other names, but that's what I called them, since we had to give everything different names the whole time anyway.

The palm of the hand, turned upward, was hollow in the middle and boggy. You could walk there only in the summer without getting wet feet.

Aleida said that strange things happened on this island, and a person would be better off not venturing there. She said that I must never go there. She didn't even know that I went that far in my canoe.

At home too there used to be places where you mustn't set foot. There were many things that you had better not do, because if you did you aroused the anger of the gods.

In Holland it was better to be invisible, and so I tried that too, although not hard enough. It wasn't as successful as I hoped, although I had already filled at least three exercise books with attempts at magic formulas. I must never be seen by people in uniform, Aleida impressed on me. I mustn't, but it was all right for her.

It was all right for her to sit with Ernst Haindl on a bench near the tennis court. The tennis court near the boathouse. The net of the court was broken, but Aleida played tennis with Ernst Haindl there anyway. She was allowed to play tennis with him, in the evenings, at quarter past eight, when it was light enough.

I would never tell anyone that I'd seen her with Ernst Haindl. Anyway, he wasn't wearing his uniform, he had his white tennis trousers on.

I didn't tell Aleida that I sat waiting and longing for the light to fade, for it to grow dark. No one would believe that anyway, of well-behaved Louise, who always wanted to go to bed early. But it wasn't Louise who was impatient, it was that other person, a passionate tyrant who was drumming on the inside of my skin, ordering me, "Hurry up, don't whine, leave that lazy person where she is."

Using a pillow and a pile of clothes, the girl with the canoe simulated the listless girl under the blankets who had to stay behind. The girl with the canoe wanted adventures. She set off, toward the dangerous island, the giants' palm. He had only to close his hand, and I would be crushed.

·   ·   ·

You made the best headway through the boggy part of Palm Island in bare feet. In that area, full of potholes and fissures, there were small wispy willows everywhere. In the middle was a hill where it was dry and where the trees were thicker and taller. Dates and a heart with an arrow through it were carved into them. I intended to take a pocket torch with me and read these names letter by letter and copy them into my notebook, but I forgot the torch every time. And in this place there was so much that demanded my attention.

There was a hut. Not just a slapdash hut that had been knocked together by boys, no, it was a structure that must have braved the elements for many years. It was weathered and strong.

On a wooden platform, borne by a number of thick round feet, about as tall as a large man, as tall as some of the trees around, stood the hut, which was actually a tree house among the crowns of the tall, but not the tallest, trees.

The steps leading up to it and the veranda and the balustrade were made of willow. They hadn't worried about being cut down and sawn into pieces to make stairs or a balustrade. They simply went on growing. For me this was the nicest thing about the tree house, the fact that it was growing. There were real leaves on it, which fell off in the autumn, but in the meantime the fence had become a lot bigger, and had even gained branches, which would produce leaves in their turn. The tree house was alive, and how! In a number of years it would be a tree again, a colossal, marvelous willow tree on at least ten legs.

Inside the hut was a large room with wide benches along all the walls. There were pans, kettles, and a paraffin stove. In a large box one could find everything that I thought a human being needed. You could camp here for at least a week, without wanting for anything. From the sloping roof a drainpipe led down to a water barrel on the porch.

Bird catchers and fisherman had once visited the hut, but no more. Aleida said that no one went there.

After it had slipped out she asked me with a frown, "Hey, what's this, what do you know about the hut, who told you about it?"

I didn't answer.

"No one must go in that hut," she said urgently.

By now I was perfectly well aware that Bald Ben, a friend of hers, lived there. He went there and I went there, and so she went there too.

Bald Ben sat on his haunches at the table. He'd seen me when I came upstairs. "Have you come from Aleida?" he called. I nodded.

A friend of Aleida's, Bald Ben said he was. I didn't know he was called Bald Ben, but he said so himself.

"I know who you are. Do you know about me?"

"Who are you then, mister?"

"Mister, mister. Just call me Bald Ben."

At first I refused to believe that anyone was called that. He said, "It's better if you don't know what my name is, and it doesn't concern you anyway."

He wasn't nice, but nervous.

"Have you brought a message from Aleida? Tell me it then, and then buzz off."

"No," I said, "she's not supposed to know I'm here."

"Well, well. That's a turn-up for the book. So how have you found your way here? What do you want? Push off, kid."

"Yes." I was about to go. He stopped me.

"I've gone underground," he said, "just like you."

"Are we underground?"

"Yes, dammit, underground, you know that, don't you?"

"Underground? Under what then?"

Bald Ben shrugged his shoulders. "Are you quite right in the head?" He looked at me angrily. "I'll let you go this time," he said gruffly. "As long as you keep your mouth shut. First say after me . . ." He sat thinking for a long time of what I had to say after him.

Before he started talking again, I said that it might be better for him to try and become invisible like me.

"Oh dear, oh dear, oh dear. You've got a lot to say for yourself. You're not right up top, d'you know that? Has she really not given you anything for me?"

I shook my head and showed him my empty hands.

"Nothing to eat either?" he asked again. He didn't even wait for me to answer, he said, "You ate it yourself." He crumpled with disappointment. He wasn't in good shape.

"I'll bring food with me, tomorrow."

"Listen, do you think you're the Queen of Sheba? You've got a lot to say for yourself. It's partly because of you lot that I'm living like a pig here, you know." I looked uncertainly round the hut, which was so big. According to me, Barend's sty was a lot smaller and I told him so.

"Will you hop it?" he cried. "I'm off to poach some more eel."

Suddenly I recognized him. I couldn't get away fast enough, and stumbled down the stairs.

"Don't create panic, will you?" I didn't know what creating panic was, but he must have meant what he did with the eels.

Creating panic was right up his street. He created panic among the fish with razor blades. He hadn't recognized me the last time, perhaps he hadn't even seen me, but I'd seen him. And I'd seen him doing it, with the fishes. He threw razor blades into the water, handfuls, squatting on the shore of Thumb Island, where the eels squirmed through the grass, because it was so lush and damp and wet there. He sat on the edge catching them just after they'd plopped into the water again. I expect he thought it was clever catching my fish this way.

Instead of avoiding him like the plague from then on, I sailed past him once, as close to him as I dared, so that I could see his boils, the rows of boils, which created whole fields on the thin whitish covering of his body. Because the sun had shined so fiercely and for so long, his arms were red. On his sunburned arms, which he moved through the water so tempestuously making it splash, dying fishes and all, you could see that his pimples had burst. I'd never seen such huge pimples. Certainly not on Barend, the friendly pig that had such a beautiful, pink skin, with thick wrinkles and lots of stiff golden hair.

The late evening sun glinted on the water and made the razor blades glisten as they fluttered down. The fishes floated in their own blood, with cut heads and throats. He hauled them up with his keep net. He'd seen me, but paid no attention to me, and I had drifted by in my blue canoe. How often did I meet Bald Ben, whose real name I didn't know then, in the hut? I never knew his real name, his head was on wanted notices, and people talked about him, but it would be better if I forgot him. I impressed it upon myself that I'd never seen him. I thought he was a demon, but he was a friend of Aleida's, a servant of the good cause, but an enemy of the fishes.

He was a threat to my islands. Little Finger, Thumb, and Palm. In the grasslands of Thumb I'd once seen one of his footsteps, which became larger and deeper and deeper instead of gradually fading, like the footsteps of ordinary people.

He buried his rubbish on Palm, but not always, sometimes he left a pile of cigarette ends and eggshells and sausage skins behind. Not to sacrifice to the gods. You couldn't call that a sacrifice, cigarette ends, shells, and stinking skins, which disgusted even the rats.

Whenever there was another filthy heap, I buried it with branches and leaves and made it into a small bonfire. In the tree hut there were loose matches and carbide and a can of paraffin. But I would only be able to light the piles when we were liberated.

Aleida impressed on me never ever to do anything that attracted other people's attention. As far as possible I must keep well away from other people.

I sometimes met anglers in the very early morning on my way back from my wanderings. If they'd asked me what a girl of ten was doing so early alone in a boat on the water, I would have answered that I was taking eggs to the village on the other side. Aleida had said that she always used to do this, not even in the canoe, but in a rowboat, which was much harder. That's what had given her strong arms.

No angler ever asked me anything.

"You don't know who you can trust and who you can't," said Aleida, looking sad.

But I'd known things like that for ages. You couldn't trust anyone, not even Aleida.

One night at the island I was about to moor my canoe to a tree trunk, which served as a natural bollard. I saw there was already a canoe there. Not moored to the bollard, but on land, under a bush. A camouflage sheet had been pulled over it, not too tight and not too loose, exactly as you were supposed to. Even the paddle was firmly attached. I was looking at the model of mooring that Father Bakker had tried to teach me. It was a two-person Bakker canoe, I recognized it at once. Even though the name was covered, I knew that it was the *Welmoet II*. Welmoet was the name of Aleida and Hendrik Bakker's dead mother.

I pulled my canoe onto dry land a little way away and set out to investigate. I'd always thought that the island was a living thing. It moved to the rhythm of something still greater, the water perhaps. The island's breaths could be clearly felt and heard. And it was subject to moods: sometimes it seemed to be submerged in a devilish dream and then it jolted so violently that I had to grab hold of a tree so as not to fall. These convulsions took place in a charged silence and only when they were over could you hear the sounds of water and wind. Because I was thinking about the *Welmoet II*, I was surprised by such a quake and thrown to the ground. Perhaps I was unconscious for a brief moment.

When I came round, I was underneath the hut. I was sitting on the ground, between the legs. Above me I heard moaning. It could have been the dog.

I hesitated, and I was sorry that I hadn't brought Teddy White with me. Even though he was sometimes frightened and didn't like water, he was still company. It was actually a shame that besides my dog I had also left obedient Louise at home. Louise and Teddy would have made me turn around and go back.

But the girl with the canoe had got it into her head that I must be an adventurer. So I had to stay and go and investigate. With a pounding heart, I climbed the rickety steps, which were more of a ladder than a staircase.

The groaning grew louder and merged into intelligible sounds. With a jolt I recognized the language that we no longer spoke, except when there was no alternative, for the good cause or by accident.

It was German, I was sure of it. The man's voice spoke of eternal persecution and doom. The woman's voice, soothing, talked of hope and love, and the happy time that would come when the war was over.

I made myself invisible and crept across the veranda. I looked through an opening that served as a door, but didn't really want to look and couldn't see much anyway. There was a lot of squirming going on, on a settee, under a blanket. It was as if an animal were being stuffed into a big bag, and was thrashing about and kicking in an attempt to free itself. The animal became tired, the kicks slower and slower, but finally the animal managed to escape and emerged. It sat up, stretched, and split into two.

It wasn't Bald Ben she was with, or Ernst Haindl.

I retreated and floated back down the steps. I could no longer feel my body. I had an irresistible urge to laugh out loud at the fear I still felt. How could that be, when I no longer had a body, since mine was lying asleep in a bed under a skylight? I could also split into two, at will. One half of me roamed the world and could go wherever it liked. I was never in danger, because this half was invisible anyway, perhaps for good. I impressed the fact of my invisibility on myself, so that I never forgot that I couldn't speak.

"So when was that, when? Come on, think hard," my mother asked me later. I simply couldn't remember.

Bald Ben continued to elude his pursuers. He knew this area like the back of his hand, he knew the maze of canals and ditches like no one else, and he could swim like a water rat. He was forever finding new places to ensconce himself. Perhaps he was sometimes in hiding close to us, in the sty of the vanished Barend.

In the town Bald Ben had captured weapons and bumped off bad Germans, eliminated them. We heard whispers, but never knew for sure.

We knew nothing, we heard the whole story only later. Or rather we did know, but we weren't supposed to. We never knew the full truth about anything. In our twilight world, Mannie said, the mice behind the wallpaper knew more than we did.

It was bad for Ernst Haindl that Bald Ben wasn't found. According to Aleida, Ernst Haindl was not a good but a reasonable German. He hadn't put much effort into the search, because he knew it was pointless. For failing to track down Bald Ben in time, he was punished by being sent to the Eastern Front, where he lost an arm and a leg.

The manhunt was repeated thoroughly several times after the disappearance of Ernst Haindl. Bald Ben was never run to ground, but it eventually cost the lives of at least five people.

That later led me to reflect that the people in the mill and the two Bakkers might still be alive if Bald Ben had been found. But I mustn't think like that, because human lives can't be weighed against one another—in a war perhaps, but not anymore.

Tycho de Vries and his granny managed to escape from the mill. They lowered themselves into the water along the big wheel. For hours Tycho and his granny stood stock-still in the cold water.

The pursuers left a trail of devastation.

They missed scarcely a single storage space, and turned everything upside down: houses, farms or mills, barns or haystacks. They forgot the beams of the boathouse, on which we were sitting. If they had set fire to the boathouse, we would have gone and stood in the water too.

They stuck their rifle barrels into the hay, so the story went. They collected bales of straw to set fire to the mill.

It was in the summer of 1944.

TWENTY-ONE

On Friday evenings Sabbath was celebrated in the mill. Selma and old Mrs. de Vries insisted. "*Sjabbes* in a cupboard," muttered my father in astonishment. But because Selma had fallen ill and asked him to come, he nevertheless went one Friday, and after that attended more often. He took Mannie, who, in fact, like me, preferred to sneak outside when it was dark. So Mannie too returned to the mill, grumbling that this was all he needed, to become a practicing Jew when it was already too late. I wanted to go too, because Sabbath was a celebration, but my father said it would be better if I stayed with Aleida.

It was a miracle that my father hadn't gone that Friday evening of June 9. It wasn't a miracle that it was my birthday the following day, but it was a miracle that he stayed with me on that occasion to celebrate my birthday in advance. I should have invited everyone, but the thought hadn't occurred to me. We no longer made a fuss about birthdays. In the past, though, we had celebrated them with balloons and flowers and cake.

My father didn't know that I didn't mind being alone. In fact, I liked being alone, because I could then go and investigate things. What I was looking for I had no idea, but anything was better than sitting on a bed at nighttime looking straight ahead of you and practicing not thinking of anything.

He came to my little room under the eaves. It was still light outside, and the skylight was open. He sat down to write at the little table, which he had pushed under it, and wrote a birthday message for me, with lots of curlicues and a gigantic ten. I lay in bed with my head at the foot end, so that I could look through the skylight and see a section of the pale-blue sky. The section turned first pink, then lilac, then black. The birds that flew past were black already.

When night fell in Holland, I always felt that vague sense of threat, which didn't frighten me but excited me, even giving me a feeling of expectancy: what did fate have in store for us?

In the Indies there was a short dusk as night fell, but here in the wetlands the fading of the day went on and on, sometimes lasting for hours. Only then was the night fully there, in every nook and cranny. Until that time the signal stayed at danger, which was exciting. Even outside the small window hazards lurked. That night they no longer lurked, but came inside.

I was dozing off when I started awake in a roomful of greasy smoke and heard the noise of shots and cries. I was so frightened and my chest was so tight that I couldn't scream. I tried to drop down from the loft steps, but perhaps I jumped.

At the foot of the loft steps my father put me back on my feet; we got down from the loft, I no longer remember how. Perhaps he lifted me out of bed, perhaps he put a blanket round my head, perhaps I just dreamed that I jumped. My father rushed out of the room with me and carried me downstairs.

The mill was surrounded by flames; the Germans had put bales of straw around it, piled many feet high. They had dowsed the bales with paraffin and set them alight. They emptied their rifles into the mill. The fire raged all night, no one must put it out, no one could get near because of the black smoke and the suffocating fumes that surrounded the mill in a head-high cordon of doom.

Tycho's father had nevertheless staggered his way through it: he came out with his hands up and a handkerchief stuffed in his mouth. At first of course no one knew who he was, and he called out in German that he was the only one hiding in the mill, so distracting attention.

Tycho and his granny escaped.

Later, much later, Tycho pointed out to me the way they had gone. When we saw it, in broad daylight and in peacetime, we couldn't understand how they had managed it. How his granny, who was as fragile as a china bird, and who later could get so unreasonably grumpy about the fact that those damned Huns had even stolen her Hummel figures from her old house—how his little granny had had the nerve to attempt these daredevil feats, with a struggling little boy on her shoulders.

Was it conceivable that this wall of black smoke and the flames as high as a house had actually existed outside our imagination? In reality? Here by this country mill, in these charming surroundings? We could scarcely believe it.

The mill hadn't burned down, it bore no visible scars—or they had been expertly hidden.

The mill has a gray memorial plaque listing the names of those who died on June 10, 1944. Simon de Vries, who came out, and Hendrik B. Bakker, who stayed inside, to find a way out for the others, and Sebastiaan B. Bakker, who despite the ban had tried to extinguish the fire.

A little way away, where the village begins, is another memorial. This is made of two large pieces of unmilled and serrated glass, which are set upright in horizontal, black marble planes. Here, in silver letters, are the same names again and the names of others who died in the surrounding area.

It was one Friday evening when my father and I were talking

to each other cheerfully and confidently. I had nothing to fear because he was finally back sitting with me. Out of exuberance I made silly jokes; it was nearly my birthday after all! I made a funny remark about the bow legs of brother Henk and about Farmer Bakker's gray quiff. My father didn't tick me off, but he didn't respond. I didn't dare think of those jokes afterward, which is precisely why from time to time they start replaying in my head word for word.

Long before the fire at the mill, Corie started gesturing to me. Without a word she informed me she wanted a flower. She pointed to the red and orange flowers that bloomed far into autumn in vines around the well. Although everyone told me not to, everyone, even my father, I always gave her one when she sat kicking her feet like a greedy baby in her chair. One brightly colored flower, with a few leaves. She chewed for a long time on her booty, with a blissful expression on her face, which became almost an ordinary, recognizable face. I could see what she had once been like, an exuberant creature, with a vixen's nose and two round, glittering eyes.

She reacted enthusiastically to all the questions I asked her. I believed she was an oracle, because I couldn't understand a word of her replies.

The others maintained that Corie wasn't telling the future but ranting, and was garbling all kinds of texts from the Bible. Garbling those texts was quite an art. I wrote them down in my exercise book when they weren't too long and too difficult, but they usually were. "Unreasoning creatures," she could cry painfully, "born of nature, to be captured and slain!"

During the night of the fire in the mill and the following day and for perhaps a month afterward, she cried, "But the day of the Lord shall come as a thief in the night, when the heavens shall pass with thunder and the elements shall melt with heat, and the earth and the works that are in it shall be consumed with fire."

I knew for certain that she had prophetic gifts.

After the fire we became indoor people once and for all. Even more so than at first. We now lived day and night in a small, oblong room, invisible to others, a darkened room, behind blacked-out glass. The room was half underground, but still above the boathouse.

If you listened very closely, you could hear the willows whispering above us and the water lapping. It lapped around the boats that were inside. I lay on a wooden bed and hoped the bed was made of willow, because I knew that this would stay afloat if the water rose. I also knew that the willows would continue to grow if I washed up somewhere. When I made my nightly excursions, I had planted a willow branch on Little Finger, because that little island was bare. In a year's time it would be an island full of trees. The willow never stays dead for very long, and it never stays alone.

You mustn't make a movement, you mustn't make a sound, you lie motionless, with your hands folded and your eyes closed, resigned to your fate.

Teddy White adjusted better than I did; he lay as still as a rug and played dead. Now and then he produced a gentle fart, a secret sign of his presence. When it was time for me to wake up, he stood by my bed and put his head diffidently on my pillow.

He went for walks by himself, disappeared like a shadow, and came back silently and invisibly. We never saw him come and go.

"That dog's got the knack," said my father. "Better than we have."

Granny Mimi's plant, which could no longer be called by its

name either, had stood on the windowsill in the warm kitchen for a while. Suddenly it was brought here by Aleida, to this dark narrow room. She muttered that it wasn't doing very well and might revive if it could see me. It stood on the table next to my bed, and it didn't do better. I asked my father if he would cure my plant.

"You and your little *waringin*," he answered glumly. "I expect you think I'm a magician? If the life has gone out of something, I can't get it back. No one has been able to do that up to now."

I turned my head away from the plant in dismay, since that meant it was already dead.

Once I knew there was no hope left, I could no longer bear to look at the thin, dry trunk and sparse brown and yellow leaves.

Whatever had happened in the meantime, to the others and to us, no one had yet maintained that all hope was lost. Hope sprang eternal.

My father, whom I considered wise and powerful, now told me just like that, aloud, that all hope was lost and he couldn't do anything. I started crying, because my father wasn't a magician.

"Now you just make sure you get better."

"Louise wants to die."

"Louise wants to die? And why, Louise, tell me why."

It was difficult to explain to him that I didn't want to die, but that the child who was always so obedient, and always wanted to please everyone else, suddenly hadn't a clue what to do. She was too frightened to go on living. I searched for words.

"Is it so difficult to explain, Lulu?" My father bent over to me. I pulled my head back a bit, sank deeper into the pillow, tried to become invisible, and shook my head. With her voice in my head, I shouted to him that Louise didn't know what to do anymore and that's why she didn't say anything. Of course I couldn't say it in her place, because I wasn't the same as her.

He didn't understand me, however hard I tried to transmit my thoughts to him.

"Lulu, don't you want to talk? Why not then?" he asked after a while.

"Well, well." He had waited, in vain. "What's going on; tell me."

When we'd both been silent for a while, he took me cautiously by the shoulder and shook me to and fro in a friendly fashion. "What's wrong, Lulu?"

"She's crept off," I finally said with difficulty. "Louise has gone."

"Crept off? Where to?" I pointed to somewhere in my tummy, at the level of my navel. How was I to know where Louise had gone?

"Oh yes," he said. "It's your age. Perhaps. That's incurable, but it's not an illness, you know. We'll see. You won't die, my darling; you'll get over it, believe me."

He spoke cheerfully and encouragingly, gave me affectionate pats on the cheek, sat down on his own bed and said cheerfully, "Well, reading is no good in this darkness, so I'll simply tell you a story."

I loved it; I wanted to hear his voice and nothing else. I hoped he would tell me what was going to happen to us next. I didn't want any more fairy tales. It had to be reality.

"Things that really happened," I muttered.

"Things that really happened." He repeated it with a deep sigh.

"Are lots of things really going to happen?"

"Of course, Lulu, and it's bound to get better." He pulled himself together. His voice sounded firm again. "Every war ends one day."

"Even the Eighty Years' War?"

Tycho had told me about that. Tycho was four years older than I was, and he knew lots more than I did. His father and Mannie had taught him all kinds of things in the mill. Tycho wanted to teach me all kinds of things too, but my head couldn't take it anymore. For example, he said, "It starts with the fact you can't add apples and pears, do you understand that?" Although I believed him, I didn't understand what it had to do with us. In the wetlands we didn't even have any more apples or pears.

I preferred to know what was simply going to happen in reality.

"I don't know point by point," said my father, "but this war is definitely going to end." He added more softly, "And they're definitely not going to win either. They can forget about that again." He told me that it had been the same story in the previous war. Germany had lost and just as well, because as a result there had been space for a new age, which unfortunately hadn't continued. Everything had gone on in the same old way.

My father didn't want to talk about this war, which was still going on, but he was prepared to talk about the previous one, the first. He told us a lot about the First World War. He described how the surgeons at the Jewish hospital in Berlin where he worked had gone to the battlefields like miracle workers in their own train to patch up the German soldiers or to save their lives. The train was called Viktoria Luise. One carriage had been fitted out as an operating theater. My father had been eager to go with them; all the young doctors in the hospital fought for the honor of traveling on the train. At the risk of their own lives, they had pulled wounded men from the trenches and brought them to safety.

"Did you take basket people to safety too, Uncle Cees?" asked Tycho.

"Basket people? Lad, we took everyone with us who was still breathing."

Was my father telling all this to Tycho and me, who were listening to him intently on my bed, or were his stories intended for the ears of Aleida, who sat next to him on his own bed and bent over me feeding me porridge? I hated porridge. My father must have forgotten to tell her that I didn't want either porridge or milk.

I didn't know what to do with the mouthfuls and stored the food in the pouches of my cheeks, like a hamster, but it got too much and while they weren't paying attention, I emptied it silently under my pillow. They were too absorbed in each other, Aleida and my father, to notice. I listened to his voice, and sometimes fell asleep as I did so.

Bloody scenes were played out under the unwashed hands of the doctors: dying soldiers, with earth in their mouths, so that they couldn't even scream. Dying women, young and strong like Aleida, lay writhing on the floorboards of small delivery cubicles. Moonlight or the gas lamps of the great city of Vienna cast a dim light inside. Ghastly cries echoed along endless corridors, but no one heard. My father's stories, about Ignaz Semmelweis. His portrait used to hang on the wall, a photo. It also hung in this wooden room with the blacked-out windows, in which I was lying sick. Or rather not sick, but listless. The wooden cubbyhole in which I often no longer knew where I was, or didn't want to know. And didn't want to knew who I really was.

Sometimes I thought that Semmelweis was still alive and was sitting with me and telling me stories about my father, who couldn't make anyone better. It was easier to remember what you dreamed than to remember what you had experienced while awake. You sometimes didn't know if you'd experienced anything or if it had been seen and told to you by other people.

Semmelweis had dived into the water of the ditch, like Tycho's little granny, or had run outside like Uncle Simon de Vries. My father's story was about blue rooms with open doors, behind which women died screaming, women who suffered unbearably as if they were on fire, with puerperal fever from which they died, until Semmelweis discovered that he must wash his hands before treating the sick women. Everyone who treated these women must wash their hands—doctors, nurses, mid-wives—must all wash their hands, which put an end to puerperal fever.

Pain penetrated our old walls, pain and lamentations. I was convinced that it was because the wooden walls in our room weren't made of willow. The walls, with their grains and knots, were made of proud, strong trees that thought they could never be cut down. Never in their lives, the proud oaks and beeches. They were cut down anyway, and sawn up into pieces. Ever since they never stopped their moaning and groaning for a second. They simply went on raving, whether the wind was blowing or not. There was nothing that I could do for them, because their pain wasn't mine.

I was confined to my bed and wasn't allowed to go out.

Sister Corie was worse off than I was, but not now. She could struggle free of her chair and crawl on her hands and feet, this way and that, wherever she liked. She opened the door of our little room with her thick white cat's head and meowed a biblical text quickly and rhythmically.

> "*Behold the man,*
> *who has come through water and blood,*
> *Jesus Christ,*
> *not through water alone,*
> *but through water and blood.*
> *And it is the Spirit that bears witness,*
> *for the Spirit is the truth.*"

The narrow room was blacked out, with black paper stuck on the windows. I could just make out that it was Corie, and streaks of light splashed around her mop of white hair.

I took my right arm out from under the blankets and felt how far I could reach with my hands. I could reach my father's bed, which stood next to mine, pushed against the other wall, with a small gangway between us. It was an iron camp bed, on which the pillows and blankets were fluffed up and smoothed out by Aleida every day. She wanted to fluff up and smooth my bed too, but I pretended to be asleep. She bent over me as she always used to, but for a time she was so fat that the whole of her touched me, and I felt her breast and her round belly. She was even fatter than sister Corie and smelled of porridge.

At night I felt to see if my father's head, his own head, was lying on the pillow. Or had he made his clothes and the pillow into someone else and tucked him under the blankets?

Outside it shook and blustered, and strange smells squeezed in through the chinks. Everything that happened outside was part of us, was partly actually a result of our presence, as Bald Ben had confided to me. But whatever happened, we weren't allowed to know about it; it didn't concern us.

Under the ground, or behind a window with black paper stuck over it, you experienced life as if you were in a barrel that was nailed shut with pebbles in it and were being rolled along at the fair. But I only thought of that later.

My father said that we mustn't give up, but that we must keep going, keep going every day of the war, like a rider jumping obstacles on his horse.

We must look forward to the new life that was ahead of us, when the war was over, when we were liberated.

Tycho told me about the basket people from the First World War, a few of whom might still be alive. They were soldiers brought back from the battlefield without limbs, with no arms, with no legs. All they had were their torsos and their heads. They spent the rest of their lives dangling in baskets, hanging from the ceiling.

What did they think about? we wondered.

These basket people really had nowhere to go, so we mustn't complain. We weren't badly off at all, compared with the basket people.

One day Mother van Vloten brought us potatoes boiled in their skins with salt. There were two colored eggs, a red one and a yellow one, but we didn't notice that immediately. Mother said we were lucky devils.

She lit a stump of candle for us and sat down on a chair next to the bed to see how we ate. Tycho had got one egg but dropped it in alarm.

"What a hard potato," he hiccuped.

Mother Van Vloten slapped her knees with laughter.

"Easter and April Fool, both together."

We didn't dare leave the potatoes with salt.

Aleida came and brought a knob of butter.

"Today's a festival, it's Easter."

The butter was on a dish, in the shape of a melting lamb.

"For the *Pellkartoffeln*," she said. My father raised his head, but if he was astonished, he controlled his astonishment. He didn't answer when I asked what kind of festival it was. I couldn't remember our ever having celebrated it before. The five of us sat there in silence with the end of a candle, the dish of butter, and the plate of gray potatoes in which Tycho had carefully deposited the yellow egg.

Louise wanted to cheer up the others, because of the festival, and she picked up the new word as she used to do. Like a sea lion plays with a ball on its nose, she went on with it, nudging it ahead of her, *Pellkartoffeln, Pellpantoffelen, Pellpantoffeln*, until her father said to her, more weary than impatient, "Stop that now, Lulu, we've got it now."

Tycho said, "I haven't got it yet, Uncle Cees. What does she mean by *Pellpantoffelen*?"

"It's a German word for those things there." My father pointed to the potatoes, which we had put back because they were piping hot.

"Are we still allowed to understand German?" asked Tycho politely.

I asked him in surprise if Mannie had also told him the game of good, wrong, and forbidden, and he said yes. *Pellpantoffeln* was wrong and forbidden.

"That all depends on who says it," my father suddenly said sternly. He made us jump. He looked at us quite angrily. "You heard that it was Aleida who said it, didn't you?"

"It isn't wrong, because Aleida says it?" asked Tycho uncertainly.

"That's right," said my father, "when Aleida says it, it's always right."

I didn't feel at all like eating potatoes anymore, and I wasn't hungry for that matter. I may have had problems with everything, but hunger never bothered me. Aleida insisted that I take a potato anyway, which when she wasn't looking I quickly hid under my pillow.

Aleida was our angel of mercy.

My father never tired of praising her and explaining that Aleida wasn't an angel but a human being.

"She's a good human being; angels don't exist, and good human beings are even rarer than angels."

When I thought about Aleida I could see in front of me the scene when we were living with Granny Mimi and had just got to know her, and she had shown us in the kitchen how to skin a calf's tongue. She shouldn't have done that. I couldn't say a word for hours. The sad calf's head had lain on the work top in the kitchen and looked straight at me as if I could do something about it.

"You must never do that, Aleida."

"Oh, but lovey, we have to eat, don't we? This is lovely to eat."

That's undoubtedly the reason why, a couple of years later, her own bleeding head landed in my lap.

We had been liberated, but Aleida was seized. Boys and men

from the village had come and grabbed hold of her. I was sure Bald Ben was among them, singing and waving a sign.

"Oh Lulu, you can't be certain. Bald Ben! You couldn't see properly, you didn't have any glasses then," said my father later. "I don't care who they were; they were bastards."

Six or seven of them had grabbed her and shaved her head, because Aleida had fraternized with the Germans.

Of course that wasn't true. She hadn't fraternized with the Hun, but played tennis with him. All for the good cause.

The boys and men shouted that Aleida was a Hun whore, with a Hun child. It lay upstairs, in the loft, and its name was Pandora.

Aleida had laid about her with her long, strong arms, torn herself free, and run away. Crying her eyes out, she arrived on our doorstep, at her own house. Her pursuers were hard on her heels and waved sticks and garden shears and an orange scarf.

My father had immediately put his arm around her and in a couple of strides led her away from the wild mob. He had sat her down carefully on the wooden bench in front of the waterside inn next to me, who was looking at everything but couldn't see it properly.

We had been liberated, but Aleida had been beaten. She had never been beaten before; she'd never been beaten so badly in the past that she couldn't sort it out for herself. "I'll sort it out," that's what she always said, whether it was a tennis match, bearing a child, or burying a dead person. "I'll sort it out."

This time someone else had to sort it out. This time she fell over and put her head on my knees. Her head was bleeding. Aleida was at the end of her tether. It was a punishment for the calf's tongue, I thought, so I really ought to let it go on bleeding. But the calf was dead, and Aleida wasn't. I watched as red liquid welled up from the wounds with serrated edges, little areas of blood emerged and the head changed into a strange flower, a tulip that was about to drop.

The stamens were still there, the short stubble, they were her vixen's hair, blood red at the roots. Instead of petals she had loose-hanging, bloody, lobe-shaped flaps. I wanted to stroke her, but I couldn't deal with this havoc. I put my hand protectively on Aleida's battered skull.

My father came and stood next to us. "Don't do that, Lulu, let me look after it." He took Aleida by her arm and led her indoors, talking softly to her.

What had my father said loudly to the boys and men who were leaping around and taunting us? I can't remember exactly. At any rate Aleida's pursuers calmed down and went back to their village.

First he had given them a good whack with his walking stick, which had a sharp tip. They scattered, and coarse laughter rose from their throats, as if they thought it was a game; my father was much angrier than they were. He was furious. He screamed something at them about the child, which they had to leave alone, because it was his too. The child was there. It had nothing to do with good or wrong.

As I dig into my memory, like a dog hunting for an old bone, I hear my mother's voice warbling, "Men couldn't keep their hands off her."

I knew what I had to answer.

"She could beat men. She blasted all the men off the court, the German too! Anyway, she could row harder than anyone, because she had strong arms. She could juggle too, with more than three balls."

My mother replied, "She really could do a lot; she enchanted friend and foe alike, it's true."

My father had put his arm round Aleida. Everyone could see that. He had said loudly that her child wasn't a German child. "Leave her alone; that child is mine."

It was immediately gossiped around the village.

It wasn't long before the gifts started arriving. Baby clothes and a mug with a stork on it and a rattle.

"I think it's very good of Uncle Cees to say that," said Tycho to me. "He said it, but it's not true at all."

"He used to do that in the Indies too," I replied offhandedly, "give babies to pathetic and bleeding women."

"That's impossible."

I didn't care anymore. I didn't want to talk about it anymore and said that Tycho's father was brave because he'd run out when they shot at the mill, but then Tycho started crying.

Aleida the vixen was more indifferent to her cub than our cats were to their litters. I went up to Aleida's attic room and saw her child in the blue cradle. I'd seen it just after it had been born. Tycho and I had fetched jugs of hot water that we were given by Mother van Vloten in the kitchen, while my father brought out the baby.

I saw the new baby many times afterward, without the blood and without the messy, torn skin around it. Its head stuck out of the blankets, and we could just see a little collar and a white blouse. It always woke up when I came. It yawned, it opened its mouth wide, and only then did the eyes slowly open and roam around hesitantly. The child had exactly the same dark-blue eyes as the freshly painted wood. Who had painted the wood precisely that color, beautifully finished in violet gloss, and when? And why had no one told us about it before?

When my baby brother had been born in Bandung, there had been great celebrations, at my father and mother's house, of course, and also on Bali, where I was staying with Granddad and Poppy. We had been allowed to dance, everyone had danced, there had been dancing all night and we had sung Dutch songs. "Where the white top of the dunes shimmers in the sun's glow."

We had eaten Dutch rusks with aniseed comfits, and bottles of fizzy wine had been opened.

No one had given a party for Dora. Before little Pandora arrived, we'd all smelled the paint fumes in the attic, but nothing else. It had been even quieter than when the cats gave birth. The mother cats became restless before the kittens came, they meowed plaintively and started traipsing about with their hanging bellies, and then Uncle Bakker the farmer was immediately on hand to help them. And Louise.

Louise looked for soft materials for the litter, she put her own scratchy woolen pullover in, she rummaged in dusty drawers full of old rags and cobwebs, she hunted for a sturdy box that could serve as a cradle, she made herself indispensable—but she wasn't allowed to be present at the birth. Farmer Bakker would let her see the kittens only when they'd been licked clean, and were lying contentedly against their mother padding her with their paws. She was allowed in when everything was over. Louise would kneel down by the litter, put her thumb in her mouth involuntarily, and began to think up names. She thought up names like Zofira and Bamborus.

Aleida told her that Louise's father had thought of names for the child, whom she called Panda or Dora, but mostly Dorie. The child was called Pandora Serena. Louise refused to believe that her father had made up such beautiful names for this insignificant dwarf. Her father would never do that, give such a bald-headed little mite names as beautiful as he had given to big, strong, long-haired Louise.

It was much too much for a little snippet, Pandora Serena. Dorie was better, she looked no stronger than a newborn kitten. On the contrary, cats kept all the hair they had been given at birth and acquired even more. They grew quicker and became real cats faster than Pandora became a real person, and started looking like Aleida.

Pandora had rolling blue eyes, which she couldn't really focus yet, and black hair that fell out in large wads and lay in sticky clumps on the pillow, around her red head, which became balder and balder. According to Mother van Vloten, she was red from all the crying she didn't do. She bottled it all up because she was a war child.

"It's not easy being a new life in the kingdom where death rules."

Pandora never gave a peep, either of displeasure or of contentment. I looked her up and down. I didn't stroke her. Did she bring bad luck? Did she bring luck? She didn't have a father of her own, but my father had given her to Aleida.

Without telling anyone, I consulted sister Corie, whom I visited every day anyway, though of course not to get any prophetic or clairvoyant statements from her, because that was strictly forbidden. Even Farmer Bakker, who used to agree to almost everything, said that I mustn't do that. Not even now that Farmer Bakker has gone, I asked Mother van Vloten. No, especially not now, said Mother van Vloten, now especially we must respect and cherish the worldly goods and values of old Bakker as if they were our own. We mustn't under any circumstances tempt Corie to speak. It would only rebound on ourselves.

I asked hesitantly whether Mother van Vloten knew in that case.

"What do you want to know, child?"

"Does Dora bring bad luck? Or does she bring luck?"

"Mm," said Mother van Vloten, "she brings luck. She has to, because she's new life in the realm of death."

Just as in previous years, as soon as it got cold sister Corie had been put at the back of the shop, in her chair, wrapped in all her cloths and blankets, with her things around her: the table, the branches, the pile of boxes, the wooden spoons. Through a narrow window she had a view of her summer place, in the middle of the lawn in the back garden, with the sundial on her left and the old well on her right, of which you could see the old red and gray stones, because they weren't covered by the East Indian cherry, which didn't bloom in winter. Perhaps that was why sister Corie looked not at the garden but at the clouds above it.

"Pandora," I whispered to her. She wobbled a little, as she always did, and as always when someone was visiting her, she sat there with her mouth open and kept running her tongue over her lips. She suddenly looked at me expectantly with her one, still clear eye.

"Pandora Serena," I ventured.

She puffed out her cheeks, and burst out exultantly, "Dearly beloved, let us love one another, for love is from God and whosoever loveth, is born of God and knows God."

She repeated it so often that I had plenty of time to get my exercise book and write it down as neatly as possible.

If a good deed needed to be done, I rocked the cradle back and forth. Aleida came at set times, peeled the little dwarf out of her sheet and blankets, lifted her up, and looked at her, full of astonishment. "You great darling," she said, as if she had to get used to her every time anew. Then she sat down on the bed with her, made herself comfortable with lots of cushions in her back, leaned back humming, and unbuttoned her blouse. By that time my heart was in my mouth, and if Aleida had asked me something, I wouldn't have been able to answer, I was so tense. I kept asking myself if what I'd seen last time would happen again.

Even though it happened every time, I was still frightened that I was imagining it all, and that one day it would turn out never to have happened.

That applied to a number of things, for example, Teddy

White, whom I kept seeing around me. I kept feeling that he was sitting under my bed, however often Mother van Vloten said that he had been taken away by a woman who was passing because she was hungry. For a bag of potatoes, the woman had been prepared to exchange everything she still possessed, an original dance costume from Toledo.

"I did it, but why?" Mother van Vloten had sighed. "The costume would suit our Aleida very well. But she'll never wear it; she can whistle for fun from now on."

Aleida took out one of her large, heavily swollen globes and pressed the child against it. She pushed the child against the dark part, which was on the end of the globe with a few gold hairs on it. She pushed and fidgeted until the child gripped it with its lips. It wasn't a hungry child. It was a drowning person, who had just managed to clamber ashore. The child pretended to suck; it only pretended.

It kept its eyes tight shut and its flat nose disappeared and it made loud, smacking noises, but the globe didn't empty, not even by a millimeter. I could see that.

I stood between Aleida's legs and leaned forward, as far as I dared and could.

When Aleida came to "give the child the breast," as she called it, I went with her.

It was a secret of the two of us, Aleida and me. The child was there too, but it didn't join in. It didn't know what was happening. It didn't know what Aleida and I were doing, on her other side.

"Go on," murmured Aleida, "while there's enough for one there's enough for two; I've got more than enough, go on, have a good slobber, suck."

I did, but it made me shudder. It was lukewarm and sweet and it was like milk. I didn't like milk.

"Go on, lovey, that'll strengthen you."

My father had said that Aleida was a good person, so I wanted to be nice to her. But I couldn't do it; it made me sick.

I couldn't face Aleida's disappointment. I ran out of the blue attic room. I almost jumped down from the high steps, as I had in the fire, but I took care this time. Anyway this time it would be from relief.

It was May. The East Indian cherry for Corie wasn't in bloom yet, but we were free. We'd been liberated. The Germans had gone, so I could now go wherever I liked. I didn't have to stay where I was, as I had before.

Before I wasn't allowed to give a peep, but once we were liberated I could give all the peeps I could think of.

I could make as much noise as I wanted.

If I wanted, I could run everywhere and scream, back and forth on the terrace of the inn, in circuits round the boathouse, even around the mill.

In the kitchen of the inn, Mother van Vloten and Corie both sat swaying and clapping their hands. In front of them stood Teunis van Vloten, who had been taken off to Germany in the war but who had returned. He had pinched a bike and had cycled, from south of the great rivers. He'd cycled nonstop. He had lost weight, and his hair was thin, but he still felt like a champion on the bike. He had come for Aleida; he wanted to see Aleida.

"Lad, you did the right thing. How happy she'll be," stammered Mother van Vloten with tears in her eyes. To me she said, "Go and get Aleida. My, won't she be pleased!" With little nudges she led me out of the kitchen. When we were outside on the gravel path, she raised one finger imperiously. "Remember, don't say Teunis is there, remember, it must be a surprise for her!"

In the attic Aleida had finished feeding the little mite, she had buttoned her blouse and was sitting unusually still on the bed with the child in her arms. I went up to her, but not too close. Aleida looked at me above the almost bald head of Pandora Serena. Her face had started beaming as soon as she saw me.

"Teunis van Vloten is here; he's sitting in the kitchen." I said it hurriedly, as if I were making a confession.

I always admired Aleida's muscles, the way they rippled under her smooth skin whatever she did. In a supple, wavy tempo, as if they weren't muscles but creatures performing an impromptu dance.

The muscles in her arms undulated upward as Aleida put Dora in her cot.

She stood up, turned to me, and let her arms hang down, so that her muscles moved from top to bottom.

"Go and say I'm not coming." She said it in a determined tone. She hadn't had to think about it for long. She sounded like what she was again, a winner.

"Lovey, will you do that for me? Go and tell Teunis I don't want to talk to him."

I was excited that I was finally able to do something for Aleida that wasn't an effort for me, and I ran back downstairs, where I could already hear Teunis's voice on the gravel path, in the middle of a long story about his cycling adventures.

My news came as a bombshell. There was a deep silence, which was broken sharply by Mother van Vloten.

"She always had lots of airs, did Aleida. She'll live to regret it."

Corie began talking like an oracle. Teunis had sat down in a daze and drummed his fingers on the table, making the glasses on it tinkle.

Over the top of this noise he cried out, "Calm down, you women, it'll all come good. She's a thoroughbred, is my Aleida."

He nodded to me and grinned. "I don't mind those funny whims. So there."

Perhaps I should tell him that Aleida wasn't a horse but a vixen. Vixens are too clever for everyone. But Teunis must make his own mind up.

Anyway, he was sitting there again singing in a good-humored way and accompanying himself by tapping the glasses with a spoon.

My father had gone to the village with Tycho to get news at the town hall about the fate of Uncle de Vries, who might have survived the rifle shots. There were rumors that he wasn't dead but had been captured and taken to a place called Westerbork. Perhaps he was still alive.

In the distance I could hear music. This was a very different kind of drumming and jingling than Teunis was making on the table and the glasses.

The oracular garbling of the two women in the kitchen went on and on. I no longer had to listen to this.

Crunching as loudly as possible, I ran down the gravel path to the garden of the boathouse, I passed the water well and the beech tree, whistling shrilly. Then up the stone steps that led up to the top of the small dike.

I stood on the road down which we'd come a couple of years before. We got to this point and no farther. Not a step farther. The road was gray and surrounded by the misty green of the wetlands. On the right lay the canal, with willows with narrow silver-gray leaves on either side of it. On the left the pond, with the water lilies. They were open. At the end of this road was The Hague; I hadn't forgotten that.

I whistled for Teddy White. If he were anywhere, he would hear me and come.

In the far distance I could see something moving that looked to my eyes like a tangled ball of cats that was quickly rolling closer. They seemed to be black-and-white cats, playing with sticks and balls, but it might well be a real band.

A marching band, with hooters and banners, ahead of our liberators.

When would they get here?

I would go to meet them right away. Then I could continue on to The Hague in one go. I didn't look round anymore. I looked ahead.

My journey back began.

Helga Ruebsamen was born in 1934 in Jakarta, Indonesia, and spent her early childhood on Java. In 1939, her family traveled to Europe and stayed in The Hague throughout the war. She worked as a journalist for *Het Vaderland,* a newspaper in The Hague, before becoming a freelance writer. She is the author of five collections of short stories and two previous novels. *The Song and the Truth* is her first work to be published in English.